"Offbeat, intriguing." —*Philadelphia Inquirer*

"Eerie, thrilling, and wonderfully original: a mad killer wreaks havoc in the arcane world of fine art. Marvelous!" —James Neal Harvey, author of *By Reason of Insanity*

"Take a tour of the big-time art world, from Venice to Istanbul to Florence to New York—pursued all the way by an unknown person who slashes up paintings and people. I found the tour fascinating, the slasher horrific."
—Robert Daley, author of *Prince of the City*

"A literate plot, graceful prose, lovely settings, and tantalizing glimpses into the competitive politics of the art world . . . a villain who could give Hannibal Lecter a run for his money. An outstanding novel."
—*Booklist*

"Lieberman writes an elegant sentence, as always, and his art-world detailing, especially of maneuverings and backstabbings, seems splendidly on target." —*Publishers Weekly*

"Lieberman's knowing portrait of the international art world, the tautly placed plot, and his two complex, believable protagonists make this a highly effective work." —*Kirkus Reviews*

"A grim and tense scenario." —*Hackensack Record*

"The suspense builds wonderfully." —*Anniston Star*

By Herbert Lieberman

NOVELS

The Adventures of Dolphin Green
Crawlspace
The Eighth Square
Brilliant Kids
City of the Dead
The Climate of Hell
Nightcall from a Distant Time Zone
Nightbloom
The Green Train
Shadow Dancers
Sandman, Sleep

PLAYS

Matty and the Moron and Madonna
Tigers in Red Weather

THE GIRL
WITH THE
BOTTICELLI
EYES

HERBERT
LIEBERMAN

St. Martin's Paperbacks

THE GIRL WITH THE BOTTICELLI EYES

Copyright © 1996 by Herbert Lieberman.

Library of Congress Catalog Card Number: 96-5193

ISBN: 0-312-96406-4

Printed in the United States of America

St. Martin's Press hardcover edition / August 1996
St. Martin's Paperbacks edition / February 1998

10 9 8 7 6 5 4 3 2 1

For Jean and Adrian Marcuse

THE GIRL
WITH THE
BOTTICELLI
EYES

PROLOGUE

It was hot, so they left the doors open. If you stared at them for a while, you could see the waves of heat rising off the damp stone walk just across the threshold. Sunlight streaming through the branches of an olive tree outside washed the marble entryway in thick shadows of black and gray. And beyond the door, a jagged line of dome and corkscrew shapes stood silhouetted against a sky of dazzling blue.

It was nearly 5:30 P.M., and within the Church of St. Stephen, a tiny Christian church in Istanbul, it was a half hour to closing. St. Stephen's is a little-known structure dating back to the time of Bajazet I. An extension of stone fortress built during the Crusades, it sits astride the western slopes of the Golden Horn. Never a major attraction to the general run of tourists, unlike Hagia Sophia, the Blue Mosque, the Dolmabahçe Palace, or the Topkapi, the church is known mostly to Turkish Christians and to art historians who come there from all parts of the world to view its chief attraction—the splendid Byzantine murals and mosaics over seven centuries old.

During this particular afternoon, the flow of tourists had been light but steady. Now, at this late hour, only a handful of people still lingered in the fast-fading light of the basilica.

St. Stephen's sole security guard was an aged sexton. Imprisoned in a thick robe of gray twill, clearly hot and tired, the poor man did his best to fulfill a guard's function. With the sun slanting westward and the great clock in the tower outside the church ticking off the few remaining minutes until closing, the sexton had grown noticeably restless. Shifting from one foot to the other, he watched the visitors circle the little area, view the various exhibits hanging there, light votive candles in the vestibule, then file out through the open door. On his face, he wore that expression of sullen resentment so characteristic of underpaid petty functionaries the world over.

One of the visitors lingered longer than the rest. A shape-less gray figure—ill-kempt but respectable—he wore a long, transparent raincoat of some synthetic substance—the sort that can be folded into a neat square and slipped into a jacket pocket. On the coat in question, the squares of the fold lines showed clearly in the straight gridlike ridges running both the length and width of the coat.

This person's most prominent feature was a headful of bushy hair of nondescript color. A rather large pair of yellowish incisors protruded ever so slightly over his lower lip, forcing the mouth into an expression of fixed petulance.

In one of the tiny chapels off to the side, scarcely observed, the man stood riveted before a small painting. Executed in oil and tempera, in the thirty-two-by-forty-seven-centimeter category, it was attributed to Botticelli. The subject was a portrait of the good Centurion whose slave Christ heals, as told in the Gospels of both Matthew and Luke.

Here, the Centurion is seen in a simple three-quarter pose. Attired in a pale white belted tunic that barely hints at the muscularity of the figure below, his face is long and sharply lined, with high cheeks and eyes that convey a mixture of both power and gentleness. Upon the viewer, he turns the shrewd, vigilant gaze of a wise man, a knower of arcane things. It is a look of keen and disarming intelligence.

The man poised before this painting was now the last person in the church. Anyone near him would have been struck by his total absorption in the subject. A dreamy expression on his face, he muttered words half-aloud to himself, oblivious to his surroundings, or to the fact that the church was suddenly empty and that the sexton was now glancing with frank impatience in his direction.

In the next instant, the man's arm rose. Something bright and metallic shot from the bottom of his sleeve. The sexton watched with fascination as the shiny object leaped upward to the top right-hand corner of the painting, then, with a single uninterrupted slash, plunged diagonally downward to the bottom left corner. A noise like ripping cloth followed.

The motion was repeated, this time starting at the upper left-hand corner, then once more descending with a fierce, rhythmic rage, over and over again.

Manship was in Munich, at the Alta Pinakothek, viewing paintings, when he was informed of it. Twenty-four hours later, he was back in Istanbul at the Church of St. Stephen, surveying the wreckage. The little chapel in which the painting had hung was cordoned off. A variety of forensic specialists and Turkish police padded noiselessly about, carrying out their duties. Though tourists were still permitted in to view other parts of the church, there was all about the place an air of hushed reverence, like a mortuary to which people have come to pay final respects to one recently deceased. As of yet, the police had picked up no suspects.

By means of an official pass authorized by the Turkish government, Manship was allowed into the chapel. He stood there now, silent and grim, gazing at the painting, the thing he'd viewed whole and gorgeous less than a fortnight ago. As a curator and the man charged with the responsibility of bringing the painting to the United States for a massive Botticelli retrospective at the Metropolitan Museum, he was beset by a horde of practical questions. First and foremost was to ascertain the degree of destruction sustained by the painting, then to determine whatever reasonable expectations he might have of repairing it in time for the exhibition's opening in late September.

When Manship entered the church that morning, a blush of healthful pink had suffused his sharply angled features. Over the course of a few hours, his pallor had drained to something like that of old parchment. Less than two weeks ago, he'd left Istanbul ecstatic, having successfully negotiated terms for the painting's temporary loan, the first time this startling Botticelli, virtually unknown in the West, would be exhibited. Now, in this ancient little church full of the dank musk of centuries, he was back again to see what might be salvaged from the pitiful ragged strips hanging on the wall there still in their frame.

Though the painting was unsigned, Manship had no doubt what it was. Layered with dust, encrusted with five centuries of grime, it hung in a dark niche at the rear of the tiny chapel, illuminated by no more than a few votive candles guttering in the damp, cryptlike air. But not even grime and dust and the absence of decent light could conceal the unmistakable brushwork, the streaks of dazzling color leaping like flames from out of the ruins of it.

It had taken his breath away, finding it there like that. Old Yampolski had talked about it on several occasions. But who listened to Yampolski these days? Manship had thought it was nothing more than an old man's (albeit a brilliant old man's) flight of fancy. A leading figure in the field of fourteenth- and fifteenth-century European painting, Yampolski was said to be failing rapidly, along with his memory and whatever meager worldly fortunes he'd managed to accumulate as an art critic and historian.

Manship had been so thrilled with the find that in a burst of gratitude he'd rewarded the old man with the job of writing the catalog for the show, his chief motive being to put some much-needed cash into his former teacher's pocket.

The next morning, the *Centurion,* packed in crates specially designed to control temperature and humidity, then entrusted to the care of a team of trained couriers, lifted off the tarmac at Istanbul International Airport en route to Italy. Cabled ahead from Turkey, Signor Emilio Torelli cleared his work schedule and readied his staff and atelier to receive the badly mutilated canvas. Torelli was a genius. In the field of restoration he was looked upon as something of a miracle worker, his name uttered with a kind of hushed awe. He ran his shop on the outskirts of Florence in much the same manner as large urban hospitals run first-class emergency wards.

Torelli was Manship's only hope. The *Centurion* had become the exhibit's first casualty. Manship was determined there would be no others.

PART ONE

ONE

"Twenty-five, twenty-five. Do I hear thirty? I hear thirty. Now I have thirty. Do I hear thirty-five? Gentleman over there in the corner with the handsome yellow necktie. Splendid. Thirty-five is my bid. Thirty-five. Come now, let's not be shy. We can do better than thirty-five for this excellent museum-quality sketch. Forty is surely not too high. Lady Beresford. Splendid. We have forty. Forty thousand, then. We have forty thousand."

The voice of the auctioneer droned on, piping numbers while the low murmur of some eighty or ninety people gathered in the small airless hall rose and fell upon his every intonation.

It was midsummer in London and the private Sotheby's salon was packed with perhaps a dozen more bodies than it was ever intended to contain. Dusk coming on, an elderly white-haired attendant tottered around the room, lighting the small electric sconces that lined the walls at intervals.

"Sixty-five. Sixty-five." The auctioneer's voice prodded, taunted, and caressed.

Mark Manship sat there, knees crossed so lightly, they scarcely seemed to touch each other. His thatchy mane of salt-and-pepper hair had barely begun to recede at the forehead, and there was a certain elegant emaciation in the drawn, pallid lines of his face, like a Greco saint. Tall, gangly, boyish-looking, even in his late thirties, he seemed uneffaced by time.

Alert and upright in his chair, hands clasped in his lap, he gave an impression of innocence and inexperience that may have been just a bit disingenuous.

"*Quatre-vingt.*" The words issued from a long, Gallic face belonging to a man known to Manship as the director of the Louvre. Manship's eyes wandered upward to the ceiling above him. It was a Baroque ceiling, bronze and coffered into separate panels in which raised friezes depicted various mythological stories. Just above him, several plump cupids, their cheeks swollen, puffed into coach horns.

"Eighty. We have eighty," cried the auctioneer at the block. "Who'll give us eighty-five?"

The object of all this attention was a small Madonna drawn by Botticelli in the late fifteenth century. It was one of a series of thirteen small line sketches executed by the painter at the request of his powerful patron, Lorenzo de' Medici.

"Note the curious mixture of vigor combined with delicate refinement," said the auctioneer. His name was Philpot. "The verticality, the unbroken linear perfection, the absolute confidence of the stroke—" Philpot was much given to talk like that. It was his stock-in-trade. "Truly an excellent example, ladies and gentlemen. Mint condition. Eighty-five. Come now. Let's hear you. Eighty-five. Very good. Right over there."

Manship continued to sit with his hands folded in his lap. He seemed as removed from the bidding as he was from anything else going on at the moment. He gazed everywhere but at the drawing. Out of the corner of his eye, he glimpsed his counterpart at the prestigious Getty Museum smiling sardonically back at him. Manship nodded to the man and received a deep, ceremonious nod in return.

"I believe that was your hand then, Mr. Manship?" said the auctioneer.

"It was."

"Splendid," the auctioneer enthused, for he knew the real bidding had at last begun. "Ninety is now the bid of the Metropolitan Museum," he croaked happily.

The presence to Manship's left moved abruptly. "Ninety-five."

"Ninety-five from Mr. Allenby of the Getty."

The action in the hall froze for a moment while everyone gazed at Manship.

"One hundred thousand," came the bid.

"One hundred. We have one hundred thousand pounds, ladies and gentlemen."

"One hundred and five," cried a heretofore-unheard voice behind Manship and to his right. It was Carstairs of London's National Gallery.

"One hundred and five from Mr. Carstairs."

By then, most of the private, unaffiliated bidders had dropped out. Several of the attendants, including the char-women and even the gray-uniformed guards, sensing drama, had gathered at the entrance.

Mr. Philpot, showing a large gap-tooth smile, beamed down from his place on the block. Manship's hand rose again.

"One hundred and ten," cried the auctioneer. His eyes swept the room, darting back and forth from Carstairs to Allenby. "We have one hundred and ten. Do I hear fifteen? Fifteen. Let's hear fifteen."

A Japanese gentleman, up until then a silent presence, hoisted a tremulous finger. If there was anyone Manship feared, it was that one.

The man on the block pounced. "One hundred and twenty," he cried, his cheeks flamed. "We have one hundred and twenty thousand pounds."

"Twenty-five," Carstairs countered. Nothing of his face moved but an eyebrow.

Manship sat quietly. They were carooming toward two hundred and thirty thousand dollars now. He felt the spite-ful smile of his colleague from the Getty and imagined with some amusement the "shocked indignation" of the Met-ropolitan trustees. His finger rose again.

"Is that thirty, Mr. Manship?" said the auctioneer.

"It is."

"One thirty, then. We have one thirty."

"Thirty-five," said Allenby, but this time Manship was certain he detected hesitation.

"We have thirty-five from Mr. Allenby," the auctioneer cried, and stared hard at the curator from the National Gallery. But by then, Carstairs had little stomach for more. He shrugged and shook his head.

"Thirty-five, then. The bid holds at one thirty-five." Mr. Philpot's gavel inched upward above his head. He was watching Manship, who was watching the ascent of the gavel.

Just then, the finger of the silent Japanese gentleman rose again, this time to one forty, intended as a preemptive strike. A gasp pulsed through the hall.

Trustees be damned—Manship's finger cocked up to meet the challenge. "One forty-three, three." He heard his voice come back at him across vast distances.

The auctioneer was in a transport of ecstasy. People at the back of the hall had risen from their seats to see better.

The ball was once again in the Japanese gentleman's court. The man on the block gazed intently at him. "One fifty. One fifty is the call." The gavel resumed its slow ascent. An unearthly silence roared in on them. "Going . . . going . . ." All eyes watched the Japanese gentleman, his face an impassive mask as the gavel reached its apogee then plunged downward, striking the block with an awesome crack. The challenge had gone unanswered.

"One hundred and forty-three thousand three hundred pounds it is. To Mr. Manship and the Metropolitan Museum."

He was suddenly surrounded by a flood of well-wishers— perfect strangers surging forward, pumping his hand, thumping his back.

"Bravo."

"Well done, sir."

A band of gallery officials swarmed down upon him. There were papers to sign, questions to answer, forms to complete. Sotheby's director, Hiram McCallish, came steaming up. He was a large Scot with a ruddy face and a scrawl of veins raking each jowl.

"I knew you'd take it, Mark. Once you get something in that pigheaded mind of yours. And frankly"—he

glanced sideward at the Japanese gentleman in the corner—
"I'm always delighted to see one of that lot routed for a
change." McCallish had been a prisoner of the Japanese in
Malaysia during the closing months of the big war, and
there was no love lost there.

Manship signed several documents while a wolf pack of
shouting reporters encircled him.

"When does New York get to see your show, Mr. Manship?" asked the correspondent of the *Daily Mail.*

"With any luck at all, the third week in September."

"Do you think you'll have everything you planned by
then?"

"If I know him, he will," McCallish said. "He might
even resurrect old Botticelli for the event."

They laughed and Manship handed the big Scot the Metropolitan Museum's check for $229,000. McCallish held it
at arm's length, inspecting it.

"May we have one of you smiling at the check, Mr.
McCallish?" asked a photographer. A flashbulb ignited before anyone could refuse.

A man from Lloyd's came up. He already had the drawing in tow. It was wrapped in simple brown tar paper. Two
armed guards stood behind him.

"You'll take good care of that now," said Manship.

"Yes, sir. It leaves tonight for Florence by special courier."

"Mr. Torelli will be at the airport to receive it."

"He'd better be," said the Lloyd's man, laughing. "Just
sign here, if you will, sir." He held a standard policy form
out for Manship. "You'll want the same half million again,
I presume."

McCallish shooed them all away. He took Manship by
the arm and steered him through the lingering crowd just
starting to drift off. "Come on up. I've something nice
chilling on the ice."

Manship let himself be guided into a narrow little coffin
of an elevator that swayed and cranked its way haltingly

up to the penthouse of the Sotheby building where Mc-
Callish's private suite of offices was located.

"Claude says you have the Lemmi frescoes. How'd you
manage that?"

"It wasn't easy."

"I don't doubt it." McCallish dabbed at his neck with a
wad of tissue. "Old Baudreuil is damned near impossible.
You must have promised him all of Eighty-sixth Street."
He sighed. "And the *Duveen Madonna?* I suppose you've
got that, too?"

"Hollander ran it down for me in Bruges. Needs a bit
of retouching, but otherwise . . ."

"Wizard, dear boy. Wizard." There was a look of genuine wonder in the old Scot's rheumy eyes. "And the Chigi
sketches? What number are you up to now? There must be
some fifteen, if I'm not mistaken."

"Thirteen. With this one, I've now got nine."

McCallish hummed in admiration. "Hard to believe that
thirteen Botticelli drawings could have gone unseen for so
long."

"Not all that hard when you consider they've been scattered all over the map for five centuries. No one knew what
they were."

McCallish laughed scornfully. "Incredible. Simply incredible."

The director's long red nose whistled as he peeled the
lead capsule from a bottle of Pol Roger. The cork popped.
"Commissioned by Lorenzo himself, were they not?"

"Lorenzino, actually. Lorenzo the Great's cousin, the
fellow who commissioned the *Primavera* and the *Venus.*"

McCallish's face purpled as he bent stiffly from the waist
to pour champagne into a pair of chilled flutes. "Done before 1500, I should say."

Manship's brow wrinkled in thought. "Somewhere between 1490 and 1497." He reached up to accept a glass.
"The line is quite different from the sort of thing Sandro
was doing after 1500."

"Christina of Sweden figures in there somewhere, doesn't she?" McCallish smacked his lips, savoring the wine. "Oh, I dare say, that's lovely."

"She bought eight and bequeathed them to the Vatican."

"Those beggars give you much trouble?"

"They were very decent, actually. No problem."

McCallish sipped. "They can be prickly about loans, you know."

A police siren went whooping past outside.

"And the remaining four? Where were they?"

"In the hands of an Italian bookseller in Paris. Fellow called Molini, who sold them to William Beckford."

"Oh yes, of course. My father knew Beckford. Great collector. First-rate eye. Odd sort of chap."

"And Beckford's estate passed them on to his daughter."

"The Duchess of Hamilton. Well . . . you know the rest." Manship raised his glass to permit another half flute to be poured.

When they had settled into the pair of commodious facing settees, McCallish extended an open humidor of Churchills, one of which Manship accepted. There followed some fumbling with a balky butane lighter. Shortly, the air grew thick with the rich, earthy odor of good Havana.

Succumbing to the effect of vintage champagne and a fine cigar, McCallish closed his eyes and leaned back into the cushions. "Where to from here?"

"I'm off to Paris tonight to pick up another of the drawings."

"Old DeMornay, I imagine. That leaves three to go."

"That's the rub. I don't know where those last three are. I've got a few leads, but they're thin, and I don't have much time. Right after Paris, I'll make a dash over to Berlin."

"Berlin?"

"The German police. The last they heard of the sketches, they were in Leipzig. Probably stolen during the war."

"Their art-theft division might be helpful there."

"I'm already on to them. They've very generously promised to open their files to me."

McCallish blew a luxurious column of smoke into the air, then grew solemn. "Heard all about that mess in Istanbul last week. Nasty business. What do you make of it?"

Manship thought a moment, then shook his head. "I don't know what to make of it."

When he reached his hotel in Carlos Place, the concierge handed him his cables and a list of phone messages. Manship went directly up to his room and drew a hot bath. Immersing himself in the healing potion of suds and steamy water, he gradually felt the jagged shards of nerves subside and nearly drowsed.

But into those easeful moments crept the thought of the attack on the *Centurion* the week prior in Istanbul. He wondered if it was an isolated incident or if it had something to do with the upcoming Botticelli show. He knew that there were people in the art world, so-called colleagues in lofty positions in other museums, even his own at the Metropolitan, who resented the show, whose smiles were venomous, and who cordially wished to see it fail—for no better reason than that it wasn't their own. Manship didn't whine about such things. He simply took it as a fact of life. Call it envy, competitiveness. In the museum world, it went with the territory. But would a colleague go so far as to vandalize a world-class painting in order to detract from the good fortune of another curator? Manship found that far-fetched and put the thought out of his head.

He turned instead to more pressing matters—namely, the show scheduled for an opening in New York in late September. He'd been given the job of mounting a Botticelli retrospective on the occasion of the 550th birthday of the great Renaissance master. It was to be the largest and most comprehensive exhibition of the Florentine painter's work ever assembled under one roof.

Manship had worked feverishly on the project over the

past five years—buying, borrowing, tracking down all of the major paintings the world over—something over one hundred canvases. Most of them were already in New York, or else in Florence undergoing restoration. Those already in New York were being cataloged by scholars and assembled by the leading specialists in the field. Lighting experts were even then at work rewiring the entire second floor of the Metropolitan in order to present the paintings in the most advantageous illumination. Lawyers were drawing up contracts, hammering out terms for both sales and loans.

All of the major museums of the world were contributing to the show. The Louvre had promised the *Guidi Madonna.* The Lemmi frescoes were coming from Belgium and the *Corsini Madonna* from the National Gallery in Washington. The *Saint Sebastian* had just been flown across the Atlantic from the Staatliche Museum in Berlin. The papal frescoes were due from the Vatican and the predella panels were coming from the Accademia in Florence. The Uffizi itself was to make the major presentation with the medallion portrait of Cosimo de' Medici, the tondo *Madonna of the Pomegranate*, the *Adoration of the Magi,* and the two breathtaking masterpieces, the *Primavera* and the *Birth of Venus.*

The final and most difficult job was still incomplete. It had been left to Manship to gather from a host of widely scattered sources some thirteen drawings, all executed by Botticelli as warm-up exercises in preparation for the painting of the *Chigi Madonna.* The painting itself was en route from the Gardner in Boston. Having all thirteen drawings was considered by the museum directors to be an absolute imperative. The drawings had literally been lost for centuries; hence, their appearance at the museum was generating the most excitement. Every major newspaper, periodical, and scholarly journal was sending representatives. The media coverage planned was rumored to be staggering, since the show was to be the highpoint of the Metropolitan's year. On the success of it depended whether or not Manship

would replace soon-to-retire William Osgood as the next
director of the Metropolitan.

Manship had been a curator for the past dozen years of
his life. In and out of several notable museums until, at
twenty-six, he was catapulted into the sort of splashy fame
that only the arts seem able to bestow. A wunderkind, he
was appointed curator of Renaissance painting at the Metropolitan Museum of Art and, in a short time, as everyone
had warned, he'd roused the ire of older generations of
curators whose careers were then sliding into the twilight.

In the pursuit of his duties, he was tireless. He would
travel anywhere to see a newly discovered Verrocchio,
Piero, or Titian. A brilliant administrator, idolized by those
who worked beneath him, he was one of the first curators
empowered to bid at auctions and private sales on multi-
million-dollar works of art, a privilege entrusted to few of
his peers.

In something just under five years of his appointment, he
had transformed the museum's Renaissance wing from an
indifferent melange of second-rate Italian works into one
of the most stunning and cohesive collections of Quattrocento painting in the world.

There was no doubt he had done well. Articles were written about him. He was photographed at thousand-dollar-a-
plate fund-raisers and power restaurants, dining with
society ladies all with three names. He loathed that side of
the job, but that was the bread and butter. That's what kept
the museum's doors open over three hundred days a year.

Certainly he had enemies. Any man in as powerful and
as coveted a position was bound to. But he also had friends
in high places and knew how and when to use them. His
future was bright, and after the autumn opening of the Botticelli extravaganza (depending on its outcome, of course),
it should be many times brighter. A seat on the board could
not be far behind.

Over the past months, he'd wheedled and cajoled and
bullied the bulk of the paintings and drawings for the ex-

hibit out of estates and from professional dealers all highly experienced at the art of extracting valuable concessions from ambitious curators. Assembling all thirteen drawings of the Chigi series for the show would be the topmost feather in Manship's cap.

Still, three of the full series defied detection. Manship had already exhausted all of his sources, save one, as well as a small fortune trying to track them down. Nearly a million dollars had already been expended on that aspect of the show alone. That afternoon at Sotheby's, bidders had forced the price of one of the drawings into the stratosphere. Manship had gone well over his budget and would undoubtedly have to go back to his superiors for additional funding. The prospect didn't please him, since begging was not Manship's strong suit. He'd already had several scorching wires from Osgood expressing the ''dismay'' of the trustees over his ''reckless extravagance.''

Well, what did they expect? They wanted the whole series, insisted upon it. Did they think the world was made up of philanthropists and do-gooders all just panting for a chance to lay their priceless works of art at the exalted feet of the Metropolitan? And for what? A smile? A pat on the back? A pair of complimentary passes to the big show and a letter of commendation from William Osgood III? Not even a little something you could send to the Internal Revenue Service at tax time in the hope of a much-needed deduction was that enticing.

He laughed bitterly, suds sliding down the length of his long, bony frame as he rose from the tub.

TWO

"I've been watching you for several days now."

"I know you have."

"You do? Was I that obvious?"

"Yes. I kept wondering when you'd finally get up the nerve to approach."

He laughed at her bluntness and watched her drain her coffee.

"Do you come here every day?"

"I like the coffee here."

"Can I buy you another?" he asked.

"If you like. And I could use a roll and butter while you're at it." She spoke without looking at him.

Pointing to an assortment of baked goods, he signaled the counterman. A scratchy announcement sounded over the PA system, totally garbled in the vast, high-ceilinged hall. All the same, people rose hastily from their stools, dropping coins on the countertop, and scurried off to various passenger gates where buses, idling their engines, spewed diesel fumes into the air and waited to carry them off to their destinations.

He watched her pounce on her food with ravenous hunger. He was certain she hadn't eaten for days. She was pathetically thin and her clothes were not all that fresh. She could be no more than twenty-four or twenty-five, he judged, though she looked closer to forty; she was still attractive, but in a tired, badly used way, and with that sullen look of availability.

"You know why I've been watching you?" he asked.

She stared straight ahead, dabbing a napkin at her heavily painted lips with an almost laughable elegance. "No. But I can imagine."

He caught the world-weary note in her voice.

"I mean it. Seriously."

"Yes, of course you do."

"Your eyes."

"My eyes?"

"Yes. They're Botticelli eyes."

"Who?"

"Botticelli—the painter. You have the very same eyes as his Venus and his Primavera."

She listened, not bothering to conceal the smirk, merely wondering why a gentleman like that, well dressed, urbane, obviously educated and wellborn, would resort to such a pitiful pretext to pick up a woman. In all of her years haunting boulevards, hotel lobbies, and now, sadly, bus stations, she'd never heard anything quite so naïve.

"So what exactly is it you want?" she asked, eager to get to the point.

"I want you to model for me."

"You're an artist?"

"Yes. There was a pause, which gave heightened emphasis to the words that followed. "I'm an artist."

How many times had she heard that before? Men identifying themselves as artists, photographers, talent agents, one man who had even described himself as an internationally renowned couturier—all seeking a special look that she had precisely. Such elaborate, absurdly transparent schemes just to achieve such a simple, uncomplicated end. It was all so unnecessary. Why couldn't men just say what they wanted?

"And you want me to pose in the nude, no doubt?"

"I didn't say that."

"But that's what you have in mind, right?"

"No. You can wear your clothes. What you have on is fine. All I'm interested in are your eyes."

"My eyes. How romantic." She unleashed a high, shattering cackle that brought nearby heads around. He could see in the lines suddenly creasing her face that she was older than he'd first guessed.

"It's only for a few hours," he said. "I'll pay you well."

"How much?" She turned suddenly to stare into his

eyes. Her own eyes danced flirtingly. They had about them
an edge of ridicule, possibly even contempt.

He mentioned a sum.

She was impressed. "Just to paint my eyes? Nothing
more?"

"Nothing more. Just the eyes. It will take only a few
hours."

She appeared to consider, all the while her eyes apprais-
ing him up and down.

"You're not one of those crazy people with strange
tastes?"

"No." He laughed. "No. I assure you, I'm not one of
those."

"Let's see your money."

He removed a billfold from his inner pocket and withdrew a pair of 100,000-lire notes, then placed them before
her on the counter.

She seemed to catch her breath and the tip of her tongue
slid along her lower lip.

"Where is your studio, Mr. Artiste?"

"Over in Parioli. Just a few minutes from here by cab.
Come, I'll show you." He dropped a handful of coins on
the counter, then smiled and took her arm.

TORSO OF UNIDENTIFIED WOMAN
FOUND IN TIBER

The body of a young woman between the ages of thirty
and thirty-five was discovered by fishermen in the Tiber
today. In the vicinity of the Hospital de la Infanta, the
body was naked and appeared to have been dead
several days.

Pathologists are checking local dentists for charts in
an attempt to make a positive identification. "It's not
unusual for bodies to be found in the river," said Chief
Inspector Mario Buonofaccio. Unusual in this case was
the fact that the eyes of the young woman had been

excised from the skull, making this the sixth such cadaver to be discovered over the past twenty-four months. All have exhibited the same disfigurement.

—*Il Repubblico*, Roma

THREE

It was 9:00 A.M. and Rome's Galleria Pallavicini had just opened. Given that it was a Tuesday morning following a long holiday weekend, not many people were expected— at least not at that hour. Perhaps around noon, a lunch-hour crowd might wander in from the stifling alleyways to linger in the air conditioning and stroll about for a few idle minutes before returning to their offices.

The few guards on duty, scattered here and there in the different galleries, were still having coffee and paid little attention to the solitary figure moving through the labyrinth of corridors. A large, somewhat ungainly man, he shambled rather than walked, giving the impression of someone in the early stages of some neurological disorder. Although the day outside was brilliant and clear, the man carried an umbrella and wore a badly rumpled raincoat. He was virtually alone on the upper gallery, and the sound of his cork-soled shoes squeaked like a sponge on the parquet floors.

A short time later, an unfamiliar sound reached the ears of a drowsy attendant lingering over a morning cigarette in one of the small alcoves off the main gallery. At first, he scarcely attached any significance to it. It was only a short time later, when the disturbance persisted, that he realized it was the sound of cloth ripping.

Even then the attendant was slow to respond. Perhaps that's what saved his life. Had he arrived a few moments earlier, he would have come face-to-face with a large, menacing individual, arms threshing back and forth in a kind of scything motion, a low growling sound rising from him as he went about his work. When he had finished, long strips of canvas dangled from inside the frame of the painting, still quivering, like the entrails of something living that had just been eviscerated.

The object of that savage act was Botticelli's *Transfiguration*. As stunning today as when first painted five hundred years ago, it now hung in ruins.

When the guard finally did arrive, the worst had already been done. Rounding a corner and turning into the gallery, he stopped abruptly, watching the last of those long, sweeping strokes, a bemused expression on his face, as though he couldn't quite grasp what he was seeing.

Just then, the arm shot straight out and the guard glimpsed something bright and metallic at the end of it. It was a thick, short blade, hooked at the end like a kris. The police later identified it as a "knife of the sort used by carpet installers."

When the raincoated figure had stopped flailing his arm, he stood still for a moment, breathing heavily, staring up at the canvas, as if appalled at the destruction he'd wrought. Sensing someone approaching from behind, he wheeled in time to see a figure bearing down on him. The guard came fast, slightly stooped, in position to tackle. Just before impact, the knife wielder stepped neatly aside. Off balance, the guard lumbered past as the hooked end of the blade flashed forward, scooping a gout of flesh the size of a golf ball from the man's cheek. A hole opened just beneath the eye and in seconds a jagged red circle began to widen across the floor. Attempting to recover his balance, the guard slid and went down in his own fluids.

From an adjoining gallery, another guard heard the scuffle and came running. He arrived in time to see his fellow worker floundering on the floor, one hand to his face. Blood spouted from between the injured man's fingers as he tried to stanch the flow. Turning, the guard saw a figure fleeing headlong through the main corridor to a stairwell. He watched him start down the stair, the tails of what appeared to be a raincoat flying behind him.

The guard never gave chase. What he saw on the floor at his feet must have been that unnerving—a fellow worker and close friend, arterial blood fountaining from a crescent-shaped gash that left most of his right cheek hanging in a flap. Bone from beneath the cheek and eye socket gaped outward from the wound. The guard used a handkerchief and later his own tie as a tourniquet to stanch the blood until help could arrive.

Several blocks away from the museum, in an alleyway between two large office buildings, the fleeing figure scrambled out of the oversized raincoat, its inner lining padded with a series of small cushions to provide an illusion of bulkiness to its wearer. This illusion became more apparent when moments later the individual slipping off the coat and a wig turned out to be a slight, wiry fellow with closely cropped gray hair. He was short as well, an impression confirmed when he stepped out of a pair of high-ankled shoes and stood on the cold alley pavement in his socks. The shoes were custom-built, so engineered that it was impossible to tell from a casual glance that the person wearing them was walking on four inches of cork lining concealed in the vamp and inner sole of the shoe.

Despite the fact that the immediate area of the Pallavicini was already filled with the whoop of police sirens, the man carefully packed the coat and elevated shoes into a small overnight bag he carried.

As a final touch, he removed from his mouth a dental bridge comprised of large, protruding yellow incisors, revealing beneath them perfectly normal ones. Then, crisply neat, about him an air of brisk composure, he exited the alleyway and boarded a streetcar heading out along the Via Appia Antica on the way to Ostia.

MASTERPIECE DESECRATED AT THE PALLAVICINI

Guard at Museum Slashed Trying to Rescue a Botticelli from the Razor of a Madman.

A museum guard lies in critical condition at the Hospital della Sorella Misericordia, the victim of a vicious attack at the hands of a razor-wielding madman. Guido Ponsorotti lost the sight of his right eye when the optic nerve was severed during a deadly struggle with a man discovered in an upstairs gallery slashing at Botticelli's *Transfiguration.*

According to experts from the Vatican Museum, the painting can be restored, but damage done to the eyes of the Virgin in what appears to be an unsuccessful attempt to have removed them from the canvas may well make it impossible to restore the work to its original glory.

Police authorities here have noted a rash of similar mutilations of masterpieces over the past several years and are now coordinating information with Interpol investigators in St. Cloud, France.

The *Transfiguration* was due to travel to New York, one of the paintings selected by the Metropolitan Museum of Art for its upcoming Botticelli exhibition in September.

—*Quotidiano,* Venezia

FOUR

"Well, there you have it, and I'm glad to be rid of it. Phuh." Monsieur Étienne DeMornay rubbed his hands vigorously, as if washing some unpleasant substance from them. He was a small, nervous man with an unnaturally high color. He talked expansively, using his arms. "I don't mind telling you, it hasn't been easy."

That was the Frenchman's code language for, I think you owe me more than the price we originally agreed upon.

After years of dealing with DeMornay, Manship knew the code words only too well. "I didn't expect it would be," he said.

"I've given the better part of a year to locating this." DeMornay pointed to the small pencil drawing mounted on an easel. "Through Italy, Holland, Canada, and, finally, the unnumbered account of some ponce in Switzerland. . . ."

"A gangster?" Manship inquired.

"Worse. All you had to do was look at the man. Phuh." He made that curious sucking sound again to convey his disgust. "It's cost me the friendship of several researchers and a top-notch restorer. Wait till you see his bill."

Manship could sense his own bill mounting by the minute.

"And then to have that—that creature barge in here to my gallery. Right in broad daylight. I thank God there were no people here. I run a respectable establishment."

"It must have been awful." Manship took a stab at commiseration.

"I want it out of here now. Take it out."

DeMornay was one of those individuals who go about with a look of chronic injury. Only when large sums of money crossed his palm did the expression change, usually to that of a kind of religious transport. It was almost beatific. Manship often wondered if there was a Madame DeMornay and, if so, what ghastly indignities she was forced to endure each day at the hands of her husband.

"He didn't actually lay hands on you?" Manship asked.

"My dear, he didn't have to. It wasn't necessary. His eyes were hurtful enough."

"His eyes?"

"*Horrible*," DeMornay snapped in French. "Mad. Cruel. *Horrible*. Phuh."

They were standing in a private room located in one of the many wings of DeMornay's renowned galleries on the Boulevard Raspail. Just outside this room were halls and corridors, individual salons crammed with superb paintings, statuary, silver, gems, porcelain, medallions, rare first editions—a treasure-house of the ages. But the room in which they stood was a simple affair, virtually unfurnished except for a half a dozen Louis Quinze chairs arranged in a semi-circle on a fine old Savonnerie. The walls were bare and stark white. There were several powerful halogen lights placed on tracks high up on the ceiling. They all pointed to a single spot at the head of the room. Above them was a clear skylight, through which the brilliant sunshine of a Parisian August streamed down upon them. A Botticelli drawing, the object that morning of Manship's business at the galleries of DeMornay, had been set up before them on a small easel. Not a particularly fine example of the master's hand, it nevertheless represented the fourth Madonna of the Chigi series and thus, in the light of Manship's thinking, took on special importance as a curiosity, if not as great art.

Manship lit one of his panatelas. "You say he did offer to buy it?"

"Yes. For fifty thousand francs more than I'm getting from you. But I stuck to my deal." DeMornay's voice was an irritating mixture of wheedling and self-righteousness. "I told him very clearly that I had a written commitment to you and that I intended to honor it."

"What did he say to that?" Manship asked.

The Frenchman thumped his head with a pudgy fist.

"What did he say? I told you what he said. Merely that if I sold to you, I'd have cause to regret it."

"Was this person French?"

"He spoke French. Rather good French at that. But with an Italian accent," DeMornay added almost as an after-thought.

The story bore with it a certain whiff of fabrication. The Frenchman was embroidering the tale a bit in preparation for the kill. Manship had dealt enough with DeMornay before to know that he was perfectly capable of doing just that sort of thing when it came time to settle up.

"I tell you, Monsieur Manship, this won't be cheap."

Manship could scarcely conceal his impatience. "Why didn't you call the police?"

"Why didn't I call—" The red in DeMornay's cheeks turned an apoplectic purple. "In the first place, the fellow stormed out of here like a tornado. By the time I could grasp what he'd said, he was gone. In the second place, I didn't call the police because if you do, they come round to ask questions. The moment they appear, the press lice soon follow on their heels. In a business of refinement such as this, that's fatal."

"I see," said Manship. He was seething inside. "How much do I owe you, Étienne?" He had taken out his pen and checkbook.

DeMornay's eyes widened. "How much? You know how much. It's all in the contract."

"I'm under the impression you're disappointed with that figure."

The Frenchman grew apologetic. His voice took on a piteous quality. "Well, you know very frankly, my dear—I don't make a penny on any of this."

"Yes, of course," said Manship. He began to scribble in his checkbook.

"With unexpected expenses, many times I must spend my own money. I don't even charge you." His eyes fixed on Manship's checkbook as he spoke. "It's been a disaster for me."

Manship handed him the check. A smile of surprised pleasure illuminated DeMornay's face when he inspected it.

"That's awfully decent of you, dear fellow."

"The least I can do is meet the price of my competition." Manship closed his checkbook and extended his hand.

"You're going?"

"I'm afraid I must. I'm very busy."

"I don't like to see you go off this way."

"What way?"

"Angry. I can see you're angry."

"Angry?" Manship's eyes opened wide in bogus puzzlement. "Whatever gave you that idea?"

DeMornay looked sheepishly at the American. "Can't I at least give you lunch?"

"I'm sorry," Manship said, in a way that closed the question for all eternity. "I have a previous engagement. I'd appreciate your seeing to it that the Lloyd's people pick up the drawing this afternoon."

"Of course, dear fellow." The Frenchman rushed ahead to open the door. "I take it they know what they are to do with it?"

Manship turned and smiled almost impudently into DeMornay's face. "I think we can depend on Lloyd's to do the right thing. Good day, Étienne."

Standing outside the DeMornay galleries in the dazzling August sunshine, Manship took his bearings, figuring his next move. It was late morning of a working day and virtually impossible to get a cab, so he decided to walk to his hotel.

Crossing the Boulevard St. Germain, he entered the Rue du Bac and walked slowly, skirting what was left of morning rain puddles. The sound of piano music rained down from somewhere up above. For the briefest moment, all of the sunlight was eclipsed by the brick overhang of two adjacent buildings, and where an alley let out onto the street, a man was seated on the ground. He sat on a badly soiled coat that had been folded up to serve as some sort of cushion, leaning his back against the wall of the building. A clochard, he played something melancholy on an ocarina. Passing him, Manship saw that the man had rolled up his trousers to expose a pair of plastic artificial legs with kneecaps made of stainless-steel balls. The pale pinkish orange of the plastic made Manship a bit queasy.

The clochard greeted him by tapping his plastic legs with the ocarina. A dull, hollow thud came forth from somewhere inside them. Manship peered down into an ancient, haggard face framed in a wreath of lanky gray hair, imparting to its owner the look of an Old Testament prophet. One of the pale blue eyes was covered with a gray, milky cataract, like the blank, sightless orb of a dead fish.

The clochard held his hat up to Manship and smiled, flapping it at him, while at the same time revealing a mouthful of ruined teeth. Manship fumbled in his pockets and scooped up a few francs, which he dropped into the hat. When he stepped back out of the alley, the sun had once more flooded the Rue du Bac, and moving down the street, Manship could still hear the thin, reedy strains of the ocarina behind him.

Back at his hotel, Manship went directly to his room and placed a transatlantic call to Osgood.

"Can you hear me, Bill?"

"Just barely. It's a lousy connection. Where are you?"

"Still in Paris."

"The Pallavicini business?"

"You heard?"

"It's bizarre," Osgood said. "I don't like the sound of it."

"The next move should be Scotland Yard and Interpol."

"Is it that serious?"

"I can't be sure," said Manship. "But first Istanbul, then Rome. And just now something pretty strange here." Manship proceeded to tell him about the DeMornay incident on the Boulevard Raspail. "With DeMornay, however, I take the story with a grain of salt. Probably nothing to it. At any rate, I hope to reach Berlin later today for one last crack at those three missing drawings."

"You think there's a chance?"

"Who knows? I've got one card left to play. It would be a shame not to at least try while I'm here."

"I don't know, Mark. This thing in Rome and Istanbul . . . What do you make of it?"

"I don't know what to make of it," Manship said, loosening his collar and kicking off his shoes. "You think they're connected?"

"We spoke to Lloyd's today," Osgood hurried on, "about increasing our coverage."

"Probably wise," Manship reflected aloud. "While we're on the subject of money, I'll need some additional funds."

There was the sound of a throat being cleared, followed by a yawning silence from the other side of the Atlantic. Finally, Osgood spoke. "I was up to see Van Nuys Tuesday. I brought up the matter of more money. He practically laughed in my face. We've already exhausted most of the usual sources—the National Endowment, Pepsico, the Wallace Funds."

"Was it a complete negative?"

"I wouldn't say complete."

Manship took a deep breath. "How much?"

There was another clearing of the throat. "A hundred and seventy-five. Maybe two hundred at the outside."

"I need more." Manship felt a rush of heat beneath his collar. "I had to pay a hundred above what I'd planned to in London."

"A hundred?"

"Some old samurai was bidding me up. And then

DeMornay decided to roll me for 'unspecified' services. . . .''

Osgood made a clucking sound that might have been either disgust or despair. "What's left in the kitty?"

"About two hundred and fifty thousand."

"With the new funds, you should have between four hundred and four fifty."

"What happens if I get lucky and locate the three drawings?"

"Try to arrange for a loan, with an option to buy somewhere down the line."

"If we do that, we're going to lose them."

There was another pause; then Osgood spoke. "I'm afraid you're just going to have to make do, Mark." Osgood sounded rushed. "I've something to tell you. There's been a development here."

"A development?" Manship's antennae rose. He saw red flags waving.

"Van Nuys called me in yesterday. Very excited. Apparently, they've located a woman in Florence. Supposed to be the great-great-great——I don't know how many—granddaughter of the Simonetta. . . ."

"Oh Christ," Manship groaned.

"I know what you're thinking. But the lady has documents, credentials, family heirlooms."

"So did a half dozen Anastasias."

"Granted. It sounds far-fetched, but this is different. This one's the real thing."

"They're all the real thing, aren't they? Until invariably, they're proved not to be."

"For Christ sake, Mark. Don't give me more hassles. I don't need that now. I've had a shitty day. My stomach lining is in shreds. The old man's been on my back all week. You know what this little beano means to him. As of the close of the fiscal year in July, we're running a deficit of three million dollars. The board's not in the best of moods. If this show's as much of a flop as the last two,

Van Nuys is out. And if you ask me"—his voice dropped to a harsh whisper—"so are we."

There was a pause as both men listened to each other's breathing. When they spoke next, they did so simultaneously, their words colliding over the crackling phone wires.

"Well, what does he want?" Manship had begun to simmer dangerously. "Wait—don't tell me. I'll tell you. He wants me to go to Florence and bring this lady back alive. Right?" Not waiting for an answer, he plunged straight on. "Then, on opening night we're supposed to get her all gussied up like the Primavera in a diaphanous tunic, weave cornflowers through her hair, and have her stroll among the distinguished gathering, followed by an ensemble of lute and sackbut players from Local Six oh two, in velveteen leotards, while the TV cameras lunge after the procession like famished pirhana, snapping photos for the six o'clock news."

"Shit," Osgood muttered.

"My sentiments exactly."

It wasn't that Manship didn't understand the mentality behind that sort of thing. On a practical level, he understood it only too well. On some other level, deeper, more visceral, he hated it with every bone in his body. But, of course, there was the inevitable budget crisis. Year after year, it was always the same thing—the harangues, the binges of penny-pinching, the veiled threats, the hand-wringing that usually foreshadowed draconian layoffs. They'd been in budget crises for the last six out of seven years. Each fiscal year began with some new cloud hovering above them.

There was the guaranteed donor money; it came from the city, from corporations and foundations, and from a grudging pittance from the federal government. It could cover just so much. The rest had to come from subscribers and people walking in off the street. You had to get people into the museum some way. A megashow was one way to do it. The Simonetta was the hook.

It had a certain kind of romantic, if not tacky, appeal—

one of the great beauties of all time, a mistress of prominent
Medici and great artists, the source of court and papal scan-
dals. Savonarola, the mad monk, believed her to be the pure
incarnation of evil. She was believed to be Botticelli's probable model for the *Birth of Venus* and the *Primavera,* and,
what's more, the *Chigi Madonna.* And all of this set against
the splendor and pageantry of medieval Tuscany. It was the
stuff advertising copywriters and public-relations hacks
dream of, just the sort of thing to catch the interest of a
bored and jaded media.

Manship could see the press releases now being cobbled
together by the publicity wizards; some spicy tale, mostly
apocryphal, about the great-great-——whatever she was—
granddaughter of Isobel Cattaneo, known to history as the
Simonetta. What was the matter with him? Couldn't he see
it was box office?

"Bill, I'm up to my ass in problems here. There's a
million and one details still left. . . ."

"You don't want to go to Florence," Osgood bellowed
into the phone, "don't go."

Manship had to hold the receiver away from his ear while
the rest of the tirade blew on.

"What if she refuses to come?"

The pause that followed told him that Osgood had never
seriously entertained such a possibility. "She'll come, all
right," he finally said, full of brash assurance. "She's broke
and alone."

"So am I."

"The difference is, you have an expense account."

Manship ignored the barb. "Okay. Enough. I know the
rest. Just get me Venus's telephone number."

"Wait a minute. I've got it right here. In Fiesole. Name's
Cattaneo."

A short time later, Manship called for his bill and had
his bags brought down. His plane to Berlin was due to leave
in less than an hour.

FIVE

"Are you sure?"

"The records are quite clear."

"There can be no mistake?"

"Those are the drawings, are they not?"

"They appear to be, although you can't be certain with photographs."

"Yes, of course." Major Von Marle, head of the art-theft division of the German Bundeskriminalamt, nodded sympathetically.

"The old man . . ." Manship resumed.

"Streicher?"

"Dead?"

"He died in Spandau." Von Marle flipped through some papers. "In 1982. Convicted in Nuremberg in 1946 for high crimes against humanity."

The major rattled off a series of dates, indictments, and convictions in his crisp, uninflected English.

"So you would never have known about the drawings if it hadn't been for the murder of the son."

"Correct." Von Marle inserted a cold, half-smoked Marlboro into a cigarette holder and relit it. "After all, if you're bright enough to smuggle priceless masters out of Italy in 1940, you're not going to be so foolish as to exhibit them on a wall in your home in Germany."

"His son did."

Von Marle smiled wearily. "Much to the poor fellow's regret. The moment old Streicher died, the foolish boy hauled the drawings up out of storage and plastered them over his walls for all the world to see. I can show you the house. It's in Leipzig."

"That won't be necessary." Manship dismissed the offer with a wave. "Have they ever found the fellow's murderer?"

The major riffled through a stack of files at the bottom of his desk drawer. Whistling softly to himself until locat-

ing a particular file, he plucked it out with an air of triumph.
"Ah, here we are."

Glasses perched at the crown of a closely cropped pate,
he lip-read to himself, peering periodically over his frames
at Manship, who was seated opposite him.

"According to this report, it was a case of robbery.
Someone had evidently heard that the drawings were there
in the house and relatively unprotected. He, or they, broke
in on the night of October ninth, 1987, with the intention
of taking them and were surprised by the son and his wife
returning home after a night out. Both were killed. Horrible,
filthy business. Blood. Mutilations." The major lowered his
voice to a discreet whisper. "The woman's eyes were
gouged out."

"Gouged out?"

"That's what it says here. Care to see?" Von Marle
opened the folder and slid it across the desk. Manship let
his eye drift down over a long official document written
partly in German, partly in English. Attached to that were
several fairly graphic police photos, which he declined to
view at all.

"Something wrong?" the major asked, amused at what
he took to be American squeamishness.

But it was not this report or the grim photographs that
had upset Manship; rather, it was that business of the eyes.
He was thinking of the mutilations in the paintings at St.
Stephen's and the Pallavicini.

"Any witnesses?" he asked.

"Not according to this report."

"Anything else taken?"

"Other than the drawings, nothing. The matter was reported to the police, who referred it to us. Once it was
determined that they were masterworks stolen during the
war, naturally we became involved."

"Eleven through thirteen," Manship muttered to himself.

The major's caterpillar brows rose up above the rims of
his eyeglasses. "Pardon?"

"Nothing. Just talking to myself. Any suspects?"

"None to speak of." Von Marle gave a tired shrug, then seemed to spark. "Wait." A hand rose as if to keep Manship in his seat. "Just one moment, please."

"Yes? What?"

The major did a half turn in his swivel chair and reached back into another file behind him, where he rummaged about a bit. When his chair squealed around again, his face was red and he dangled a slim folder.

Manship, scarcely breathing, watched the thin, strong fingers flip with remarkable agility through a stack of papers.

"Ah, yes, here it is."

Manship leaned forward.

"A special unit of our division," von Marle began, "devotes itself solely to the recovery of art stolen during the war."

"Yes, of course. Our own FBI and U.S. Army intelligence have such a branch, too."

"There was so much of that unfortunate looting then." The major shook his head regretfully. "During the occupation here, the Russians were the worst offenders along those lines.

"Ordinarily, we would not have pursued the matter," von Marle went on, "but work of this quality, by an artist of this stature, we were not prepared to forget quite so quickly."

"Of course." Manship waited breathlessly.

"I remember the case very well, Mr. Manship. As a matter of fact, I was in charge of the task of seeking out paid informants both here and in the Berlin underworld in order to put together a profile of the guilty party."

"And?"

"Interesting. Several of our most reliable sources, quite independent from one another, were all certain the assassins were Italian. Possibly even Corsican."

"You speak of more than one."

"Indeed. So we were led to believe. I seem to recall

something about some group there—a handful of disaffected fascists, holdovers from the Mussolini era. The typical failures and misfits you find in such groups. Never got over the humiliation of defeat. Determined to redeem all works of Italian art, the heritage of the motherland looted during the war. You know the drill. That sort of typical folderol.''

Manship pondered a while. "Presumably, then, this group would still have the drawings.''

"I should think so. We were not successful in recovering them. And the last attempt . . .''

Manship waited, barely moving.

"Several of our people—top agents, highly responsible— they never returned.'' The major seemed tired now, and his mouth drooped at the corners. "Simply disappeared. We tried for months after to find them. Never a trace.''

There was a moment of silence while the two men appeared to weigh the significance of this last detail.

"You don't happen to have the name of the organization?'' Manship asked.

The major shrugged. "If I did, I don't any longer. May I interest you in some refreshment? I have an excellent plum brandy.'' He held up a bottle of slivovitz.

"That's very kind of you, Major.'' Manship rose. "I've a plane to catch to Florence and I'm running late already. May I take these?'' He pointed to the photos of the drawings on von Marle's desk.

"By all means. I have no further use for them.'' The major smiled somewhat sadly. "Good luck with your exhibition. I wish I could come,'' he added somewhat wistfully, and raised his glass to Manship as the younger man waved good-bye from the door.

Before checking out of his hotel in Berlin, Manship called the number in Florence Osgood had given him. He was unable to reach Isobel Cattaneo herself but spoke to a housekeeper who knew little, if any, English. Their conversation went on in halting, demotic Italian, from which he was able to gather that the signorina was out and not expected back until much later that evening. He left his name and said he would call again when he reached Florence. Having spelled his name for her the sixth time, he had no great hope that the signorina would ever receive his message.

Late that afternoon, checking into the Excelsior, he was given a room with a terrace overlooking the Arno. It was sunset and already the city had begun to glow in the burnt pinks and russets for which it is famous. The streets below Manship's window were thronged with shoppers swarming along the embankment. Motor scooters snarled up and down the cramped alleyways, a clanging counterpoint to the basilica bells just chiming vespers.

He made himself a Cinzano and soda from the well-stocked refrigerator in his room and strolled out on the terrace to watch the scullers darting over the motionless water with the speed and airy weightlessness of waterbugs.

Sprawled on his bed, he tried the Fiesole number again. Again, he was unable to reach the signorina, but this time he was told by the housekeeper that she would be able to see him at four the following afternoon.

He went out briefly for dinner, then returned to the hotel and went directly up to his room.

No sooner, it seemed, had Manship closed his eyes that night than he was wakened by a call from Osgood in New York, out of breath and talking too fast.

"Listen, Mark. They're thinking of canceling the show. They think it's a security problem. Lawsuits . . ."

"Lawsuits?"

"If there should be any trouble during the run of the show . . . If someone were to get hurt . . . We couldn't exactly claim we didn't know there was a problem. I've been on the phone with the underwriters this morning. And our lawyers, too. They say we'd be liable big-time. What with thousands of visitors streaming in and out of here every day, we can't possibly monitor everyone's movements. Already they're talking higher premiums.'' His manner became conciliatory, almost wheedling. ''Come home, Mark.''

Manship was tempted. No more planes, he thought. No more airports and hotels. No more avid estate lawyers and conniving gallery owners. His own bed. His beautiful little converted mews house on East Eighty-fifth Street, just across from the park.

''I intend to,'' Manship said finally. ''Just as soon as I finish up here with Torelli.''

''Mark!''

''Don't worry about it, Bill. I'll be fine. I promise you. I suppose you know—we're not going to have those last three Chigi sketches.''

''I don't care about that anymore.'' Osgood sounded resigned. ''About the money, I can't get you any more than maybe two hundred at the outside. Van Nuys won't budge.''

''We'll make do. Look, I'll finish up here tomorrow and get right home on Tuesday. Who did you talk to in Istanbul?''

''Hakim himself. It's pure chaos over there. They blame us for the *Centurion*. Also the guard at the Pallavicini lost an eye.''

''Good God.'' Manship gritted his teeth.

''Don't do anything foolish,'' Osgood warned. ''Let the police do it all. Whoever is behind this looks like a dangerous nutcase.''

''I'll be fine.''

''Don't take any risks.''

''I trust no one.''

''That's because you've been working in museums too long.''

They both laughed grimly.

"Look—do as I say," Osgood went on. "Come right home."

"I will, Bill. I told you. It's just for another day. I need to talk to Torelli. I have to see the damage to the *Centurion* and the Pallavicini canvas for myself. Then, of course, there's your Simonetta look-alike. I've an appointment with her tomorrow. You still want me to run her down?"

There was another of those long, weighty pauses. When Osgood's voice came again, it bore a tired sigh of resignation. "You may as well, since you're there already."

BODY OF WOMAN DISCOVERED IN ASHES OF BURNED-OUT CAR

The woman whose cadaver was found in a burned vehicle on the autostrada between Naples and Castello de Mar was first thought to be the victim of an accident. Police now suspect, however, that this is a case of homicide.

Forensic experts report that the body was burned beyond recognition. Autopsy reports have disclosed that the eyes had been forcibly removed—almost surgically pared—from the skull. . . .

—*Il Messagero,* Rome

Colonel Ludovico Borghini sat at his desk, affixing his signature to a stack of documents. He sat stiffly and scarcely moved his hand. Mostly, the papers were solicitations for funds, addressed to a well-guarded list of private benefactors who contributed substantially to his work.

A direct descendant of the powerful Renaissance family of Sforza, Borghini never used the title Count, to which he was fully entitled, but insisted on being addressed by his military rank of colonel—to which he was in no way entitled, since he was not, nor had he ever been, a member of any official military body recognized by the Italian government. An incorrectable astigmatism had kept him from a career as a professional soldier, a fact he looked upon as the central sorrow of his life.

Instead, he was a full-time member of some vague paramilitary group made up of disaffected middle-aged men and a smattering of aimless youths, all of whom seemed to enjoy getting dressed up in surplus army fatigues once or twice a month and strutting about like soldiers.

More zealous than the others and therefore willing to work harder, Borghini was given the title Colonel and some nebulous authority to act on the group's behalf.

Self-denying by nature, the colonel was a man who scorned physical comfort and made few concessions to adversity. The office he occupied was small and windowless, its walls constructed of plain concrete block, unadorned by anything that might possibly be construed as decorative or frivolous. The few bits of ornamentation permitted there fell more naturally into the category of official furnishings. These consisted of a signed photograph of Benito Mussolini to Borghini's father, Count Ottorino; a photograph of Ludovico Borghini and his father taken at the family villa on Lake Maggiore; and, centered on the wall directly above the plain pine desk, a black banner upon which the insignia of a mailed fist of iron appeared to rise high in an attitude of threat. Above the fist, woven in gold, were the words *Il Fèrro Pugno*. Below the fist, set in flowing cursive on an arc, was the motto: *Tutti per la Patria*.

Anyone perusing the small family photo would immediately have been struck by the resemblance of the son to the father. Not the son as pictured in the photo, to be sure, but the black-shirted fifty-year-old man of the present, seated that moment ramrod straight at his desk, affixing his tight, cramped, oddly runic signature to dozens of documents.

In the photographs, his father wore the uniform of an Italian cavalry officer of the crack Risorgimento Brigade. The ascot, the knee-high leather boots, and the peaked Tyrolean cap worn at a swaggering angle low over the forehead gave the impression of a vain man who took himself quite seriously.

As for the pale youth standing beside him, reaching barely to his father's hip, that was a different story. Undersized for his age, he, too, wore a uniform—a custommade exact replica of the count's. Squinting into the sunlight, the child appeared to be making a heroic effort to appear taller than his barely three-foot frame. The cost of that effort could be read in the tense grimace of the youth's face. From the photograph, it was at once evident how much the boy loved and feared the father.

Ludovico Borghini had never married. He never felt the need for wife or children. Such homely virtues clashed with what he thought of as his predestined calling. His only family were the men of the Pugno, his comrades in arms. Regarding the motherland, they were politically and philosophically like-minded. Feeling the same dissatisfaction as Borghini did with the sloppy, undisciplined tenor of life in Italy since the close of the war, Fèrro Pugno had little use for democracy. Their concept of civilized life most closely resembled Imperial Rome under the Caesars.

In Count Borghini, present-day Italy produced something akin to nausea. To see the lawless, unkempt citizenry flow-

ing like raw sewage down the streets of Italy's most beautiful cities—prostitutes and drug peddlers; petty thieves
battening on tourists, haunting the parks and boulevards;
degenerate, indolent youth with far too much money in
their pockets, devoid of any sense of national pride, reeling
from drugs, lolling on the grassy slopes of the Borghese
Gardens in various states of undress, copulating openly like
dogs; women dressed as men and, worse yet, men dressed
as women—in short, doing everything in their power to
offend: It made him sick to his stomach.

It was close on to midnight when Borghini completed
his paperwork. His back ached from having sat at his desk
typing for several hours. Slipping off his eyeglasses, he
rubbed the bridge of his nose between two fingers, then
massaged his bleared eyes with the back of his fists in a
slow circular motion.

He'd not slept for sixteen hours. He longed for bed but
was determined to review his work once more before turning in for the night. Sighing, he pulled a heavily edited
sheet of foolscap from the platen of an ancient typewriter,
lowered his eyeglasses back onto his nose, and proceeded
to read.

> . . . and so, let no man doubt, the Fist has a long arm
> that can reach out wherever it wishes and squash the
> enemies of the motherland. Those enemies know who
> they are. They sit in the ministries and parliament.
> They think their exalted positions exempt them from
> retribution. To those benighted fools, the Fist wishes
> to disabuse you of all such notions. We will reach you
> anywhere—in your powerful offices surrounded by
> armed protectors; in the sanctity of your homes sur-
> rounded by friends and family; in the streets; in your
> fine chauffeured limousines; in cafés as you take your
> pleasure. The Fist can strike at any time. Betray your
> countrymen and you become the enemy of your coun-

try; hence, the enemy of the Fist. To defy the Fist is to do so at your peril.

In the matter of Proposition 13459, the Fist advises Parliament to say *no.*

Finished, the Count lit a small di Napoli cigarillo, wafting the smoke ceilingward with an air of weary contentment. Almost as an afterthought, he withdrew from the bottom drawer of his desk a dark manila folder. Across the face of it, written in large red crayon letters, was the name BOTTICELLI.. Beneath that, in a small, cramped hand, was a subhead: *Exhibition. New York. Metropolitan Museum. Sept. 22, 1995.* The date had been heavily underlined in black.

Opening the folder, a sheaf of newspaper clippings slid out onto the desk. With a short sideward stroke of the hand, Borghini spread them out, like a casino baccarat dealer, into a rough fanlike arrangement.

The pile before him consisted of a stack of articles all taken from the Italian press. Arranged chronologically, some dated back two or three years. Their frequency increased as they proceeded forward to the present. On many of the clippings, the features of Mark Manship figured prominently. There were additional photographs of the curator that Borghini himself had taken surreptitiously.

The articles with rare exception dealt with the forthcoming Botticelli retrospective to be mounted by Dr. Manship at New York's Metropolitan Museum. In the articles, he was quoted liberally, providing such information as his plans for the show, which works he hoped to purchase outright for the occasion, and those which he hoped he could secure on loan. In addition, many of the journals had presented in meticulous detail Manship's itinerary while in Europe. Much of this data was underlined in heavy red crayon.

The colonel lingered a while over the clippings, reading and rereading several of them, and growing increasingly angry as he did so. By the time he was ready to leave, he'd worked himself up into fairly high dudgeon.

Abruptly, he rose, turned out the light, and stomped out of his office.

SEVEN

Manship was scarcely prepared for what followed after he tugged the pull-chain bell at the front door of the gray, somewhat down-at-the-heels Villa Tranquillo in the Via Prospecta in Fiesole.

It was the woman herself who came to the door. He had no idea why he'd assumed that someone else would appear or, for that matter, what had made him think that the great-great—whatever she was to the Simonetta—would be a fortyish, somewhat drab spinster getting through life, trading on whatever benefits might accrue from being a direct descendant of the exalted Vespuccis and Cattaneos.

Far from it. Isobel Cattaneo was a much younger woman—Manship estimated somewhere in the late twenties to early thirties. She was unmarried, to be sure, but hardly drab. Nor was she especially beautiful, at least not in the sense in which that word is generally understood. He could see the resemblance to her illustrious forebear at once, but if he had not been forewarned to look for it, chances are that he would have missed it.

For one thing, she did little to call attention to the similarities. If anything, she went out of her way to play them down. Instead of the flowing gold tresses of the Primavera, Isobel Cattaneo's hair was pulled back and pinned up almost mannishly. She used little in the way of cosmetics and dressed as though she hadn't given a moment's thought to what garment she'd put on that morning.

Overall, the effect was somewhat slapdash. Further, it was clear she'd made no special effort to put on appearances for him.

She met him at the door in a long flowered skirt, a loose peasant blouse, and a pair of thong sandals that flapped disconcertingly on the cold tiles as she walked.

She apologized for not having been in when he called, shooed a drowsy cat from a tatty armchair so he could sit, and offered him tea.

"I'd love a cup," he said, gazing about at the dilapidated interior while she fussed about somewhere in a distant kitchen. He heard the clank of pots and pans, followed shortly by the whistle of a teakettle down a darkened corridor. Moments later, she reappeared, carrying a tray, and beckoned him to follow.

"Outside is better." She glanced over her shoulder at him, an oblique apology for the widespread disorder of things. "The housekeeper." She sighed and rolled her eyes. "She's young and a bit scatterbrained. Her family's been with us for years."

They turned a corner and went out through tall French doors into a garden. It was bounded on either side by a pair of high stucco walls squared off at the bottom of the lawn by a stand of tall, feathery cypress. The fourth side, where they now stood, was a stone patio at the rear of the villa, where a cast-iron table and a pair of canvas lounges sagged in a state of shabby disrepair.

Highlighting the garden at its center was a narrow, rectangular reflecting pool, its shallow water scummy and choked with lily pads. Clay pots of tangled agapanthus sat along its granite coping and, in the center of the pool on a pedestal, a moss-stained marble cupid with a shattered nose plashed a lazy stream of water through its genitals into the pool below. All about the place, unattended beds of irises and yellow ranunculuses thrived vividly despite near-total neglect.

"I still have no idea what you want of me," she said, pouring steaming water into a majolica pot when they'd settled on the patio.

"Mr. Osgood told you nothing—"

"He said something about an art show. It was all a bit vague."

She spoke a perfect unaccented English. For their purposes, he thought, that wasn't good. The American media idolized the foreign and mysterious.

"This is to take place at the Metropolitan Museum in

New York," he explained. "Botticelli. Five hundred and fiftieth birthday. He didn't say anything to you about that—Mr. Osgood?"

"Yes, he said something like that."

"In September. About four weeks from now."

"Yes, yes." She placed two biscotti on a plate and handed it to him. "But I still don't quite see what all this . . ."

The note of feminine helplessness struck him as disingenuous. She was anything but helpless.

"For one thing, I can't afford . . ."

Ah, now it comes, he thought. The money thing, of course.

"There'd be no question of your paying," he explained. "We'd handle all expenses, travel to and from Italy, lodging, food, all per diem out-of-pocket expenses, plus a small honorarium for your time." (He was careful to use the euphemism for salary.) "It's only a matter of your being there opening night and, possibly, a week or two after. You might be asked to sit for a few interviews."

"Interviews." She looked up warily. "My English . . ."

"Is fine." He smiled. "Perfect. Believe me. Too perfect."

She made an odd face at him.

A door slammed from somewhere inside. Moments later, a dark, surly-looking young man, a scurf of plaster powdering the shoulders of his denim shirt, stuck his head out through the French doors. He shot Manship a somewhat-disapproving look, then proceeded to ignore him.

They rattled off some Italian between themselves, from which Manship detected a note of strain. When the young man turned to go, he half-nodded to Manship before disappearing into the gloomy darkness of the villa.

She offered nothing by way of explanation for the interruption, but sat erect, teacup poised at chest level, waiting for him to continue.

"As I was about to say, it won't be unpleasant. We'll

try to make it as painless as possible for you.''

If he thought he was winning her over, in point of fact, she'd grown markedly cooler.

''What will I have to do?'' she asked, as though she suspected something illicit.

''Nothing much. Just stand around and look like your famous ancestor.''

''I don't look like her at all.''

''There are some who'd dispute that,'' he said, and sensed her annoyance. ''Did I say something wrong?''

''It's just that it all seems so . . .''

''Irrelevant,'' he concluded for her. ''Perhaps it is. What's wrong with a bit of irrelevance every now and then?''

''Nothing at all, if you like that sort of thing.'' Her irritation increased. ''I hate this.''

''I beg your pardon?''

''This . . . this . . . connection to some famous ancestor who means nothing to me.''

''Like it or not, I'm afraid you're stuck with it. It could have been a lot worse.'' He laughed, but she didn't. ''What do you know about her?'' he asked, changing the subject.

Her head came around, sending a rush of color to her cheek. ''I know what everyone else knows, and that's not much. Only that she came from Genoa. She lived in Florence in the final decades of the fifteenth century. Her beauty was celebrated, not only by the common folk but by the major artists and poets of her time.''

His confusion had been growing steadily. He'd been expecting an altogether different response to his invitation.

''The usual thing,'' she went on. ''I know what is common knowledge—her marriage to Marco Vespucci, her love affair with Botticelli, with Jiuliano de' Medici, and all the others. She was not particularly discreet. What's the big attraction anyway?'' Isobel Cattaneo asked, the red flare at her cheeks deepening. ''I fail to understand it. No one outside of Italy has ever heard the name Simonetta. Only here is she known; looked on as a sort of minor icon; celebrated because her face is immortalized in a few great paintings and also because she happened to be clever enough to sleep with the right men.''

She made a disparaging face, as though the whole thing was beyond her. Here, a direct descendant of the Simonetta was at great pains to distance herself from her famous forebear. It puzzled, irritated, and surprised him.

Manship's head tilted slightly to the side as he studied her. "Have you had the connection traced?''

"My parents and grandparents have.''

"Through a certified genealogist?''

"Of course.''

"May I see the trace?''

She shrugged indifferently. "If you like.''

The expression on her face made him feel silly, so that he thought it wise to abandon the subject. "Would you take your hair down for me?''

"What?''

"Your hair. Would you take it down? Unpin it?''

"Are you insane?''

"A bit, I suppose. Anyway, please indulge me.''

She looked at him, not knowing whether to ask him to leave or to call her friend upstairs for help. At last, she shook her head and sighed, then slowly reached up and removed several bobs from her hair. In the next instant, it all tumbled round her shoulders like a shawl, the sheer volume of it far more than he'd suspected from the tight, severe upsweep with which she preferred to present herself.

He stood there, chin in hand, tilting his head right and left. He walked away from her a short distance, then came back. "Well, I must say, I don't see that much of a resemblance to your famous ancestor.'' All the while he spoke, his eyes kept studying her. "What do you do, by the way, if I may ask?'' Manship said.

"Do? What do you mean, do? You mean for a living?''

She seemed on the verge of lashing out again, then appeared to draw back. "Some acting. Some modeling. But, professionally, I'm an actor." She said it proudly, almost defiantly. "That is, when I can find work."

"Is that often?"

"Not often enough. There can be some thin times."

"Are they thin now?"

"For the moment, I'm between roles. In all truth, however, it's been a fairly long moment." She laughed ruefully.

Her laugh lingered on the air, but when Manship took out his wallet and started to peel off bills, she looked mortified.

"What in God's name are you doing?"

"Oh, come—it's nothing, really."

"Absolutely not. I'm not in the habit of begging."

"This is hardly begging. Just a small advance on your salary."

"What salary? I haven't accepted your offer. And what's more, I don't intend to. I have one or two prospects here that look quite promising. . . ."

Her voice trailed off as if she knew her boast conveyed little conviction. She went on now in a more conciliatory vein. "It's awkward for me right now." She looked uneasily up at one of the leaded windows. "There are things pressing."

His eyes followed hers to the window. "Have you ever been to New York?"

She shook her head no.

"Despite the fact that it's a bit crazy there, it's a wonderful place," he said. "Much theater, and lots of people who can move you ahead in that area. I know some of them."

Her mouth fell open and she gaped at him. "You can't really believe I would agree to come for that reason?"

For the first time during their conversation, he sensed her pride and realized what a crude enticement he'd offered. It made him feel shabby.

He put his cup down on the cast-iron table and rose with

a sigh. "I'll be with our restorer all day tomorrow. Don't answer now." His manner was contrite. "Sleep on it. Then have dinner with me and we'll talk again."

She made a wary face. "What does this mean—'sleep on it'?" She pronounced the words as though he'd proposed something indecent.

In spite of the tension of the moment, he laughed. "An idiom. It means don't rush to judgment. Think about the offer a while before you decide anything."

Outside in the narrow streets, the sky was brushed with streaks of russet. A soft violet dusk had rained down like wine decanted slowly through water. It cooled the air and brought with it the scent of heliotrope and fennel. The shuttered windows of nearby dwellings had been thrown open as if to breathe in the approaching cool of evening. Lights twinkled everywhere and darkness carried with it the sounds of supper being prepared in countless kitchens—the clatter of pots and pans, cutlery and dishes being laid out on tables, mothers at the open-shuttered windows, calling tardy children home for the night.

He was looking for a taxi stand, but his movements through the narrow, winding street seemed aimless, desultory, like a man who felt he'd mislaid something but wasn't quite sure what.

Over and over, he replayed in his mind the scene in the villa, trying to analyze what had happened. He couldn't escape the thought that he'd committed some awful gaffe— brandished money, treated her cheaply. He knew he'd gone there with the hope that the woman would decline the offer he'd been ordered to propose. Now his greatest fear was that it seemed she might.

EIGHT

"The moment we had your wire we knew something was amiss."

"It was only intended as a warning. I didn't want to alarm you."

"Surely," said Signor Torelli. "We understand. As for the Pallavicini *Transfiguration,* we can handle it."

"You can?" Manship felt hope leap in his heart.

"Surely. When I first saw it, I tell you, my heart sank. When we examined it, we saw that the slashes are not as bad as they look at first. The cuts run with the grain. We can sew them. They will be hardly noticeable." Signor Torelli looked at him uneasily. "Unfortunately, I wish I could say as much for the *Centurion.*"

"When did it get here?"

"They had the Pallavicini Virgin here that same day. With the St. Stephen's canvas, the Lloyd's people carried the *Centurion* by hand from Istanbul the day after." Torelli wiped his brow with an immense handkerchief. *"Tragico,"* he grieved.

Signor Torelli was a small man with elaborately curled mustaches and droopy dark eyes that had the look of over-ripe muscat grapes. He had a disconcerting habit of starting most of his sentences with the word *surely.*

"Can I see them now?" Manship asked.

"Of course. We'll drive over to the shop together."

"Is it far from here?"

"Oh no. Fifteen, maybe twenty kilometers. We're there in twenty minutes, or a half hour." Torelli skipped spryly round the office, picking up papers, struggling into his jacket.

Manship had been standing near a pair of French doors, staring out into the courtyard. Now he turned and gazed at the hyperkinetic little Tuscan.

"When do you think I can have the paintings?" Manship asked.

. It was then the Friday morning of what promised to be a very warm day. Signor Torelli had already melted visibly through his seersucker suit. His tongue flicked out serpent-like over white parched lips. He tilted his head and studied Manship warily.

"As you know, Mr. Manship, restorers are pathological liars. Lateness is a matter of principle with them."

"I understand," said Manship.

Torelli rattled on. "I've been on the phone to them a dozen times in the past two days. One day they tell me one thing; the next day it's another."

"I must have them at least one week before the show, Mr. Torelli."

For some odd reason, Torelli glanced at his wristwatch. "One week." He swallowed hard. "Surely. I promise it, Mr. Manship. Believe me," he muttered. "Surely, you shall have them. This time no ifs or buts."

Manship feigned satisfaction, but years of dealing with restorers, as well as gallery owners, had made him skeptical. "That gives us ample time to fetch the drawings and paintings and have them on the plane with me by noon to New York."

Manship rose abruptly and stretched his legs. "Then everything's settled. I should like now to go out to the shop to look at the paintings for myself."

"Surely—with great pleasure," said Torelli.

The old gentleman, visibly relieved to have done with the ticklish part of the meeting with the "Metropolitan fellow," dialed three numbers on a private telephone. Then, leading Manship out through the shadowy high-ceilinged gallery and locking the doors behind him, he opened the door of a gleaming white vintage Daimler parked just outside on the graveled drive and invited Manship to enter. That done, the old man scurried around to the driver's side and, with much huffing and puffing, maneuvered his paunch in behind the wheel. "Don't worry, Mr. Manship," Torelli said, expanding his chest. "Monday morning.

Bright and early. Surely, it's a promise. And when Torelli
promises . . ."

They set off with a lurch.

They drove north from the city over a landscape of green
terraced hills dotted with the umber-colored silhouettes of
ancient family palazzos. Patches of vineyards and groves
of olive trees scattered bright splashes of green over the
brown undulant humps. They wound through tiny villages
with empty streets and squares, where all the shop windows
were shuttered against the blinding noonday heat and the
ubiquitous clock towers, like the hands of sundials, cast
their long needle shadows across the vacant, broiling pi-
azzas. Out once more on the narrow lanes of countryside,
the only hints of habitation were the occasional drowsing
goats tethered beneath trees, or the eerie tinkle of cowbells
clanking through the scorched afternoon.

In less than a half hour they reached the restorers. Accompanied by the chief conservator, a Ligurian by the name
of Panuzzi, they toured the shop, a series of large intercon-
nected work spaces where various craftsmen chiseled at
statuary and daubed and matched paint onto fraying canvases. A workforce of nearly a dozen young men attired in
plaster-dusted jeans and denim aprons shouted back and
forth, chain-smoked, drank endless paper cupfuls of coffee
and Pelligrino water, laughed raucously above the chink of
hammers and chisels, and hurled good-natured insults at
one another as they labored over their appointed tasks. To
Manship, they seemed boyish and inexperienced, unatten-
tive to the rigors of their highly demanding work. But after
even the briefest inspection of the final product, he had to
admit they were masters.

Seeing the paintings had a tonic effect on Manship. For
the first time in several days, his spirits lifted. The work
already done was more than anyone could have reasonably
hoped for. They'd moved quickly, particularly with those
things most damaged. Moreover, the restoration was first-

rate, flawless, without looking unnaturally new.

As his eye wandered over one of several versions of the Madonna, Manship waved a hand lightly through the air above it, as if to whisk away some barely perceptible mote of dust. For a moment, he permitted his finger to linger with a slight tremor over the surface of the canvas: Withdrawing a jeweler's loop from his pocket, he carefully inserted it into the socket of his eye.

Torelli and Panuzzi hovered breathlessly behind him. "Note the line running along her throat, Signor Manship," the chief conservator remarked. "And the shading defining it. Exquisite, no?"

Manship had just been studying that same area. He wondered how long it had taken Botticelli to render just the right balance of line to shading. Did it require hours and hours of exasperating trial and error, or had the old master dashed it off with an effortless twist of the wrist? Manship tended toward the latter opinion. His loop ranged up and down the canvas, then swung horizontally left and right. "The reds down in the lower right . . ."

"Yes, yes, I know." Signor Panuzzi was crestfallen. "They appear pallid now. That's because of the age and condition of the material beneath. Botticelli's reds by no means. But when I finish with them, Mr. Manship, I swear to you by the ghost of my dear departed mother, Botticelli himself could not tell the difference between Panuzzi's red and his own."

Torelli laughed nervously and dabbed his immense handkerchief at the back of his neck.

When they came to the Pallavicini painting, it was a different matter entirely. Far more grave, but Manship was pleased with the work that had been done so far.

"Not bad, ay, Signor Manship?" Torelli asked hopefully.

"I think it will be fine," Manship said after a moment, spirits rising.

But later, standing before the *Centurion,* he was bereft,

like someone who'd come to a morgue to identify the body of a loved one brutally violated. No one spoke for some time, awestruck by the degree of rage inflicted on the work. And yet, beneath the long, jagged gashes, within the very tatters and ribbons of canvas spilling out from beneath the frame, vivid glimpses of the glory of the painting still endured.

"*Tragico,*" old Torelli murmured again.

"What can you do for it?" Manship asked after a while. His mouth dry as cotton, he stood with his back to the two men, staring up transfixed at the destruction. But he knew the answer already.

Both of them cleared their throats, but it was Signor Panuzzi who spoke. "We can sew it back, match threads and paint to the original canvas. But I must be honest. It will never be right. Too much of the material is destroyed. The eyes—just look at the eyes."

Manship gazed up at the gaping holes in the canvas where the eyes had once been.

"I can repaint the eyes, Signor Manship," the voice stammered behind him. "But they will never be Botticelli eyes. The same with the Pallavicini. I can't replace those eyes. I'm merely a restorer. Botticelli was a god."

They finished off with some minor details, then walked out of the shop. At the moment, the workmen were outside, having their lunch at a long stone table in a grove of lemon trees at the back.

Manship grew suddenly grave. "You will promise me, Signor Panuzzi, and you, too Signor Torelli, never to let the paintings out of your sight while they're here in your possession."

"That, I can assure you, Signor Manship," Panuzzi said.

"Surely." Old Torelli nodded, touched by the solemnity of commitment.

"If someone comes nosing about, asking questions," Manship went on, "you will notify the carabinieri at once.

And call me." He pressed his personal business card into Panuzzi's big paint-spattered hands.

At the conclusion of their business, Panuzzi invited him and Signor Torelli to sit down and join him and the work crew for lunch. There were flasks of ice-cold Frascati, loaves of crusty round Tuscan bread, bottles of mineral water, plates of hard, tangy goat cheese, black and green olives. Over a small fire nearby, the men were roasting chunks of sweet fennel sausage. The savory odor of burning fat and apple wood made Manship hungry.

NINE

"I was sure you wouldn't come."

"I didn't intend to."

"But you did all the same."

"To be perfectly frank, I was fiendishly hungry."

He looked at her as if to gauge the depth of her seriousness, then laughed out loud. "Well, you're nothing if not blunt. Let's order."

The place he'd chosen was on the left bank of the Arno in that vaguely arty section of narrow alleys clogged with cafés, boutiques, and craft shops, lying between the river and the Boboli Gardens.

Recalling how she had bridled the afternoon before when he'd tried to tempt her with a hint of influential friends, he was careful not to select anything too flashy or imposing. Small, cozy, informal, warmed by a large woodstove on which bread was baked, the restaurant was what the Florentines call an *enoteca*. They offered good wine, better-than-average Tuscan fare, and the waiters were friendly.

He told her about his day with Torelli and his plans for the show in New York, scheduled to open in a few weeks. Careful to avoid any discussion of the part she might play in this, he spoke instead of the logistics of acquiring the necessary paintings—a job made up of equal parts of wheedling, begging, and twisting arms.

The work yet to be done in barely four weeks' time was formidable. Publicity, advertising, and, most crucial of all, hanging the show so that its arrangement would not only flow smoothly from one gallery to the next but also track chronologically the stylistic development of the artist.

He told her about the incidents in Istanbul and Rome but later regretted it. Mutilated old masters and near-fatal human injuries were not exactly the sort of enticements designed to encourage a young woman to cast her lot with you.

Lastly, he spoke of the three missing Botticelli drawings

and the unfortunate gap they would cause in the full series of thirteen which had never before been exhibited as a group. This was to be virtually the series debut before the public. He had to admit that, from all appearances, the odds were greatly against his ever getting his hands on the missing three.

He had spoken that day to the Interpol people at St. Cloud, telling them what he'd learned from von Marle, the art-thefts-division head in Berlin. They discussed the German's belief that the thief or thieves had been Italian, possibly Corsican, and part of some quasi-military organization with vague connections to the loosely knit, nearly extinct Italian Neo-Fascist party. The people at St. Cloud had listened politely but were not impressed.

All the while he spoke of the theft of the three Chigi sketches in Leipzig, she remained perfectly silent. But slowly, the drowsy eyes widened and grew alert.

"This organization . . ." she interrupted.

"*I* don't say it's an organization that's behind it. The Germans do. It could just as well be some solitary malcontent full of personal grievances and working out his own agenda for redress. I rather tend to that theory myself."

Her brow arched. "Agenda for what?"

"Social change, perhaps. I don't know. It could be anything."

"Murder, theft, the mutilation of priceless masterpieces— that doesn't sound like just anything." Wine had punctured some of her reserve. "It sounds too planned, orchestrated, carefully worked out. Tell me, what did the Germans learn?"

"Nothing." He refilled her wineglass. "Moreover, several of their own people who'd traced the drawings to Corsica and then Rome subsequently disappeared."

"And so?"

"Nothing," he said again, tight-lipped, reluctant to go on. "The Germans lost interest or, what's more probable, funding to carry on the search. They just gave up."

She picked idly at her salad. "There are groups like that still around, you know."

"Groups?"

"Neofascists—little cells of them. Squadre d'Azione, Ordine Nuovo, and Avanguardia Nazionale. Men like Almirante and Pino Rauti. Elitists. They live in the past, these people. They want all foreigners out of Italy. They swagger about in black shirts and wear pistols on their hips. They blow up public buildings, railroad terminals, labor union headquarters. Italy for the Italians, that sort of thing."

"Where do they get their funds? Who finances them?"

"There are some very wealthy people in Italy who would have preferred to see the war go the other way—industrialists, aristocrats, even some intellectuals. You'd be surprised at some of the names. People who wouldn't be caught dead in the presence of such riffraff as the Squadre d'Azione but who subscribe on the sly to their agenda."

Manship scoffed. "But they were around in the sixties and seventies, making bombs and conducting domestic sabotage. They're mostly gone now."

"Mostly," she agreed. "Even hate dies without some encouragement. But you're right—most of the big neofascist groups are gone. Yet there are still stubborn little pockets of them left over from the war. Their numbers are minuscule. Only the die-hard lunatics have held on. But they're the most dangerous, the zealots."

Manship slowly twirled the stem of his wineglass between two fingers. "I understand all that. But what I still fail to grasp is what possible interest such groups would have in Renaissance paintings."

"It's not money, if that's what you're thinking. They don't steal these works of art with the intention of selling them for great sums of money. That's not their game."

"Then what is?"

She gazed up at the ceiling as if organizing her thoughts. "These people are xenophobic. They see themselves as heirs of Caesar, and Italy still as the Roman Empire before

Charlemagne. These paintings are Italy's greatest heritage, its claim to the greatness of its past. When Squadre d'Azione steal such paintings, it's not for profit. They're not quite so simple. When they steal, it's to hold the paintings hostage.''

"Hostage?" Manship looked perplexed. "To whom?"

"I mean, to use them as a form of ransom to compel the government—''

"To do what?"

"To write laws more favorable to the organization's agenda.''

"Such as?"

"Well, say, immigration or tax laws, work rules excluding certain 'undesirable' ethnic types.''

Manship's fingers spun the stem of his glass more quickly. "I see. But if, as you say, they hold these paintings in such esteem, why mutilate them?''

"To impress the culture minister of the seriousness of their cause. Already there are a number of those in Parliament sufficiently intimidated to listen. Ah, here's the antipasto.''

They were silent as they watched the waiter spoon generous servings of cold eggplant, onions, olives, artichokes, tomatoes, boiled eggs, sausage, and sardines onto their plates. When he left, she resumed speaking between forkfuls of food.

"There are people in Italy who see themselves as great patriots, who resent foreigners who come here with the intention of carrying off our art. These people are prepared to take steps, often very violent steps, to prevent that from happening. With people such as this, art has become a very powerful weapon.''

"Hence the threat to destroy it." Manship set his fork and knife down on his plate. "But that's insane.''

"I agree, but these people *are* insane.''

"What about the government?"

"Powerless. Corrupt. Many of the ministers and magistrates have been paid to look the other way. And others, particularly the police, are, in fact, privately sympathetic to the ideas of these people. Many of the older police were collaborators of Mussolini during the war."

Manship tilted his glass back and tossed off his wine. "How do you know these things?"

"Because some of these very people we speak of I knew in my university days. Some I occasionally still see. We run into one another on the street. We have a drink. They trust me because my family represented a part of this country's past they would like to restore. In fact, at one time I was one of them."

His surprise amused her.

"It was just for a brief time. I was very young, and one of the leaders of the movement showed me great kindness at a time when I needed *kindness*."

She'd given that last word distinct emphasis.

"You don't see that person anymore?"

"No."

"Why is that?"

"I don't know. Things happen. People change."

"You or he?"

"I don't believe I said if it was a he or a she."

"You didn't, but it was a he."

"Yes. And to answer your question, both of us changed, I would imagine."

She whistled a stream of cool air on her steaming tagliatelle, then, with a soft sucking sound, swept her spoon clean.

When she'd finished, he was suddenly aware that she was looking at him oddly.

"What is it?" he asked. "Is something wrong?"

"Would it be all right if I had just a touch more of the tagliatelle? And perhaps a bit more of the veal, too?"

Her sudden shift in talk made him laugh out loud. "When's the last time you ate?"

"About three hours ago."

He laughed all the harder.

When they'd brought her the tagliatelle, he sat thought-fully at the table, watching her. He marveled that anyone that ravenous could be so elegant and thin. When she'd finished, he folded his hands and propped his chin on them. "You haven't told me whether or not you're going to New York with me."

"I'm not," she said matter-of-factly, then put her fork down beside her plate. "That's awful of me, isn't it? Eating such a sumptuous dinner at your expense, then declining your offer. I should have told you before I'd had a spoonful of anything." She seemed genuinely upset.

He tried to look unfazed, but in truth, he hadn't been expecting that. And now what he felt was more than dis-appointment. He wondered what he'd tell Osgood. "I don't suppose there's anything I can do to change your mind?"

She shook her head, causing her gold loop earrings to sway gently against her cheeks. "It serves no earthly pur-pose, and, as I told you, this is an awkward time for me."

"It's none of my business," he said, "but who was that young man at your place yesterday?"

"You're right," she said firmly. "It is none of your busi-ness." Then, regretting her brusqueness, she added, "It's my problem. I'll deal with it myself."

While they had coffee and she a sorbet, he studied her. The long, angular face seemed more Nordic than Italian, more Modigliani than Botticelli. For some reason, he felt sad, unable to think of another thing to say. The long si-lence between them heightened the sense of awkwardness.

"I suppose, then," he said, "given what you've just told me about these people, I'm also at some risk."

"As someone in the business of carrying masterworks of art out of this country, I should think you are."

Her frankness was disarming, yet bracing—like a blast of cold air that clears cobwebs from one's brain.

"I'm flying back home on Monday," he said, signaling at the same time for his check. "If, for any reason, you

have a change of heart, give me a ring.'' He scribbled his
number at the Excelsior on the back of his business card.
''You can also reach me at the museum. My number's right
there on the card. ''Oh, and here''—he rummaged in his
inside pocket—''take these.''

Looking down at the envelope, she recoiled slightly.
''What's this?''

''Reservations for a round-trip flight from Milan to New
York.''

''But I've already told you—''

''Yes, I know.'' His manner grew curt and businesslike.
''The ticket's good for the next two months. If you don't
use it, I'd appreciate your mailing it back to me. The show
opens on the evening of September twenty-second.''

She thrust the envelope back at him, but he evaded it,
instead seizing her hand and pinning it to the table. ''Please.
Just hold on to it. That's surely not too much to ask.''

They sat that way for a moment, he still pinning her
hand, she staring hard at him until the tension in her arm
relaxed. When he released her hand, she opened her bag
and crammed the ticket into it.

By then, he'd signed the bill and had had his credit card
returned. With a swift, almost angry motion, he drained the
dregs of his espresso and rose. ''May I take you home?''

''It's better I go myself. If you'll just have them call me
a taxi.''

They sat, not speaking, until the waiter shortly reappeared and told them the taxi was out front.

They edged their way out through a narrow aisle of fes-
tive late-evening diners packed cheek by jowl into the cozy
little enoteca. Manship noted a large, unkempt gentleman
with closely cropped sandy-colored hair in a distant corner
of the restaurant. Seated by himself, he was poring over a
wine list. Manship had no idea what had drawn his eye to
him. But in the next instant, she was talking again and he'd
forgotten the man entirely.

*   *   *

It was still early, at least early for Florentines, who tend to dine late even on weekday nights. The evening was warm. Manship felt full from dinner and peeved at its unsuccessful outcome. Instead of taking a taxi, he decided to walk back to the hotel.

His way took him across the bridge, crowded with shoppers and strolling couples. All the way down the embankment to his hotel, he was plagued with a feeling of annoyance, impatience with himself, a sense of having fumbled some crucial maneuver. He was not accustomed to such feelings. Had he misplayed his hand? Had he overplayed it? He'd more or less taken it for granted that if his offer was proffered, it would be accepted. When it wasn't, he was surprised, but not unpleasantly. Quite the contrary. That was the puzzling part of it.

And, after all, hadn't he gotten what he wanted? She wasn't coming. It had worked out just the way he'd hoped it would. So why was he annoyed, upset? In truth, the woman's presence in New York at this time could only have been a huge nuisance. Moreover, it would have cast over the event an air of something faintly cheap. Not that she was cheap. She was the furthest thing from that. He admired her refusal to be used, and thereby cheapened by the event. She'd declined money even at a time when, from every indication, things couldn't have been all that flush for her.

Still, how to explain that to Osgood; worse yet, to Van Nuys, with his stolid Dutch burgher's mentality that couldn't conceive of anything in the world that couldn't be had for money.

When he reached the hotel, it was close to midnight. The lobby was jammed with guests returning from dinner, the theater, and concerts, all thirsty for tea or a nightcap in the bar.

When he asked the desk clerk for his key, he was also handed an envelope with his name scrawled across the face of it. Opening it, he found a sheet of hotel stationery with the day's date and the time—11:20 P.M..—noted on the top—all but a half hour ago.

It was written in a large, open hand, with the sort of roly-poly letters one associates with the handwriting of a child. When he saw the name Cattaneo (that's the way it was signed, just the surname) affixed to the bottom, his heart leaped.

"When did Signorina Cattaneo come by?" he asked the clerk.

"She didn't, Signor Manship. The Signorina phoned and asked if I would give you the message. I merely took it down as she dictated it."

"I see. Thank you," he said, staring at the letter but not actually seeing it. He still hadn't read it—only the signature at the bottom, which had been written by the clerk. Taking several steps backward from the desk, he turned toward the elevators. "Good night," he said.

"Good night, sir," the clerk replied, staring after him.

She's changed her mind, he thought, and for some inexplicable reason, he felt disappointment. She's thought things over and called to tell me she'll be on the plane.

He'd deliberately put off reading the message until he'd undressed, washed, and slipped into bed.

Dear Mr. Manship,

I hope you will forgive me, but I cannot get your three stolen drawings out of my mind. You may recall I mentioned to you something about friends I had at university who were a part of those groups we discussed tonight at dinner.

I thought, if you had time, it might be useful to call on one of them, whom I occasionally still see. His name is Aldo Pettigrilli. I don't have the number, but your concierge will get it for you. He lives in Rome, 18 Via Sestina. Tell him you are a friend of Isobel and ask if he won't give you fifteen minutes or so. You'll find him a bit odd, but in matters such as this, he's quite knowledgeable. He may be able to help you locate those drawings. I feel I owe you this for having made such a pig of myself at dinner.

Good luck with your show in September.

All best,
Cattaneo

Once more, he experienced that strangely ambivalent sense of annoyance—wanting her to go back to New York with him, yet impressed that she'd stuck firmly to her decision not to. He had no intention whatever of barging off to Rome on a wild-goose chase. For one thing, he hadn't the time. The show was waiting to be hung. He was already seriously behind schedule, and here she was, offering him no more than some possibly diverting chat with her friend on the history of post–World War II neofascism in Italy.

He reached for the phone to call and thank her for her kindness. It was past midnight, but she would still be up, particularly since she'd dictated her message to him such a short time ago.

"*Pronto,*" the operator trilled. "*Numero, per favore.*"

"This is Mr. Manship, room four oh three." Then, instead of calling Isobel, he asked, "Would you kindly get me, in Rome, the number of Signor Aldo Pettigrilli, eighteen Via Sestina."

Even he was surprised as the name leaped with astonishing ease to his lips.

That night the voices woke him again. He'd been dreaming of the eyes again, the empty, sightless orbs. But then upon waking, they seemed to recede into the distance, until only the voices remained. One was a man's voice, the other a woman's. They sounded as though they were engaged in some sort of row. The voices floated up from somewhere below. They were muffled as they poured through the plaster of the walls.

Borghini's damp hand clutched at the border of his quilt. He shrank down deeper into his bed, trying to drown out the shouting. He felt small and lost and helpless. Once again, he felt the old tightening in his throat. It told him he was about to cry. But he knew he mustn't cry. Papa hated it when he cried.

TEN

It was easy, almost too easy, and Manship always distrusted the easy.

He'd spoken to Pettigrilli, who had reluctantly agreed to meet him for lunch in Trastevere. Taking an express train down from Florence early the next morning, Manship arrived in Rome at noon and took a taxi directly to the little trattoria Pettigrilli had suggested they meet at shortly after one o'clock.

Aldo Pettigrilli was a lean man—anorexically thin, with sunken cheeks—and strung tight as a wire. He had the sort of pale, translucent skin you associate with either stern asceticism or terminal illness. He walked stooped forward from the waist, as if he had back trouble. He seemed distracted, his eyes roaming restlessly around the small room as if about to discover someone there he didn't care to see.

Exasperatingly, there were times during the lunch when Manship was certain he was on the brink of learning something of value. But then suddenly, so fleetingly that he thought he'd just imagined it, something like a cloud fled across the surface of the man's eyes. He grew cautious, sullen, kept looking over his shoulder. When Manship introduced the subject of the missing Chigi sketches and revealed what he'd learned from von Marle in Berlin about the quasi-military Italian group suspected of stealing them, Pettigrilli grew strangely distant. Manship had the feeling that under different circumstances, less public and open, the man might have felt freer to talk. There were times he believed Pettigrilli might actually know something. But if he did, this was clearly not the place he was about to disclose it.

When they parted, somewhere close to three, it was Pettigrilli who rose first from the table, as if he'd stayed too long and was expected elsewhere. He fumbled in his pockets as if intending to pay his share of the bill, but when Manship waved the offer aside, he barely protested, asking only to be remembered to Isobel. This was not the moment, Manship thought, to explain that he had virtually no expectations of ever seeing the lady again. They exchanged cards and promised to keep in touch if they had any information to exchange. Manship had little hope they would.

They said their good-byes outside the restaurant, with Manship shaking a limp, moist hand, then entering a taxi.

It was only after he'd settled back into the overheated black leather of the backseat that he glanced down at Aldo Pettigrilli's card and noticed that something had been scrawled there in pencil above the printed address. Toward the end of lunch, when they'd exchanged cards, Pettigrilli had indeed scribbled something onto his card. Manship had thought nothing of it at the time. It was the sort of thing people typically do when they wish to make a correction or update information. What he saw there on the card now, however, looked like something else entirely.

It was an address: 14 Via Corso Margutta, in the Parioli district of Rome. Called Quattrocento, it appeared to be a gallery of some sort. Knocking on the glass partition separating driver from passenger, he handed the card through a money chute to the startled cabdriver and pointed to the address.

The window in front of 14 Via Corso Margutta identified the establishment within as an art gallery. PURVEYORS OF FINE ART. read the gold decal letters appearing in the lower-right glass pane of the window. But when Manship shaded his eyes from the sun to peer into the darkened shop, what he saw looked to be more on the order of a small picture-framing establishment.

The drafting tables, the coffered tin ceiling, and the carpentry tools—saws, chisels, and sharp cutting instruments suspended from a long trellis above the workbenches—all said as much. Pots of glue and sheets of glass sat everywhere, and then, of course, there were the innumerable empty frames stashed along the walls—carved walnut, ormolu, gold leaf, gesso, dark Bavarian elm bent into the rings of a cartouche for the framing of tondi. It was all quite familiar to him.

There were also, to be sure, some fine paintings in evidence. Even in that gloomy late-afternoon light, Manship's well-trained eye picked up several decent examples of the seventeenth- and eighteenth-century schools, mostly Italian and Flemish. But these did not appear to belong to the gallery; most likely, they were only there awaiting the skilled hands of the framers.

Manship had been around long enough to be able to distinguish framers of pictures from purveyors of fine art. There was a pretense of an art gallery here, but a feeble one at best. Moreover, the building situated at 14 Via Corso Margutta, although located in the exclusive residential district of Parioli, was tucked off in a side street that ended in a cul-de-sac. There was something vaguely louche about the place. Crammed in between a warehouse and several other shops of equally dubious character, the tiny establishment gave a distinctly down-at-the-heels impression.

The sign hanging lopsided from a rubber band on the front door bore the word *chiuso* scrawled in crayon on a piece of cardboard. But a light left on in the back suggested that someone might yet be in the shop.

When he yanked the little bellpull at the side of the door, he could hear its high, hollow jingle rattle through the dusty shop, but he saw no sign of anyone hastening to respond.

Several times, he tugged at the bell, with much the same results. At last, he concluded that the light had been left on more for purposes of security than illumination.

The desolation of the street and the light at that hour imparted an air of something vaguely disquieting. The few additional shops in the Via Corso Margutta all bore similar placards on their front doors, all with the word *chiuso*. It was, of course, August, and everyone in Italy was either off at the seashore or up in the mountains. The heat was suffocating and those few shops that remained open generally closed down between the hours of twelve and four.

Still, it was unusual not to see a soul about, as if the weather had chased everyone indoors. He followed a lank, sullen alley cat that limped around to the back of the shop as though eager to share with him some particularly fascinating sight. There, he found a pair of unemptied trash cans brimming over with cord and torn wrapping papers all heaped atop shards of broken glass.

Peering into the back door through dusty windowpanes, he saw more frames stacked against the walls, along with more paintings, prints, and watercolors. The single burning light he'd seen through the front door, he now saw from the perspective of the rear. It was a naked bulb dangling at the end of a long, frayed wire. It cast a pale bluish light onto the head of a stairway that appeared to lead down into a basement.

Nothing unusual, he thought. But somewhat odder, from where he stood peering through dust-clouded glass panes, was the peculiar odor seeping out from the crack beneath the door. At first, he assumed that it was the fumes of framer's glue.

For some reason, he grasped the doorknob. Despite the great heat of the day, it was cold and clammy to the touch. He experienced the curious sense of watching his own wrist, as though it were someone else's, make a half rotation to the right. He felt the bolt click beneath his hand, drawing his arm forward as the door unexpectedly opened.

It didn't open fully. His arm checked it at a point just wide enough for him to poke his head forward and in. Like the doorknob, the air inside was unnaturally cool—even cold, though Manship could see or hear no sign of an air conditioner. And there was that smell, acrid, medicinal, like ether, or possibly formalin.

"Hello," Manship addressed the shadows. His voice in that chill sepulchral silence seemed a desecration. "Hello. Anyone here?"

It crossed his mind that he might enter, look around.

After all, why had Pettigrilli sent him here if he hadn't felt that some clue to the missing Chigi sketches might be found on the premises?

Then he thought of burglar alarms—not only the irksome ones that make loud whooping noises but also the silent ones preferred by so many of the better galleries in the States, with direct hookups to the police. He imagined himself trying to explain, in his barely serviceable Italian, his presence in the empty shop to some frowning carabiniere. A shop so obviously closed. Why would the police believe him? If he were the police, he certainly wouldn't believe him.

Something about that chill, cluttered space just beyond the door unnerved him—the naked lightbulb glowing dim blue at the end of that long, frayed wire; the utter desolation of the place; that indefinable air of something menacing, something instinct urged one to get away from as quickly as possible.

When at last he did leave, he moved quickly.

In his haste, his hand hit the top of one of those brimming trash cans, dislodging a bit of torn wrapping paper. It drifted idly to the ground. Curious now, he stooped to retrieve it. It was a badly torn brown manila envelope. It bore the postmark Linz, sterreich, dated a full month ago, and was franked with Austrian postage stamps picturing views of the Tyrol. The name of the addressee was still intact. The name was Borghini.

Once in a cab, he realized he was quite shaken. He could still smell that unpleasant medicinal odor. It seemed to cling to his clothing and skin. He knew now what it was. Not glue. Not ether. Not formalin. It was asafetida, a smell he associated with the small midwestern pharmacies of his youth, where he'd jerked phosphates and ice cream sodas to pick up a bit of extra cash. Its principal use was as a disinfectant, to control germs in places where the sick and ailing were known to be. It was used not only in pharmacies but also in hospitals and doctors' office, and, of course, funeral homes.

ELEVEN

High at the uppermost point of the Palazzo Borghini, Count Ludovico Borghini stood in the center of a room, staring upward. The place in which he stood was not actually a room, but a glassed-in cupola turned into an office. From the colonel's point of view, the office provided two highly desirable features: One was the splendid prospect of Rome as seen from the top of the Quirinal; the other was the total isolation from the rest of the house, providing a privacy indispensable to his work.

As elsewhere in the palazzo, the furnishings were spare. Other than the fine old Second Empire pear-wood desk and a tall upholstered chair that looked like a medieval throne, there was nothing. Entering the room, one had the impression of a monastic cell occupied by some silent, uncomplaining penitent who'd given over his life to meditation and self-denial.

That impression was heightened by the single decorative note permitted there. On the wall above his desk hung a full-scale reproduction of Ghirlandaio's rather forbidding portrait of Savonarola.

Borghini often thought that had he lived in Florence during the fifteenth century, in that troubled time, he would have been proud to stand shoulder-to-shoulder with the mad monk and die with him in the flames of the auto-da-fé. One of the *piagoni,* one of the mad monk's weepers.

The palazzo had been built in the early twenties by Borghini's father, Count Ottorino. In siting it, he had selected one of the highest points in Rome, the top of the Quirinal, with a prospect of the sprawling city as far as St. Peter's.

The palace had been conceived at a time when the principal impulse of architecture deferred to the monumental. All construction was intended as a not-too-subtle reminder of the grandeur of the state.

With its four stories, twenty thousand square feet of Car-

rara marble, salons, sitting rooms, galleries, boudoirs, kitchens designed to provide vast banquets, Palazzo Borghini,
in scale and design, had succeeded eminently. At the time
of its completion, journalists had been sent there from
newspapers and periodicals to photograph and write about
its many wonders. Its endless winding corridors had known
leaders of state, poets, and artists. D'Annunzio, a U.S. president, and even Il Duce had all been guests there.

For the Count, Palazzo Borghini was rife with ghosts.
He'd been born there and come of age, romping with little
friends, steering tricycles and hoops down its labyrinthine
corridors, flying kites out on its vast, rolling parklike
grounds.

His mother had died there and she and his father were
buried in a small private cemetery on the grounds. The
specters of aunts and uncles, grandparents, and vanished
cousins wandered the hallways. On certain nights when his
head swam from too much wine, he swore he could hear
laughter, the wheezing of his grandfather Raffaello's accordion torturing some long-forgotten Neapolitan street
song, and his aunt Lucia's frail, warbling accompaniments.
Sometimes she would venture a little Puccini, something
short from *Gianni Schicchi* or *Turandot,* her favorites. He
could hear the rough, slightly drunken voices of the men
arguing politics in the billiard room after dinner, or out on
the bocci court under the olive trees on the back lawn, their
laughter drifting in through the open terrace doors on one
of those stifling Roman afternoons.

At such times, he imagined he could smell the odor of
dark bitter coffee laced with anisette. He associated the
smell of anisette with his mother, who loved fennel, grew
it in profusion in her gardens, and flavored many of her
most savory dishes with it.

The aroma of fine old Havana cigars, Borghini associated
with his father—the big humidor of Monte Christos on the
Colonella's desk, always full and perfectly moist. He could

still feel the shock of pride he experienced the first time his father had offered him one.

Today, with the Borghini dynasty mostly dead or scattered in disarray on foreign soil (one of the last survivors was said to drive a taxi in a large American city), and the count himself unmarried, in his fifties, hobbled by chronic debt, the palazzo had been allowed to run quietly to seed.

Save for the sullen youth who lived there with him, there were no other occupants. Serving as a kind of man Friday, the boy functioned as everything from bodyguard and chauffeur to cook and personal valet.

Bruno Falco—Beppe, as the colonel affectionately called him—was short and bulky in stature. While clumsy, he was also immensely powerful. He had a soft, round face, seemingly boneless and of ambiguous gender. It wore a blank and unchanging expression that many found unsettling. A waif of the streets, informally adopted by Borghini, the boy had the sort of rash fearlessness ideal in a bodyguard. In matters regarding his master, his loyalty was slavish. But along with the loyalty, there was a residue of resentment, unspoken but nonetheless real, born from the tough independence of Roman street life. Yes, he resented taking orders from anyone—even the colonel.

Dusk coming on fast, the interior of the cupola had grown thick with shadows.

"It's all right, Mother. I'm fine now. I know what must be done and I will do it," Borghini whispered at the encroaching dark.

Laying down an old quill pen, Borghini rose from his desk. Just behind the chair where he'd sat was a narrow area of wall framed between two strips of ornate molding. One had to look closely to discover inset between those strips the faint outline of a door.

The colonel drew a chain of keys out of his pocket and fished about in search of one in particular. It was a small gold key he inserted into the tiny opening that served as the lock of the door. Snapping his wrist sharply, the click of tumblers could be heard as the door swung open.

Peering into the darkness beyond the threshold, Borghini appeared to waver for a moment, then entered and closed the door behind him.

He stood there for some time, his back pressed hard against the door. The voices of children at play drifted up from somewhere in the street below.

His eyes now adjusted to the dark, he groped for the electric switch. Flicking it, the lights came on, not at once, but slowly, as in a theater when the curtain goes up. The light didn't come from overhead but, rather, from behind the walls. It cast a pale phantomish glow like that of pictures viewed on an X-ray screen.

It was a long, narrow room that the colonel now occupied. The walls on either side were made of long glass panels divided into separate compartments, each roughly three or four hundred square feet in area. Each a kind of large glass tank, it was what museums call a diorama, used for display.

A rail of teak ran the full length of the wall on each side, preventing observers from coming any closer than two or three feet to the glass, though few observers other than the colonel had ever been to this room. The low hum of an electrical generator, barely audible, flowed outward from somewhere behind the glass.

He'd been sitting there for several hours watching her. They didn't speak. They didn't have to. At such moments, their communication with each other was complete. He was content merely to watch her work. He could sit there like that and watch for hours.

Outside, the sky was lowering, streaked with a threatening green-gray pewter. Periodically, thunder rumbled down off the craggy peaks above and seemed to bounce and roll up to the very wells of the chalet on Lake Maggiore. It was warm and the windows were open. He could smell the lake, and the air stirring the curtains carried with it a promise of rain.

His father was gone—off on one of his business trips. He wouldn't be back for several days. That's the way the boy liked it—just him and his mother, alone in the chalet, peaceful, watching her work. The brush moved back and forth, so he could hear its faint scratching over the canvas. Then came the lines of color, gorgeous color—trailing out magically behind her brush, like the feathery letters streaming out from the exhaust of a skywriter.

He'd watched this particular painting take shape over the past several months. His mother worked from an open book of art reproductions and from sketches of the original she had copied at the museum. It was a Botticelli Madonna and Child. An angel stood before the two, bearing a bowl of grapes. Next to them was a window that opened on a prospect of ruins high on a hillside. An old chapel sloped sideways near its crest. Terraced meadows led up to it. At each level of meadows, farmers hoed and scythed, and horses ploughed. Cows and sheep grazed. A mythical representation of Tuscan fecundity underscored the principal image of the child at its mother's breast. The painting, entitled the *Chigi Madonna*, appeared to be finished except for the eyes, which his mother had done over and over again, painting them out, unable to reproduce them to her satisfaction. Where the sensuously protuberant eyes of the original were supposed to be, only a gray emptiness filled the vacant sockets.

Colonel Borghini stood, back pressed hard against the door, eyes half-closed, as though trying to recall something. Voices rolled down the long corridor and faded beneath his feet somewhere on the floor below. The sole occupant of that dark cavernous space in the upper reaches of the house, he gave the impression of frightened, vulnerable smallness.

In the first diorama to his right, two life-sized female figures appeared to be hurrying across a wooded landscape.

Both young and fair, the one in front brandished a saber, its blade glistening with blood. The one following close behind bore a woven basket on her head. Clearly visible inside the basket was a severed head. A small white card, framed on a pilaster to the right of the diorama, carried several typed lines in a small, formal print.

JUDITH RETURNS FROM THE
ENEMY CAMP AT BETHULIA
Botticelli, ca. 1470, Uffizi, Florence

Anyone having even a passing familiarity with the famous painting would have been astonished at the faithfulness to detail. Only the scale had been altered to make the characters life-size. But beyond that, everything was meticulously rendered—the gowns the two women wore, the design, the color, the manner in which they were draped on the figures—all copied to perfection.

The diorama itself was lit so as to replicate perfectly the washed-out yellows and bluish greens of the original. The skin tones of Judith's face and throat, as well as the serving maid's, had the flushed, vibrant look of people who'd been running hard for some time. One could almost see the arteries pulsating beneath the skin. No less was the effect of the blood at the edge of Judith's saber blade. It looked newly shed—sticky and wet.

The next diorama featured Botticelli's *Mars and Venus*. The lovers lay on a bed of grass and cushions. Both exhausted from recent lovemaking, Mars slept while the goddess of love, satisfied and tranquil, studied him enigmatically. All about them, cupids disported themselves.

Borghini continued his slow, proprietorial walk down the central aisle, acknowledging, one after the other, his own lovingly rendered re-creations of some of the highest points of fifteenth-century Italian painting.

It had taken Borghini decades to assemble and mount his collection. Each diorama represented a monumental labor

in itself—some having taken up to three or four years before all of the elements were located and the many intricate
steps completed.

Nothing comparable to this existed anywhere else in the
world—a shrine devoted exclusively to the works of Botticelli, not Botticelli on wood or canvas, but rendered in
human scale, three-dimensionally, more lifelike than the
paintings themselves. There were some twelve or thirteen
of them.

Intimately familiar with each representation, Borghini
didn't pause long at any of the *tableaux vivants,* but moved
directly forward to one of the larger dioramas situated near
the end of the hall, where at last he stopped.

The little white card at the right identified the scene
within: MADONNA OF THE EUCHARIST, ca. 1472, also known
as THE CHIGI MADONNA. For the most part, the major elements of the painting were already there, in place—a clay
model of the angel with a wreath in his hair, a blond infant
Jesus with pudgy pink thighs and arms, reaching with outstretched fingers for the grapes. However, the place the Madonna herself was to occupy contained only a wire armature
representation to suggest the figure and its position when
the permanent installation could be made. Faceless and
stiff, the wire model was a silent rebuke to the colonel, still
unable to find the crucial element he sought in order to
complete the scene.

Colonel Borghini was a decisive man. He loathed vac-
illation, as his father the count had taught him to. In all
things, in every aspect of his life, he had the professional
soldier's aptitude for swift, decisive action. But in this particular instance, he felt paralyzed by the task. Mere representation here would not be enough. The work must
transcend that. It had to take on a life of its own.

Moreover, Botticelli had been his mother's god. At the
time of her death, she'd been at work on a version of that
very painting. Never able to satisfy the ideal of it she held
in her head, she'd painted the Chigi over and over again,

agonizing over each detail. She'd never completed it to her satisfaction and now her son was determined to execute his own version of the work as an homage to the woman he looked upon as the principal force in his life.

Ragged by the problem of the Chigi, the colonel continued to move about in front of the glass cage, trying to penetrate the mystery of Botticelli's perspective. When all of his efforts failed, he threw up his hands in disgust and strode to a little door at the rear of the hall that led around to the back of the dioramas. Entering another door, he stooped and entered the diorama itself.

Though the scene within depicted the lush green warmth of springtime, the temperature inside the glass case had been chilled down by means of refrigerants to a frosty seven degrees Celsius.

Puffs of vapor streamed from the colonel's nose as he took up a position between the angel and the infant Jesus and tried again to situate the Madonna in a way so as to be most faithful to the painter without ruining his perfect perspective.

Standing there in the cool bluish shadows surrounded by gods and goddesses, nymphs, and centaurs, ancient kings in mythological gardens and biblical landscapes, Borghini was in a world half-fantastic—such as he had always wished to inhabit. As a child taken to museums by his nursery maid or his mother, he would imagine himself suddenly disembodied and walking into such paintings, becoming a part of each scene—one of the immortals. This childish dream would often come true while at work in one of his dioramas. He could become one of the players in his own creation.

"Come quickly, Mama. Get dressed."

"Silly child. The bus doesn't leave for three hours. There's plenty of time."

"Mama, come. We must get there early. The Museum doors open at ten. If we get there before the crowds, the

guards may let us in. Like the last time. Remember? Come.
Please, Mama. Put down your knitting. Hurry, get
dressed. . . .''

The hollow voices receded, fading and slowly dying
throughout the untenanted upper floors of the palazzo.

Later, seated in the small chapel just off of the vast gardens,
Borghini listened to voices fading, waves of memories
sweeping in upon him. The chapel had been the site of
family events for years. It was there, the colonel recalled,
that parents, aunts and uncles, sisters, cousins, distant relatives, old patriarchal figures, gnarled, stooped, reeking of
camphor, had all gathered for such family events as bap-
tisms, weddings, deaths.

Laid out in the classic cruciform of a basilica, the tiny
chapel contained nave and transept and chancel. Stone vir-
gins and transfigured saints gazed down from niches. A
series of peeling, badly faded, little-known Giotto panels
hung above the narthex door.

The colonel recalled being taken there as a child, his
damp hand clasped in the knotty arthritic fist of his grandfather Claudio, being led into the chapel, trembling, slightly
overwhelmed at the honor of having been admitted there
amid the gathering of elders, and feeling very proud.

It was only after his mother's tragic death—a death that
thrust the family into the national spotlight, forever marring
its name with scandal—that young Ludo ceased to go there.
Then, having actively shunned the place for years, as an
adult never particularly religious, he was drawn back to the
chapel.

Shortly after his father's death, Borghini stripped the
chapel of all of its religious trappings, and in defiance of
old Count Ottorino's wishes, he had turned it into a shrine
in memory of his mother.

Borghini had filled the little chapel with memento mori
of the contessa—old sepia photos, lace gloves, pressed
flowers, the contessa's wedding veil, her jewelry, her opera

glasses, sheets of music, theater bills and old librettos she cherished, all exhibited in rows of glass vitrines. The walls were hung with many of her own paintings, copies of those by her beloved Botticelli.

In the center of the room, once occupied by rows of dark walnut pews, several glass cases had been given over to objects of a more unusual nature. Among dozens of such items was a vintage World War I bayonet. Another was a diamond pendant watch, its crystal face shattered, its dials stopped at 12:31. Another was a blue painter's smock, made of some rough utilitarian fabric, a shapeless stain of something earthy brown smeared across its front. Out of the center of that stain, the ragged ends of time-yellowed thread curled outward from what appeared to be a long gash made by something sharp.

Lining the walls of the chapel, stacked on marble consoles, were copies of old magazines and newspapers, yellowed by time, crumbly to the touch. Portraits of the Contessa Borghini stared out from their pages, her kindly patrician features radiating intelligence and warmth. Above those portraits, banner headlines screamed the words *morta, assassinata, oltraggio.* Below were portraits of his father's dark, scowling features, the villa at the summit of the Quirinal cast in mourning, hearses drawn up to the massive oaken front doors. Throngs of mourners stood crouched beneath umbrellas, huddled near the entryway, sleeves bound in mourners' armbands of black bombazine.

A headline from the Vatican press featured the words of the Pope, expressing regrets and profound sympathy for the family during their time of loss.

It had become his custom of late to spend several hours each week in the little chapel. Having scorned it for years, he now found the place to be a genuine comfort. When he was upset, when he was puzzled or confused, angered by a world that had become totally alien to him, he sought the solace of the chapel.

Seated in one of the few remaining pews, eyes closed,

forehead cushioned in an upright palm, he appeared to be
praying. He was not, however. Lost in thought, he heard
the voices of ghosts, of friends and family long gone, whispering all about him. There, he could summon up the memory of his mother. Mama. Beloved Mathilde. He would
imagine the music room of a winter's evening, the small
child, adorned in overly pretty clothing, propped up in his
mother's lap. She would place the chubby, little-boy fingers
in the steel strings of the harp, then, guiding his hands,
strum. The sound of it, rich and deep, resonated in the pit
of his stomach and made him giggle.

Later, standing beside her, at her knee, or sprawled on
the floor, surrounded by tubes of paint, brushes, swatches
of discarded canvas she had given him, he would spend
hours sketching flowers, tiny houses, cows and dogs, joyous
daubs of color, all the while humming to himself, as his
mother, just above him, labored over the detail of some
great Renaissance master, but mostly Botticelli.

"Mama . . . Come, we must get there early. . . . Please,
Mama. Put down your knitting. Hurry. . . ."

Later, when he rose from the pew and walked out of the
little chapel, he felt renewed, like a man who'd gone to bed
exhausted and rose refreshed: relieved of all doubts, all the
uncertainties that afflicted his days like a swarm of angry
gnats.

Out in the garden, dusk had gone to full darkness. Rags
of mist draped the trees. It was still hot, promising to be
an uncomfortable evening. But Count Ludovico was un-
daunted. Ready to go.

POLICE PSYCHIATRISTS ATTEMPT TO DRAW A
PROFILE OF THE "TRASTEVERE HORROR"

Fetishist, obsessive-compulsive, demonist, serial killer,
these are some of the words police have used to

describe the nature of the person believed to be responsible for the disappearance of dozens of people over the past several years. Preying mainly on the homeless and derelict, the "Trastevere Horror," as he is now known, because his ghastly activities appear to center about that area, remains a stubborn riddle for the police and the carabinieri.

Striking without warning in the vicinity of the train station, where vagrants are known to congregate in the early hours of the morning, or in the notorious district of the Caracalla Baths, haunted by prostitutes after dark, the "Horror" has so far eluded detection. Only the remains of a handful of his victims have ever been found; each victim has had its eyes excised.

Police psychiatrists have been asked to suggest profiles of the sort of individual who might be capable of such acts. Professor Hugo Iardi of the faculty of the School of Medicine at the University of Bologna has drawn a strikingly vivid portrait of an individual outwardly unexceptional, shy, withdrawn, quite possibly even refined. Both rigid and spiritual, he might well be capable of acts of bestiality.

According to the professor, the complete absence of any sign of sexual interference with the victims prior to or directly after killing them lends a unique dimension to the case.

—*La Stampa*, Turin

PART TWO

TWELVE

What about a couple of wall washes here for the Predella panels?"

"Too dark. You'll get glare."

"Not if we keep the wattage down. Maybe a row of forty-watt fluorescents with UV filters, say."

"It's got to be soft. I want the overall feeling of this room soft."

"It'll be like goose down. Trust me, Mr. Manship."

"I do," Manship said, full of misgivings. "Just so there's no glare."

They moved on into a larger gallery, their footsteps clattering loudly in the vast silences of the empty museum. Manship led the way, followed by a hyperkinetic young man with a light meter bobbing around his neck and scribbling notations on a clipboard. Esteemed as a genius in that rarefied world of lighting designers, he was never referred to by anything other than his surname—Frettobaldi. His professional cards, embossed on rich creamy matte, advertised to the world, "Frettobaldi—the Leonardo of lighting."

"No doubt you'll want track rails in here," Frettobaldi said, entering the gallery, twirling slowly around and around, his light meter held above him like the torch of liberty. "Four, at least, I'd judge. One for each wall. Ten units per track." He resumed scribbling on his clipboard.

"Ten? My God. This isn't a night game at the stadium. We don't want to send people home with night blindness."

Frettobaldi had a much-publicized reputation for fulminations. He took himself seriously and expected others to behave in kind. He had a volcanic temper. He did not take well to opposition. But the Metropolitan was a big commission, and prestigious, so that in this instance, some rarely exercised streak of practicality in the "Leonardo of lighting" urged accommodation.

They moved on to the next gallery.

"This is the western side of the building, am I right, Mr. Manship?" Frettobaldi strode toward the huge panoramic windows, thrusting his light meter up into inaccessible corners. Outside could be seen the skyline of Central Park West floating dreamlike above the treetops of the park.

"I have a lot of early things planned for this room. Drawings, sketches," Manship attempted to explain. "They're pale, faded, very fragile. You're going to wash them out even more if you use tracks. Just give us some plain filaments here. No ultraviolet, please."

"Too hot. Too hot, Mr. Manship. You said yourself the stuff is old. You use filaments here, you're going to melt the stuff, for Christ sake."

It was always this way with Frettobaldi. Manship had lit many shows with him. First came the intimidation, the naked assertion of will. When that didn't work, Frettobaldi reverted to tantrums and then fierce sulks. But in the end, when the job was done, the show mounted and lit, Manship was glad to have suffered the ordeal.

"Can you give me a spot for *Pallas and the Centaur?*" Manship tactfully changed the subject as they turned into another gallery. "I really want to knock eyes out with this."

Frettobaldi planted himself before the painting, tilting his head this way and that, studying it from every conceivable angle. "This is a big item, Mr. Manship, something you want to play big. What I see here is high-focus lighting, something with a lens system—something you can throw a cool beam with a hundred feet. Maybe a hundred and fifty. I can light that baby like a marquee. Pow. Pow. Pow."

Frettobaldi jabbed the air with a fist to demonstrate the dazzling effects he would achieve. It was hard for Manship to tell Frettobaldi he didn't want quite so much pow, pow, pow.

"I wouldn't care to see anything too . . ." Manship began his cautious defense.

Mercifully, like salvation itself, a slimly elegant young

woman had poked a head of close-cropped ginger hair into the gallery. "Oh, there you are."

It was Emily Taverner, his assistant, fresh out of graduate school, full of that brusque, self-assured efficiency of the young overachiever, accustomed to the constant fawning of parents and professors.

"I've got Dr. Yampolski down in your office, Mark."

"Good. Tell him I'll be right along."

Almost apologetically, he turned back to Frettobaldi. "Can we continue a little later? This old buck in my office was one of my teachers at the Institute. He's proofreading catalog galleys and he's running late."

"I'm running late, too." Frettobaldi glanced at his watch and fumed.

"Give me twenty minutes," Manship said. "I'll get rid of him."

Even as he said it, he knew he was lying.

"Alec. Nice to see you again."

The professor, seated in a deeply cushioned wing chair, made a faint nod and mumbled something by way of greeting. He was a tiny, compact man in his late sixties, with a meticulously barbered beard and rough pawlike hands more suited to a bricklayer than a world-renowned art historian. A trim cane of malacca with an ivory-knobbed head leaning against his knee lent an air of old-world panache.

Manship squandered about five minutes on obligatory chitchat—gossip from the gallery and auction-house worlds, news about mutual friends with whom he'd collided on his recent travels to secure paintings for the show.

"You've got the Lemmi frescoes, I hear." Yampolski beamed.

"Yes, indeed."

"And I take it you found my *Centurion* where I told you?"

"Indeed I did, Professor. Just where you said it would be." Manship smiled feebly. He hadn't the heart to tell the old man the fate of the painting. Before Yampolski could spin more problems, Manship steered him to the prickly business of deadlines past. Shortly, the air between them sparked with tension.

"But I never—"

"Alec, you did. You promised those galley proofs."

"You've no need to tell me what I promised. I know what I promised. But you misled me."

"You did know that the printer's deadline for all catalog copy was the second week in August," Manship chided gently.

"Of course I knew, dear boy. But I also told you I was taking the last two weeks in August to go to the shore, did I not?"

"You did, Alec. You certainly did. But you also assured me that wouldn't interfere with the deadline."

Yampolski's face reddened. The rooster wattles quivered beneath his trimly bearded chin. "But you promised me a few weeks' grace. You said a few weeks would be no problem."

"Perfectly true. I did promise that, I grant you. But we're a bit beyond the grace period now, Alec. We're talking three weeks here."

Shortly past noon, Manship was up on the second floor, signing shipping orders and taking delivery on a truckful of paintings just arrived from Torelli in Florence.

By 2:00 P.M., the hangers had arrived and had to be dealt with. Just as he'd started down to join them, Emily Taverner buzzed him on an intercom to tell him that *The New York Times* was on the phone, trying to arrange passes for a sneak preview before opening night. Not to mention, she went on breathlessly, the fact that his desk was strewn with "call back" slips from colleagues, friends, gallery owners, proprietors of top auction houses—everyone who imagined they were owed a favor from him—all trying to wheedle not only opening-night tickets to the exhibit but also to the black-tie midnight dinner to be held on the museum's roof-top as well.

Emily Taverner went on to report that a Mr. Leonard Rackholm, a local real estate tycoon who donated up to a quarter of a million dollars to the museum annually, had asked for twelve more tickets, in addition to the customary two he'd already been sent for himself and his wife. It was an outrageous request, but with benefactors in the category of Mr. Rackholm, one tended to pay somewhat greater attention.

Somewhere near 4:00 p.m., Manship was seated at the desk in his office, talking with the caterer confirming last-minute details for the affair. A sleek Greek gentleman with a lofty attitude, Mr. Tsacrios had brought along with him a stack of menus, photographs of past extravaganzas, and a portfolio of testimonials from all manner of luminaries— celebrities, statesmen, politicians, and social lions he'd managed to please in the long course of his career. "People who matter," Mr. Tsacrios proclaimed importantly.

With him came a badly rattled, overworked assistant who had carried in a precariously balanced tower of cardboard boxes containing, as the great man said, a variety of samples for Mr. Manship's personal "delectation."

Smile never wavering, Mr. Tsacrios unveiled each of his creations with a flourish. "Brie *en croûte*," he trumpeted, "blinis caspianis," then offered Manship morsels of each.

"And, of course, the wine." He flourished a leather-bound book thick as a telephone directory. "You'll want a white for the crab. Nothing too big or overpowering, mind you. May I suggest the Chablis. And then something red and positively sinful for the lamb."

By the time they'd settled on wines and chosen the silver and china patterns, Manship's head was spinning.

THIRTEEN

The late-afternoon September sun had already set. The western sky behind the dark silhouette of the apartment building known as the Dakota across the park had turned a molten orange.

He'd been up and running since five that morning and now, as dusk crept through the branches of trees, Manship paused for a late-afternoon espresso at his desk. The hot, bitter pungence of it triggered a throwback to Florence a few weeks earlier—narrow, choked streets, lights coming on in the shops, people streaming along the riverfront. Recalling those fleeting images of the old Tuscan city, he felt a pang of regret he was at a loss to explain.

He thought for a minute with a shudder of dread what he would do for dinner. He was alone, as he usually was. Mrs. McCooch, his housekeeper for a dozen years, was across the way at 5 East Eighty-fifth Street, the little brown Victorian mews house he'd occupied from the first day he'd come to New York. It had been left to him by his uncle Rupert, an idiosyncratic millionaire doorknob manufacturer who'd never married, along with an annual stipend for taxes and upkeep. The bequest was made out of Rupert's justifiable fear that on the salary of a museum curator, his hapless nephew, his brother's only child, was doomed to a life of grungy indigence. His generosity had been motivated out of a sense of duty, for his brother, it seemed, had been just as hapless as his nephew.

At that hour, Mrs. McCooch would be getting ready to go home to her garden apartment in Queens. Having put a comb through her hair, then perching the little gray pillbox hat atop her head, she would put the finishing touches on a light, cold dinner for Manship—sliced ham, sliced veal, or sliced whatever, along with some limp greens and a tasteless greenhouse tomato, all entombed under Saran Wrap, then tucked neatly like an airline meal into the refrigerator, ready for him when he got back. She had been

Rupert's housekeeper before and, like the little mews house, Manship had inherited her, as well.

It was nigh onto 8:00 P.M.. as Manship was getting ready to leave. He puttered about, finishing up odds and ends, then reviewed a freshly typed version of his annual departmental budget for the coming fiscal year, already a week past due.

"You're still here." Bill Osgood ducked a head in.

"So are you, I see."

"If I am, we're about the only two fools dumb enough still to be hanging around at this hour."

"Maybe Van Nuys will put a little something extra in our Christmas envelopes."

Osgood sauntered forward, a lanky Texan whose sharp granity features seemed more suited to the Marlboro man than to a museum director. The simple, almost colloquial line of patter belied the half a dozen or so college degrees, one a doctorate in art history and two or three others in business administration from the most prestigious institutions. He was also a Rhodes scholar and a lawyer, for good measure. Just forty, he was the sort of man who, after a distinguished career, is usually sent off to Washington to head some powerful committee on the arts.

"Watcha got?" Osgood slouched into the chair opposite Manship, craning his neck for a glimpse at the papers spread out on the desk.

"Budget stuff."

Osgood made a disagreeable face.

"Did you get a chance to speak to Van Nuys?"

"For over an hour."

"And?"

"You're not gonna like it."

"So what? I never like it. I only want to know if he's going to try and meet us halfway."

Osgood propped a cowboy-booted foot up on the edge of the desk. "The chairman asked me to tell you that he wants the biggest and best show in the history of this institution and respectfully declines to pay an additional pfen-nig for it. Moreover, he asked me to wish you well.''

''Bugger the chairman,'' Manship muttered, and went back to his budget.

''In all fairness,'' Osgood went on, ''he's sunk more money into this show than anything the museum had done since the Degas. The point is—''

''Skip it, will you, Bill. I already know the point.''

''Van Nuys is on the spot, too,'' Osgood went on, de-termined to complete his thought. ''You've got to appre-ciate the fact—''

''Sure, sure. I appreciate it. We've been running at a loss for the last three years. We're presently carrying a deficit of slightly over three million dollars. Local Sixty-two of the Museum Workers Union is threatening a strike and Mr. Van Nuys has the board nipping at his buns.''

Osgood's frown widened into a begrudging grin. ''Say, that was pretty good.''

''I practice.''

''And when you take over my job, you'll be able to sit in my seat and do a more graceful job of telling some smart-ass hotshot curator the cupboard's bare.''

Manship took a long, sober look at him.

''Pay heed, Mark,'' Osgood added. ''My term here is running out. I've already informed Van Nuys I have no wish for reappointment. You're shortlisted, along with Col-bert and Klass, for the next directorship. You've lots of friends on the board, but also two powerful enemies—Van Nuys being the most powerful. He can be overridden, of course, providing you don't blow this Botticelli gig. Van Nuys wants to have his name vindicated with a succès d'estime. When he goes, he wants to go out like a Roman candle: All glory. Not out the back door.''

Manship brooded as he scanned a column of numbers. Then at last, he spoke. ''By the time you leave, this place will be a financial shambles. We'll all be selling ties at

Bloomingdale's. Hopefully, Van Nuys, too, pompous old shit.''

Osgood tilted his head back and hooted at the ceiling. ''Frankly, I'd been thinking more along the lines of a night-school typing course at Katie Gibbs myself. The girls are prettier there than at Bloomies.''

Manship's fingers fiddled idly with the grinning netsuke monkey on his desk. He'd had it since college days, a present from Uncle Rupert, whose other passion after door-knobs was the Orient. For Manship, it served as a pacifier in troubled times, with possible talismanic overtones, as well. ''Any plans for dinner?''

''I was going to dine with the ex–Mrs. Osgood. But she canceled at the last minute. I take it a better offer came up.''

''Come back and have a bite with me. Mrs. McCooch always leaves something decent lying around the refriger-ator. It's not Bouley, but there's generally enough for two, and there's a fairly decent bottle of wine chilling in the fridge.''

William Osgood III uncoiled his long, seemingly joint-less legs and rose to his full six and a half feet. ''Beggars can't be choosers, I guess. Are you ever going to tell me about this Cattaneo gal?''

''Oh, our Simonetta? What about her?''

Osgood flashed him a leering wink. ''You tell me.''

Chucking some papers into a battered briefcase, Manship rose and started for the door. ''She, my friend, is a piece of work. I'll tell you all about it on the way over.''

FOURTEEN

"When did you learn this, Aldo?"

"I've known about it for some time."

"Who else knows of it?"

"Maybe two—maybe three others. His closest associates."

"Can they be trusted?"

"To the extent that you can trust crazy people. Who else would be drawn to such an organization?"

Aldo Pettigrilli lifted his cup of tea and sipped. As he did so, Isobel noted how his hand trembled.

They were seated on the flagstoned patio behind the Villa Tranquillo. Isobel wore jeans, a sweatshirt, and sandals. Pettigrilli sat in a badly rumpled suit, the collar of an unlaundered shirt poked up above his soiled lapels. There was a touch of the ludicrous in a man so attired extending a pinky finger as he sipped tea.

Isobel tipped the steaming spout of the teapot into his outstretched cup, refilling it as she continued to speak. "And, I take it, you don't believe that anyone else knows?"

"That Borghini has the drawings?" Pettigrilli shook his head in the negative. "And in future, Isobel, please don't send any more of your friends to me regarding that matter. It's my neck that's at risk here. Moreover, may I ask, why in heaven's name you would send this Mr. Manship to me in the first place?"

"Rumors, Aldo. That's all. You used to run with that bunch."

Pettigrilli regarded her with an air of haughty disbelief.

"Have you told anyone else, Aldo?"

"Whom would I tell? I can't very well go to the police."

"Why not?"

"Are you mad? I told you, these people are crazy. You know that as well as I do. They kill the way you and I eat or breathe. It's nothing to them."

"You think they would kill you if they knew you knew about the drawings?"

"In a minute. Dead—kaput. And I don't mind telling you that your knowing—"

"Puts me at risk, too." She sighed. "So knowing that, you told me anyway."

"I told you because you sent me this man, asking me very specific questions about those drawings." Pettigrilli banged his cup down on the table. "Oh, come on, girl. I just gave him an address in Parioli. I told him nothing."

"And you have no idea whether he actually went or not."

"No. That was the end of it. I walked out of the restaurant and washed my hands of it entirely. Now I regret having even given him the address. If he's serious about locating those drawings . . ."

"He's serious. Take my word for it."

Pettigrilli brooded into the palms of his hands.

"Let's assume he went." Her eyes closed, focusing hard on something. "If he'd found something of importance, wouldn't he have notified one of us? You or me?"

"No doubt you." Pettigrilli fretted. "I left no forwarding address."

"But if he'd found something truly of significance, wouldn't he have first notified the police?"

Pettigrilli paled. "The police?"

"Surely. That would have been the most logical thing. The drawings are stolen goods, and he couldn't very well have gotten them out of the country—not to mention exhibit them—without first notifying the police."

The thought of the police plunged Pettigrilli into a fit of gloom.

"But since we've both heard nothing," Isobel went on, "I can only assume he found nothing in Parioli."

Pettigrilli's hand rose in protest, then dropped back limply into his lap. "What exactly is your interest in these drawings, Isobel?"

"None at all," she shot back.

"They're of no financial interest to you?"

"None whatsoever."

"And they have nothing to do with the gentleman?"

"The gentleman? Oh, you mean the curator chap." She laughed. "God no."

Pettigrilli's mouth curled into an unpleasant smirk.

She went on, ignoring the smirk. "He's a perfectly decent fellow. He gave me supper once, and I thought it would be nice if his show were to be a success."

"Of course."

"Don't be bitchy, Aldo," she said, then changed the subject. "Do you still see any of that crowd?"

"The Pugno?" He made one of those consummately Italian gestures with his hand. "*Finita la commèdia.* Seven years is more than enough for me."

"And, besides, the world has changed."

He conceded the point, then nodded gloomily. "Trouble is, they haven't. They never change. They're still waiting for the ghosts of Almirante and Pino Rauti to arise so they can all put on their uniforms and go goose-stepping up and down the Forum." Pettigrilli lay a palm against his flushed cheek and laughed bitterly. "Borghini is madder than ever. Better I'm out of there, and my advice to you, Isobel . . ."

"Yes?"

"Don't go near him. Stay far away. Don't go poking about in Parioli if you know what's good for you."

"You think I'm mad?"

Eyes squinting, he watched her, nodding slightly to himself. "A bit, yes. That's your appeal. That enchanting, tricky madness of yours. That's why he's always been so drawn to you. One madness infatuated by another."

"I was young and a bit seduced by the whole thing."

"So were we all. It *was* seductive—the unity, the power, the oaths, the cabala, the great mission. All very glamorous in a kind of stupid, juvenile way."

His eyes closed and he appeared to have drifted back

over the years to better times. A smile played around his lips as he savored memories. But then the eyes shot open. The old petulance returned and he was glaring at her. "Take heed, Isobel. Hear what I say. Stay far from Parioli. Don't go near Palazzo Borghini. You wouldn't recognize it today. It's a house of horrors."

FIFTEEN

"The thing about tanning is that so few realize what an art it is. It goes back to the Bible—Genesis Three, twenty-one, I believe. 'Unto Adam and also his wife did the Lord God make coats of skin and clothed him.' Then, of course, came the Egyptians and Hebrews. Your Jews were no slouches there. Direct records date back to the building of the pyramids, nearly five thousand years ago. There's an early recipe of the Arabians that tells of first putting the skins into flour and salt for three days to cleanse them of all the fats and impurities. And I bet you didn't know that the first settlers in America were taught tanning by the Indians. The Crow and the Navajo in particular were masters at skin dressing. They made their own flensing knives from the leg bones of certain animals. It was the Crow who developed the technique of removing hair by applying lye made from their campfire ashes, then rubbing the skin with a mixture of brains and liver. If we have time, I'll show you that today."

Colonel Borghini paused in his dissertation to thrust his pole into a lye pool, stirring it along the bottom until several limp, sodden objects lumbered up to the rippling surface like creatures roused unwillingly from deep sleep.

With his pole, the colonel prodded each object to the edge of the pool, where he knelt to inspect. Then with a twist of the wrist, he pushed them back out on his pole to the middle of the pool, where, with a few slow circling motions, they sank noiselessly from sight.

"Think. Just imagine." Borghini resumed his lecture, moving forward, deeper into the cellars beneath the Quattrocento galleries.

The boy, trailing behind him, listened, his eyes riveted to the spot where the objects had sunk beneath the surface of the pool.

"To take something dead and make it live again. That's no small feat, ay, Beppe? Not unlike what great artists do with paint and canvas. That's what art is, no? Creating life out of dead matter. But the tanner takes it one step further. He preserves matter in such a way so that it is no longer subject to the laws of entropy—decay.''

Borghini whirled suddenly. The boy reared back so as to avoid collision.

''But today, my young friend''—Borghini's pedagogical drone resonated through the endless caverns winding beneath the Via Corso Margutta—''today we're light-years beyond our ancestors. Where they practiced the art with primitive tools, we are privileged to work with the most advanced instruments. Things virtually indistinguishable from those in the surgeon's kit. Scalpels, forceps, skinning knives, flensing beams. The very finest.''

The colonel paused before a tall glass vitrine in which hundreds of various knives of countless sizes and shapes hung from shelf hooks.

Young Beppe stood just behind the colonel, struck silent, as if in the presence of something holy. He was not unaware of the honor bestowed upon him—being invited there to share in such mysteries with the maestro himself, the lord of this underworld.

''The flensing beam.'' Borghini paused before a long, curved wooden object. It lay against a sawhorse, and appeared to have been fashioned out of the staves of an old wine cask, the sort in which vintners age Chiantis and fine old Barolos. He slapped it affectionately with his hand as though it were some dear long-lost friend with whom he'd shared numerous adventures. ''This, my young buck, is our operating table.''

Eyes tearing from the lye vapors wafting off the pool, Beppe, still awestruck, continued to gaze about at the surroundings.

It was a sizable area, every inch of it crammed like some disorderly curio shop with great cumbersome shapes—from the most prosaic, such as tables and shelves and benches, to others far more esoteric.

From the ceiling, suspended by means of ropes and pulleys, were plaster casts of torsos, appendages, arms, limbs, heads. A shelf just behind them contained dozens of masks—faces fashioned out of papier-mâché. Along another wall stood large open bins in which were stored objects that appeared to be bones of every anatomical type—femurs, ulnas, tibiae, scapulae, clavicles.

Another shelf directly above that was lined with glass canisters, each filled with pale yellowish liquid, within which floated a variety of small round objects.

Passing closer to get a better look, the boy was startled to see, somewhat magnified by the thickish walls of their glass containers, what appeared to be the pupils of eyes staring out at him.

Off in an entirely different area, bolts of rich fabrics—silks, cottons, batiks, woven materials, some as elaborate as old tapestry—were stacked high in a musty corner. Nearby were huge barrels brimming over with every conceivable type of button—brass, ivory, bone, wood.

Other shelves contained jewelry—rings, amulets, bracelets, pendants, chokers, brooches, tiaras, earrings—some of diamond, some of pearl. On the floor stood a huge barrel crammed with crucifixes of every imaginable variety, from the most crude to those studded with precious and semi-precious stones.

"Over here is our wardrobe area." The colonel beckoned the boy on. Before him stretched aisle after aisle of plain pipes, from which hung an endless array of gowns, doublets, jerkins, breeches, tunics.

There were shoes, too, stacked high on tables. Old shoes, the boy noted, such as people no longer wore today—boots, buskins, sandals that laced up the length of one's calf, and old clogs of wood that looked cruel to wear.

All the while the colonel spoke, Beppe had been unable to avert his gaze from something he'd glimpsed out of the corner of his eye. Approaching it, it took on the appearance of a large towel or, possibly, an article of dirty, discarded clothing. It was draped over what the maestro called a "flensing beam." Coming closer, Beppe, for some reason, felt his heart race with a strange excitement.

The color of weak tea, the thing draped on the beam hung slack, edges of it grazing the floor. Obviously, it had once been wet and appeared now to be drying out. Nearby, a vat of fluid of some sort dripped noisily into the shadows. A gradual awareness of what he saw made the boy giddy, made him want to laugh out loud.

He had to hurry to catch up with the maestro, who'd disappeared into a dark curtained-off area. Stepping somewhat hesitantly through the draperies, he stood there, his eyes adjusting to the dark. Up ahead, the colonel was looking up at an illuminated scanning screen. On it had been mounted dozens of eight-by-six-inch color slides. Running left to right were contact sheets showing a man and a woman in time-lapse sequence. They appeared to be in a restaurant, eating. Two or three slides showed a waiter serving food and pouring wine at their table; in several, it was possible to glimpse other diners at nearby tables. The last three slides in particular were blowups of the woman herself.

"Pretty, ay?" Borghini remarked to the boy standing just behind him."

"Yes, maestro."

"How old, would you guess?"

"She? Oh, between twenty-five and thirty."

"Closer to the latter than the former. But close enough. And the man?"

"Late thirties to early forties, maestro."

Borghini pondered. "He looks older than he may actually be. Scholarly type—soft, sedentary, bookish, lazy. Given to good food and drink. That type ages quickly. What line of work do you suppose he's in?"

The boy thought a moment. He knew he was being tested and that much depended on his answer. "A professional of some sort—a teacher perhaps, at the university. He doesn't look Italian, though. His suit and haircut are American."

"Bravo." Borghini laughed appreciatively. "And the young lady? What do you make of her?"

"Do you mean what she does—her line of work, maestro?"

"Precisely."

A faint, almost impudent smile creased the corners of the boy's mouth. "Something in the theater? A performer of some sort?"

"Not bad, Beppe. Not bad." The colonel flicked the button of a VCR and vivid colored views of the same young woman, demonstrating cosmetics in a television commercial, flooded the screen.

"Who is she, maestro?"

Borghini's gaze lingered a while over the images, then slowly lifted as he flicked off the machine. "I've known this one for years, Beppe. Had my eye on her for a long time, although she doesn't know it. However, she will soon."

The boy gave a faint smile.

Borghini laughed and slapped the boy playfully across the cheek. "*Molto bravo*, Beppe." He clapped lightly. "I think it is time now for your first lesson. What do you say?"

"Very good, maestro."

"We start small, ay?"

There had always been cats. The cellars beneath the Quattrocento galleries overflowed with them. Borghini had always encouraged them, leaving makeshift entryways in the sides of the building just large enough for the numerous strays outside to creep in at night, drawn by the warmth and shelter, and by the scent of rats and other small rodents that occupied the place in abundance.

Borghini himself would put out food at night—gizzards, fish crumbs, bowls of milk. He had a genuine fondness for cats, and they for him, sensing in him a generous provider. The one that rubbed against his leg now purred when he bent down to scratch her head, stroking backward and completing the stroke with a long, lingering caress of the tail.

She was a plump young calico—playful, affectionate, with white blazing running from the forehead to her pink rubbery nose. She licked the back of his hand when he knelt to lift her; then, cradling her in his arms, he nuzzled her with his nose.

The boy watched transfixed as the maestro chucked the cat's chin with his finger and whispered into her ear. By the time they'd reached the big copper sink and the boy had turned the spigots on full force, the cat was in a state of ecstasy.

"Good kitty. Good girl," Borghini cooed affectionately. "We're going to have our bath now. That's a good girl. What a good girl. Just a bit more there. That's good, Beppe. That's fine. Just beneath the rim there. You don't want it any higher. Now, if you'll turn off the spigots. Good. And if you'll be so good as to hand me that can of putty there. Good. Open it."

The colonel had placed the cat gently down on the drainboard and proceeded to roll up his sleeves. The cat, head tilted sideways, watched him with a mixture of curiosity and obedience. Borghini continued to talk to the cat gently, soothingly, all the while drawing her closer with his free hand.

"Now watch closely," the colonel instructed as he dipped a finger into the putty. "We must be certain to seal off each orifice so there will be no stains on the skin."

The cat squirmed as he inserted a plump gob of the putty into her rectum. The squirms grew increasingly violent, accompanied by yowls when he inserted more putty by means of cotton swabs into her nostrils and ears. By the time he'd started to fill the oral cavity, she was actively struggling against him—gagging, trying to scratch him with her paws, which he held firm in one hand.

Borghini was quite adept at the operation. He'd done it often enough so that he had perfected a method of holding the terrified animal in such a way that it could never get at him.

Sensing the danger she was in, the cat struggled fiercely. But Borghini's hands, unnaturally large for a small man, were strong and quick. "Now for your bath, kitty."

He continued to coo as he lowered the cat into the water. Fascinated, Beppe watched her front legs stiffen and shoot out as if trying to fend off the water. In the next moment, she slipped beneath the surface. The boy watched the clear outline of the creature fade to a watery white blur beneath the surface as she churned frantically with her legs. He could see the creature pinned to the floor of the sink, the maestro's two hands interlocked about her middle.

"Good, kitty. Good girl," Borghini cooed softly. The boy thought he heard a note of grief in the maestro's voice as the cat struggled more feebly in his grip.

The last act of life young Beppe saw was the animal hunching its back, retracting its head into its shoulders. The powerful hind legs appeared to sag and relax as the creature slumped.

Still holding the body firmly, the maestro bent forward, squinting his eyes so as to peer beneath the surface. "Good girl, kitty." He shook his head sadly. "You see, Beppe," he continued, still gazing down at the cat under the water, "the key to it all is never to let them suffer. When you dispatch them, you must be quick and merciful. Do you understand?"

"Yes, maestro," the boy replied, trying to ignore the rush of warmth between his legs.

Sixteen

"I'm sorry. I fail to see your point."

"It's not all that complicated."

"Then explain it to me again."

They sat in Walter Van Nuys's office—Van Nuys, Osgood, and Manship, although Manship didn't sit. He was up and down, on his feet most of the time, then retreating to his chair, a long streak of angry red flaming each cheek.

It was a big office, pompous and presidential in every way. The principal function of its design was to impress visitors and intimidate subordinates. Van Nuys himself sat at a large formal desk of the size and type upon which declarations of war and treaties of peace are usually signed. Heightening the effect were the exquisite Persian carpets, priceless paintings from the museum's own collections, and rare bibelots—everything from Chinese jade pillboxes and Greek funerary jars to a collection of eighteenth-century Italian music boxes—displayed all about.

Manship took a breath. Then, with a shrug of despair, he began to restate his position for the third time that morning. "I'm opposed to opening the show one week early for several reasons, the most obvious being that with all we have left to do, we can't possibly be ready by the fifteenth. The lighting alone—"

"And I've already told you, hire more electricians. Work all night. Pay time and a half."

"I was under the impression we were trying to save money rather than spend more."

"Not quite the same thing, Mark," Osgood inserted, trying to head off the fatal collision he knew was coming. "I think what Walter is saying is that he's willing to spend the extra money it takes to open the show a week early because the additional revenues the museum will realize as a result will probably be ten times the amount expended on a half a dozen or so additional electricians working overtime."

"We're expecting upward of twenty thousand visitors a day to see the Botticelli," Van Nuys interrupted. "Twenty thousand. That's a hundred and forty thousand dollars per week. That approaches a half a million dollars in admissions, not to mention the thousands of additional meals served in the restaurant. We're talking here three-quarters of a million dollars to our badly depleted coffers. Nothing to be sneezed at."

The mention of large sums of money had turned Walter Van Nuys florid. He was a small, fleshy man who tended to wear his custom-tailored shirts a size too small, which may have contributed to the impression he gave at that moment of swelling dangerously.

"My second point," Manship went on, "is that the Botticelli was originally conceived as the five hundred and fiftieth celebration of the painter's birthday. There's a powerful symbolic significance to opening the show on precisely that date. I realize this is a point that will elude ninety-nine out of every one hundred visitors who attend the show."

"If they give a damn at all," Van Nuys fumed.

"They probably won't, but it's a point that won't be lost on the dozens of critics, teachers, scholars, gallery owners, and other museum heads who'll be watching us closely. By this, I mean the movers and shakers, the opinion makes whose articles and reviews and word of mouth will spell the difference between success or failure."

There was a moment of strained silence in which the chief executive officer's narrow, nearly invisible eyes, sunk deep within the pouches of flesh, slowly opened. They pored over Manship with a mixture of impatience and dislike.

"What sort of success exactly did you have in mind, Mr. Manship?"

"The same as you, I'd like to think." Manship could see Osgood desperately signaling him to soften his tone. "I want a commercial success, just like you. I want to see this institution's finances put on a sound footing, so that we can all sleep better at night and get about our jobs. But I'm afraid the only way you'll have a commercial success here is if this show is widely reviewed by the media. It must be perceived by the general public as a truly *important* event—important with a capital *I*. It has to be written and spoken about everywhere as *the* thing. The *must-see* show of the season. Then, and only then, will you have people lining up outside the front doors from opening until closing.''

Van Nuys didn't speak. Instead, his stubby fingers drummed his desktop, beating a lively tattoo, as if calling up reinforcements from the rear for a war he was certain was to come.

A far more skillful diplomat than Manship, one fully versed in the art of corporate politesse, Osgood could see all the battle flags flying.

''Walter, I do think Mark may have a point here, although I don't fully agree. . . .''

Van Nuys's great dome of a head rotated slowly, turning on its thick neck with the stiff, creaky motion of some robotic device. ''Oh? Tell me. What is his point exactly? I confess, it escapes me.''

''Well, what I think Mark means is—''

''You don't have to tell him what I mean.'' Manship, on his feet again, interrupted. ''I already have.''

''Hold on, Mark.'' Osgood attempted to guide him back to his chair. ''Let me do this, please.''

''Let him speak if he wants to.'' Van Nuys sat motionless, hands folded, stolid and imperturbable as a Buddha.

''If it's my resignation you want,'' Manship roared, ''I'll have it on your desk by closing time tonight.''

''Will you shut up, Mark?'' Osgood glowered.

''If Mr. Manship would like to talk resignation, I'm perfectly amenable,'' Van Nuys went on smoothly.

''Thank you. Mr. Manship does not care to talk resignation,'' Osgood fired back. ''Mr. Manship has a major exhibition to mount in barely two weeks' time. If he wishes to resign after that point, that's entirely up to him. Although I do think that would be a mistake for him, as well as for this institution.''

The drumming of Van Nuys's fingers accelerated on his desktop. ''Just what the hell is the point you're trying so hard to make, Bill? And failing dismally at it, I might add.''

''I'm trying to say that I think Mark has a great deal to contribute to this institution—not only for the present but for years to come.''

''That may be, and then again, it may not. I hasten to add, however, that his scorn for all matters fiscal is not particularly a trait one seeks in a future director of a major museum.''

''You've no need to worry on that score, Mr. Van Nuys,'' Manship shot back. ''I have no wish to be the director of this or any other institution. Not now, and not anytime in the foreseeable future.''

Van Nuys smiled faintly with an air of some relief. ''I take your point, Mr. Manship. In any event, the question is academic, since the position is not open at present and, hopefully, won't be for the foreseeable future.''

Van Nuys glanced at Osgood, who at that moment appeared extremely unhappy with the direction the discussion had taken.

Speaking now, he was visibly rattled. ''To get back to the original question we came here to resolve . . .''

''We do appear to have strayed,'' Van Nuys agreed. ''I must repeat, it's the wish of the board, based on the best advice of our financial officers, that the Botticelli open on the fifteenth of the month rather than on the twenty-second.''

''Impossible,'' Manship said. ''Advertisements already printed with one date will have to be recalled and reprinted with the other.''

''Not all that complicated.'' Van Nuys smiled broadly from behind clasped hands. ''Publish notices in the *The New Yorker, New York* magazine, and the 'Arts and Lei-

sure' section of *The New York Times,* rescheduling the affair for the fifteenth. Make announcements over WQXR
and the Arts and Entertainment network.''

Manship's jaw dropped. ''Invitations have been sent out
to four hundred guests. We can't possibly guarantee reaching every one of them. The caterers will have to be res-
cheduled. They run a business, too.''

''I'm not concerned about their business. I'm concerned
about ours.''

''The fifteenth is a little over eight days away. I can't
possibly have this show lit and mounted by then.''

Van Nuys was implacable. A faint smile lingered on his
lips. The razor-slit eyes rose lazily and fixed him with a
mean pleasure. ''I'm disappointed in you, Mr. Manship.
I'm accustomed to everyone singing your praises around
here—'Oh, yes, Manship . . . very capable fellow.' 'Oh yes,
Manship . . . if anyone can do it, *he* can.' I regret to say, I
haven't found that to be the case. It strikes me that from
the outset of this project all I've had from you are reasons
why one thing or another can't be done.''

A cloud had begun to darken over Manship's brow.

''First,'' Van Nuys continued, ''you failed to bring me
all the Chigi sketches.''

''Oh, come now, Walter,'' Osgood interceded. ''That's
unfair.''

''You've got ten out of the original thirteen,'' Manship
fumed. ''You know perfectly well the reasons why the
other three couldn't be had.''

Van Nuys's smile had slipped into a broad smirk. Manship continued in spite of it.

''This will be the first and largest group showing of these
sketches ever. The other three are probably gracing the
walls of some mafiosa chief's villa in Calabria.''

''Sounds to me as though you just lost your nerve, Mr.
Manship.''

''Come on now, Walter,'' Osgood interrupted. ''This is
really uncalled for.''

"What's more," Van Nuys jabbed on, "you consistently overpaid for works that any skilled negotiator could have secured for far less. You have this formidable reputation for negotiation, so we trusted you to negotiate."

"Next time, send some other skilled negotiator who'll nickel-and-dime more to your taste," Manship shot back.

By then, Osgood had given up any hope of polite arbitration between what were clearly two adversaries bent on mauling each other. He sat back helplessly now and watched the situation deteriorate.

"Moreover," Van Nuys went on, all traces of civility gone, "I asked you to bring the Simonetta woman back with you for the opening. There again you failed me."

"It wasn't for lack of trying," he said bitterly. "I wanted her to come as much as you. . . ."

"That isn't the way I heard it, Mr. Manship."

Osgood addressed his boss sharply for the first time, "What I told you was that Mark didn't want anything superficial to detract from the intrinsic importance of the occasion. And I must say," Osgood added with a certain pointedness to his voice, "I'm sympathetic to that point of view myself."

Manship flung his hands up in despair. "It's all academic now, anyway. She's not coming. She hasn't the slightest interest in the show. She's made that quite clear."

"Perhaps you weren't persuasive enough," Van Nuys taunted. "Not sexy enough." He tossed his great head back and laughed. But it was a cheerless laugh that broke off quickly, rippling away into jagged edges. The fingers resumed their rattle on the desktop and the CEO was once more all icy efficiency.

"Am I to understand, then, Mr. Manship, that you won't accommodate the financial officers of this institution and move your opening night up one week?"

"That's correct." Manship didn't blink an eye. "And if that's unsatisfactory to you and the board, as I said before, you have my resignation." His manner was quite civilized.

There was no rancor to it. Just a simple statement of fact.

A moment of silence followed. Even the rapid drumming of fingers on the desktop ceased. Van Nuys appeared unfazed, but one could sense a keen mind calculating quickly behind the jutting brow. He was about to answer Manship's challenge when Osgood headed him off.

"I should add, Walter, that if Mark's resignation is accepted by the board, they can have mine, as well."

It was at this point that Van Nuys blinked.

SEVENTEEN

It was 6:00 P.M. A weary, sullen tide of workers streamed from office buildings, homeward-bound. Early September, Rome, but the temperature and humidity felt closer to July.

Isobel Cattaneo lay wearily against the backseat of the taxi. It was not air-conditioned and the leather seats were hot. The driver, a fiery Sicilian, sat sweltering in his undershirt, cursing the demonic, heat-crazed traffic. The front windows were rolled down as if to gather any available breath of air.

Isobel's head rolled right and left against the backseat. Eyes closed, head pounding, she was certain she was about to be sick with the next swerve of the car. The thin shift she wore was damp with sweat; the elastic of her light undergarments chafed her skin.

She'd had a bad day. In fact, a bad three days, shooting a TV commercial for a line of "quality" plumbing fixtures: "Lumenetti's Luxury Kitchens and Bathrooms." Worse than the kitchens and bathrooms was the arrogant young director, convinced he was Fellini and given to tantrums and intimidation.

It was the sort of thing she'd done far too much of in the past and swore she'd never do again. This time when her agent called, she'd declined. When he called back within an hour to say that he'd extracted the promise of an extortionate sum from the producers if he could secure her services, she'd declined again. The agent was relentless. If she'd just do this job as a favor to him, he guaranteed he'd never book her for such a thing again, and, moreover, he'd have a play for her in the fall.

All of her better instincts had been to say no. But if the promise of a play in the fall was genuine, she would somehow endure.

It seemed that the story line of the commercial involved a reenactment of Botticelli's *Birth of Venus*. Isobel in a transparent body stocking was to rise from the sea in a

Lumenetti bathroom sink sculpted into the shape of a scallop shell. No doubt that's why the producers were so determined to have her. Most Roman casting directors, when looking about for a classic Renaissance type, invariably thought of Isobel Cattaneo first.

She didn't mind the near nudity. She was used to that, as well as to Italian male directors with their well-known penchant for contriving reasons to get an actress out of her clothing. She was more angry with her agent, who apparently had so little regard for her acting skills as to permit her to get dragged into the situation in the first place.

But what particularly bothered her was this neophyte young director with his shrill voice and his mincing, lisping manner grandly ordering her about. No doubt his uncle was Mr. Lumenetti. That's the way such things generally worked.

Add to all that the fact she'd had a call that afternoon from Fiesole. Erminia was nearly hysterical. Tino had taken money from her purse. He'd come in from the studio, filthy and muttering. Something about his gallery owner cheating him out of his commissions. When she'd told him he was tracking up the kitchen floor, which she'd just washed, he threw a glass at her. This was the second or third time he'd stolen from her purse. She would not come back to work unless the signorina reimbursed her. She knew it was hopeless to expect him to pay her back.

Isobel sighed. Between the heat of the cab, the obnoxious little jingle director, and now Tino's pathetic pilferings from a poor housemaid, it was all getting to be a bit much.

She knew it was time to get rid of Tino. The whole thing was misbegotten from the start. What had ever possessed her? Of course, he could be quite charming. But, recently, with luck running against him, the charm was more likely to become abuse, and expressed in ways she could no longer tolerate.

What had she been thinking when she'd brought him home, permitted him to move in? His ways were uncouth.

Wherever he went in the house, he left a trail of debris behind him. Expecting people to clean up after him, he behaved like a spoiled child. Part of the time he was sullen; the other part, nasty. It was time to face facts. She had to get rid of him, even if it meant getting the police to throw him out.

The throbbing of her head distracted her from her brooding. When she looked up again, she was surprised to see it had gone full dusk. Lights had begun to flicker from the windows of buildings and shopfronts. Buses now lit gasped past, crammed to the gunnels with passengers limp from the heat, clinging to overhead straps and looking as though they were pasted to the windows.

The taxi was climbing a hill, actually hurtling upward, quite fast. The heavy traffic around the Forum had given way and the driver gunned the engine. All the while he hurtled forward, he kept muttering to no one in particular.

They were on the Quirinal, climbing the steep cobbled embankment of Via XX Settembre. They had to cross it in order to get back to her hotel. Something in her became excited in ways not entirely pleasing to her. With that came the odd sensation of time sliding backward, along with the streetlights zooming past outside the taxi.

She was ten years younger, having just completed with honors her second year at the university. Sitting in a ball dress in which she felt foolish, in the back of a taxi, just as she was now, she was going to a dinner party at Palazzo Borghini. Her first time there—the count himself had invited her.

He'd come to the university as a spokesman of the National Alliance. There'd been violent protests when it was learned that he was to speak. Christian Democrats and Communists kicked up an awful row. Chanting and shouting rose outside the lecture hall: "FASCISTO . . . FASCISTO . . . FASCISTO."

It had been an unusually warm day. The windows in the

lecture hall stood open to catch what little air there was. "FASCISTO. FASCISTO." The simple word shouted over and over again drifted upward from the quadrangle below along with the wail of sirens. The police had cordoned off the mobs, threatening at any moment to charge the building.

The man at the center of all of this chaos, the man she'd come there to hear, Count Ludovico Borghini, was a member of one of the most ancient and venerated families of Italy. He was an admitted fascist and despised. His family was said to have been closely associated with Mussolini during the war, and had collaborated with the Germans during the occupation. The colonel himself argued for a curb on many of the rights of the people, a curb on the waves of Third World immigrants currently flooding the country, a curb on the press, and an expansion of powers for the police and the military.

Borghini's views were deemed to be so extreme that even members of his own family had publicly disavowed them. At the time Isobel came to know him, he was already an outcast. That, doubtless, was part of the attraction for her. So was she, and by her own choice.

She watched him on the podium where he stood, a prematurely gray, impeccably tailored presence. Small. Smaller than she. Having read so much about him and knowing his views when she first saw him, she came close to laughing. It was simply so incongruous.

A great deal of what he said she scarcely understood. He spoke about politics, the church, Italian history, particularly that of the fifteenth century. When he spoke of Savonarola, his eyes appeared to glow. Afterward, she went up to the podium, where a few others milled about, asking him questions. All the while he spoke, he kept glancing at her, until she became keenly aware of his interest, his eyes holding hers, so that after a while some subtle thread of understanding had bonded them. After the others had drifted off, she finally approached him.

For a man with such hateful thoughts (much of his thinking was hateful to her—elitism, exclusivism, right is
might), she was nonetheless drawn to his longing for an
Italy long gone, for a less cynical, less mercenary Italy, for
people who placed the love of ideas above the love of
things. After all, she had come from one of the powerful
merchant families herself and was diametrically opposed to
the glib, fashionable new socialism that many people of her
age and class had embraced.

Later, he gave her his card. "If you get to Rome someday, call." She sensed that he liked her.

A motor scooter shot past the taxi and cut out in front of
them. The driver blared his horn and jammed on the brakes.
There was the squeal of metal grinding and almost instantly
the smell of burning rubber. She was hurled forward, hard
up against the back of the front seat, shaken but unhurt.
The driver's head was out the side window, spewing obscenities after the driver speeding rapidly into the gaudy
twilight up ahead.

They sat pulled over to the side, where the driver scribbled something into his book. When she looked out, she
was startled to find that they had stopped almost directly
across from the Palazzo Borghini. She asked the driver to
pull over for a moment.

The place was not as she recalled it. For one thing, it
now seemed closer to the street—almost exactly where the
Via del Quirinale crosses the Via della Quattro Fontane.

That first night when she'd gone there, she recalled a far
more gracious expanse of open space around the palace.
She was surprised now to discover that it was wedged
somewhat clumsily between two official-looking buildings,
dwarfed by one and overshadowing the other.

Her first impression, years before, was that it was a
larger, more imposing structure. That might have been due
to the fact that she was younger and more impressionable,
more inclined to amplify and romanticize things.

Looking out the taxi window, the place looked a bit tatty—unkempt, unattended to. The gardens, at one time a source of pride to the Borghinis (and Contessa Borghini's particular joy), had been allowed to run to seed.

In fact, the whole place, still impressive as architecture, had the down-at-the-heels look of derelict property. If not for the single light glowing faintly in a corner window, she would have guessed the place was unoccupied. There was a dark, inhospitable look about it, a rueful air heightened by the spear-point wrought-iron gates that stood shut and unwelcoming against the approaching night.

Just beyond the gate and standing off to the side of the large circular drive, she glimpsed a vintage Hispano Suiza. Battered and looking every bit its age, the car, once the pride of the late Count Ottorino, was a sure sign that Borghini himself was in residence, no doubt the lone occupant of the corner downstairs room where the single light burned against the vast façade of the building.

"Signorina?"

The note of impatience in the driver's voice roused her from her musings. The man was hot, still infuriated by the motor scooter driver who'd nearly wrecked them, and, no doubt, anxious to get home to his family and supper.

"Yes. I'm sorry. Drive on," she said.

As they pulled out, she glanced back in time to catch the notched outline of the palazzo against the pale, starless sky of early evening. Turning a corner into the Via Francesco Crispi, the last thing she saw was the tiny orange light flickering in the vast encroaching darkness.

Isobel had misread the significance of the single light flickering that night in a corner window of the Palazzo Borghini. Quite naturally, she'd concluded that the colonel was in residence—somewhere behind the massive masonry of the building.

In point of fact, Borghini was not there. He was, instead, some six or seven miles away, gathering with a handful of young braves at an hosteria in the Parioli district not far from the Quattrocento galleries.

It was a Friday night, the end of the workweek for Borghini. There were no activities scheduled for the next day, and so the colonel felt a certain sense of release. Tonight, he was surrounded by a handful of young louts around whom he felt most comfortable. With their shaved heads and black shirts, they were of that ilk known to the freedom-loving Italians as "Nazi skins." What these twenty-year-olds found so irresistible in a middle-aged colonel was due in large part, no doubt, to the fact that he spent freely, and then, too, with the colonel there was always the promise of excitement.

Here was Luccabrava; Buonofaccio; Vicenti Picarello, known among his fellows as "the Whip"; Baddamente of the gentle nature and fists of steel; Canova; Corsi; Tenuto, who bore the sobriquet "the Spokesman," so called for his eloquence in articulating the political and moral platform of the group. Finally, there was young Beppe, the baby of the group, perhaps the rawest and most untamed, the one to inspire most caution.

They'd gathered there at roughly 8:00 P.M. and proceeded to eat and drink with a certain seriousness. The staff in the kitchen and the waiters had all been put on the alert. The colonel was known to insist upon perfection. That was all right, of course. But more disturbingly, the group as a whole had a reputation for unpredictability.

By nine or half past nine that evening, the maestro's tongue had grown looser. Encouraged by his *banda,* he'd launched into a number of pet diatribes—the fading glory of Italy; Italy as a Third World nation; why Italy must forsake industrialization. Industrialization had fouled everything about them. Italy must return to an agrarian economy; Italy must go back to monarchy. Republicanism had failed Italy; the professional bureaucrats who governed the nation were inept and corrupt; the streets of Rome were an open sewer, swarming with rude Third World blacks and other undesirable ethnic types, all plundering the national treasury. Such people produced nothing but dirt and social problems. Any gesture of generosity they viewed as weakness and an invitation to demand more. He likened these *immigranti* to a running sore.

Mesmerized by his own eloquence, Borghini pounded the table. The youths grew raucous. The innkeeper, who knew Borghini, began to show signs of nervousness. But he also knew the man well enough not to interfere. Borghini's "louts" could be quite nasty when the honor of the maestro was challenged. So instead, he brought out plate after plate and bottle after bottle—his oldest and finest Brunellos and Barolos.

Offended by the noise, other diners asked to have their tables changed or paid their bills and left. But by then, Borghini and his small clique of admirers were too drunk to notice.

Sipping his after-dinner grappa, his tongue loosened and he grew more relaxed. He leaned back, tie loosened, collar opened, and began to speak of his mother. Each sentence would begin: "My mother used to say . . ." or "My mother was a great one for . . ." He would turn next to his father. "My father, of course, was one of the original founders of Salo—I might say *the* original founder. . . ."

After his mother and father, in order of importance came Savonarola, the mad monk who had burned books and paintings in fifteenth-century Florence because they fostered a worldliness that led to atheism and immorality.

Savonarola would usually coincide with the appearance of his third grappa. By the fifth, the colonel would be maudlin. For those who'd sat through these intimate little suppers with him before, they knew this to be the signal for him to lapse into meandering reminiscences, by which time tears would glisten in his bleary eyes.

It was nearly midnight when they lurched out of the little hosteria, leaving in their wake a litter of broken glass and spilled food. The area about the table where they'd dined looked as though a herd of cattle had pastured there.

The colonel had signed his IOU over to the innkeeper, assuring him that payment would be in the mail the next day. The innkeeper could do little more than nod his head deferentially, a queasy smile frozen on his face. He well knew that payment would be a long time coming, if, indeed, it ever came at all. He also knew it was best to swallow his bile and say nothing, rather than tangle with the colonel and his boyish thugs. To be sure, one dared not go to the police, for the colonel had friends in high places, and if some poor aggrieved innkeeper were so rash as to file a complaint, the next day he might find his license to operate suddenly withdrawn—the reasons given, health violations or some trumped-up, nebulous charge.

Full of wine and grappa, the maestro, having eaten and talked himself out, expressed a desire to walk. The night was cool. A breeze had started up off the river and felt like a kiss rushing past his feverish, pounding temples.

The group surged out onto the street, singing bawdy songs. People out for a stroll, returning from cinemas and late-night dinners, gave them a wide berth. They made a fairly menacing picture—six or seven burly louts, not exactly unkempt, but bordering on it, accompanied by a smallish middle-aged man swaggering along with a cocky stride, all apparently relishing the uneasiness they caused in any passerby.

Somewhere near the old Jewish quarter, hard by the Tiber, the group had started to jog, then run. Someone had snatched an old newspaper out of a trash can and, with bits of string salvaged from carton wrappings found in the gutter, fashioned a ball from it. Shortly, they were barging down the street, playing soccer—kicking their paper ball and banging off one another, their hoots and jeers rising upward into the gaudy night, the small, slight, older individual in the group far more boisterous than his younger companions. He was determined to show that not only could he keep up with his young bucks; he had the physical stamina to exceed them by far.

In the vicinity of the Via Monte de Cenci, they grew more riotous. People on the street, coming out of Piperno and da Giggetto, looked anxiously for taxis and tried hard not to notice.

Not far from Piperno, one of them kicked the paper ball, exploding it into a blizzard of downward-drifting confetti, dusting their hair and the collars of their jackets. They punched out at the slow, drifting white stuff, flailing the air like shadow boxers and roaring with delight. When the blizzard had slowed to a few stray wisps swirling idly about them, the group suddenly looked up, to find themselves in front of the Jewish temple—the old Sinagoga Ebraica on the Lungotevere dei Cenci.

Angular, massive, and thrusting, the ancient masonry loomed above them, jutting out above their heads into the street. Dark and silent, it appeared to sleep deep within the mystery of centuries past.

Realizing for the first time where he was, the maestro gestured for all of his revelers to be silent. He pressed a finger against his lips as if calling for respect before this venerable house of worship.

At once, the group fell silent. They watched the maestro intently, with glints of mischief in their eyes, anticipating that something special was about to take place.

In the next moment, Borghini, a wicked smirk across his face, tiptoed stealthily up the front steps. The others watched, transfixed, as the small, plucky figure opened his trousers and urinated against the big oaken front door of the ancient building.

Cars swept past, speeding up the Lungotevere, momentarily lighting up the strange scene, then sped on. For the little *banda,* it was different. They roared with delight, cheering on their patron—the maestro, a figure of striking dignity, his trousers open, underpants extruding through the unbuttoned fly, pissing against the front door of an ancient, holy building.

Suddenly, they broke out into cheers and hoots of laughter, rushing the door, baying like cats, all urinating at once.

From there, they proceeded north along the river embankment in the direction of Hadrian's tomb. They sang marching songs and had begun a game of leapfrog down the streets. A few blocks up from the synagogue, one of the youths stumbled, nearly toppling over. When he went back to see what he'd stumbled on, he discovered it to be a foot sticking out from the doorway of a florist's shop. On closer inspection, the foot was found to be attached to the leg of a vagrant asleep under a pile of newspapers in the doorway.

"What have we here, lads?" Borghini waded into the group, pushing the others aside. He jabbed the newspapers skittishly, as if fearing he might soil the tip of his shoe with some filth below. A faint groan arose from somewhere beneath the papers. "I believe we've stumbled upon another victim of social injustice."

There was sniggering and some boyish shoving as the group surged in closer around the doorway.

With the tip of his boot, Borghini swept the assorted odds and ends of paper aside, revealing beneath them the figure of an elderly man sleeping. Borghini knelt down beside what appeared to be a mound of rags. "Who has a match?" he asked.

Tenuto, crouching above the maestro, ignited a butane lighter and handed it down to him. Almost at once, a shaft of pale orange light rose from the ground up, casting a wavering light on the walls and ceiling inside the doorway. The shadows of the flame, greatly magnified, danced all about them.

The old man sprawled on the ground stirred drowsily. Half-rising, he fell back again, covering his eyes against the sudden unwanted light.

From where he was kneeling beside the old fellow,

Borghini could smell the fetor of cheap wine and old clothing in which the man had fouled himself.

"He stinks," Luccabrava muttered.

"Shit his pants," another remarked.

Borghini moved the lighter down close to the old fellow's face. It was a worn, tired face, deeply lined, scored even in sleep with the cares of a lifetime. He'd been cuffed about some; one of his eyes was swollen and purple; clots of dried blood spattered his forehead. The face itself was wreathed in a halo of filthy white beard. A gash of something crusty and yellow marked where the mouth ought to be. Within that gash, a ruin of brown stumpish teeth was just visible. A limp hand grimed with filth barely held on to a paper bag, out of which the neck of a near-empty bottle protruded.

No longer quite so amused, Borghini's face had taken on a profoundly sad expression, as if there on the ground within that narrow frame of the doorway, he'd glimpsed the clearest picture of man's fate. One of Giorgione's Christs flashed before his eye—the *Deposition from the Cross*. He gazed long and hard at the scene, as if trying to memorize every shadow of it, each detail.

The Count rose and again jabbed the sleeping figure with his booted toe. "Hey, old man. Get up."

The next time, it was a kick, placed squarely in the ribs. It must have hurt. The old man yelped and half-rose, then rolled to his side, trying to protect himself.

"Get up, you old shit. Get up." Borghini grew furious.

The others crowded about, laughing. Borghini started kicking him again. "Come on, you stinking, lice-ridden bug-life. Get up."

The old man was either too drunk or too far gone to respond. He'd huddled himself into something like a fetal position, resolved to take the beating if only they'd let him sleep.

"I think we shall do this old man a favor." Borghini had

lapsed into the expansive locutions of stage farce. "I think
he's earned it. Wouldn't you say, lads?"

"He has indeed, maestro," young Beppe agreed. "This
poor old trooper has been a victim far too long."

The others crowded in, sniggering. A few of them kicked
the prone figure.

"Far too long, maestro."

"It isn't fair."

"How can we repay him for all he's been made to suffer?"

"What can we do to redress the wrong, maestro?"

"I think," the colonel began, his head tilted sideways as
he mused aloud, "we shall do this poor tragic soul the
supreme honor . . ."

"Yes, maestro. . . ."

"The supreme honor, yes, maestro."

"We shall martyr him," Borghini said, his features
aglow with a beatific light.

Cheers and roars of delight went up. Cars roared up the
Aventino.

"By all means. Let's martyr him. He's earned martyr-
dom."

They'd taken up the chant, their voices rising boyish and
giddy above the roar of the river below.

"Luccabrava," Borghini cried. "Get me some ash. Over
there in the trash cans."

A number of trash cans had been put out for the collection in front of a nearby office building. The trash had already been burned in the building's incinerators, and the
residue left behind was a cold mound of powdery ash.

Luccabrava, a stout, eager youth in his early twenties,
returned with a huge fistful of the stuff, which he offered
to the maestro. Borghini, regarding the opened fist with a
look of quiet pleasure, moistened the tip of his finger with
his tongue, then dipped it into the powdery mound, twisting
it right and left several times until it was covered with a
dark grayish paste.

Once more, the colonel knelt beside the sprawling figure, who was now snoring faintly, hiccuping a brownish fluid into his flowing scraggly beard. Smiling down and leaning over him, the colonel carefully inscribed the letters INRI across the old man's forehead. When he'd finished, Borghini leaned back again to admire his work. Then he stood. "Okay, lads. Lift him."

Hands reached out, grabbing the old fellow at different parts of his body. Borghini himself took the area under each armpit. For some reason, the taller boys had gravitated toward the feet and lower limbs, the net effect of which was that the body was hoisted with the legs higher than the head. Indeed, the area of the head, where Borghini alone stood, hung low; the long mane of filthy white hair drooping almost vertically downward swung from side to side, sweeping the cobbled roadway across the Lungo.

Airborne and in motion, the old man appeared to waken, to sense finally some hint of danger before him. In his fear, he started to moan and thrash about. But they held him firm, marching across the Lungo in the direction of the embankment. All the way, they sang cheers and old party rallying songs.

"Hey, what's up?" The old man flailed helplessly. "What's going on? Give an old wreck a break, will you! For Christ sake."

"We intend to, father," Luccabrava reassured him kindly, "a big break."

The others howled with delight.

A shallow stone wall marked the embankment. It served as a kind of guardrail for the safety of pedestrians. Beyond that lay a steep dirt parapet towering some seventy feet above the Tiber.

In the darkness, one could scarcely see the river below, but its churning could be heard. Recent heavy rains had swelled it, and its badly roiled current thrashed about, slapping hard against the rocks and boulders littering the streambed. Where the foaming current swirled past, it was possible to see whitecaps bobbing downstream like tiny fleeting phantoms.

Reaching the embankment, they peered down over the stone wall. The roar of it had sobered them for a moment as they stood about silent and puzzled, not entirely certain what to do next.

"All right, lads," Borghini barked. "Hoist this bag of shit high. We'll launch him up to heaven in grand style."

They did so eagerly. The old tramp was fully awake now, panicked and thrashing his legs.

"Listen—I meant no harm. Let me go. I'll be out of your way in a minute." The whites of the old man's eyes rolled in his head.

"Over the side with him now, lads," Borghini directed. "That's good. Good. Now hold him aloft there just like that till I give the signal to launch him."

Borghini could hear the old fellow whimper as they hoisted him over the top of the wall and held him dangling and kicking, eyes glaring down at the yawning space below. Leaning out over the wall, the maestro shouted to him above the roar.

"It's better this way, old soldier. Better than some cold doorway at night. You're going to like where you're going. The gates of heaven. Far better than this piss hole down here. Trust me on this, old chap." He snapped off a sharp military salute to the scrawny figure squirming above the dark void.

"All right, lads. One . . . two . . . and three."

For the briefest moment, it looked like a large bird hovering in space. Then there was nothing, just a black emptiness where seconds before the old tramp had squirmed and wriggled like a hooked fish.

In the sky across the river, still glowing red from the lights of Trastevere, Colonel Ludovico Borghini watched in wonder a hand holding a sword. He watched it cleave the clouds, moving slowly back and forth as if saluting him. There was thunder and a rush of rain and he thought he heard a child crying.

EIGHTEEN

"Well, I must say, you always did have a gift for surprise."

"Trust me, Mark. I didn't plan it this way. If there was some other alternative . . ."

"Well, there isn't. And don't be ridiculous. I'm delighted to see you."

"Sure you are. I can see the gnashing of teeth under that big welcoming grin of yours."

"Here, give me your bag." Manship snatched the light overnight carryall, nearly yanking her over the threshold. "Go inside by the fire. You're soaking wet."

"I didn't pack a raincoat. This all happened so fast."

"Bad things generally do."

She followed him into the living room, her quick, shrewd gaze darting left and right in appraisal. "Looks about the same. You still have those mothy old drapes, I see."

"And always will, if I can help it."

She smiled at his annoyance. "Mrs. McCooch taking good care of you?"

"Reliable as clockwork. Still goes home for the weekends." Manship stood there at the foot of the stairs, holding her bag and looking at a loss. He watched her go to the fire, kicking off her shoes and dropping to her knees on the rug beside it. "A fire. Heavenly."

"Just drying out the place. We've had rain for a week straight." He started up the stair. "I'm putting you in our— my room. I'll take the guest room."

"Absolutely not." She was on her feet, bounding after him. "Mark—I can't stay if you do that. The guest room is fine for me. As it is, I feel guilty enough. . . ."

He was about to protest, then shrugged. "Have it your way. Pour yourself a drink. You know where everything is. I'll be right down."

Moments later, he was back in the living room. She was seated on a cushion on the floor, sipping a sherry, stretching her legs before the fire. The static electricity of her stock-

ings brushing against each other gave him an oddly arous-
ing sensation.

"When did all this happen?" he asked, pouring himself
a sherry. "Was it expected?"

"Oh, yes. He'd been failing for the past year. The doctor
told us it could be anytime."

"You don't have to believe this. I was fond of your
father." He dropped into the big wing chair opposite her,
sliding down into his characteristic tailbone, cross-kneed
slouch. "Even though I'm sure he couldn't abide me."

"Let's face it, Mark. You weren't quite the son-in-law
he'd bargained for."

"I wasn't a banker, a broker, a world force, if that's what
you mean."

"None of the above." She laughed.

"Just an impoverished curator. Have you had supper?"

"Just a doughnut at the airport."

"You must be starved. There are some eggs. I can throw
a salad together."

"Sounds perfect."

He started into the kitchen. She followed him through
the long, narrow hallway, on past the big swinging kitchen
door that made a gulping sound each time it opened or
closed.

"This is very kind of you, Mark. I swear I didn't plan
this."

"How do you plan death? It just comes."

"If I could've gotten a hotel room . . ."

"Anything even just okay is three hundred dollars a
night, and they don't have the decency to throw in a cup
of coffee for that. Ah," Manship proclaimed, peering into
the refrigerator. "You're in luck. Mrs. McCooch has laid
in some fresh raspberries. And there's a bit of Stilton left
over from the other night."

Her ears pricked. "Did you have guests the other night?"

"Not what you're thinking. Just Bill Osgood."

Manship plucked an endive and a cucumber from the vegetable bin.

"He'd be more fun for me than you." She followed after him with a cruet of oil and vinegar. "He still looking for a new wife?"

"Yes. . . . Well, maybe not a wife, but a full-time sleep-in lady friend. If only he could get the old one out of his hair."

"She still so ditsy?"

"Yes. Still. Omelette or over easy?"

"Over easy's fine. I like my yolks runny."

"I know perfectly well how you like your yolks." There was an edge to his voice. Their gazes bumped, then held a moment. She looked away first.

"Tell me about your big Botticelli show. There was a cover story in *ARTnews*."

"Did you read it?"

"Partially," she paused, considering. "Typical for them—you know, pompous."

"In that case, you know more about the show than I do. I didn't read the story."

"Sure, sure. If I know you, you probably bought a thousand copies of the magazine and mailed them out all over the country."

"There's not much to tell." He cracked eggs into a sizzling skillet. "It opens on the twenty-second. I've been on it for a couple of years."

"What is this mysterious series of drawings you've been running down?"

"Oh, you mean the Chigis? Nothing mysterious about it. They're just that. A series of sketches—thirteen. Botticelli did them in the 1490s. Preparation for painting the *Chigi Madonna*. Never before shown. I've only been able to find ten."

"How come?"

"Don't ask. I'm just about sick of the whole thing by now." He tossed salt on the gently pulsing yolks. "Speak-

ing of shows, I read about yours in the *Times*. Pretty fast
company for a little girl from Scarsdale.''

"I got lucky, I guess. The Getty was doing a show of
female American moderns—O'Keeffe, Frankenthaler, Al-
ice Neel, Susan Rothenberg—you know, the usual suspects.'' She went on, animated, much revived from the
drowned rat that had washed up on the doorstep shortly
before. "They asked me if I wanted to show. I wasn't sure.
I said I'd call back in twenty-four hours. I called Jane out
in the Hamptons and asked if I should do it. 'Of course
you should, you idiot.' '' She rattled on, imitating the
throaty locutions of an old artist friend. "Well, you know
Jane.''

"So?''

"So I got back to the Getty the next day and said, 'I'll
be delighted.' ''

He set out the eggs and tossed the salad, then sat across
from her and watched her devour them—greedily, the way
she did everything, as if she didn't expect to be around
long and had no idea where she was going next.

He marveled at how pretty she still was. One of those
serendipitously lucky people for whom everything just falls
into place, she had looks, talent, opportunities—all with no
special effort on her part. Still young, too, just thirty-four,
she never took many pains with her looks. It wasn't typical
magazine prettiness, either, but something else—hard to put
one's finger on. She had a long, narrow face, angular, with
good bones; a bladelike Roman nose, a straight line down
from the forehead with a little break at the bridge; a bony,
thrusting chin; a slightly snaggled front tooth; a wide expanse of shrewd, darting eyes that never seemed to rest.

When he first saw her he was a young instructor at the
Art Institute; she was five years his junior, a painting student from downtown auditing his course but only sporadi-
cally attending it.

She had what was called in those days "attitude," which
was generally held to be a sense of superiority predicated

on no visible body of accomplishment. At an earlier time, they'd have called it "brass."

At the close of the semester, he gave her a *C* and told her she was wasting time. She apologized for making a nuisance of herself and for having played "the smart-ass brat" (her words), which she freely admitted she'd been playing most of her life and getting away with it.

They started seeing a great deal of each other (not regularly—they both continued to see other people at the same time—but a great deal, nonetheless).

As courtships go, theirs was brief. She'd married him over the strong objections of her parents, who were mercantile and would have preferred someone like-minded. Maeve was, after all, an only child, and since she showed little inclination to take over someday the substantial commercial real estate enterprise the Connells had amassed over the years, the hope was that she'd be clever enough, or at least cooperative enough, to choose a mate who would.

Needless to say, she didn't, marrying instead the young curator of Renaissance painting. Overeducated, attractive enough, he had some promise—however, unfortunately, the kind that brings great distinction but little in the way of material reward, which was the only kind the Connells understood.

Just months after their marriage, her phenomenal rise began. She started showing in galleries in TriBeCa and SoHo. Almost instantly, she was written about in the right periodicals and journals, and in the sort of glowing terms that older, far more experienced painters would sacrifice a limb to see written about themselves.

In the course of two years, her prices rose exponentially. Shortly, she was installed at the best galleries on Fifty-seventh Street. She was an item in trendy periodicals like *New York* magazine, as well as such tony ones as *ARTnews,* where heavy reputations are established. She was by no means yet "major" but highly regarded sources claimed she was well on her way to becoming just that.

At that time, Manship was putting in ten hours a day as a curator at the Metropolitan. At night, he was writing a monograph on Giotto, destined to become a classic in its own right. He was also teaching in whatever spare time he had. He, too, was spoken of as "immensely promising," but only within narrow curatorial circles and with none of the glittery media fanfare that trumpeted his wife's accomplishments. He was eclipsed, to say the least.

Far more troubling than the fact of being eclipsed by his wife was the feeling of being consumed by her, which eventually spelled doom to their marriage. Manship was not a particularly envious man. He didn't begrudge her an inch of the limelight in which she was then basking. He was making his way, too, but in a world far less generous with praise and far more adept at betrayal, and he needed every spare minute of his own time just to keep his back covered.

"You haven't said a word about Tom." Manship rose and carried off her empty plates.

"What about him?"

"Is he all right?"

"Well, you know Tom. Just as long as business is fine, he is."

"And is it?"

She accepted the bowl of raspberries he offered. "Since I haven't heard anything to the contrary, I presume that it is."

"And everything is"—he reached for the apposite phrase—"good between you?"

She gaped at him, her mouth full of berries. "Oh, Mark . . . if that isn't you to a tee. You're not really concerned?"

"Why shouldn't I be? Just because we're no longer married doesn't mean I no longer care about you. I just hope everything is . . . fine."

At first, she thought he was being sarcastic, then realized he was absolutely serious. "That's sweet of you, Mark. Well, you know, it's not exactly Romeo and Juliet between Tom and me, if that's what you mean."

"What is?"

"But, then again, we're fond of each other, respect each other's work, each other's needs. What can I say? It's a life. I'm not exactly crazy about Tom's kids. I'm not over-joyed when they breeze in on us unannounced, fresh from their wanderings, and stay and stay, until Tom gives them each a big check and with the next breeze sends them all packing."

"And you," Manship probed. "What about you?"

"What about me?"

"Are you planning to have kids anytime soon?"

"Me?" She threw her head back and hooted at the ceil-ing. "Oh, Mark."

"What's so funny? You're still young enough. I should think you'd want that."

"Motherhood?" Surprised by his sudden earnestness, she became that way, too. "I honestly don't think I'm right for it. It would be unfair."

"To the child?"

"Of course to the child. And then, what about me?"

"What about you?"

"Well, you know my life, how I am. After my work's done for the day, there's not much left over for anyone else."

She could be, and generally, was, brutally frank in her assessment of others. He'd never heard her be so frank about herself. It took him aback, so that he had to cast about for some fresh conversational ploy. "And other than that?"

"Content. I'm content. My work goes well. My health is good." She'd recovered her poise and once again she was smiling that amused, frankly mocking smile. "There now, are you satisfied?"

In answer, he rose and cleared the dishes. She took up whatever silver and soiled napery remained, then followed him to the sink. "This thing may take a week or two. There's the funeral and all the arrangements. The lawyers have to do their thing. My first job in the morning is to get myself a hotel room.''

''Don't be silly. You'll stay here.''

''I couldn't possibly. It's a terrible inconvenience. What with your show coming up and all . . .''

''Forget the show. It's no inconvenience. You'll stay. The matter is settled. I'll tell Mrs. McCooch to make up the guest room and stock the cupboard for two.''

''Are you sure?''

''Of course I'm sure.''

''That's kind of you, Mark.'' She touched his arm lightly. ''I'd feel much better about it if you weren't so angry.''

''Angry? I'm not angry,'' he shot back, then laughed at the contradiction between his words and the tone of his voice. ''At least, I'm not angry at you.''

''Well, then, what *is* bothering you?''

''Nothing.'' He brooded a moment, then shook his head wearily. ''Nothing important.''

NINETEEN

"Goodbye, Aldo. You were really never much of a soldier."

They watched the bony, naked shape slip soundlessly beneath the surface of the pool, then disappear in a gentle swirl. Borghini winked at his young apprentice.

"No one saw you, Beppe?"

"No one, maestro."

"You're certain?"

"The street was deserted. We just drew up and asked him the way to Frascati. When he came up to the car— *woosh*." The boy made a whistling sound. "We had him inside in a minute."

"Did he make much of a fuss?"

"He was too frightened, maestro."

"He wept, you say?"

"When he caught on who we were and all, he offered us money to let him go. When that didn't work, he pleaded."

Borghini chuckled at the thought of his old associate pleading. He reached behind him for one of the long bamboo poles leaning up against a nearby wall. He thrust it into the pool, and its tip quickly encountered something solid not far beneath the surface. With a deep dipping motion, the colonel pushed down hard against it, making a grunting sound as he did so. Almost at once, the murky surface surrounding the pole appeared to drop, then swirl in a counterclockwise circle as Borghini sent the pole plunging deeper.

The boy watched the roiled surface spread out and slap noisily at the edges of the pool. He stepped back to avoid the highly caustic fluid from splashing his shoes. He watched, not moving, never once lifting his gaze until the swirling vortex near the center of the pool grew still once more. By then, the colonel had returned his pole to its place among several others resting against the wall.

"In a few days," Borghini said, wringing his hands dry on a dirty towel, "our beloved, late-lamented Pettigrilli will be ready for the flensing beam. And then, my dear Beppe . . ."

"Yes, maestro?"

"Can you guess what is next?"

"Yes, maestro." The boy spoke with the quiet, unquestioning obedience of an acolyte in a sacred order. "You will then have to fetch the young lady in the photographs."

Ludovico Borghini touched a candle to the small cigarillo clenched between his teeth and splashed another finger of grappa into his glass. It was nearly midnight. He sat at the dinner table, exhausted after a day of strenuous activity.

He'd scarcely eaten since morning. Having returned muddy and exhausted less than an hour ago, he found Beppe had left him a bland, rubbery piece of chicken and overboiled vegetables. There was even a slice of commercial cake for dessert. He gazed at it in disgust, then pushed his plate away and resigned himself to the simple pleasure of bread and grappa.

His thirst for that fiery white liquid had sharpened considerably over the past months. Its benefits to him were not inconsiderable. It had the power to quell in him the gnawing, fretful ache of life he carried about with him each day from morning until night.

A pleasant drowsy sensation had started to flow upward from his feet, radiating outward into his limbs and chest and settling finally behind his eyes. The effect was to muffle all of the jarring, dissonant noises from the street outside. He knew from the numb little circle erupting at the center of his forehead that it would soon be time for him to go upstairs to sleep. It was a particularly pleasing sensation to him—but not for the sensation in itself. He liked to recall that as a young man Fra Girolamo, the mad monk Savonarola, while casting about for some direction in life, had dreamed that while he slept a stream of icy water had poured relentlessly down on his forehead. When he woke, Savonarola felt purified, cleansed, and renewed. From that point on, he knew precisely what his life's work was to be.

Though his eyes had begun to droop, Borghini pulled out from inside his rumpled tunic a set of photographs and, like a hand of whist, fanned them out on the table before him.

The familiar features of a young woman on the Ponte Vecchio swam before his woozy eyes. He had to struggle to focus his gaze. One had her browsing at the outdoor stand of an inexpensive jeweler. Another had her stepping from a bus near the Baptistry. Each shot, candid, unposed, registered some specific reaction in her strikingly expressive face—everything from indifference to a kind of veiled sorrow. In several photos, she chatted with a vendor. . . .

"You can have her, Ludo."

"I prefer the other, Papa."

"But that one has no breasts. Why don't you take the one with the good breasts. Or possibly even the *negra.* Signora, bring the *tutzone* here for a moment. Look at those thighs, Ludo. But be careful. She could crush you between them."

Borghini's eyes scanned every line of that well-remembered face. He knew each crease, each shadow. Over the years, the face had changed. No doubt of that. When still a girl just out of university, there'd been a kind of radical spark in her look. There was a defiance to it, a certain inclination to challenge authority and break laws.

Here now, in a dozen or so candid photos, he saw an older, more self-assured woman. Still young, to be sure, not yet thirty, that fever that once burned in her appeared to have been cooled by time and circumstances. The need to make her own way, to get on with life, had tempered the rebelliousness and opened her to accommodation.

No doubt she would marry soon—some professional

man, a lawyer, an engineer, perhaps, or a university teacher. Some upstanding, safe, prosaic dolt who'd give her six children and a house in the suburbs. They'd go to the seashore in the summer. Shaking his head, he belched, bringing up a sour chyme of undigested grappa that burned the back of his throat.

"Well, what are you waiting for? Go on. I won't bite you. Here . . . give me your hand. What's the matter with you? Don't be silly. I'll make it good for you. I won't hurt you. Here, now give me your hand. Now squeeze and rub. Back and forth. Very gentle. That's it. Be nice. A girl likes it when you're nice. Good. Very good. See? It's not so terrible. I can't believe this is really your first time. And even your papa has to bring you. How old did you say—"

"Fifteen."

"Fifteen? Oh my. That feels nice. Keep going. Hold me close. Don't you like it? What's the matter? Don't you like a black girl? I can show you things no white girl can. Here, let me—Oh, what's wrong? We haven't even begun and already . . . Oh, forgive me. I don't mean to laugh. I'm stupid. Wait—let me wash you off. You don't want the old man to see."

From somewhere upstairs in the far reaches of the empty palazzo, Borghini heard the old grandfather clock strike the hour. Reaching into his pocket, he pulled out a crumpled, dirt-stained piece of paper on which had been written a note in a large, childish scrawl. During the past several weeks, he'd read it over and over again, each time with a sense of slowly mounting anger.

Maestro,
    No mistake. It was Pettigrilli at the signorina's place. I followed him there to Fiesole. They sat outside

in the garden. They drank tea and I watched from behind a bush. He stayed about an hour.

Beppe

Borghini crumpled the note in his fist and flung it across
the table. "So," he muttered. "There is no longer any
doubt. It had to be Isobel who sent the museum fellow
around to the gallery. What was he looking for? Isobel
knows nothing about the gallery; she's never been there.
But Pettigrilli, that pukey little *strunz,* had. Often enough.
And he told her, ay? Well, now we've taken care of Pettigrilli and his long tongue. And as for you, my darling
Isobel," he cooed drunkenly at the snapshots fanned out
across the tabletop, "it seems our paths are soon to cross
again."

That night, while he lay in bed upstairs in the dark, the
eyes appeared on his wall. He watched them float past
him—large, staring, disembodied. They would glide so
close, he could see the hairs on the lashes and brows. A
pale bluish aura seemed to emanate from somewhere within
them, and as they dipped and swerved past, he could feel
the cool trail of air left behind in their wake.

The first time he'd seen the eyes, as a small boy, not
quite ten, it had frightened him. But over the months, then
years, it occurred with increasing frequency, and by now
he'd gotten used to it, actually come to like it. He even
looked forward to their next appearance.

TWENTY

True to his word, old Torelli came through with a timely delivery of the newly restored paintings. They arrived a full eight days before the scheduled opening—plenty of time to hang and light them.

The uncrating of the paintings themselves had something of the breathless drama of a bomb being defused. A small, select group had gathered early in the room where the crates had been delivered by a handpicked unit of the premier art-crating specialists in Florence—people whose sole job was limited to the crating and uncrating of priceless objects of the most fragile nature.

Among the group gathered there were Osgood, Emily Taverner, Pat Colbert, curator of Early American art, and René Klass, curator of Impressionist painting (thought to be Manship's only two serious competitors for the directorship of the museum), and, of course, Manship himself.

Silent, Manship watched crowbars and claw hammers applied to the tough wooden packing containers. Reluctant to speak lest he interrupt the concentration of the unpackers, he appeared to wince with each groan and ripping crack of the wood.

When at last both paintings were out, propped up against the walls of the room, a hushed awe had fallen over the assembled audience. Shortly, they began to tiptoe around the canvases, checking each from various perspectives.

Osgood was the first to venture an opinion. "Damned if I can see a seam or a telltale line in that *Transfiguration* to show where they sewed it."

"It was in shreds a few weeks ago," Manship said. "Take my word for it." To himself, he recited a paean of gratitude to old Torelli and particularly to Signor Panuzzi, whose eyes had filled with tears that morning in Florence as they viewed together the awful desecration visited on the two Botticelli paintings.

It was when they turned to the *Centurion*, which had

been savaged in Istanbul, that things got sticky. In accordance with Manship's instructions, no effort had been made to repair the damage. The canvas simply hung in strips.

"Good God," murmured René Klass, a small, dashing, high-energy type.

"Pretty, huh?" Manship remarked bitterly.

Emily Taverner shuddered.

"Bizarre," Osgood murmured. "Simply bizarre."

Pat Colbert stared down at the ruined *Centurion.* "I'm surprised Torelli didn't try to repair this. Surely there are some decent photographs of the original from which to work."

"There are," Manship agreed. "And he wanted to. But I wouldn't let him."

Manship's sudden revelation was met with a mystified silence.

"What are you going to do, then?" Klass asked.

"Surely you're not going to hang it this way," Colbert added.

A small, bitter smile flickered at the corners of Manship's mouth. "Why not?"

"You're kidding," Klass said.

"I'm perfectly serious."

Silence followed—this time not merely mystified but uncomfortable as well. Feet shuffled and awkward gazes were exchanged. The air grew thick with tension.

"But why?" Klass demanded. "What's the point? It's grotesque. People will be upset by it."

"That's the point. I want them to be," Manship countered. "I want everyone to see and understand just how irreparable the loss every time a work of art is savaged in this manner."

For the moment, Manship's argument appeared to have squelched the potentially dangerous skirmish that had nearly broken out between the two curators.

"What about the missing Chigi sketches, Mark?" Colbert asked.

"What about them?"

"How do you intend to handle that?"

"We'll have photographs of the missing originals, along with an explanatory note off to the side providing background on the situation. If we can't show all of the original works just as Botticelli sketched them, at least we can supply an idea of the order in which they evolved in his mind."

Once again, Manship won the day. Even Klass, who felt obliged to be combative in the presence of his younger, more controversial colleague, thought it prudent, at least for the moment, to back off.

"Good afternoon, Captain."

"Good afternoon, Mr. Manship."

That was their customary greeting, a tacit pact between the two, stipulating that Manship must address Chief of Security Leon MacWirter by his former army rank of captain, for which in turn MacWirter would agree never to address Manship as Dr. Manship.

"Everything shipshape with you, Captain?"

"Couldn't be better, Mr. Manship. We're just now finishing up installing more cameras for sweeps and bumping up those electronic systems already in place."

"Fire and panic controls?"

"Likewise. All covered," MacWirter explained as darkness crowded up against the office windows. He raised a clipboard to eye level and proceeded to read aloud from it through a pince-nez perched at the tip of his nose. A pince-nez on a retired U.S. Army captain in the final decade of the twentieth century spoke volumes regarding the idiosyncratic nature of the chief of security.

"We're installing a dozen or so more photoelectric eyes," he went on. "And we'll be running closed-circuit TVs throughout the second-floor galleries."

"Glass-breaking sensors, microwave motion detectors, infrared devices?"

"All in place, sir."

Manship massaged the small netsuke monkey on his desk. "I trust we won't be relying too heavily on velvet ropes as barriers this time, Captain."

"No, sir." MacWirter laughed at some private joke between them. "For the most part,' we'll be going to laminated safety-glass screens."

"That laminated stuff, how effective is it?"

"Not a hundred percent, I'm afraid. As barriers, they're mostly a psychological deterrent. Let's put it this way. A real four-star nutso with mischief on his mind could get around it easily enough."

Manship stroked his chin thoughtfully. "That's what I wanted to talk to you about."

MacWirter cocked a caterpillar brow.

"Your people," Manship went on, "You feel they're up to speed?"

"You know them all well, as I do, sir. They're a good bunch."

"Is good good enough? Are they good enough to catch certain mannerisms in visitors?"

"Mannerisms?"

"Characteristics of potentially dangerous types—something that would alert you before they do harm?"

MacWirter's brow cocked higher. He put aside his clipboard and leaned forward. "You're trying to tell me something, aren't you, Mr. Manship?"

Manship sighed and rose. He proceeded to pace around the office. "This Botticelli exhibition, Captain. It should be treated much like any other important exhibition we've done before. There are, however, a few things, details, that make this show a bit different."

In the next several minutes, Manship proceeded to inform the chief of security of his experiences on his recent trip abroad, particularly those in connection with the stolen Chigi drawings. Lastly, he described in minute detail the mutilation of the two Botticellis destined for the show.

MacWirter appeared more impressed by that final disclo-

sure than by anything that had preceded it. He shifted uneasily in his seat. "Was anyone hurt during these two
incidents, Mr. Manship?"

"One guard was severely injured."

"Do you know the weapon used on them, sir?"

"The same used to mutilate the paintings."

MacWirter's beetling brow lowered. "I appreciate your
apprising me of the matter, sir. I take it, then, you've been
considering laying on some additional outside security people for the run of the show."

"I confess, the thought crossed my mind."

Manship could see that the man was clearly troubled, as
though his own performance had been called into question.
"There'll be close to two hundred works of art."

"One hundred and ninety-six, sir."

"Precisely—and I gather you can only spare ten of your
people to cover the show. That's roughly twenty paintings
per man. Far more than anything they typically do."

"Yes, it is, sir."

"In addition, more than ninety percent of the show is
made up of loans from the most influential collections in
the world—the Prado, the Louvre, the Mellon, the National
Gallery, the Getty, the Uffizi, and so on. You get my drift,
Captain. Imagine if anything were to happen to any one of
these paintings. They're priceless. Irreplaceable."

"I'm well aware of that, Mr. Manship."

Manship dropped back into his chair and folded his arms.
"Look, I don't want you to take any of this personally."

"No, sir."

"I have the highest regard for you and your people, Captain. You know that. But I've asked the board, and they've
agreed to pony up an additional two hundred and fifty thousand dollars to hire a bit more security for the duration of
the show."

"How many additional would that be, sir?"

"Ten," Manship said, the figure at the tip of his tongue.

"That's a bit more than a bit."

Manship rubbed the netsuke. "Given the fact that the Botticellis are irreplaceable on the open market, wouldn't you rather err on the side of too many than too few?"

MacWirter brooded on that a moment. "I see." None too happy, he sighed and slapped his knee. "I'll call the Pinkerton people first thing in the morning."

"They're the best?"

"Top-notch, sir. Sticklers on every detail. Right down to the candidate's attitude."

"Attitude toward what?"

"People, museums. They check each candidate for evidence of antisocial behavior."

"Police records all checked?"

"Obviously that. Temperament's very important, too. They look for people who can act calmly in emergencies. . . ."

"What about individuals who can sustain power of attention over long periods of duty?"

"Very much so, sir. Also people accustomed to dealing with children and unruly teenagers."

"People bent on mischief," Manship added pointedly, "what about those?"

"Yes, sir." MacWirter nodded. "Particularly those."

TWENTY-ONE

Both men wore aprons and rubber gloves. Each had a surgeon's hat (a sort of snood) on his head. Added to that, Borghini wore a pair of high-magnification surgeon's glasses. They had small black cubes affixed to the lenses.

The two worked quietly, the colonel hunched over his work, Beppe hanging back, ill at ease, but overcome with the heady sensation of donning apron and robes. A bead of sweat glistened on the boy's forehead, his eyes were riveted on the object splayed out on the surgical table.

The only sounds to be heard in the damp, winding cellars of the gallery in Parioli were the steady drumming of water streaming from a spigot into a steel sink and the high snipping sound of shears. In addition to the scissors, laid out on a narrow rectangular table at right angles to the operating table was an array of surgical instruments and esoteric tools. They included a claw hammer, a tack hammer, a crosscut saw, a ripsaw, a paring knife, tweezers, a pair of side-cutting pliers, a pair of wire cutters, a surgeon's bone snip, a surgeon's cartilage knife, a scalpel, a butcher's skinning knife, a quiver of stainless-steel needles of assorted sizes, a hacksaw, a small ball-peen hammer, a drill set, an upholsterer's regulator or spindle, various sizes of small files, one medium-fine wood rasp, and one skin scraper for use on large skins.

With his boxy black surgical spectacles jutting forward from the bridge of his nose, Borghini's latex gloved hands moved swiftly up and down the length of the cadaver. Working with bone snips in one hand and a cartilage knife in the other, he alternated both with deft skill.

Already the top of the skull had been trepanned by means of the circular handsaw. A mass of cortical matter was exposed just beneath the cut, and the skin of the scalp had been pulled forward and down over the face, in much the same way a glove is stripped from a hand. The three-day bath of lye had done much to loosen the skin and subcutaneous tissue from the bony frame just below, By means of scissors, tweezers, and bone and cartilage cutters, Borghini now completed the task of separating the skin from the skeletal structure.

He'd already separated the skin from around the neck and was working with utmost precision to do the same with the skin around the throat and clavicle.

While the colonel snipped and sawed, it was young Beppe's job to pull back, exerting a gentle but constant downward pressure on the skin just freeing up as the maestro sliced it away from the carcass. The beads of sweat on the boy's forehead were not the result of exertion. They were a mixture of keen excitement and fear—fear that if he pulled too hard, or not hard enough, the skin might snag and thus tear, an outcome the maestro cautioned would not be tolerated under any circumstances. The maestro was at great pains to stress that at the conclusion of that day they must have a complete skin from head to toe, unbroken and in perfect condition.

Beppe's eyes burned from the lye fumes wafting upward off the surface of the pool. His discomfort made him focus all the harder on the swift flashes of the maestro's knife as it went about its work.

In the days following, Borghini seldom left the galleries in Parioli. Working upward of seventeen hours a day on one of his "re-creations," he would practice what he'd come to think of as his great "alchemical" skills—the art of transforming death into life.

With a complete skin separated from its carcass, the remaining skeleton would then serve as the foundation for constructing a framework.

During that crucial period, Beppe never left the maestro's side. Initially queasy from the scissoring of flesh and laying back of skin, in a short time he'd become remarkably adept at carrying out his master's directions. Not only had he a

natural finesse, Borghini observed, but he had overcome his
first few qualms as well.

For the boy, it was a whole new world of wonders. In
his mind, he'd entered the secret rites of some sacred ritual.
Before the colonel had discovered him and brought him
here, Beppe had been running with a pack of wolves in
Trastevere, a group whose nightly work had outraged and
sickened the good citizens of Rome. That was merely
child's play, the boy now thought, aglow with a sense of
tremendous pride. In a matter of days, the maestro had
raised him to a level of consciousness he had no idea existed, beckoning him to a universe so rarefied and mysterious, so replete with fresh possibilities as to make his flesh
tingle.

The first day after the skinning, as the pelt dried, they
spent applying layers of modeling clay to the skeletal
framework. Borghini was at great pains to demonstrate the
art of applying the clay so that each curve, each indentation
of the original, would be perfectly duplicated in the final
product.

The skeleton stood upright, held in position by wood
blocks chockered up about the feet and held erect by a thin
adjustable pole inserted through the pelvic synthesis. Then
threaded upward to the top of the skull, the pole's length
was adjusted by means of a screw clamp at its midpoint.
Loosening the clamp enabled one section of the pole to be
telescoped into the other.

"Don't apply clay just to fill up spaces," Borghini instructed the boy. "The clay has to conform to the framework of the body, just like human flesh." He took a great
lump of clay, kneading it in his fist, then tearing it into
pieces. "Apply your clay. Work it on in layers. Where the
ribs are, put the clay on thinner so that the viewer can
appreciate the configuration of the rib cage. No, no *cre-
tino.*" The maestro gouged out the clay the boy had just
applied and flung it off to the side. "How many times must
I tell you? Let your hands sculpt. Just don't throw it on.

Sculpt. Mold. Shape. If it's done right, the clay will be so perfectly melded to the frame beneath that you should almost feel the shock of something live quivering beneath your hand. Ah, good. You see? There you have it. Now when the clay hardens, it will fall between each rib exactly the way the actual flesh fell there in life. Better.'' He tugged the boy's ear lobe so hard that he winced. ''Better. Now go ahead. Do it yourself.''

Before the day was over, they'd completed the clay form, never leaving the upraised platform where they worked. They took their lunch there, wolfing down sandwiches and gulping coffee while they knelt and stooped and stretched over the figure already sculpted into a rough approximation of the position it would assume in Borghini's diorama—that of an angel in Botticelli's *Chigi Madonna.*

When they left the cellar workshop late that night, they applied a coat of plaster of Paris to the clay form. By early the next day, the plaster mold had hardened. Ready to be removed, it peeled away from the form easily, ready for the next step in the procedure.

For a break, they ate toast and fried eggs, swigged coffee noisily, then cut sheets of burlap into long strips and glued them, layer after layer, inside the plaster mold. After that, they could do nothing more but permit the mold with its burlap liner to rest for a period of forty-eight hours. Returning two mornings later, they filled a tub with warm water and soaked the mold.

After several hours of soaking, Borghini and the boy carefully lifted the mold out of the tub. It rose dripping, sloughing off water, like some mummified thing that had rested for eons, buried in ooze at the bottom of a deep glacial lake.

Scarcely daring to breathe, they carried the form back to the surgical table and placed it there. With a ball-peen hammer and a light chisel, the maestro then tapped gently at several key points along a line visible only to him—a line running from the parietal lobe to the anklebone.

Finally, with a definitive tap, like a pianist playing the final note of a complex sonata, Borghini delivered the coup de grâce. A sharp crack sounded, followed by a tearing noise, and the mold fell open into perfect halves. Revealed below was a hollow burlap mannequin, an exact replica of the clay form that served as a template of Aldo Pettigrilli's body just as it had appeared in life.

After what seemed an interminable time of studying the mannequin, Borghini, tottering slightly, lifted it out of its plaster shell. The boy moved to help, but the colonel waved him off with a sharp sideward snap of the head. Borghini handled it as though he were carrying the eggs of a hummingbird in his palm, all the while his feverish eyes swarmed over it, searching for weak points, for any slight imperfection.

Young Beppe hung back, not daring to speak. What was going on during that moment was a kind of communion between the maestro and the burlap figure, and the boy recognized with a shock of resentment that he'd been excluded.

Borghini had been studying the figure tilted stiffly sideways on the surgical table. With that crucial part of the operation over, all of his former passion and enthusiasm seemed gone. Instead, something like anger had overtaken him. It left the boy puzzled, thinking he'd done something wrong. But if he had, he couldn't say what. The mannequin, to him at least, appeared to be a literally perfect re-creation of its living model.

"Tomorrow," the maestro murmured, his jaw taut, his manner uncharacteristically curt, "the skin."

The next morning began bumpily, the maestro still tense and out of sorts. Unexpected sounds, the light in the cellar, his instruments—everything infuriated him. They spent a full hour and a half aiming and adjusting floodlights on the mannequin so that the contrast of light and shadow would approximate precisely those conditions of light present in the dioramas at the Palazzo Borghini.

By 10:30, they were ready for the final step, fitting the tanned skin onto the mannequin.

The skin lay draped over the flensing beam, exactly where they'd left it four days before. Treated with oils and acids, it had dried perfectly; now when Borghini lifted it gently from the rungs of the beam, it was amazingly supple and pliant, smooth to the touch.

The next hour was spent slathering a thin white paste over the mannequin, lubricating it thoroughly, then pulling the tanned skin over it, much the same way a sock is drawn onto a foot. It was that final step that seemed to be the source of the maestro's great vexation. To the boy, that final step in the procedure seemed relatively easy, far more so than many of those preceding it. But the maestro didn't see things quite that way. Several times, just as Borghini was about to begin lifting the skin off of the beam, he'd suddenly replace it and return to the mannequin, playing light, tremulous fingers over every inch of it, seeking spots in the burlap on which the skin might snag.

By late morning, they began in earnest. At first, their progress was slow and faltering; then it gradually went forward with increasing confidence. Beppe scarcely dared move, occasionally making unwanted sounds. Each time, the maestro's head snapped around and he glowered at him. When the maestro's eyes were angry, they could freeze the marrow of your bones.

Shortly past noon, the entire skin had been fitted onto the mannequin. It was only then that Borghini appeared to relax.

"Beautiful, no?"

Moving swiftly around the platform, he viewed the figure from every possible angle. It could be stood on its own feet now, some six feet tall, one arm extended as though hailing a friend.

Borghini kept circling the platform like a nervous, prowling cat. Kneeling down and covering an eye to view it from beneath, he would suddenly bolt up and circle it again, hopping in his boyish excitement.

Suddenly, he stopped dead in his tracks and clapped his hands. "*Fantastico*," he shouted, his laugh echoing through the dark, cobwebbed cellars.

The rest of the afternoon was spent in fitting and adjusting the skin on its burlap frame, removing unsightly ridges or bumps, tucking in and tightening areas where the skin was either baggy or drooped on the frame.

On his knees, with pins in his mouth, Borghini looked like a tailor. He seemed tireless. He took no lunch. Long, unbroken hours of bending, stretching, lifting, and punishing concentration seemed to have animated rather than tired him. By dusk, he was whistling something softly to himself. Hours later, he was still skipping lightly about. "What time is it, Beppe?"

"Ten-forty-five, maestro."

He shook his head in disbelief. "Christ. Let's go get something to eat."

They ate at a small nearby hosteria, Borghini reeling off lists of things still to be done as he spooned a creamy fettuccine into his mouth.

Later that evening, they returned to the gallery. Back down in the cellar, they fashioned a bed of excelsior and sheets. Then, taking elaborate care, they wrapped the figure inside it. Carrying it upstairs took the better part of an hour. It had to be jockeyed and coaxed along beneath the low overhang of the stair. Negotiating bad turns and narrow corners, Borghini spat angry, rapid-fire instructions at the boy every inch of the way.

Finally, out in the alley where the Hispano-Suiza waited, they created another bed for the figure, this time out of three or four tarpaulins folded over several times across the backseat to absorb unwanted shocks.

By 2:00 A.M., they were back at the Palazzo Borghini,

essed in a business suit, and knotting his tie.
out from the kitchen, munching a slice of
on't we look spiffy.''
past, stirring a faint breeze in his wake.
called after him. ''Dinner tonight?''
here. I can't go out. I'm too busy.''
ook,'' she said, her voice fading as the front
''Anyway, I'll try to,'' she added somewhat

yellow call-back slips were stacked up on his
entered his office that morning. Emily Tav-
rked ''urgent'' in red pencil under a message
ldi, suggesting that once again the Leonardo
s unhappy with some aspect of the museum's
ned that it threatened to smother his obviously
genius.
n a half dozen periodicals, including *Time,*
RTnews and *New York* magazine, had all re-
ission to preview the show. Michael Kimmel-
New York Times had requested an interview
t Manship call back.
tack and appearing somewhat more ominous
s was a cryptic message from Van Nuys, ask-
p by later in the afternoon. Van Nuys seldom,
l. It was more his style to walk in unannoun-
a breezy manner, then drop some bombshell
Manship felt a spasm clench his bowel.
y a cursory glance at his mail, he instructed
he would take no calls and see no visitors
notice. When she started to protest, he clicked
wn on what he sensed to be a slowly sim-
rapidly coming to a boil. He knew where
eading. The problems were real, but he would
with them in the only way he could, and that
time.

having carried the burlap figure up several flights of stairs to the top of the house, where it would take its preordained place in Borghini's *tableau vivant* version of Botticelli's *Chigi Madonna.*

Once they'd settled the mannequin into the approximate position it would occupy in the diorama, they stood for some time admiring it. Already the holy infant was in place, along with a wire armature of the Virgin Mary. The infant Christ had been fashioned from a child the colonel had purchased from a teenage prostitute working near the Caracalla Baths. He'd kept the child a few days, growing quite fond of it, feeding it special treats and tickling it until it giggled happily. He cried when it became time to dispose of it.

In the background stood several farmers, formerly vagrants collected at the railroad terminal and lured out to Parioli with promises of food and work. Anchored into varying positions, they stood alongside a number of farm animals, sheep and oxen grazing on a hillside. The animals had been found at slaughterhouses outside of Rome. And now Aldo Pettigrilli, or what remained of him, had taken his place within the vignette as the heavenly angel of the *Chigi Madonna.*

Though the features of the mannequin's face were an exact replication of Pettigrilli's, the sockets where the eyes were to be were empty, mere hollow cavities sunk into the forehead. Borghini had removed the eyes from the corpse before its immersion in lye. He had already taken perfect molds of them to be reproduced in glass. By means of color swatches, he'd matched the color of the pupils and irises of Botticelli's angel; now he would paint directly onto the glass molds.

Tomorrow, if all went well, he and Beppe would spend the day at the palazzo, working inside the diorama. He would teach the boy how to use the brushes and oils not only to touch up the faded areas of the skin but to restore the vibrancy of life into flesh already tinged with the gray pallor of death.

"Well, Beppe, what do you think?"

The boy was too overcome to reply. "*Fantastico,* maestro," was all he could manage.

Borghini laughed and clapped the boy on the back. "Tomorrow we paint. I'll put the brush in your hand and a tube of paint at your feet. There are still the eyes to take care of and the wardrobe to match with the original. Then we're finished with this one." Borghini glanced slyly at the boy. "Then, Beppe, what do you think comes next?"

"The Madonna, maestro," the boy answered eagerly. "You'll want the one in the photographs on the Ponte Vecchio for that."

T

The Chigi drawing
collector of informat
so-called Anonimo
part of 1496, for Bot
francesco de' Medici,
had also commission
Birth of Venus.

All thirteen drawing
inches, were publishe
must be one of the mc

It was going on four i
off the living room of 5
ship was wide awake, his
printed fresh-off-the pres
mered on a small electric
and illustration captions
words with his lips as if
intent.

That was the sight that
down the stairway the foll
of Manship's pajamas an
robe, she was on her w
McCooch was already uj
pened to glance across tow
halt.

"What the hell are you
"Reading."
"Aren't you supposed
"I'm on my way this in
looking up. "Just going u
She gazed after him as
two at a time, then disap
top of the stair.
When he clattered bacl

was shaved, dr
Maeve cam
toast. "Well,
He whizzec
"Hey," she
"Sure. But
"Fine, I'll
door slammec
ruefully.

A dozen pale
desk when he
erner had ma
from Frettob:
of lighting w
design. It see
inexhaustible
Critics fro
Newsweek, A
quested perm
man of *The*
and asked th
Atop the s
than the othe
ing him to st
if ever, calle
ced, feigning
on his desk.
With bare
Taverner tha
until further
the phone d
mering pani-
things were
have to deal
was one at a

With that, he turned off his phone, then slipped into the deeply padded swivel chair behind his desk.

It was going on 5:00 P.M. when he reemerged from his office. He'd worked straight through without a lunch break. Stepping out into the outer office, he found Taverner, already moving toward him, clipboard in hand, an expression on her face somewhere between hysteria and relief.

"Are you all right?" she asked, as if he were a diver who'd just come up from a long submersion.

"Barely," he said grimly, then flashed a wry smile. "What did you think I did in there, slash my wrists?"

"The thought did cross my mind."

"I take it we're nearing Armageddon."

"Nearing, and on a direct collision course." She waved a slip of paper at him.

"If that's from Mr. Van Nuys . . ."

"He's called three times."

That got Manship's attention. Already his mind had played out a half a dozen unpleasant scenarios. Turning sharply on his heels, he strode back into his office and put the call through.

Mr. Van Nuys was in conference, his administrative assistant informed him. He'd call back the moment he was free.

Manship's fingers drummed his desktop for several moments, then, for reasons not entirely clear, he began rummaging through his drawer for his address book. He scarcely knew what he was doing until he'd dialed the long-distance operator and gave her Isobel Cattaneo's number in Fiesole, where it would be going on 11:00 P.M.. Late to call, but not outrageously for Italy.

Sitting there listening to a succession of bell tones and a burst of rapid-fire Italian captured momentarily in crossed wires, Manship felt a surge of free-floating anxiety.

The phone was ringing on the other end. He thought of hanging up before she could answer. Three rings, four, then a fifth. He was certain she wasn't home. Almost relieved, he let it ring several times more, berating himself for calling. He was about to hang up.

"Pronto." The voice came low, drowsy, a bit annoyed.

"Miss Cattaneo . . ." He could hear the quaver in his voice. "Mark Manship in New York. I know it's late. I hope I haven't . . ."

Her response lagged, so that he wondered if he had awakened her, or, more dismally, if she simply didn't recall anyone by that name.

"You know, the Metropolitan Museum fellow." He laughed uneasily.

"Yes. Yes, of course. That Botticelli thing."

He was certain he'd detected a note of irritation.

They exchanged a few awkward pleasantries.

"Did you ever find your missing drawings?" she asked.

"The Chigi sketches? No, I'm afraid not. I did see your friend in Rome."

"Yes, I know. He was here last week. He told me he'd seen you. He said he'd given you someone to look up."

"That's right. He did. Some sort of a gallery in Parioli."

"The Quattrocento. I know it. And did you contact them?"

"Yes—well, not exactly. I went there. But the place was closed. They were off on vacation."

"Yes," she said almost apologetically. "Everyone in Italy is at that time. I'd completely forgotten."

Their conversation sputtered on as if they'd run out of things to say.

"I have no special reason for calling," he said, certain she was waiting for him to renew his pleas that she appear in New York as some sort of featured event at his opening. He was determined to make no such plea. "I just wanted to say hello," he went on, realizing at the same time that 11:00 P.M. was a strange time to call just to say hello.

"I see," she said with a cool brevity, and let it hang there like that.

There was another longish silence. He could sense her irritation. She hadn't the foggiest notion what he was driving at. For that matter, neither did he.

"I was just checking . . . I mean, rather, I had a funny intuition." It was all coming out wrong, but he couldn't stop himself now. "I just wanted to check and see that you were okay."

"I can assure you I am."

"You are?"

"Why wouldn't I be? What exactly were you worried about?"

He realized he couldn't tell her what he was worried about. "Nothing in particular," he said. "As I say, I just wanted to say hello."

"That was nice of you. And, as I say, I'm fine. Just fine. Thank you very much."

He laughed nervously. "Yes, I can hear you are. Well, I'll say good night then."

He found himself hoping she might prolong the conversation, and providentially, she did.

"I still have your plane tickets to New York," she said. "Do you want me to send them back?"

"No. Not at all. You keep them." His generosity sounded a bit too eager. It smacked of the bribe. "You may change your mind someday. Oh . . . I don't mean about coming for the show," he hastened to add. "You might just want to visit."

"Yes," she said, and let it drop at that.

"If you do come . . . for whatever reason, I hope you'll call."

There was another of those lengthy pauses.

"Well, then. I guess I'll say good night," he said again and feared he'd come off sounding pathetic.

"Thank you for your concern," she said, and rang off with an abrupt, almost rude click.

He sat there for several seconds longer, the phone receiver still pressed to his ear. Outside the big skylight window of his office, the dusk had begun to gather, and as it fell softly over the park, he felt dejection overtake him. Brooding on his disastrous attempt at a friendly call to Isobel Cattaneo, he felt what a jackass he'd made of himself, then wondered why he even cared.

He was jarred from these gloomy thoughts by the phone ringing on his desk. It was Helen Mirkin, Van Nuys's assistant, calling to tell him that the great man was free.

Climbing the short flight of stairs to Van Nuys's suite, Manship felt as though he were mounting the gallows.

TWENTY-THREE

After she'd hung up, Isobel stared at the phone, a puzzled expression flickering in the shadows around her eyes.

She'd been sitting out on the terrace when the phone rang. September had cooled the ovenlike nights and it was so much more pleasant outdoors than inside, where the airless rooms and the tile roof of the old villa held tight to the heat of a blistering hot summer.

She fully intended to go back out a bit longer before turning in, then decided to stop first in the kitchen for a piece of fruit. Munching a chilled pear on her way back out to the terrace, she collapsed with an almost-voluptuous languor into one of the battered old lounges.

She had the place to herself for the night. That was a luxury in itself. Erminia had gone home for a few days to her family in the north, and Tino was gone now, hopefully forever. She was glad to be rid of him.

He'd glowered at first when she told him it was over. He made threatening sounds, followed by gestures, going so far as to put rough hands on her.

That's when she told him about the lawyer and her intention to file charges against him for theft, not only of Erminia's money but also of some of her own, which she could prove he had taken. The lawyer, she told him, had also suggested that she press charges of menacing and battery for the several times he'd struck her. Of course, she hadn't been to a lawyer. She couldn't begin to afford one.

Tino laughed, but there was more bravado to his laughter than substance. When she picked up the phone and proceeded to dial the police, the façade crumbled.

She ordered him out that night, even going so far as to help him pack his few messy belongings. The threat of police and litigation had been too much for him. Gone were those well-practiced sullen looks he placed such stock in.

Seeing him out the door, she slipped a small bunch of lire into his pocket, enough to keep him going for a few weeks, long enough to find himself some sort of gainful employment, or, what was far more probable, another young woman with means enough to take care of him for a while, and naïve enough to believe that he was some sort of genius, wounded by a callous world, and whom only she could save.

They said good-bye and she watched him walk down the graveled front path, his meager shabby bag banging at his hip. He looked chastened and lost, like a small child who'd misbehaved and was being sent to his room. Several times, he glanced over his shoulder, hoping to be called back, but no call came.

Stretching luxuriously in the lounge, she let the chilly juices of the pear drip in tiny runnels at the corners of her mouth. Licking them with the tip of her tongue, she savored the sheer joy of being alone and at peace on such a perfect night. She laughed out loud at the whole awful episode, put it down to a lapse of good sense, and vowed she'd never permit such nonsense to repeat itself.

Her thoughts returned to Manship, his curious, unexpected call. She frowned into the flower-scented shadows of her garden, brooding over her need to be unkind to him, and wondered why. He'd certainly never been unkind to her, his only crime being that he offered her a job, which she took to be an insult.

It was then she heard the noise. She paid no attention to it. It was a dull, thudding sound, nondescript, something like a book dropping. She imagined it came from somewhere out on the street and so ignored it. The second noise, however, was far less ambiguous. It was the sound of a door opening, and it came from somewhere inside the villa.

It couldn't have been Erminia. She'd spoken to her that afternoon on the phone. She was miles away at her grandmother's farm up in the north, not due back for several days. Tino was what came first to mind.

"Tino," she called into the shadows behind her. "Tino."

There was no answer.

She rose and strode into the house, prepared to be stern with him. Most of the lights were out, which was the local custom on summer nights, since it kept the house cooler. A single light glowed dimly in the front-hall vestibule, and another in the long, narrow corridor leading to her bedroom.

Though she heard no sound, she was certain someone was in the house. She stood perfectly still, unmoving, like a stag spooked by a hound in the bush.

"Who's there?" she called out into the stuffy darkness. Impatient, angry, beginning to feel fright, she took a step forward into the parlor. "Tino . . . is that you? Don't play games with me, I warn you. . . ."

There was another sound, this time a sharp crack, as if someone or something had struck wood. The noise made her flinch, then shrink backward. In that instant, framed in the ormolu mirror above the mantel, a figure stood.

It wasn't Tino.

She was aware that her mouth was dry and that she had no voice.

"Who—" The rest of it stuck in her throat while she watched the figure in the mirror take a step forward into the room. Watching the figure even as it watched her, she saw what appeared to be the outline of a young man of average height with a somewhat boxy, athletic frame.

She was about to cry out when he smiled at her. That was the first time she saw his face. Youthful, it was, even sweet, like a young boy's. Seeing her fright, he put a finger to his lips as if to say, Hush.

Slowly, with no hesitation, he stepped into the room, coming toward her, still smiling, his finger pressed to his lips. Far from threatening, the movement of his body was sinuous, mesmerizing. In that moment, a sound came from behind her, from out on the terrace.

She whirled around in time to see two more of them.

The two entered the villa from the terrace outside, quietly closing the tall louvered doors behind them.

It was the smell that awakened her. She recognized it at once. For a fleeting instant, she was five years old again, in a doctor's office. Her mother stood above her, holding her arms while a man in a white gown of some sort, features blurred by a surgeon's mask, held a white cloth over her nose. It was that odor she smelled now—ether. Then the pinwheels—pretty, vivid colored circles like kaleidoscopic figures—spinning before her eyes.

She heard herself scream and then woke with a terrible headache. She was aware of lying flat on something hard and cold, unable to move. A large wad of gauze or something had been stuffed into her mouth. It forced her jaws open and held them that way at an unnaturally wide angle, so that they ached.

She knew her hands and ankles had been tied. Then it occurred to her that, in addition, she'd been wound cocoonlike into what felt and smelled like a dirty piece of carpet. It covered her papoose-fashion from her toes to the top of her head. Only her face was exposed.

She knew she was in a truck or a van, stretched out on the floor in the back as it bounced and jostled along. The springs of the vehicle had to be practically shot, since the impact of its tires with each pothole in the road wrenched every bone in her body.

She could see up and out through the panel windows above her. She knew they were on one of the big four-lane autostrada running north and south out of Florence. She could hear the woosh of automobile tires streaking past, headlight beams momentarily flooding the cabin of the van, then sliding past. In the pale gray light of first dawn, she could see the rooftops of government housing projects, and laundry drying over the balcony banisters of top-floor apartments. She judged it to be somewhere past 4:00 A.M.

Then she recalled the night before, the three of them in

the house, suddenly around her, swarming all over her. And then the cloth over her face and that smell. The front door, of course. She had never locked it. One had no reason to.

Someone was speaking up front, then someone else, the voices drifting sleepily backward into the van. She could smell cigarette smoke. Someone was laughing.

By tucking her chin above the border of the rug, she could roll her eyes forward and just barely make out the tops of three heads side by side in the front seat. She knew who they were—not them personally, but where they came from and who had sent them. Her recent talk with Pettigrilli came back to her and there wasn't a doubt in her mind.

She knew where she was going and why. It was that business with the museum chap. How rash that was. Why had she ever started up with him?

How ludicrous. All she'd done was to try to help him locate three small sketches of great importance to him, and of absolutely none to her. And to risk something so stupid as to reopen the whole thing with Borghini in order to achieve that. And now these people. And all because she'd done a stranger a small favor. He'd been nice to her and she had wanted to reciprocate. That was all. There was nothing to it. Now it was going to cost her dearly. She had few illusions about Ludovico Borghini. His reach was long, his tastes bizarre. He had a long memory, and one didn't want to be so rash as to meddle in his affairs.

"Never do that again."

"Do what?"

"You know what I mean. Countermand my orders. I tell the boy to do one thing. You tell him he doesn't have to."

"If you're talking about that bunch in the *vicinato* . . ."

"Never mind that bunch. They're fine boys—his age, good families. A little rough, perhaps, but that's the way of young boys."

"They're louts. Little hoodlums bent on mischief."

"He needs a bit of mischief, if you ask me."

"I won't have him associating with that sort."

"And I won't have him turned into a pansy. What will he come to with you dragging him off by the hand to opera houses and art galleries every day after school? Talk about a bad sort. Degenerates, the pack of them."

"You mean my friends, I take it."

"Your words, not mine."

"That crowd you call degenerate—some of the finest painters on the continent—de Chirico, Salemma, Tanguy . . ."

"I know perfectly well what they are."

"What are they, Otto? Tell me."

"Never mind. I'm telling you, I won't have my boy grow up to be some feckless dilettante. Sitting around galleries with effete people sipping tea, talking art. I won't have that. For God sake, isn't he prissy enough without your—"

"Stop shouting. . . . He'll hear."

"Good. Maybe it will shake some sense into his empty head. Pay heed, Mathilde. Don't cross me again. It undermines my authority in the boy's eyes, and I won't have it. I won't have it. I won't—"

First came the dull thud and then the scream. The scream was more one of fear than of pain. Then two more thuds and his father shouting. And more screams. His mother's screams. Panicked footsteps. Scuffing, stumbling, as if someone was running from someone else, dodging blows.

Seated barefoot in his pajamas at the top of the stairs, the boy cringed, his heart banging so hard in his chest, he thought his ribs might crack. Sometimes he would wake in the middle of the night, having heard them quarreling in the upper reaches of the palazzo. It would so unnerve him that he would get up and wander through the sprawling labyrinth of intersecting corridors, knuckling the tears from his eyes, unable to get back to sleep.

Years after, when they were both long dead, he would still awaken, hearing the voices and those fearful noises, the harsh, dull thuds, four, five at a time, in quick succession, the sound of flesh impacting on flesh, the bang of something heavy falling to the floor.

After all those years, it still had the power to unnerve him. And just as he'd done as a child, he would get up and wander the corridors, through the salons and sitting rooms, whose costly furnishings had now been either sold or shrouded beneath dusty sheets. His way invariably took him to his mother's room, where he still expected to find her.

It had been left precisely as it was the day she died—the tall four-poster with its embroidered tester, the old Savois vanity, its mirrored top littered with perfume bottles and cosmetics.

After all those vanished years, he could still sense her presence in the room. Throwing open the doors to her closets, he would inhale the musty smell of her clothing mingling with the faded scent of perfume and paper-dry, long-dead sachet.

"I won't have it. . . ."

The voice racketed down the stair again and along the empty corridors, slowly fading across the spate of years.

"I won't have it. . . ."

Borghini rose, shaking his head as if to slough off whatever bits of sleep still clung to him. It was dawn. He'd slept, seated at the dinner table, a plate of barely touched food before him; beside that was a near-empty flask of grappa. Still in his clothing from the night before, he was rumpled and smelled of perspiration.

He heard voices again, but this time they were real. One was a woman's voice, a mixture of outrage and defiance, alternating with frightened sobs.

In the next moment, a figure propelled by someone just behind came stumbling into the room. The figure was blindfolded, hands bound behind. A mane of tawny hair fanned out over its head and lay flat across the cheek, partially concealing the face. But he knew who it was.

Beppe stood in the doorway, looking larger beneath the

low lintel than his actual five-foot-five frame. He gazed across the room at the maestro, beaming like a proud puppy who'd just retrieved a stick and was awaiting his master's next command.

"Well, Isobel," Borghini said, grinning agreeably. "It's been a long time, hasn't it?"

TWENTY-FOUR

It was 10:00 P.M. Emily Taverner's back hurt and her head ached. She'd been going flat out since eight that morning, and she was stretched to her limit.

They were reviewing a list of last details before zero hour, exactly one week hence. Tie open, feet up on the desk, Manship, tilted back in his chair, read aloud from the list. Taverner buried her head in her clipboard and checked off items.

"For the media opening, does the press list include a cover release?"

"Yes."

"Containing full details of the exhibit?"

"Yes."

"What about a few quickie releases dealing with features on persons associated with the exhibit?"

"We have the one on the Mayor and Mrs. Giuliani. Also the one of the special banquet for the membership at Gracie Terrace."

"What about the Tisches and Salomon Brothers? Their funding of past exhibitions, et cetera, et cetera."

"We're putting the finishing touches on bios of the Tisches and also one of Warren Buffett."

"Don't forget to mention the Wallace Funds and also Mr. and Mrs. Laurance Rockefeller."

"All covered."

"And the PBS segment?"

"Scheduled to be aired the night before. I told you all of this yesterday."

"I know you did, damn it. There's no need to keep reminding me." He stared down into his lap for a long moment, then looked up. "Sorry about that," he said, and hurried on. "What about feature stories?"

"Three scheduled—*ARTnews*, *Newsweek*, *New York* magazine, *The New York Times* wants to do something on the Chigi sketches."

"I can't talk to them now."

"To none of them?"

"Not now. I don't have the time."

"But, Mark, that's insane. There's been too much advance hype to simply ignore them all now. It will look funny."

"Let it look funny. I can't help that."

"The *Times* also mentioned this Cattaneo woman you met in Florence."

Manship groaned and rubbed his red-rimmed eyes. "How the hell did they hear about her?"

"Someone evidently leaked the story about your going to Fiesole. If she is who she says she is . . ."

"Of course she is. She's got all the papers to prove it."

"What a pity. That would have been *the* perfect guest spot."

"Well, it ain't gonna happen." Manship sulked. "I spoke to her again this afternoon."

"Why won't she come? What reasons does she give?"

"She doesn't give reasons. She just won't. She's made that abundantly clear. She simply has no wish to be paraded around here like some kind of trophy. So let's just forget about it."

"Is she as beautiful as—"

"Her great-great-great-great whatever she was."

"Grandmother."

"Whatever." Manship brooded. "Well, if you ask me, she's no Primavera. No Venus." He thought a moment, then seemed to relent. "Oh, I suppose she's pretty enough. Frankly, I didn't even see the resemblance until—"

"Until what?"

"Until she took down her hair."

"She took down her hair?"

"I asked her to. And sure, it would have been fun to have her here for the opening. But I can't seem to make Van Nuys or anyone else around here understand that our Miss Simonetta has zero interest in playing any part whatsoever in this exhibition. Don't worry. I'm not concerned. We'll do just fine without her.''

It all came boiling up in one long, breathy screed. Now that it was out, he realized how much it had been bothering him.

Emily Taverner could see that at once. She could see other things, too, regarding the Cattaneo woman that had perhaps not yet occurred to Manship himself.

Before they finally broke for the evening, they went over the general mailing list and studied the seating plan for the trustees at the opening-night banquet.

In the morning, they'd be meeting with one of the whiz-kid creative directors from Chiat/Day, the museum's advertising agency. They would look at banners and billboard layouts, stickers, lapel pins on which the timeless visage of the Venus would appear, as well as designs for bus and subway advertising.

When Manship finally crept home that evening, it was going on midnight. He'd put Taverner in a cab, feeling strangely tongue-tied, torn between his desire to thank her for all of the unpaid time she'd put in and his inability to apologize for being short with her. He knew he had. Rather than the acid tongue he'd occasionally meted out, the girl deserved a medal for all of her superhuman efforts on the show's behalf.

Coming up on 5 East Eighty-fifth, he was startled to see the little mews house all lit up and aglow. The impression from out on the street on a damp, chill night was like a Christmas card—all cozy and welcoming, as if just beyond the leaded windows Scrooge might well find old Fezziwig there dancing a quadrille at a party, as drawn by Boz.

Opening the front door, his key still in the lock, he stood for a moment, stooping slightly over the threshold, surprised to hear voices drifting at him from the kitchen. One was Maeve's; the other was a man's. He didn't recognize it until he'd pushed open the swinging door into the kitchen and saw Bill Osgood seated opposite Maeve at the kitchen table. They were lingering over a glass of wine, with the litter of supper plates strewn out between them.

"Well, this is a fine time to be showing up." Maeve gazed up at him. "Weren't we supposed to be having dinner tonight?"

"Oh, Christ." Manship thumped his forehead. "I got tied up at the office. Completely forgot."

"I sat here like an idiot twiddling my thumbs until nine o'clock, when Mr. Osgood came along and was kind enough to sit down in your place."

Osgood smiled like the Cheshire cat, his face flamed from a healthy infusion of wine and cutlets. "I sure lucked out tonight, old buddy. I just stopped by to drop off some revised figures for the advertising budget and poor Mrs. Costain here said you'd stood her up for supper. I was perfectly prepared to settle for rancid tuna salad out of my refrigerator, but she was good enough to ask me to sit in for you, you rude thing—and since I had no plans for supper, I told her I'd gladly do such. Glass of Riesling, old buddy? This is an '83 Auslese. It's a honey."

"I know. It's from my cellar."

"You have marvelous taste." He waved the half-finished bottle at Manship.

"There're still cutlets left over, and I bought some lovely fresh asparagus at the market today, though you don't deserve it." Studying him more closely, Maeve frowned. "Come sit down, Mark. You look like you've been horsewhipped."

He came forward uncertainly, sagging into a chair between them.

Osgood poured him a glass of wine. "Maeve and I have just been arguing. . . ."

"Not arguing, Bill. Discussing."

"Right. Discussing," Osgood conceded, clearly feeling his wine and full of himself.

"What's your idea of a museum, Mark?"

"A museum is a lunatic asylum," Manship said. "Handsomely decorated."

Maeve made a face, as if there was a bad taste in her mouth. "If it's any good, it had better have a sense of the past and some ideas about the future."

"You mean the sort of thing with four bare walls, track lighting, and some plasticine balls and radiator caps strewn over the floor in a cunning arrangement?" Manship plucked a bread stick out of a tall jar and chewed gloomily.

"What about a row of TV sets, all chattering at once, or maybe some old boards and planks strewn on a skate ramp," Osgood threw in with spiteful relish. "A nest of tangled multicolored neon lights blinking. Blink, blink, blink."

"At least it makes a statement," Maeve shot back.

"So does a mound of dog doo," Manship grumbled. "Now, if you don't mind, let's quit all this. I'm getting depressed."

Osgood and Maeve exchanged troubled glances.

"I'm sorry," Manship murmured, crestfallen. "Forgive me. That was uncalled for."

"What's wrong?" Osgood asked, moving a step toward him.

"What's wrong? Well, if you must know, I feel shitty. I'm so sick of this goddamned show, by now, I seem to have forgotten the reasons for wanting to put it on in the first place."

"You're pushing yourself too hard, Mark." Osgood looked concerned. "It's not good for you or for the show."

"The work's got to get done." Manship started to rise, then sat back down. "There're a million and one things left to do and not enough hands to do them. I sandbagged poor Taverner tonight. She didn't deserve it. She's been working like a dog. There's just too goddamned much for the both of us."

"It'll get done," Maeve said.

Osgood splashed another two inches of Riesling into

Manship's glass. "Had another dustup with Van Nuys, too, I gather."

"That was only this afternoon. How did you hear?"

"News travels fast, old buddy. The tom-toms were still beating in the PR department when I left tonight. He still wants you to move up the opening date?"

"Sure he does. And the way things are going right now, I'm inclined to ask for a week's postponement."

"You didn't say that, I hope."

"I sure did." Manship gave a short cheerless laugh. "He got red in the face. His wattles quivered like some old turkey's—you know the way he gets." Manship did a passable imitation of the board chairman working up to apoplexy.

Shortly, they were all in stitches.

"Frankly," he went on in manic fury, "I was hoping to prod the old boy into a stroke. Nothing serious, mind you. A small aneurysm. A mild cerebral hemorrhage. Something to disable him temporarily until after the opening."

"You'll have one before he does," Maeve said. "You look awful."

Osgood studied him a while. "Looks better than when he came in. The wine's put some color back in his cheeks."

"I'll say one thing." Manship dabbed a napkin to his lips. "The moment this show is launched and up on its feet, I'm gone. Out of here."

Removing soiled dishes from the table, Maeve stopped dead in her tracks, gaping down at him.

"You don't mean that," Osgood said.

"I sure do. Van Nuys and I are rapidly approaching the time where we're going to have it out. He's packing bigger guns than I am, so I'm not looking for any victories. I just want to get out of here with what's left of my sanity and stomach lining."

"You've given the place twelve years," Maeve argued. "You've done so much for it."

"What a waste. What a god-awful waste," Osgood muttered.

Manship's fork fiddled idly in his salad. "I've been mulling this thing a long time now, Bill. I really don't belong here. It was fun for a while. It's not fun anymore."

"As you know," Osgood went on in his slow Texas twang, "my term is up here next fall. I'm going home to Texas after fifteen years in the big city. Looking forward to doing nothing more for a long time than maybe some part-time teaching at the university, and lots of tarpon fishing down in Baja. All of which suits me just fine."

Manship had heard this sort of thing before. It was pure Osgood, doing his Lyndon Johnson imitation at its most treacherous best.

"I've already notified Van Nuys in a notarized letter that you're my personal choice to replace me as director. I won't pretend that he was overjoyed with my selection, and, to be absolutely frank, I, too, have reservations about it. He prefers Klass or Colbert, and I can see why. Colbert's about as amiable as an ice pick. Doesn't stand a chance, far as I can see. Klass is amiable and very corporate; you're not. He's political; he plays the game; you don't. He does what he's told. He's a good soldier, a team player. You're none of the above. And, most important to the bean counters in charge around here, Klass has a healthy respect for money—how to get it, how to spend it. You, my friend, are a walking budget deficit."

Manship took the criticism with good grace. "In that case, René should have the job. He'll enjoy it far more than I ever could."

"But *you're* the better man for it," Osgood countered. "Better qualified. A far wider range of expertise. Less academic than either Colbert or Klass, with far more vision of what this institution is and where it should be going. And, of course, temperamentally you're far better suited to take on the constant bickering of the board. René will cave in to anything they want. But most important, you're better suited for the job of putting the business of this museum, which is Art with a capital *A*, before a wider public. Call it flare, if you like. Panache. None of the others have it.''

Manship sat quietly, hands on knees, listening. It was his future that was being discussed. At his age, in that highly specialized field, one could not bounce around too much without raising eyebrows, not to mention questions as to one's professional steadiness.

When at last he rose, his eyes were fixed straight ahead. He started toward the study.

''Mark,'' Maeve called after him, a faint quaver to her voice. ''How about a slice of nice fresh cobbler for dessert?''

''No thanks. I've got some work to finish up.'' He was aware of their eyes following him as he closed the door behind him.

Seated at his desk, a stack of advertising rush copy before him, there was the taste of something bitter in his mouth. That silly talk with Maeve about museums, then that pious lecture from Osgood, ending with a report card scoring his strengths and weaknesses and outlook for the future. How he hated it all, the striving and the nauseating business of getting ahead. And now, suddenly, Maeve and Osgood. Why did that rankle so? Clearly they'd struck up something that night. More power to them. Both were trapped in unsatisfactory situations—hers dying, his already dead, with batteries of divorce lawyers gorging avidly on the corpse of the marriage. Why not reach out if they both felt something?

Toward dawn, sheer exhaustion took him up to bed. Shortly after he'd fallen asleep, he was awakened by the sound of an ambulance siren whooping its way uptown to some dangerous precinct farther north. The room was still dark and he'd been dreaming of a pale, golden-haired creature skimming toward him over the surf in a huge mollusk shell. Why in heaven's name had he called her? What a fool he must have sounded like. Hemming and hawing and bumping along, he'd carried on like some pimply adolescent making his first call to a girl.

Trying to reconstruct Isobel Cattaneo's features in his mind, he found, to his surprise, that he couldn't. Physically, she remained a vague, shadowy outline to him. Yet how similar in outlook they were, the two of them. Both alone in the world, unsettled, unanchored to anything, still en route somewhere, both dissatisfied with the progress of their journeys to date. Was that the reason behind his strange affinity for her? As discouraging as their talk today had been, he was certain he'd not seen the last of her. And in the back of his mind lurked a sharp, inescapable sense of some impending danger hurtling toward them.

TWENTY-FIVE

"I want to give you the benefit of the doubt, Isobel. But you make it hard for me."

He sat at a large desk in his study. The chair she sat in was small, low to the ground, very much like a child's chair, so that she had to sit with her knees up. For contrast (and to make a point), Borghini sat in a large, imposing chair. Attired in freshly starched and ironed army fatigues, he conducted the interview in his grand, inquisitorial manner. The child's chair had been his own nursery chair almost fifty years ago.

His last words resonated with an ominous ring—"you make it hard for me"—her panicky thoughts had been racketing ahead at a dizzying speed. She still wore the simple skirt, blouse, and sandals she had been wearing in Fiesole when they'd taken her.

The irony of it all was that the last time she'd seen him was right here in this dark, sprawling palazzo on the Quirinal—ten years ago.

She marveled at his youthfulness, his unlined face. But now, behind that grand, self-important desk, he looked smaller to her—almost doll-like. Morbidly sensitive about his height, she recalled, he always wore elevated shoes adding at least three inches to his frame. Today, she noted, he wore combat boots, spit-polished and buffed to a high sheen, trousers bloused into them in military fashion.

His gaze fastened on her, full of patience and bogus sorrow. On first meeting him, that expression could be extremely appealing. But to know Borghini was to know never to take what you saw for granted. Behind that gentle, pitying gaze lurked stratagems and treachery, secret agendas, far too byzantine to imagine.

"I was fond of you, Isobel." He shook his head regretfully. "I had hopes for you."

Above and just behind her, she could sense the other one, an unseen presence whose slow, regular breathing she could feel at the back of her neck. She knew it was the boy. That's all he was, a boy, seventeen or eighteen at most, with a pink-skinned baby face as of yet untouched by the razor. Rarely, she noted, did he leave his master's side.

Nor did she fail to note how he looked at her. She'd seen it the night before when she'd discovered him in the front hallway of the house. He crouched then like a cat on its nocturnal prowl. Unpredictable, he could pounce at any moment. There was something deeply unsettling in his eyes.

"Why did you send that man to me, Isobel?"

"I didn't, Ludo. I told you that."

He waved a scornful hand at her. "No, you sent him to that scum Pettigrilli, who sent him to me."

"How was I to know that Aldo would send him to Parioli? I thought he might have some clue as to the whereabouts of those drawings."

"Which is as good as sending him directly to me. Where else would that rodent turncoat send your American friend for information of that sort if not to me? Not very subtle, Isobel. I would have hoped for better from you. More coffee?"

She shook her head wearily.

"Beppe, fetch the Signorina another *caffè latte*. And for me, another grappa."

She heard the boy's padded footsteps withdraw behind her, followed by the loud click of a heavy door closing.

Borghini's interrogation resumed. "Tell me again about this man, Isobel. What is his name?"

She looked away, gnawing the inside of her lip, determined not to show how frightened she was. "Manship."

"Louder, please, Isobel. You're mumbling."

"Manship. Mark Manship." She made an effort to enunciate each syllable.

"What exactly is this Mr. Manship's game?"

"As I said before, Ludo, he's a curator—for the Metropolitan Museum . . . in New York. Something of a scholar, I gather. He's putting on an exhibition in New York."

"Of Botticelli paintings."

"And drawings, too. A big show. Something to do with the occasion of Botticelli's five hundred and fiftieth birthday. Some such thing. He'd been trying to track down some drawings. The Germans—"

"Yes, the Germans? What about the Germans?"

"The federal police. In Berlin—or Leipzig. I'm not sure."

"You hadn't mentioned that before. You see, Isobel. That's what makes me so uneasy about you." His gaze pinned her. "What you *do* and what you *don't* tell me. I can never be certain if that's by accident or design."

"I'm trying to tell you everything, Ludo. I'm sure you can appreciate that at the moment I'm a bit nervous."

"Nervous?" He laughed disarmingly. "Why, in heaven's name? What do you have to be nervous about?"

The boy returned, bearing a tray rattling with cups and saucers. He placed a steaming coffee before her and poured a full pony of grappa from a carafe for Borghini. He then resumed his position behind her.

"Unless, of course," the Count continued, "you lie to me. You know, Isobel, how I despise a liar. Pettigrilli was a liar. He lied to me. That's why he was discharged from the movement." He watched the effect of his words register on her face. "Tell me again about the Germans. How are they connected?"

By then, she was close to tears.

"Well . . . they . . . he went to Berlin."

"He?"

"This fellow, Manship. He went to Berlin because that was the last place these three lost Chigi sketches were reportedly seen."

"And the Germans, I take it, knew about the sketches?"

"Apparently, they'd been stolen a few years earlier from the home of a man whose father was in the Gestapo; stationed in Naples during the war, I believe. This man smuggled them out of Italy shortly before the Allies landed in Anzio.''

She paused to see if her information had satisfied him. He gave her another of his impatient waves. ''Yes, yes. Go on.''

''As I understand it, the police in Leipzig informed the Berlin police about the theft and they—''

''They?''

''The police in Leipzig, I suppose. . . .''

''Yes?''

''They suspected that the theft was carried out by . . .''

His brow lowered and he leaned slightly forward. ''By some fascist paramilitary group centered in Rome? Is that what you were about to say, Isobel?''

She stared down at her hands and finally answered in an exhausted whisper. ''Yes.'' Seated so long in the child's chair, her back and legs had begun to ache.

Borghini splashed another finger of grappa into his glass, the tip of his tongue sliding along his lower lip as he did so. ''And so, of course, you assumed that this nasty little fascist group was your old friend Ludovico Borghini's? Am I right?''

''Yes, Ludo.'' She continued to stare down at her hands.

He paused, pleased with the way his mounting indignation was taking its toll on her. ''And so you suggested, through Pettigrilli of course, that your friend come here looking for the so-called stolen sketches?''

''It wasn't exactly that way,'' she said, ''but it worked out that way.''

''It worked out that way,'' he mimicked her voice, a look of disgust on his face.

''Yes, Ludo. The answer to your question is *yes*.'' This time, she said it louder, more emphatically, with an edge of defiance that made him smile.

''You note that I said 'so-called' stolen sketches? Have you any idea why?''

"I suppose to emphasize the point that the sketches taken out of Leipzig were not actually stolen, but merely returned to Italy, their rightful owner."

"Bravo, Isobel." The colonel applauded lightly. "Very gratifying. You see, Beppe? My teaching has not been entirely wasted."

Once again, that small, fleeting smile swept across the lower half of his features. The upper half never moved. "In the case of these so-called stolen sketches, Isobel, I wish to make clear that I serve only in a custodial capacity—until such time as a new government can be formed. . . ."

"A new government?"

"Call it instead a 'New Order.' Why quarrel?" Borghini looked up at the boy and winked. "Ay, Beppe?"

"*Si*, Maestro."

Borghini turned back to her. "I've read about your Mr. Manship's show and I loathe it. Do you know why?"

"No, Ludo."

"I resent—deeply resent—the fact that such people think they can come here, loot our museums, deprive us of our heritage. We, the descendants of Caesars. Have we become so polluted? By what right?"

Borghini pounded the desktop, making objects on it scatter. "What do you want from me, Ludo?" her voice pleaded. "I've met the man twice. Once in Fiesole, at my house. The other time in this little restaurant in Firenzè. He wanted me to go to New York with him for the opening of his show."

"Because of the striking resemblance to your illustrious ancestor, the Simonetta, *whore* of the Medici." The word, in his mouth, sounded like a sneer. "And you declined his offer?"

"Yes."

"That's to your credit." Borghini's fingertips played lightly over the leather tooling of his desk. "And your friend Mr. Manship . . ."

"He's not my friend, Ludo," she repeated wearily.

"After his luncheon with Pettigrilli, your friend went out to Parioli?"

"So I gather. Aldo said he'd given the fellow the address of the gallery."

"And, of course, the fellow came right around forthwith."

"Yes," she murmured softly.

"Please stop mumbling, Isobel. I can't hear you."

"Yes. Yes. Yes," she said, this time almost shouting.

Her sudden lashing out had taken him aback. Once again, she could feel the boy's agitated breathing and see out of the corner of her eye his knuckles whiten as he clenched the back of her chair.

Borghini's fingers resumed their drumming. "Do you really think I need you to tell me that some unwanted intruder had been out to my gallery, snooping around?"

"No, Ludo," she said, trying a more deferential tack. "I wouldn't think so."

"Don't patronize me with your 'No, Ludos.' Get that long-suffering tone out of your voice. I know very well how to deal with scum like your friend. I've been dealing with that sort for a lifetime."

He pushed a snapshot toward her. It had the overexposed, out-of-focus look of something taken by a surveillance camera. He pushed several others toward her. Two or three merely showed the front doorway and the interiors of the little Parioli gallery. But in several others, sure enough, there was Mark Manship. One caught him peering into the shop window from outside, one hand over his eyes to screen out the sunlight. Another showed him with his hand poking halfway through the open back door. Both photos were grainy, had much distortion, and the features of the individual in each case were indistinct. But in a third photo, taken from the rear of the gallery, looking out onto a back alley, the figure of Manship rummaging through a trash can was clear and unmistakable.

"So," Borghini said, aglow with quiet triumph. "What am I to do with you, Isobel?"

"Let me go, Ludo," she said, close to tears. "I intended no harm. I was merely trying to do this Manship fellow a favor...."

"A favor at my expense." Once again, Borghini's fist pounded the desktop. "Because of this favor of yours, I must now worry about what your Mr. Manship might or might not have seen out in Parioli."

She swallowed hard. "From what he told me—"

"Told you? You mean you've seen him again since he's been out there?"

"No. I haven't seen him. I've spoken to him on the phone."

"When?"

"Just last night."

"You didn't say that. Why didn't you say he called? What did he tell you about his visit to the gallery?"

"He said the shop was closed, that everyone was on vacation. You saw him for yourself with your own cameras. He didn't go in."

He watched her coolly through half-shut eyes. "That's true," he conceded begrudgingly. "He didn't go in."

Her face brightened with the incontestable logic of that fact. "Well, then, you see, Ludo, if he didn't go in, then he didn't see anything."

He frowned, unwilling to accept anything quite so simple. Then, for no apparent reason, he smiled at her. It was a rather disquieting smile, unpleasantly suggestive.

"I can well see why Mr. Manship would take such a keen interest in you, Isobel. Ay, Beppe?" He winked at the boy, prompting a low, soft laugh from him. "You're very beautiful, aren't you?"

She glanced at him, puzzled. "Beautiful?"

"Oh, don't be coy. You know that you are. For as long as I've know you—what is it now, ten years?—men have

always pursued you. Some for perfectly fine motives, some ·
for less exalted ones. Even I wanted you.''

His manner up until that moment had been playful, possibly even flirtatious. Now it had suddenly taken a somewhat sinister turn. It wasn't what he'd said but the way
he'd said it, that mixture of regret and undisguised sexual
playfulness. It sent a current of ice through her veins.

· It was true, of course. Men had always wanted her. She
couldn't help that. She knew it as a young girl and then as
she grew older. Artists flocked to her, photographers, film-·
makers, potential suitors—all wishing to enter into some
kind of union.

With Borghini, she'd always known just from the way
he behaved in her presence—affecting a certain boredom,
distraction, a kind a avuncular affection—that he was
deeply attracted to her. But his attraction went beyond the
merely carnal. Had it been just that, it would have been
simpler to deal with. With him, she knew the driving force
was something else. There was always a subtext, something
unspoken but no less real because of that. In all their time
together, he'd never once laid a questionable hand on her.
She'd never quite been able to figure that out. It wasn't
· mere gentlemanly restraint. But whatever it was, her innate
· womanly intuition had warned her to give him a wide berth.

''You were close to my ideal,'' Borghini went on wistfully. ''Had things been different . . .''

He glanced up, to see the outline of the boy hovering
like a dark stain above her. ''Beppe, leave us for a moment.''

He watched the boy, somewhat resentfully, fade away
and didn't resume until the door clicked shut behind him.
Then he turned back to her. ''My mother, you know, would
have adored you.''

The sudden disclosure increased her discomfort. She
sensed more coming and sought desperately for ways to ·
deflect it.

''You were exactly what she'd always planned for me.

And you know . . ." His words trailed off into shy laughter.

"I never got to meet your mother, Ludo."

"She died long before you were born."

He came around the desk. Taking her hand, he led her up to a small settee, where he seated her. He was almost courtly. "I'm sure that's more comfortable than the baby's chair."

"Yes, much better."

"I was punishing you, I suppose. How silly. I do have a nasty streak, don't I?"

He started to pace. "Yes, Mama would have adored you. She would have fussed over you and spoiled you. She would have loved your gorgeous Simonetta eyes. She would have painted them." Lost in thought, his voice trailed off as he studied her eyes. "Of course, it was out of the question. There was the considerable age difference, and then, too, I don't believe you were prepared to live the sort of life I was in a position to offer."

She started to reply, but he silenced her with a wave of the hand.

"No doubt you've heard something of my activities."

"Yes."

"I'm still quite involved in the movement. Some six thousand of us now. All around the world and growing every year." His pacing had become circular and faster. "There are many in our country, aggrieved, humiliated, destitute, though they don't speak out. . . ."

Relieved that the topic of conversation had shifted to his work, she struggled to keep his mind focused in that direction. "Aggrieved about what, Ludo?"

"For one thing," he sneered, "agents of powerful interests, like your friend Mr. Manship. And their insatiable hunger for our most treasured possessions, for another. Take my word for it, Isobel. This Botticelli thing—it won't happen. Not so long as I have breath to breathe. We in the movement have ways of preventing it."

Splashing another grappa into his snifter, he spilled most

of it onto his desk and onto the papers and snapshots lying there. "The pack of whores who sit in the National Assembly today. We have ways of, shall we say, impressing them. This Botticelli horror won't happen, Isobel. Take my word—"

His shouting brought the boy back. The door burst open and he stood there eyeing them warily.

"Get out," Borghini shouted, and the boy fled backward, like a dog kicked by its master.

When he turned to her again, she saw in a glance the old madness in his eyes. In the next moment, he'd reached down into some lower drawer and rummaged angrily about there. All she could see was the top of his head as he rooted about at his feet, then slammed something down onto his desk.

"This, I take it, is what your friend so desperately wants." He shoved a large manila folder across the desktop. "Look. Go ahead. Look."

The folder had skidded to a halt, half off, half on the desk, part of its contents spilling out from inside. Not daring to look too long, she glimpsed a section of old parchment. Faded charcoal lines, frayed edges soon came into view. She knew what it was. She didn't have to see any more.

"You see, Pettigrilli was right." Borghini stood, his voice ringing with anger.

Hands trembling, her fluttering fingers struggled with the top leaf of the folder.

Then suddenly, there they were, in her hands. She was touching them, stunned at the nearness, the accessibility of them. There were three of them—all in the eighteen-by-twelve-centimeter category. No special care had been given to the manner in which they'd been stored. No paper overlays protected them; they were not under glass or any covering that would prevent the time-faded charcoal lines from disappearing.

"Go on," he shouted. "Pick it up. Pick it up."

With tremulous fingers, she lifted one from the folder, careful to hold it at the edges with the tips of her fingers. There was the Simonetta—that virginal, achingly lovely face, the long, exquisitely attenuated oval of it fading ghost-like into the smudged parchment.

She could feel his eyes on her, watchful, triumphant.

"That's what your friend wanted, isn't it, Isobel? He has excellent taste. Well, what's the matter? They're not fake."

"No, they're not fake, Ludo. I can see that."

She could tell it from the sure, pure sweep of the line, rendered unbroken in a single stroke, as if whoever had held the charcoal never lifted it once. No hesitation. No erasures. No overlapping lines. Just masterful control of the hand, as though some preternatural force had guided it.

Serene, timeless, devoid of any of the frank sensuality found in the *Birth of Venus* or the *Primavera,* the sketches for the *Chigi Madonna* had a fragile, chaste beauty. The infant she cradled in her arms was plump and laughing—greedy, lunging for a fistful of grapes. You could almost hear its giggles of delight.

Borghini's gaze bore down harder. "Your friend went to Parioli to steal those from me," he shouted. "And you sent him there."

"No, Ludo. I didn't."

"Don't tell me you didn't," he thundered.

"Ludo. I swear."

"If he dares come poking round again, things won't go quite so easy for him."

She was close to tears. "Ludo, please. I'd like to go home now."

He was ranting and tossing things about on his desk. "Next time he shows his face here—" He looked up, startled, as though her last words had finally registered. "You'd like to go home?"

"Yes, Ludo. I'd like to go now, as soon as possible."

"But why?" There was a look of hurt in his eyes.

She could think of nothing to say that would not offend him or send him off on another tirade.

"Isn't my house comfortable? You have enough of everything here."

"Everything is fine, Ludo. Lovely." Her voice was almost a whisper. "But I want my own home. Please. When may I go?"

He gazed at her as if not quite grasping what she'd said. "When? When?" His hands fidgeted. "Who's to say when? Perhaps tomorrow." He rose suddenly, stamping his booted feet. "Perhaps never. Beppe. Beppe," he bellowed at the closed door. "Show the signorina upstairs to her room."

She could still hear him muttering after the door had closed behind them.

TWENTY-SIX

She moved numbly down the long, musty corridor, its walls lined with the darkly shadowed portraits of Borghinis long gone. There were Borghinis epauletted and braided in military uniform, in brocades and silk and flounced shoulders, monocled Borghinis, Borghinis with muttonchop whiskers and waxed mustaches, generals and judges, magistrates and merchant princes.

The boy trailed behind her, murmuring directions in a soft, oddly suggestive way. "*Sinestra,* signorina. *Diretto. Destro.*"

She was aware of the slow, scuffing drag of his footsteps on the stone floor and could feel his eyes ranging up and down her body from behind. He kept to the rear, never once coming abreast of her or moving ahead.

Presently, they came to a door at the end of a dark hallway. The boy came forward, clanking a large ring of keys. "*Permesso,*" he murmured and brushed past her, making momentary physical contact. She thought it had been intentional.

He flicked through a number of keys on the ring, trying several before finding the one he wanted. Then inserting it in the lock, he pushed the door open. At first, it appeared to stick, as though it hadn't been opened for some time. It made a groaning sound as it swung on its hinges. The boy stepped aside and waited for her to enter before following her in.

She had expected something dismal and punitive, like a cell. What she saw instead was more like out of a fairy tale—sumptuous, palatial, everything on a grand scale. A mustiness hovered everywhere, with strong hints of camphor and faded old sachet.

At the far end of the room, a bank of leaded handblown windows extended the full length of the wall. Passing her again, the boy made his way there. Pulling a heavy braided cord, a wall of gray silk moiré slid back, revealing a vast expanse of rolling forest behind the palazzo.

"The bath is this way, signorina." Beppe moved about with the brisk formality of a hotel porter demonstrating the principal features of a guest room.

She followed him into an adjoining bathroom. It contained a shower with toilet and bidet, then a tub of marble and gilt, more along the lines of a small piscine than a bath.

Outside again in the bedroom, he opened windows to air out the place. She followed him there, then looked down. They were in a corner room on the uppermost floor of the building. Her eyes sought out balconies, ledges, any route of possible escape. There was nothing between the window and the cobblestoned courtyard below but a sheer drop of twenty-odd meters.

The boy, watching her with an odd, secretive smile, seemed to read her mind and sense her dismay. "I'll bring towels, signorina," he said with almost spiteful glee.

When he left, she could hear him on the other side of the door, clanking keys until at last she heard the rusty old lock gears engage and the bolt slide home. She found it unsettling that the boy had the keys.

Hearing his footsteps recede down the hallway, finally fading into silence, heightened her sense of desolation. The quiet that followed was so pervasive and heavy, she could almost touch it. The terrifying stillness of the house was relieved only by the sharp squeal of hawks wheeling endlessly in great wide circles overhead.

At last, she allowed herself to look a bit more closely at her surroundings. The bedroom she was to occupy was larger than the entire first floor of the Villa Tranquillo in Fiesole. An enormous four-poster bed with a silk embroidered tester mounted above dominated the center of the room. Off in one corner was a small salon comprised of an old chestnut armoire, a glass-topped coffee table, and an antique settee covered in needlepoint primroses. Nearby was a small end table. Just beneath that, she found a telephone jack on the floor. The phone itself had been removed.

In the corner directly opposite stood a harp with a music stand before it. A small velvet-covered chair stood behind that. The harp gave the impression of having recently been played, as though its owner had left the room on some errand and was due back any moment. There was still sheet music on the stand. Stooping slightly above it, she saw that it was a little sonatine of Dutilleux.

Off in yet another corner of the room, in a shaft of mote-filled sunlight, were several easels, each with a painting; adjacent to that, a long marble refectory table stood littered with boxes of charcoals and pastels, tubes of paint, jars of brushes, and a heavily spattered palette, on which blobs of multicolored paints had, over time, turned rock-hard. In addition were cans of turpentine that had dried up, spatulas for applying paint, and X-Acto knives for removing it.

Whoever had worked there had done so daily and diligently. A painting still propped on the easel—a half-finished portrait of a Florentine lady of the fifteenth century—looked to Isobel like something that had been copied—something Italian. It had that light and textured opulence, richly colored in Florentine roses and siennas. But the area where the face itself should have been had been painted out and gone over several times, leaving in its place an empty, smudge-streaked oval. The paintings were decent journeyman work, but they were the work of a copyist, and not a particularly talented copyist at that.

Farther along the far wall of the room was a large ceiling-to-floor wardrobe. Comprised of eight or nine separate panels attached by hinges, it was designed to open in an accordion arrangement, sliding back on a track.

It took her some time before she mustered the courage to open it. When at last she did, a low rattle sounded and the breath of faded flowers exhaled outward from the shadowy interior. Fine, expensively tailored clothing hung there in dazzling profusion. Couture dresses, gowns, skirts. Rows of lined, built-in drawers spilled over with blouses and sweaters. Bandboxes of hats had been stacked high on an upper shelf, along with trays of handkerchiefs, gloves, and silk scarves. The styles bespoke a fashion current nearly a half century before.

Rooted to the spot for some time, she peered into the musty shadows. A gradual but depressing awareness came over her that the room in which Borghini had chosen to imprison her was none other than his own mother's, the Contessa Borghini. There was nothing especially remarkable in that. But why, then, she asked herself, did the mere thought of it so sicken her?

Two, three hours passed. She had no way of knowing. She wore no watch, and there was no clock in the room. The silence was so total and prolonged that after a while she started to make her own noises—shifting chairs, rattling perfume bottles on a vanity top, clashing steel hangers together in the wardrobe—just for the sheer relief of sound. At one point, she plucked a string on the harp, nearly jumping back at the loud plangent note that came vibrating out at her in waves from the instrument.

After a while, she became convinced there was no one in the house. But then the boy came back. She heard the soft clump of his boots moving down the corridor towards her, then the clank of keys outside the door. Once more, there was that same fumbling until he'd found the right key and the door swung open.

"The maestro would like to see you downstairs."

"Now?"

"At once."

He was seated at a long, narrow table in the kitchen pantry when the boy brought her in. He still wore the freshly starched army fatigues. Red shoulder epaulettes and collars studded with gold eagles proclaimed his rank.

He sat before a tall bottle of grappa, a snifter of the icy liquid at his right hand. At his left lay the folder containing the Chigi sketches. From the red flare streaking his cheeks, she could tell he'd been at the grappa for some time.

"Sit," he said, his voice a muffled growl.

She slipped at once into the chair opposite him. The boy instantly took up his place behind her. Eyes bleared and grieving, Borghini began to take up his rant where he'd left off earlier.

"You say you want to go home?" He snatched up the folder and wagged it in her face. "Now that you've seen these, you can never go home."

She stared at him, unblinking, her hands and feet gone sickly cold.

Lifting his snifter, he flicked his wrist, tossing off the last of the smoking liquid that remained in his glass. "Take the signorina back to her room," he thundered at the boy, and waved them both out of his sight.

A short time later, Beppe brought a tray of supper up to her. He set it out on the small end table with fastidious care, then went into the bathroom to put out fresh towels, soap, and other toiletries. All the while he went about his work, she watched transfixed, like a doomed bird watching its ferret executioner. He never spoke. By the time he left, treading noiselessly from the room, bolting the door behind him with an emphatic click, she was shaking.

Darkness had begun to descend over the palazzo. She'd not eaten in nearly twenty-four hours. Despite her appalling situation, it occurred to her that she was famished. She walked over to the table to look at the tray Beppe had left behind there. It was one of those military things—metal and compartmentalized, with utensils that had the look of something from a camper's mess kit.

On the tray lay a slice of meat of indeterminate origin. A few limp sprigs of greens passed for a salad. Another compartment contained a tepid mound of overboiled vegetables. For dessert, there was a square of spongy cake with a dollop of something red and syrupy. She poked unenthusiastically at the food, choosing finally to have none of it but a few mouthfuls of the cake and a glass of water. She was too sick with fear to eat much more. Borghini's shrill shouts still rang in her ears—"you can never go home."

With nothing else to do, she paced the room, trying to puzzle out how and why she'd gotten there, and how best and soon she could leave. That threat Borghini had let slip about the possibility she might never leave the palazzo, she knew was no jest. He was perfectly capable of that sort of thing. Also, she knew him to be the sort that reveled in intimidation, scaring the life out of someone until he or she was putty in his hands, held for him some sick appeal. She also knew him well enough to know that if he went so far as to make threats, they were seldom idle. He'd always had wildly romantic notions of his role in the world. No matter how grandiose or impractical they might be, it was a point of honor with him that he could never go back on his word.

Even as late as that evening, she was still conscious of the smells of the floor of the van she had lain on the night before. She could also smell the moldy carpet she'd been wrapped in—smell it in her hair and clothing. So she decided to bathe.

She went into the bathroom and spun both spigots full force. The tub, more like a small pool with a steeping section at one end, would take time to fill. The spigots coughed and spat a rusty brown fluid. She let them run a while, until shortly two thick columns of clear hot water came pulsing downward into the tub.

While disrobing, she heard a low, furtive *ping*. It occurred to her she'd heard that same sound before but had paid no attention to it. She glanced up in the direction of the sound just in time to see the louvers of an air duct just below the ceiling on the opposite wall slide open.

Something in her throat caught and stuck there like a fishbone. Her mind whirled with a multitude of possibilities of what lurked behind those cold metal blades.

Still, she continued to disrobe. If someone was watching her, the last thing she intended to do was to let on that she knew. That in itself could be dangerous. But by then, there was little doubt in her mind that a pair of eyes were spying on her from behind the vent of that air duct.

Slipping off the last of her garments, she approached the bath as if nothing had happened. Then, stepping over the marble rim of the tub, she let herself slip beneath the oily surface of the water. All the while she lay there steeping, she was keenly aware of hidden eyes watching her. She had no idea whose. Earlier, Borghini had said he planned to be gone for several hours; if so, it had to be the boy. The sheer horror of that realization now came down hard upon her.

Later, stepping from the tub, she sneaked a quick glance upward, this time discovering that the louvers had again returned to their original closed position.

She was determined not to sleep. Instead, she sat up in a small rocking chair, rocking slowly, struggling to remain calm and plan what she must do. Who would know she was gone? She had virtually no contact with her neighbors in Fiesole. Erminia, vacationing at her grandparents' farm in Arezzo, would not be back for several days. There was no one else. Tino was gone. She didn't regret that. Her job for the Luménetti ad had ended the day before. No one would be looking for her.

Sitting there in the rocker, weighing her prospects, her head began to throb. She was exhausted, and despite all efforts, she at last yielded to the temptation of closing her eyes. But before she did, she went back to the place where the easel stood. She recalled seeing on the long marble table littered with paint tubes and brushes and other artist's supplies, a jar containing X-Acto knives—those long, razor-mounted holders artists use for scraping paints off of surfaces. If worse came to worse during the night, she would at least have those to protect herself. But no. Everything she saw then on that marble tabletop was precisely where it had been that afternoon except for the jar of X-Acto knives. Those had been removed.

TWENTY-SEVEN

"I heard nothing, Papa."

The high, frightened voice of a child murmured through the chill darkness.

"I heard nothing, Papa."

Borghini sat bolt upright in bed, his dazed eyes chasing after the fleeting image.

"I heard nothing, Papa."

"Forget this happened, Ludo. You saw nothing. When the police ask you, tell them you saw robbers. . . ."

"Robbers?"

"The ones who came tonight. The ones who broke into the house. . . ."

"I heard nothing, Papa. I heard nothing, Papa. I heard noth—"

"If you say anything, I'll cut your head off."

Late the next day when the colonel returned to the palazzo, he was tired but unusually happy. His eyes fairly glowed as Beppe drew his bath and helped him to disrobe. The night before, he had addressed the Milan chapter of the *Pugno*.

"Several hundred came, Beppe. You should have seen. The place was packed. They cheered me at the end. They got up on their feet. They adopted all of my proposals. Almirante was there. The old man himself. He came up to shake my hand."

Borghini lifted his foot and lay back on the bed as Beppe knelt to pull off his boot. "How is the signorina?"

"I brought her a tray in the morning. Then another a few hours ago. She eats nothing."

"Scared." The colonel hoisted each foot to permit the boy to haul his trousers down. "You don't understand that, do you, Beppe? You're never scared, are you?"

Smiling, he slapped the boy affectionately on the back.

"Is the water hot? It must be scalding. I ache all over."

"Boiling, maestro. Just as you like it."

Slipping his aching bones beneath the steamy water, the colonel groaned softly. Gradually, his head drooped and he appeared to nod off to sleep. Then, as though by some act of will, he forced his eyes back open and fixed the boy with a woozy gaze. "I've seen the way you look at the signorina, Beppe. That's not for you, my lad. Don't touch. This is not some *puta* off the streets. Hands off. I have other plans for her."

The boy shrugged pleasantly. That was his way. He was always pleasant, deeply respectful to the colonel, but with him, Borghini could never be quite sure.

Shortly past dusk, someone knocked at the door of her room.

"Yes." She half-rose.

"Signorina," the boy called back from the other side of the door. "The colonel asks if you might not join him for dinner."

"Downstairs?"

"Yes, signorina."

She took a quick glance at herself in the wardrobe mirror. "Just one moment."

She went into the bathroom and, standing before the mirror, ran a comb several times through her hair, then went back out.

She heard the key fumble in the lock. The door swung open and there once again stood the boy. His face was different tonight, she noted. That nasty, bad-boy mischievousness was gone. In its place now, she thought she saw resentment.

"I do regret all this, Isobel," he was saying as Beppe ladled steaming soup into their bowls.

Uncharacteristically casual in pale linen slacks, a silk ecru shirt open at the collar, with a foulard tied round his neck, Borghini smiled and appeared relaxed.

"I'm sure you do, Ludo. And if, as you say, you regret it, then please forget all of this ever happened and let me go home."

A weary, not unkind smile creased his face. "I'm afraid it's not as simple as that." He tapped the crystal decanter and tilted it toward her. "More wine?"

She shook her head and covered the top of her glass with her hand.

"It all seems so far away now." Borghini peered into the deep garnet color of his goblet, watching the reflection of the dinner candles shimmer in the bowl of his glass. "When you first came here to this house, wanting to join our little group."

"I was interested then."

"And now no more?"

"The violence," she said unhesitatingly. "I hated the violence."

"Revolution is seldom peaceful." He laughed wearily. "Was there anything about our program you liked?"

She thought a while, marshaling her thoughts carefully. "The emphasis on tradition, continuity, family," she finally volunteered. "The notion that people had to earn their place in the system. Fair and square advancement based on real achievement. I like all that. I liked the fact that the movement stressed intellectual discipline, preservation of cultural values, and that it insisted upon a period of military service for young Italians—men and women alike. These things I admired."

Borghini nodded and sipped his wine. "You avoided any mention of our racial theories, Isobel."

"I don't admire them."

Borghini's whiskered face crumpled into a soft smile. "At least you're honest."

Seeming to materialize out of thin air, Beppe appeared at the table, cleared the soup plates, and proceeded to serve the pasta course.

All the while Borghini talked, he observed the flash of fork and spoon as the boy served the cheese-drenched rig-atoni from a deep peasant bowl that had belonged to the colonel's mother.

"How old are you now, Isobel, if I may ask."

"I'm twenty-nine."

"So you were nineteen when you first came to me?"

"Yes."

His eyes closed as he drifted back over the spate of years.

"What do you intend to do with me, Ludo?" she asked quietly when it appeared he had lapsed into silence.

When he didn't answer, she started to ask again, but this time he stirred, shifting in his seat, then finally spoke. "Understand, Isobel. I have no wish to harm you."

The words alone, by their very tone of conciliation, were alarming.

"You have no reason to. I've done nothing to you."

"Oh, I can't say I agree with you there."

"If you mean my sending Mr. Manship to Pettigrilli . . ."

Borghini nodded. "That's exactly what I mean, Isobel. That was unwise. Unfortunate things have come about as a result."

The more he spoke, the more cryptic and incoherent he became.

"Forgive me, Ludo. I don't understand."

He glanced at her out of the corner of his eye. "I would have preferred to have avoided all of this. I like you, Isobel. Believe me, I truly like you."

The note of regret in his voice, she found unsettling.

TWENTY-EIGHT

"Miss Tessino."

"Miss who?"

Taverner put a hand over the receiver and repeated the name, this time drawing the pronunciation out into discrete syllables. "Tess-i-no."

"I know of no one by that name," Manship said. "Where's she calling from?"

"Long distance. Fiesole."

That got his attention. He made an effort at recollection but failed, then reached for the phone.

"Hello. Mark Manship here. Whom am I talking to?"

There followed a stream of frantic Italian, barely half of which Manship could grasp. "Erminia. Oh yes. Of course. Miss Cattaneo's maid. I remember now."

"*Sì*, Erminia," she said in pidgin English. "Come quick. The signorina have trouble."

"What's that?"

"Come quick," the girl repeated, this time with greater urgency, her English allowing no more elaborate explanation. "The signorina is with trouble."

Unable to continue, she reverted to the Italian, from which Manship was able to gather that Isobel Cattaneo had disappeared.

By this time, he, too, was fumbling along in pidgin Italian.

"She go," the girl repeated breathlessly.

"Go? Go where?"

"Disappear."

"You mean not return?"

"*Sì*."

"Are you sure she's not off on a job? Perhaps visiting friends for the weekend."

"No job. No visit friends."

"There was no note? No message . . ."

"No message, signor. Someone take her."

"Take her?"

"*Sì*. Someone take her."

Manship was certain he'd misunderstood. "You don't mean by force?"

"*Forza. Sì. Forza,*" the girl shot back.

It was going on 4:00 P.M. New York time, nearly 10:00 P.M. in Italy. Though the connection was perfect, Manship found himself shouting into the phone. At one point, he could hear her agitated breathing.

The story that gradually emerged, if true, was disturbing. It seemed that the housemaid had returned from a weekend at her family's farm in the hills above Arezzo and found the door of the Villa Tranquillo standing wide open. There was broken crockery around and overturned furniture.

She'd called the police as a matter of course, a formality, the way one reports a robbery or an accident. The police came at once. They filled out reports, then left. She'd heard nothing since. She'd tried next to find some closer connection. She looked in her mistress' personal address book on the phone table and found Manship's business card where Isobel had left it, along with several others.

Isobel had no living parents, no relatives, no brothers or sisters, no close friends, and no significant other, as they say. Erminia had remembered Manship from his visit to Fiesole several weeks before. She recalled having spoken to him on one or two occasions over the phone in connection with seeing the Signorina Cattaneo and imagined that he was a friend. Finally, she called him in New York because there was simply no one else to call. She was frightened for the signorina and had come to the end of her rope.

"Come, Mr. Manship." she said. He could hear the catch in her throat and the onset of tears. "The signorina is with trouble. Please. You come."

Manship glanced up, to find Taverner's puzzled frown still fastened on him.

"You come quick, Mr. Manship." the woman rattled on.

Manship shifted uncomfortably in his chair, all the while

watching Taverner as he spoke. "I can't. I'm sorry. You see, there's the show. . . ."

"Show?"

He was about to explain, then realized how empty excuses about having to attend an art show would sound in the face of the situation the woman had just described, assuming it was true, and he had no reason to believe that it wasn't. What he did doubt were the dire circumstances in which Erminia had chosen to cast it.

There had to be some plausible explanation for Isobel's disappearance. She was not an irresponsible woman. She wasn't the sort to run off half-cocked, leaving no message or telephone number where she could be reached. Still, the broken crockery, the overturned furniture, the open door, and what not—all that was a bit troubling. At any rate, even if there was some emergency, he couldn't possibly leave now. There was the show, a million and one details still to be attended to. Besides, it wasn't his place to interfere. This was doubtless some personal matter, something to do with the painter chap he'd seen briefly on his visit to the villa. He had no wish to get between that. And, anyway, who was Manship to her, or she to him, that he should be expected simply to drop everything and barge off across the ocean on a wild-goose chase.

"Perhaps after, Erminia," he heard himself say with feeble conviction.

"After?"

"After the opening."

There was a pause as she tried to fathom the words.

"Oh, yes. After," at last came the crestfallen reply.

She sounded defeated, so at a loss that against his better judgment he found himself casting about for ways to make more palatable his declining to help.

"Now listen to me, Erminia. The signorina is probably fine. Stay right where you are. In the event she shows up, call me at once. I'm going to give you my home phone number. He paused, heart pounding unaccountably. "As I said, I don't think she's in any great danger, but to be on the safe side, I'm going to call friends of mine here with contacts high up in the police. Now don't worry. Be brave. Take care of the house and the cat. I'll call you as soon as I know anything.''

When he hung up, he could barely meet Taverner's gaze.

"What was that all about?" she asked.

"I don't know," he replied after a while. He tried to tell himself that he really didn't know, but the words had a counterfeit ring to them. Ever since they'd spoken, about seventy-two hours before, Manship had been dogged by a nagging suspicion that Isobel Cattaneo was in some sort of difficulty. More troublesome was a dim but growing sense that she'd incurred this difficulty because of him.

The more he considered the recent news from Fiesole, this nagging suspicion grew into an alarming probability. It was not only the fact that Isobel appeared to be missing. The reasons for that could be entirely innocent. But now there was also the business of that strange fellow, her friend Pettigrilli, in the little hosteria in Trastevere. Manship had a sudden image of the man forking food into his mouth like a hungry ferret, all the while glancing nervously over his shoulder, afraid to speak. And then, of course, there was his own misbegotten little side trip to the framing gallery in Parioli and also what he'd learned in Berlin about the stolen Chigi sketches. That, coupled with the growing conviction that Isobel Cattaneo had been the key link in this complicated chain all made for a rather dire picture.

The moment he'd hung up on Erminia, he was on the phone to a close friend at the Italian consulate in New York. He'd got the poor man out of a departmental meeting and then on the phone to the Italian embassy in Washington. His friend at the consulate in New York must have been convincing. Manship had a call back from Washington in less than an hour.

The embassy man in Washington, a deputy ambassador, was very good, very thorough. Exasperatingly, he made

Manship repeat everything twice—spelling names out carefully. Manship kept apologizing for all the bother, laughing nervously at himself, certain he was making a mountain out of a molehill. The deputy ambassador tended to agree, but when Manship mentioned the name Cattaneo, the conversation took an entirely different turn.

As for the Cattaneos, he didn't know them personally, the deputy ambassador said, but the family was very well known throughout Italy. Wealthy Genoese merchants, patrons of the arts, cultured, civilized—all those good things. Most of the Cattaneos were dead now. No, he didn't know Isobel. The Simonetta, who of course was a Cattaneo, any educated Italian would know. As for the upcoming Botticelli show at the Metropolitan, he'd read about it in *The Washington Post* and *The New York Times* and was flattered to accept Manship's personal invitation to the opening.

Manship and the embassy man (by then they were on a first-name basis), exchanged telephone and fax numbers at home and at work. His name was Ettore Foa.

He promised to call back the next day.

TWENTY-NINE

"Otto. No . . ."

"I warned you, Mathilde."

The child cringed in bed, curling the ends of the pillow up around his ears to muffle the sound.

"I warned you. Didn't I? It's not my fault. Not my—"

Out in the corridor, bare feet running. A rectangle of bright light. Mother's room. Not running towards sounds. Running from them. On the stair, counting banister posts. Hands banging each other as he sped past. Once in the country at Nana's house, outside his window at night, the sound of a fox killing a rabbit. Panicked. Squealing. Strangely excited as he tried to visualize it.

"Otto, no. The child. Dear God, no—"

Tearing sound. Ripping sound. Loud crash. Something toppling. Papa roaring something—not words, only sounds. Then silence.

Standing there halfway down the stair. Pajamas wet. One foot starting back up, the other frozen to the riser beneath. Hands bleeding, ringing from banging banister posts. Eight. Eight posts. Nine.

Coming back up, one stair at a time. Something pulsing in his throat. Stuck in his throat. Waiting in the dark for the next scream. Loud crash. Then silence. All silence. Creeping back up toward the bright square of light.

Toppled easel. Papa's shadow big and reeling on the wall. Something long and sharp in his hand. Arm rising and falling, rising and falling. Slashing at Mama's canvas. Eyes. Eyes. Eyes. Empty spaces. Vacant holes staring out. Bright, shiny thing. Sound of ripping. Muttering. Not words. Sounds—awful sounds. Canvas opening—strips of canvas peeling from frame. Peel an orange. Peel a fig. Peel a pig. Bare ankle sticking out from bloody hem. Legs splayed open between legs of easel. Small red ribbon seeping out beneath easel. Faster. Faster. Eyes. Eyes. Eyes.

Papa looking up. Shiny red-streaked thing in hand. Cuffs

of shirt red. Red smeared across forehead. Red splashed all about. Papa gaping at me. Me running.

"Ludo . . . Ludo. Come back here, Ludo. . . ."

Running downstairs again. Banister posts flying. Footsteps pounding behind.

"Ludo . . . Ludo."

Sound of voice roaring from behind. Rabbit screaming in fox's jaws. Duck into pantry. Dark. Crashing into chair. Pain stabbing up leg. Lights on. Flooding darkness. Trapped in scullery. No place to hide. Crying. Crying. Hates me for crying. Papa lurching toward me. Holding shiny red-streaked thing at hip. Clothing splashed with red. Face awful to behold. Hates me for crying.

"Sorry, Papa. . . . Sorry." Wipe tears from eyes. Grinding knuckles into eyes. Dizzy red pinwheels spin before eyes. Eyes. Eyes.

"Forget what happened, Ludo. You saw nothing. You hear? Nothing. If ever you say anything, I'll cut your head off."

"Heard nothing, Papa."

"You tell police, robbers."

"Yes, Papa. Robbers. Robbers. Heard nothing. I swear. Nothing. Please, Papa. You're hurting me. Papa. Noth—"

Borghini woke, shaking his head. Eyes fled across the wall of his bedroom. The house was deathly quiet. He was in a cold sweat—blankets kicked off, coiled about him; his mouth dry as sand. For one fleeting moment, he was six years old again, his tiny, quaking body too small for the bed he was in. Trembling, terrified his father was about to appear.

"I heard nothing, Papa," he heard a voice say in the high fluttery voice of a child. He didn't even know he was crying.

That morning directly after breakfast, there was a sharp rap at her door. Before she could respond, she heard the dull chink of the key turn in the lock. In the next moment, the door swung open and the boy stood there, scowling at her across the threshold.

He swaggered toward her, the strained, unnatural deference of days before no longer in evidence.

"Follow me."

The brusqueness of his manner alarmed her.

"Do you have any idea why?"

"You'll know soon enough. Sit, please."

With something of a flourish, he whipped a dark bandanna from his pocket and proceeded to wind it tightly around her eyes.

"Why is this necessary?" She was determined to control her mounting fear. The boy didn't answer. She tried again.

"Where are you taking me?"

Still he didn't answer.

"Will Signor Borghini be present?"

For reply, he yanked her back up on her feet.

"I demand to know where you're taking me."

She made a valiant effort to project authority, but the dark, coarse fabric wound around her eyes served only to heighten her growing sense of helplessness and panic.

She felt his hand. It was soft, yet strong, and overly warm—actually hot. It was buried like a knot in the pit of her arm and he was yanking her across the room.

"Move."

"I can't see."

One hand thrust deep in her armpit, he proceeded to guide her.

"You're hurting me." She tripped and stumbled before him. "You're going too fast."

He neither slowed nor eased his grip beneath her arm. The back of his hand kept grazing the side of her breast. At first, she thought that was accidental, until the pressure against her breast became persistent.

They were moving fast, far too fast for someone blindfolded. Several times, she tripped, nearly went down, but the hand cupped inside her armpit steadied her and prevented a fall.

"There's a stair here," he said. "Lift your foot."

She did, and stumbled. This time, the hand cupped her breast and squeezed hard—almost as punishment for stumbling. She gasped. The pain took her breath away.

"Please. You're hurting me."

"When I say lift your foot, lift."

The hand gripping her breast moved back under her armpit. "Now lift. Good. Again."

It was a laborious climb, taking several minutes, and all the while the boy grew increasingly impatient.

"Quick." His voice was a hiss.

Two, three steps more and they were at the top of a landing. It was much cooler there than where they'd just come from—unnaturally cool. Her bare arms were goose-pimpled and she could hear the low, unbroken hum of an electric motor, probably a generator.

She felt the boy sweep past and move ahead of her. A doorknob turned: hinges squealed open. From the sound of them, she imagined a large, heavy door, not necessarily wood—more probably metal.

A firm shove at her back and she stumbled forward.

"All right, Beppe. You can take the blindfold off now."

It was almost a relief to hear Borghini's voice.

It took her a moment to realize that the blindfold was off. Her eyes, adjusting to the dimness, gradually took in more detail. The first impression she had was that of a long, narrow corridor with what appeared to be glass walls on either side. The glass was not continuous, but set in large panels.

"Come in, please, Isobel."

She heard him but couldn't see him. The voice sounded as though it came from the far end of the corridor.

"Come in. Come in. Don't be afraid."

She took a tentative step in the direction of the voice and, in that instant, a switch was thrown. Lights suddenly went up behind the glass walls. Above her, a spatter of multicolored shadows swam across the ceiling.

"Come. Come." Borghini's voice was closer now, coaxing her forward with disarming warmth.

The first thing she saw was to her left. A kind of boxlike compartment, perhaps twenty feet by fifteen, it contained what appeared to be a number of stiffly awkward life-size figures. They wore rich period costumes of silk and velvet brocade. The wall behind, serving as a backdrop, showed a view of what was clearly Florence, with the dome of the Basilica dominating the skyline. The forefront was a crowd scene in a busy marketplace, where people costumed in fifteenth-century dress mingled among food stalls and bargained with merchants. What came to mind was that she'd been brought to some sort of wax museum.

"Do you recognize it?" Borghini called out from the shadows.

She knew it was a kind of *tableau vivant.* There were vague similarities to paintings she'd seen elsewhere.

"No. I'm afraid I don't."

"It's a re-creation of a Botticelli."

She thought she detected irritation in his voice.

"Oh," she said. "I see." Not seeing that at all, although it was obvious now that the backdrop was, in fact, as she suspected, a detail of a fine old Botticelli, photographically enlarged many times.

"Come on. Come ahead." Borghini's voice crackled with impatience. "See the next."

She moved uncertainly into the aisle, her heart thudding, the boy moving behind her, uncomfortably close. She noted that he now hung behind, no longer daring to touch her. She attributed that to Borghini's presence. Otherwise, there was no telling what he might try.

Electric fans whirled in the ceiling, and there was an odd odor as they penetrated deeper.

The next diorama was a Madonna. The foreground consisted of a woman on a grassy hummock; she was praying above an infant. Nearby stood a young shepherd. In the background were pomegranate trees and the outline of a distant chapel, above which storm clouds appeared to be gathering.

"Do you recognize this one, Isobel?"

Mystified, she peered at it for some time. Aware that what she'd seen moments before was a life-sized re-creation of a Botticelli, she assumed that this, too, was some sort of re-creation. They were playing a kind of game.

"I want to say it's also a Botticelli," she announced almost plaintively, "a Madonna, but I'm not sure."

"If you said that, you'd be right." Borghini could hardly conceal his delight. He seemed almost grateful to her. "It's the *Madonna Adoring the Child with Infant St. John and Two Angels*. Come on. Come on. Let's do another."

The next was the Botticelli *Venus and Mars*. Then *Pallas and the Centaur*. She guessed one, then missed the next. They hurried on.

"What about this one, Isobel? Do you know it?"

Desperately, she ransacked her memory, for by then she realized that his greatly improved spirits were in direct ratio to how many of the dioramas she could identify. When at last she had to concede that she was unable to identify this particular re-staging, his brow lowered, and she was terrified.

On they went from one presentation to the next—the *Temptation*, the *Annunciation*, a portrait of Lorenzo Tornabuoni. Fortunately, she recognized most of them, getting better at the game as they went along.

As a student at Bologna, she had majored in art history and, doubtless due to her family background (the Cattaneo and Vespucci families had been enthusiastic patrons of the arts from the fourteenth century on), she had literally grown up surrounded by some of the finest examples of Italian medieval and Renaissance art.

There was no mistaking the big Botticelli diorama of the *Primavera*. It had been given more than twice the space of the others. Recognition in this case was hardly an accomplishment. So world-renowned was the painting, any fool would have known it at once.

That didn't seem to occur to Borghini. He was far too intoxicated with the heady business of exhibiting his work.

Finally reaching the last diorama, she found Borghini himself standing there. His slight doll-like figure, half-eclipsed by a bluish luminosity cast from inside the glass case, heightened her sense of impending danger.

He smiled mischievously, as though about to share with her a pleasant secret.

"Are all of these yours, Ludo?"

A shy smile creased his features. "In a manner of speaking—yes, I suppose I did make them."

Pleased she'd asked, he flushed with pleasure. "But I had excellent primary material to start with."

"Primary material? You mean your models?"

"Yes." He smirked. "I had first-rate models. That, of course, is critical with this sort of thing." He winked at Beppe, who laughed. "I always look for models who bear a strong resemblance to the original."

She stared back at him, uncomfortably aware that he was playing some sort of game with her, that his words conveyed an additional meaning beyond their merely literal intent.

"For instance," Borghini rattled on, "this one behind you . . ."

She turned and gazed on a scene of ancient Tuscany. The background was a terraced hillside, beyond which meadows rolled gently toward a distant sea.

The foreground of the scene was comprised of two figures. One, a fair-haired man in a pale blue tunic, had the raiment and otherworldly look of an angel. Her impression was confirmed by the second figure—a plump and rosy holy infant. The angel held out a bunch of grapes in his hand. The infant appeared to reach for it.

The mood of antiquity in the scene was broken by the

appearance of a starkly modern chair between them. On its leather sling seat and stainless-steel frame had been posed a wire armature of what appeared to be a female figure.

"It isn't quite finished, as you see," Borghini hastened to explain. "Do you recognize it?"

"It's the *Chigi*, isn't it?"

He beamed. "It's the beginning of it. But I've been unable to find just the right model for my Madonna."

She recalled suddenly the sketches he'd shown her before—the ones the American fellow from the Metropolitan was so eager to locate.

All the while he spoke, he gazed at it with a kind of fierce regret. "The painting was a great favorite of my mother's. She copied it several times. Her great sorrow was that she'd never got it right. I'm doing this as a kind of tribute to her." He took her gently by the arm. "Come. I'll show you."

They entered a small door just to the right of the diorama. She had to duck her head. From there, they walked down a narrow passageway, emerging on the other side into the scene itself.

If she'd found it cool outside the diorama, inside it was frigid. Fans whirred overhead with a low roar. That odor she'd smelled outside was suddenly sharper, more pungent. It was chemical, medicinal, something like mold or wet earth. She couldn't say what.

All she knew was that she was uncomfortably cold and trying to fight back the panic she felt slowly rising in her. The scene itself made her uneasy. She had an impulse to run. Outside the glass the boy was grinning and peering in at her as though she were some sort of window display.

"Could you sit down in that chair for a moment, please, Isobel?"

Borghini seemed almost courtly as he hurried to lift the wire armature aside and with his handkerchief dust the flakes of plaster from the seat.

Her mouth was dry and she was trembling from the cold.

She took a step toward the chair, then turned back toward him.

"What do you want of me, Ludo? You have no right to keep me here like this. I want to go." Tears welled in her eyes.

"Sit down now. Sit," he said, his manner grandly sympathetic. He guided her to the chair.

"I've done nothing to you. Why are you doing this to me?"

He ignored her, his mind intent upon the empty chair. "Would you sit there a moment. A bit to the left. Now look toward me. That's it. That's it. Perfect."

She kept talking while he settled and posed her in the chair. "I have a housekeeper. She's due back tomorrow. If I'm not there she'll be very anxious."

"Yes, of course," he said, unpinning her hair, letting it fall about her neck and shoulders.

"I'm scheduled to report to a filming tomorrow. People will start calling around and asking questions."

He stepped back to study his arrangement more critically. Increasingly excited, he moved back and forth, viewing the composition from inside and outside the diorama. He tried several different positions. Then, at last, finding one that appeared to suit him, he stepped away again. Arms folded, head cocked sideways, one eye shut tight, he studied the sight lines with the sort of absorption one sees in a chess player moments before he makes his move.

"Ludo, I'm cold," she said, rubbing her arms. "May we leave now?"

Just as she said it, she realized that in the new arrangement with herself on the chair, she was staring up into the face of the angel and that the face of Aldo Pettigrilli was smiling radiantly down upon her.

The room seemed to tilt, and just as everything went dark, she could hear herself screaming far, far away.

THIRTY

"Is that you, Mark?"

"Of course it's me. Who else would it be? Unchain the door, for God sake."

He heard the whoosh of her slippered feet scurrying down the stair, then next the chain sliding through the bolt on the other side.

"Why do you chain it?" He swept past her into the house.

"This is New York. Aren't you supposed to do things like that in New York?" She rechained the front door, then followed him into the study. "What are you doing home at this hour?"

His eyes scanned the list of messages she'd left him on the hall phone table. "Are these all the calls? Nothing from Washington or abroad?"

"If it's not there on the list, you didn't get it."

He looked up. Then, seeing her for the first time, he frowned. "What have you gone and done?"

"I had my hair cut. Don't you like it?"

He wondered that she still thought it mattered. "I'm not sure. Is it too short?"

"Maybe. A bit. I saw it on a woman in Bergdorf's this morning. I marched right up to her and said, 'Where'd you get that?' 'On the eighth floor in the salon,' she said. 'Someone called a Mr. Marvin did it.' "

"So then you marched right up there to Mr. Marvin and said, 'I'll have one of those, too.' "

"Sort of," she confessed somewhat anxiously. "Is it awful?"

"I never said that. Just a bit short. Anyway, it'll grow back. Is there anything for lunch?" He steered off into the kitchen, with her following.

"If I'd known you were coming back, I would have gotten something," she fretted. "There might be some cold

roast beef from last night. And I think there's a half a baguette from breakfast.''

"What about yourself?" he asked. "Care to join?"

She must have heard the slight plaint in his voice. It
brought her around. "I'm sorry. I can't, Mark. I'm having
lunch with Bill Osgood.''

It was his turn for surprise. "Really? How come?"

"He asked me. We're just going down the street to the
Stanhope. Is that all right?"

"Of course it's all right."

"Well, you seemed so . . . startled."

"Not at all. I think it's very nice."

"It's not awkward for you? If it's Tom you're thinking
about . . ."

"It's not awkward for me, and I definitely wasn't thinking about Tom."

"Because," she went on, "Tom wouldn't give a damn.
Tom makes his plans. I make mine. That's sort of the way
things are."

"Look, Maeve." He turned toward her. "There's no
need for explanations. I'm delighted you're having lunch
with Osgood. He's a bright, decent fellow. You'll have fun
together. He won't bother you much in bed."

The moment he'd said it, he saw the hurt on her face.
"I'm sorry, Maeve. That was shitty of me, wasn't it?"

They stood that way for a while, the two of them, neither
speaking nor looking at each other. At last, Manship opened
the refrigerator, knelt slightly, and peered in.

"I'd be happy to make you a sandwich," she said.

"That's all right, you run along. You'll be late for your
lunch."

"My lunch isn't until one-thirty. I've plenty of time."
She pulled a chair out from the table. "Sit down, Mark.
While I throw something together, you tell me what's both-
ering you."

"Nothing's bothering me." He sat despondently. "Why
do you keep saying that?"

r now. No bets on for how long it'll last. I know I
 a handful.''

 can he. Don't be fooled by all that grinning Texas
. It can vanish in a trice.''

as at that moment that the phone started to ring.

 the name Borghini mean anything to you?'' Ettore
unded rushed, and as though he was eating bites of
hing between snatches of conversation.

an't say that it does,'' Manship replied.

hat about SRS?''

hat about it?''

ands for Società Republica Salo.''

lo?'' Manship searched his memory. ''Means noth-
me, I'm afraid.''

o reason it should. But it still sends chills up the
 of many self-respecting Italians of my vintage. SRS
 extreme right-wing paramilitary organization of the
irties and forties. The headquarters was on Lake Mag-
 Count Ottorino Borghini was one of its founders and
benefactors.''

nship's fingers drummed the tabletop. ''I see, but
loes all this have to do with the whereabouts of Miss
eo?''

ur gallery in Parioli—the Quattrocento—is leased
period of seventy-five years to the SRS. The chief
 of the organization, as well as the gallery owner, is
 of old Count Ottorino—that is, Ludovico Borgh-

ship thought for a moment. ''Rings no bells here,
aid.''

dly enough, my father served with old Otto in the
mento Brigade during World War Two. By the mer-
ce, I happen to know his son, Ludo. But, then
veryone in Italy knows of the Borghinis. The family
ack to the Middle Ages. Intimates of the Medici,
 and Sforza families. The old count was one of Il

''I haven't lived with you in uneasy cohabitation for the
better part of ten years not to be unable to recognize that
whipped-dog look on your face.'' She started pulling things
out from the refrigerator and marching them over to the
butcher block. ''Trouble with the show?''

''There's always trouble with the show. What else is
new?''

''Bad blood between you and Bill?''

''If my relationship with everyone else at the museum
was as smooth as it is with Bill Osgood, I'd be riding
high.''

''Would you?'' Her question and the tone in which she'd
posed it quivered with implications. ''How about a beer?''

She didn't wait for a reply, but just planted an ale and a
frosty mug before him. ''Suck on that a while. Sandwich
should be ready in a minute.''

He watched her slice the baguette and marveled half-
wistfully at her youthful figure—long, slim legs, pert
breasts, a patrician Kay Kendall nose with the sort of elevated looks that could be characterized anywhere from
smart to decidedly arresting.

''Those calls you're expecting from Washington, and
abroad,'' she said while she sliced cold beef at the block.
''Is that why you're back here at this hour?''

''There was nothing on my message machine at work. I
just stopped back to check whether or not something might
have come in here.''

''Must be fairly important for you to leave work at mid-
day. Mustard?''

''Horseradish, if you've got it. There should be some in
the fridge. Yes. You're right. The calls are important.''

The beef sliced into a small neat pile, she removed the
toasted baguette from the oven and proceeded to stack the
meat inside it. ''Sure you won't have some of that nice
honey mustard?''

''Horseradish is just fine, thank you.''

He watched her as she set a straw placemat before him,

the good odor of soap and starch emanating from her freshly laundered blouse. He tried to reconcile this domestic image of her with that of the dynamic, high-profile, eagerly sought-after young American artist with exhibitions scheduled for the next half-dozen years in all the major capitals of the world. Here she was, making a roast beef sandwich for him in his kitchen. He resisted the temptation to touch her.

She set the sandwich down beside his mug of ale.

"What was your morning like?" he asked.

"Do you really care to hear?"

"I wouldn't have asked if I didn't."

"I was at the lawyer's office at the stroke of nine. Apparently, my father made a sizable grant to the Frick."

"The Frick?" Manship laughed, his mouth full. "I'm sure that was intended as a smack in the face to me."

"Don't be silly. Daddy happened to love the Frick. It had nothing to do with you or the Met. After the lawyer, I was at my gallery until roughly eleven-fifteen, arguing with that stupid ass Plesdish. This is the last show I'll ever do with him, and I told him so."

Manship gulped ale. "And off to Bergdorf's for your rendezvous with Mr. Marvin."

"I hadn't planned to go, but I was passing by on my way uptown and thought I could use a nice blazer to wear to lunch today."

"For Osgood?"

She started to protest, then turned her head slightly sideward and laughed. "Yes. For Osgood."

He thought it was a charming gesture. "You're getting clothes-conscious in your old age, Maeve. In my time, you scorned personal adornment, thought it very bourgeois. Liked to go about in soiled, paint-spattered jeans, announcing your life's calling and your moral superiority." Manship chewed thoughtfully. "What a nice change. I wonder if old Bill knows how honored he is."

"Oh, Mark, don't."

"Don't what?"

"Don't be mean."

"I'm not being any such thing. You[...] Osgood's a lucky fellow to be going to l[...]

She frowned. "And don't feel obliged [...] to me. You've been sweet to put up wit[...] time. Except for that—"

"Bitchy thing I said a few minutes bac[...] and bed. I didn't mean it. I don't mean[...] say. You know that, Maeve. I don't kno[...] me."

Manship gulped the last of his ale and s[...] she pressed him back gently with her han[...]

"I guess I wasn't very good to you on[...] then, all I thought about was career and [...] there first. The next exhibition. The next [...] prize. Didn't matter particularly what it [...] as I'd won it. There was so little time l[...] For anything."

He fiddled with a paper napkin, wadd[...] "You've come quite a ways since then, M[...] I'm not proud. I tell everybody I knew y[...]

She laughed, then rose and started to [...] "Proud? Of me? If you knew what a g[...] I've made of things. Try spending a ni[...] me. That's if you could find one where [...] home together at one time. If you tho[...] driven, you want to try Tom Costain—[...] with his beeper and cellular phone, his [...] ing twenty-four hours a day."

She gazed off at some indetermina[...] cooking island and the sink. "Let's [...] more."

He regarded her a moment, slow[...] his sandwich. "Well, in any event," [...] glad you and Bill are hitting it off.'[...]

"F[...]
can b[...]
"S[...]
charr[...]
It [...]

"Do[...]
Foa s[...]
some[...]
"I[...]
"\[...]
"\[...]
"S[...]
"S[...]
ing t[...]
"[...]
spine[...]
was [...]
late [...]
giore[...]
chief[...]
M[...]
what [...]
Catta[...]
"Y[...]
for a [...]
officer[...]
the so[...]
ini."[...]
Mar[...]
I'm af[...]
"Od[...]
Risorg[...]
est cha[...]
again, e[...]
dates b[...]
Borgia,[...]

Duce's right-hand men. Right after the war, he was tried as a war criminal and sentenced to life imprisonment. After serving six years of his sentence, he hung himself in his cell on Galina, off the coast of Sardinia. As for Ludo, whom I knew at school, he's a bit shadowy. Dropped out of sight years ago. Some sort of self-imposed isolation. His problems, I gather, have much to do with the father and his possible implication in the death of Borghini's mother. Quite a scandal at the time. Are you still there?''

"Yes, of course," Manship said, his fingers drumming somewhat faster on the desktop.

"Forgive me." Foa laughed. "I grow long-winded. This was all by way of introduction to the matter of your friend Signorina Cattaneo."

"Have you located her?" Manship asked, trying to manage the tremor in his voice.

"Not exactly. However, as you know, the police have been up to her place in Fiesole."

"What exactly does all this mean?"

"Nothing good," Foa reported bluntly. "The police had the impression she was taken from the house by force, since the doors were open and lights had been left on. In any case, the housemaid mentioned a young man—Miss Cattaneo's companion, whom she apparently just sent packing. A young fellow by the name of''—Manship heard the crinkle of paper through the wires—''Tino Grimaldi—a painter manqué who lives mostly off the generosity of gullible young ladies."

"I know. I met him."

"The police picked him up at a lodging house in San Gimignano. According to my sources in Firenze, the fellow knows nothing of the whereabouts of the signorina. He accused her of stealing money from him; then, for some inexplicable reason, he broke down and started to cry. To make a long story short, they checked out Grimaldi's story. For now, the police believe him, but they're keeping him under surveillance."

"Isn't it just possible she left town on a job, or went off with friends for a few days?"

"Many things are possible. Miss Cattaneo may well be off with friends somewhere, or on a job that requires her being out of town. I understand she does quite a bit of that."

"Yes. She's an actress. Small jobs in films, theater, commercials, things like that." Manship reported that hopefully, trying to allay his own fears.

"Possible, but not probable, given the manner in which the villa was left—lights on, doors open, a window in the back broken."

"A broken window? You didn't say that before."

"I know I didn't," Foa grimly conceded.

For a while, they listened to each other's breathing.

Foa resumed. "Now, what is more probable—"

"Yes?"

"Given the fact that after you'd told Miss Cattaneo about your search for the missing Botticelli sketches—"

"Yes?"

"And she sent you down to Rome to speak with a signor . . ."

Again Manship heard the rustle of paper on Foa's desk in Washington. "Pettigrilli," Manship said, completing the sentence for him.

"*Giusto.* Aldo Pettigrilli. We had the police check him out, too."

"And?"

"He turns out to be a small-time gangster with a long list of petty convictions. Nothing very impressive—pickpocketing, shoplifting, minor larcenies. The police in Rome tracked him to his last address, which turns out to be a doss-house in a decidedly disreputable section hard by the Tiber." And here the deputy ambassador paused as if for emphasis. "It turns out that Pettigrilli is also missing. The manager of the doss-house claims they haven't seen him for days. They're quite miffed. He's behind on his rent several weeks. They think he skipped out. However, if he did, I should add that he left all of his belongings behind.''

There was another long, weighty pause before Foa spoke again. ''Did you know any of this?''

''About Pettigrilli, no. About Isobel—Miss Cattaneo—I had a hunch she was in trouble,'' Manship explained, his hands suddenly clammy and cold. ''Don't ask why. I don't pretend to be clairvoyant.''

Foa sorted and filed data in his busy, well-organized head. ''And the last contact you had with Mr. Pettigrilli was just before you went out to investigate the little framing gallery in Parioli?''

''The last and only,'' Manship confirmed. ''So shouldn't we—''

''We're already a step ahead of you, my dear friend,'' Foa reported, sounding expansive and pleased with himself. ''Regrettably, since Borghini comes from a prominent Roman family, even with my extremely sympathetic contacts high up in the magistracy, it will be a bit sticky securing the necessary warrants to enter the premises.''

Manship's fist clenched round the receiver. ''But that woman may be in grave difficulty.''

''Yes, yes. I quite understand. If it's of any consolation to you—''

''Very little of what you've told me consoles me at this point.'' Manship could hear the edge in his voice and regretted it.

''*Giusto*. I understand. What I wished to convey, however, is that I have also been on the phone to your insurance underwriters, the Lloyd's people in London. At our urging, they, too, contacted the police through their Rome office. They were put off in the same way by the Italian authorities, just as we were. The Lloyd's people are understandably anxious about the damage already done to two of your Botticellis, and now with your show coming up, they are eager to forestall the possibility of any further incidents.''

''Do they believe there's a connection between the Quattrocento gallery and the missing Chigi sketches?"

"They do, as well as the attacks on those two paintings. They've now applied directly to the office of the British ambassador in Rome to make specific inquiries along those lines."

Manship gnawed the inside of his lower lip. "But how long will all this take? While these drowsy bureaucrats are pushing paper back and forth across the Continent, this poor woman's life may be hanging by a thread."

"I share your concern. The young lady must be a long-standing friend of yours."

"As a matter of fact, I've met her all of two times."

"Indeed." Foa chuckled. "Those must have been two very memorable meetings. However, for whatever it's worth," the deputy ambassador hurried on, "I can tell you that in Rome a polite inquiry from the chief representative of the Court of St. James is more apt to rouse the drowsy constabulary, as you so aptly put it, than anything from a Roman official of comparable rank. Sad but true." Foa sighed. "Stand by. I'll call you as soon as I have something more concrete."

Manship gazed at the receiver for some time after he'd put it down.

"What was all that about?"

Startled, Manship turned. He'd completely forgotten that Maeve had followed him into the library when the phone rang. "Oh, you still here?"

"How could I leave? I got caught up in the plot."

Manship rose and started out.

"Aren't you going to tell me what's going on?"

"I've got to get back to the office."

She tripped after him. "Does it have something to do with those missing Botticellis?"

"In a manner of speaking."

"Oh, Mark. Don't be so goddamned secretive. Who's this woman you're talking about? What's happening to her? It sounds awful."

"It could well be."

Something about the way he'd said it alarmed him as much as it had her. When she spoke again, her voice was strangely tender. "Someone you met, Mark? Someone you care for?"

He would have liked to respond, to share it with her. But the pity of it was, there was so little to share. "Oh, I don't know, Maeve. Run along. You're going to be late for your lunch with Osgood."

He let the knuckle of his finger graze her cheek. "Get on to the Stanhope now. We'll talk tonight."

"Will you be home?"

"I have to be. I'm expecting this important call."

THIRTY-ONE

When the eyes floated past him this time, he could feel the current of air left behind in their wake.

"I heard nothing, Papa."

"When the police come . . ."

"Yes?"

"You tell them you were sleeping."

"I heard nothing, Papa."

Shouts. Screams. Terrible scuffling sounds. Pounding footsteps. The crash of something heavy toppling over. A ripping sound.

Standing in the doorway. A small child in a flannel nightshirt, a tiny, wraithlike figure. Wide-eyed, staring, silent. Eyes following the rise and fall of the bayonet blade. Strips of canvas peeling from the frame. The easel tilted. Descending with a crash. Mother's slippers—velvet, mother-of-pearl fleurs-de-lis woven on the instep. He could see the sole and the bare calf of her right leg where her gown had slid upward above the knee, a faint blue tracery of vein scrawled across the milk white skin. The rest of her not visible; sprawled beneath the toppled easel.

"I saw nothing, Papa."

In the morning, the house full of people. The hushed air of excitement. Uncle Adriano. Aunt Annamarie. Police coming and going. Prowling through the house. Poring through everything. Cars outside jammed into the driveway, out onto the boulevard. Papa in Mother's room with the police. Coming toward him, Papa and a big, lumbering man with opera buffa mustachios. Signor Bollata, Papa's attorney, ringed by carabinieri. Questions. Voices, hushed, respectful. Questions. Questions.

"Ludo." Papa spoke softly, with a carefully studied kindness. "This is Inspector Bravazzo of the carabinieri. He wants to ask you a few questions."

The inspector knelt. His big, meaty hand rumpled the

boy's hair. "Last night, Ludo . . . did you hear anything? Noises? Shouts? Anything?"

"I heard nothing." The boy stared up at him blankly.

"Did you see anything? Don't be frightened, Ludo."

Puzzled, the boy looked up at his father for guidance.

"It's all right, Ludo. Answer the inspector."

He saw something flicker in his father's eye and felt his bowel turn. "I heard nothing. I was asleep."

The boy rubbed his eyes and started to cry.

Count Ottorino was mortified.

"That's all right, Ludo." The inspector patted him on the shoulder. "You can go back to your room now."

"Can I see Mama?" the boy asked.

"Not now, Ludo. Do as the inspector says. Go back to your room, son."

Hesitating a moment, the boy glanced back and forth from his father to the inspector, then turned and ran from the room. Outside the door, he hovered in the hallway, trying to hear what was being said.

"You see, inspector," Signor Bollata was saying, his chest swelling with importance. "A robbery. It's perfectly obvious."

The inspector gazed for a time at the attorney. When at last he spoke, it was with a weary forbearance. "But if it was robbery, as you say, why was nothing taken? There had to be some other motive."

"The robbery was interrupted while in progress," Bollato persisted, a fixed little smile twitching on his face. "So, of course, nothing was taken. By then, the count was already there, fighting off the assailant."

The inspector cocked a skeptical brow. "In his wife's room? What of great value would a robber hope to find in the Contessa Borghini's studio? And then, too, the murder weapon, the bayonet, belongs to the count."

"But the count has already explained." Signor Bollato, still smiling, struggled to contain his exasperation. "The man no doubt entered at the ground-floor level, through a window. Somehow he got into the count's gun room, right off the library. Got hold of one of the bayonets there.''

''This man . . . this alleged robber,'' the inspector hypothesized. Signor Bollato's eyes opened like huge blooming peonies.

''Alleged? Can there be any further doubt? What else would you call the fellow? A vagrant? A drifter? An *ubriacone*? They loiter like roaches by the dozens around the train station. They sleep on the ground and befoul themselves in the streets. Scum of the earth. A disgrace to the nation. . . . Alleged?'' The attorney gave a scornful laugh and flung his hand in the air.

The Inspector said nothing by way of reply, merely turned his back on the attorney and once again addressed the count.

''I'm sorry to have to persist. I know what a sad time this must be for you. Please understand, it is my responsibility.''

''Of course, Inspector.'' Count Ottorino dabbed the back of his neck with a foulard he'd unwound from his throat. ''Please continue.''

''You're a trained soldier, Colonel. From what I can see, you appear to be in excellent condition.''

''I'm quite fit, if that's what you mean.''

The inspector paused. His eyes narrowed as he framed the next question in his mind. ''How, if I may ask, could a trained professional like yourself permit this homeless, pathetic drifter to get away?''

''He had a bayonet.'' Signor Bollato thrust himself protectively in front of the count. ''A twelve-inch blade. He'd already used it on the contessa.''

The inspector gave the counselor one of his most patronizing smiles. ''But my good man, when the fellow fled here, he was not even armed. The murder weapon is still lying over there in the corner.''

''I heard nothing, Papa. Nothing . . .''

The words spilled from his lips. They came at him in waves, over and over again, echoing through the gloomy quiet of the dining room.

Beppe appeared at the door. Peering in to see if anything was amiss, he came forward into the room and began to clear dishes from the table.

"You were not hungry, maestro?"

Borghini mumbled something, then dismissed the boy with a wave. He rose stumbling from the table, then took his glass and grappa bottle and went lurching off toward the library.

For the last few days, ever since the girl arrived, the scene had played itself over and over in his head: preceded by an aura, a kind of warning signal, its symptoms a cold numbness at the center of his forehead, followed by a sense of dissociation from his immediate surroundings, as though he were no longer anchored to his own body.

Next came the eyes floating in midair, then distant cries and the sound of something ripping. Finally, the half-painted Madonna would come into view, his mother's Madonna. He could see isolated parts of the face—a nose, an ear, the right quadrant of the head. Thin strips of canvas drooping from a wood frame; everything slashed, cut loose from everything else—and there, the eyes, gouged from the canvas and dancing like spirits before his dazzled gaze.

Each time the scene replayed itself, it returned with additional details. His memory of that morning decades past grew sharper, more vivid with each passing year. His father, now dead, was never prosecuted for the murder of his wife, but was later convicted of treason by a war crimes tribunal and imprisoned. Inspector Bravazzo, now dead, had been swept off into some bureaucratic backwater in malarial Calabria, dying young, more out of disappointment than infirmity. And, finally, there was the bewildered Neapolitan drifter, seized in a reeking *gabinetto* at the bus station, arrested, and convicted for the murder of the Contessa in the

Palazzo Borghini on the Quirinal. No one had ever questioned the legitimacy of the charges that had been fabricated against him.

Four years later, Ludovico Borghini, all of ten years of age, killed the first of what was to be long line of homeless, basically defenseless people. The first time he did it, he was with several other youths, prowling the streets after school. In a mean section of the city, they came across a man lying drunk in an alleyway. Barely conscious, singing softly to himself, his shirtfront covered with vomit, he drooled spit. Trembling with fear and a strange excitement, young Ludo carried out the execution with a can of lighter fluid and a match.

From that time on, he acted alone and his preferred method of execution was a bayonet—one he had lifted from his father's prized collection of military memorabilia. Frequently, after the deed was done, he would render the victim's face unidentifiable by carving it into a thatch of fleshy strands peeled back from the bones beneath. Sometimes he would excise the eyes. The exercise, which over the years had taken on the form of a ritual, invariably left him in a state of exhilaration.

THIRTY-TWO

She woke in the dark and thought she was home in the big four-poster bed in her sun-drenched upstairs bedroom in Fiesole. But the air she breathed gave off a close, rank smell. When she inhaled, she felt a stinging in her nose and mouth. Behind her, she could hear the soughing of a clammy wind pouring through a hole somewhere.

Then she remembered.

First Borghini, then the boy. Then the big glass case, three sides of it encompassed by a scene of medieval Tuscany, and opposite her in a loose white gown, a dead, smiling Aldo Pettigrilli, extending an apple toward her. At the memory of it, a bubble of sour chyme rose in her throat, along with the nagging doubt whether she'd actually seen it.

She had no idea where she was, nor any recollection of how she'd gotten there. It appeared to be a cellar, a rather large one, and she was lying on a cot that smelled faintly of cheese. Attempting to rise, she discovered that she was strapped to the cot by what felt like heavy leather restraints—belts, no doubt, three of them. One was wound around her ankles, one across her chest, and one girded so tightly over the abdomen, it made breathing difficult. Resting on her chest, her hands had been clasped together and bound with cord in an attitude of prayer.

Next to her skin, she felt a coarse, scratchy fabric. Even in the dark, she knew it to be burlap—a kind of rough-hewn, makeshift thing that may well have been originally a sack for flour or vegetables. With a rush of shame, she realized she was completely naked beneath it. The shame was slight compared to the anger she felt over the cruelty of her captors. It took a certain exquisite perversity to put someone naked, bound head to toe, in raw burlap. The sensation, she felt, was comparable to having a thousand fire ants crawling over one's naked flesh, all biting and tearing at you at the same time. It made her want to dive into ice water or walk through flames.

Movement to scratch herself was impossible. Within limits, she could move her head and neck, and with a slight, begrudging leeway in the belts, she could move her arms and legs just barely enough to maintain circulation. Something large and silky, like a scarf, had been tied across her mouth and around the back of her head to gag her.

To add to her discomfort, she became aware that her eyes were burning and had started to tear. She attributed that to the same thing—the sharp, almost onionlike smell that burned the inside of her nose and mouth.

The place was full of a whole range of nondescript but highly suggestive sounds. The sort of creaking, ambiguous scurryings you'd expect in a cellar. Periodically, she'd hear what she thought to be a lapping noise she associated with an animal. The sound was sporadic. It came and went. The next time she heard it, it sounded to her like wind passing lightly over the surface of a pond. She had no idea what the sound might be and was left with a disturbing range of possibilities as to its source.

The notion that she was in a cellar was heightened by the occasional passage of footsteps overhead or a door opening or closing. Later, she heard a phone ring, a burst of laughter, then someone talking softly above her in intimate, conspiratorial tones. Another door opened, followed by the sound of something heavy being dragged across a bare floor.

An hour passed. Struggling to move, she rolled her head backward until at last it hung half on, half off the edge of the cot. Looking behind her, upside down as it were, she glimpsed a pencil-thin stream of light sifting through a small aperture in an outside wall no more than ten feet behind her. Through it, the wind alternately whistled and sighed.

She lay like that for a time, strapped to the cot, eyes burning, her limbs inflamed by the relentless gnawing of

burlap fibers against her bare flesh. Staring upside down at
the tiny disk of white light like a star in the evening void,
she wondered how she could reach it. She hadn't the vagu-
est idea what she would do if by chance she did.

She'd long given up hope that Ludovico Borghini had
any intention of freeing her. Nor had she any further illusions about why she'd been brought there, or how they
intended to use her. The sight of Pettigrilli embalmed in
that large glass box told her all she needed to know.

She flinched when something brushed against her bare
leg. Her stomach shot upward into her throat and the sound
of her muffled shriek seeped out from beneath the silk gag.
She heard a purring noise and then she was staring into the
face of a cat perched on her chest, regarding her curiously.
Seeing it there was something of a relief. It could well have
been a number of less pleasant things.

It was a dark, slatternly creature, underfed, with wash-
board ribs showing beneath its mothy coat. Nothing like
her pampered and beloved Fanny. If she could have petted
it just then, more for her comfort than the cat's, she would
have done so.

Lying there strapped to the cot and watching the cat mew
at her, she recalled that when it first rubbed against her leg,
her immediate reaction had been an involuntary lurch away
from its touch. She'd felt her stomach and chest press hard
against the middle belt, then, in turn, the belt exerting an
equal and opposite flow of pressure downward against her.
It had the feeling of a foot on her chest, but, in that instant,
she was certain she'd felt the belt give.

Felt it and actually heard it. It was a creaking sound,
suggesting that the leather was old, dry, and stiff. If so, it
might well have loosened from the exertion of the strong,
sudden pressure. Either that or, possibly, in her sudden
lurch, the prong of the buckle may have torn one of the
punch holes open wider.

To check whether it had been merely her imagination,
she tested the belt again with another lurch upward. She

felt the buckle strain against her chest. The leather indeed creaked and this time for certain slackened a bit more.

She repeated the movement several times, finding each time that with every additional thrust, her arms, bound beneath the belt, won a bit more purchase. The amount of it was begrudging, but it gave her something to think about other than herself. She was grateful for that.

An additional bonus was that along with a slightly increased freedom of the upper arms came a similar increase in the movement of her hands. Bound together with thin, rough cord abrasive enough to tear the skin, her hands moved more freely with the few millimeters of space she'd won for her arms.

It was encouragement, if nothing else. Now she swiveled and twisted her wrists left and right, not caring that she was scraping skin from the back of her hands as she did so. After a while, her hands began to sting and burn, but it was nothing compared with the countless stings of the burlap biting at her bare flesh.

She kept up the action on her hands and arms, hearing from time to time a clock chime somewhere up above. The cat, which had slinked off into the shadows, returned. Sidling up against her flank, he purred, then sweetly shoved his forehead hard up against hers, as if inviting his new friend to scratch him.

All the while overhead, there was a constant shuffling of feet and a variety of ambiguous noises. Mostly, it was a bumping and scraping of heavy objects, sounding like something being drawn back and forth across the floor. There was a good deal of chatting and laughter, some hammering of nails. It all sounded quite harmless. It was only down there in the clammy darkness with no idea where she was or what fate awaited her that the true nightmare of her situation existed.

Some time later, possibly an hour or so, the cellar door opened and a shaft of light streamed down the string of rickety stairs. Footsteps clumped heavily down. Lights went on. The sudden illumination made her blink and close her eyes. When she opened them again, she flinched. There before her was the improbable sight of a figure got up in harlequin dress. It was a Pierrot, complete with dunce cap and a bell that jangled whenever he moved. The figure hovered above her, limp and rangy as a rag doll, with a face painted in white grease. Rouged and lipsticked, with a nose that ended in a cherry-colored rubber tip, the figure smiled down at her, alternately playful and menacing. The smile made her stomach turn. Even the garish clown mask couldn't conceal the mocking, nasty grin of Beppe Falco.

Aside from the terror she felt, the sight of him there, prancing, jingling his mad cap, darting back and forth at her in oddly jerky crablike motions, sickened her. He saw her fright and he enjoyed it.

In addition to Beppe, she had the first fully illuminated view of her surroundings. The fact that it was a cellar came as no surprise; the size of it did. It was high and cavernous and appeared to reach back for great distances beneath the joisted ceiling.

Mannequins and old suits of armour stood about in a variety of frozen poses. From wood racks above hung a vast array of what appeared to be carpenter's tools glinting like tiny stars into the shadows. Added to that were barrels and wardrobes, armoires crammed with all manner of strange objects.

But by far the most unsettling thing she saw was something she couldn't identify at all. Out of the corner of her eye, she glimpsed the dark, smooth surface of something. Spreading out for an indeterminate distance behind the prancing figure of Beppe, this thing gave the appearance of a large stain. At first, she thought it might be linoleum or carpet or the cellar floor itself, varnished to a sleek, gleaming black.

That impression was quickly demolished when the stream of air that whistled through the tiny aperture behind her suddenly kicked up and the large stain, to her amazement, began to move. Starting as a ripple, somewhere near the center, then slowly gathering momentum, it traveled outward, finally reaching the edge of its border, where it made soft lapping sounds like that of a cat drinking milk.

If it had been the boy's intention to frighten her, he'd succeeded. Strapped down to the cot, her mesmerized gaze followed the harlequin bobbing, spinning, feinting at her like a snake weaving toward a spellbound rabbit. On one level, she thought the whole thing silly, childish; on another, sickeningly sinister. What strange need did it fulfill in this boy? Was it some elaborately ritualized ceremony he had to carry out before he could do to her whatever it was he intended to do?

Several times during the course of this strange ceremony, he put his face close to hers—so close that at one point she could smell the oil base of the greasepaint smeared over his face, as well as the cloyingly sweet odor of cheap rouge that had been applied over the paint. With each pass, his face came closer to hers. She squirmed on the cot, trying to avert any contact with him.

She thought about screaming loud enough through the silk gag to be heard upstairs. Not an easy thing, but assuming she could, what reason had she to hope that the people up there weren't aware of, and fully in accord with, what was going on down below in the cellar?

All of that whirled through her head with dizzying speed—three or four scenarios played out to their logical conclusions, one more unpleasant than the next. A certain amount of unpleasantness, she felt she could manage. But the sudden image of Pettigrilli and all the others frozen for all time in those cages of glass went far beyond mere unpleasantness.

When she looked again, the boy was standing above her. He had stopped his ceaseless moving and was gazing down at her, hands clasped above his chest, a look of curious sorrow on his face. For one cruelly hopeful moment, she thought that he was relenting, that he was about to release her. Borghini had thought the whole thing over and instructed the boy to give her a good scare, then send her home.

But in the next instant, without warning, he pounced. Pushing the gag up over her eyes and nose, he brought his mouth hard down on hers in a bruising kiss. The initial impact was so great, she thought for a moment he might have broken her tooth.

Struggling to avert her mouth, she felt him trying to cram his tongue between her lips. She clamped her jaws hard together. When he couldn't open them with his tongue, he literally pried them open with his fingers and this time plunged his tongue deep inside her mouth.

His breath was disgusting, a mingling of fish and cheap brandy. His hands were all over her. She flailed and writhed beneath the punishing weight of him. When it occurred to her that the gag no longer covered her mouth, she began to scream, then felt his thumb and forefinger clamp her nostrils together. With his own mouth mashed down hard on hers, he had effectively cut off her air. She began to gag and choke. Then, realizing her danger, she grew still at last.

When she'd stopped struggling, made no further attempt to cry out, he unclasped his fingers from her nostrils, yanked the gag back down over her mouth, and rose from the cot.

He stood above her a moment, regarding her coolly. The clown no longer seemed quite so playful. From the pocket of his harlequin costume, he withdrew a small dark object and held it behind his back. Approaching in a mincing gate, he dangled something before her. It was a dead mouse. When he reached the side of the cot, he swung the small gray thing back and forth by its tail with a kind of pendulum motion. Then, stooping above her, he lowered it to her face, letting it graze her forehead and eyes, then inscribing with it slow, lazy circles on each cheek and around the sockets of her eyes. Full of childish glee, he lowered it until the dry little snout of the creature appeared to be balanced on the tip of her nose.

Through some act of sheer defiance, she never winced. She showed none of the terror or revulsion he so eagerly craved. Her intransigence excited him all the more, as though the battle lines had been drawn between two clashing wills. To demonstrate his complete command over her, he drew the dead rodent slowly across her lips, back and forth, over and over again. It had a sweet, rotten smell.

When he left, he lay the mouse on her chest and clumped heavily back up the stairs, turning off the lights behind him.

THIRTY-THREE

No work of art, particularly those afforded the
designation of "masterpiece" can be said to belong to
any individual. Museum, gallery, corporation, or like
institutions that happen to collect and exhibit works of
that stature serve only a temporary custodial function
in their care. Such masterworks belong rightly to posterity and to those who inhabit that time. The destruction, therefore, or disfiguration of any work of art is a
crime against mankind. . . .

Manship looked up from his typewriter. It was nearly 4:00
P.M. and still there'd been no word from Ettore Foa, the
Italian deputy ambassador. In fact, with the opening of the
Botticelli exhibition scarcely forty-eight hours away, Man-
ship's phone was conspicuously silent. That in itself was
ominous.

He'd been working all day on his essay on theft and
vandalism of art. When completed, it would be enlarged,
reproduced on long mats, framed in plain aluminum strips,
then hung alongside the painting of the St. Stephen's *Centurion* with its irreparable gashes and horrific excised eyes.
Distasteful as it was, he had to agree with Van Nuys and
René Klass that the mutilated masterpiece would introduce
a jarring note into an otherwise-celebratory event. But,
hopefully, he told himself, the sight of this glorious painting
reduced to shreds might just possibly serve as a sobering
tonic to a complacent public that had come to take its great
art for granted.

All the while he wrote, he kept glancing at the phone,
willing it to ring—a silent plea to Foa to put him out of
his misery of waiting.

Foa was not in Washington earlier that afternoon when
Manship called. When he asked where the deputy ambassador was, he was brusquely informed that Signor Foa was
out of town. Whomever it was he spoke to was not au-

thorized to say where he was, or when he was expected back.

So the writing of the essay that he'd postponed far too long became therapeutic. It took his mind off of troubling events. Yet all the while he wrote about the missing eyes in the Botticelli *Centurion*, it occurred to him that what he saw instead were the almond-shaped sea blue eyes of Isobel Cattaneo, their rueful, piercing gaze coming to rest upon him. They bore precisely the same expression they had that night when she sat across from him at the tiny *enoteca* in Florence. He had a distinct, almost preternatural sense of her presence nearby, as though she were looking over his shoulder. At first merely transitory, the sensation persisted and grew more intense.

Anyone who politicizes a work of art to further his own political agenda . . .

His fingers stumbled over the keys of the ancient Royal as he attempted to recapture the thread of his thought.

. . . has probably subverted the intent of the artist. Once a painting is judged by posterity to be a masterpiece, it ceases to have any national identity, any territorial boundaries. Its subject matter has achieved universality and can no longer be said to belong to any specific time or be appropriated on behalf of any cause in which people may hope to enlist it. It may then be said to have entered into the history of civilization, thus becoming untouchable.

"Isobel," he heard himself murmur, then was startled to realize he'd never addressed her by her Christian name before. The name sounded strange on his lips.

Sometime later, finishing his essay, he yanked the paper from the roller and plunged headlong for the door. Flinging it open, the first thing he saw was Taverner's startled face.

Manship flew past her, barely pausing to drop the copy of his essay down on her desk. "That has to be at the printer's by six tonight. If anyone wants me, I can be reached at home."

He watched her eyes flare. "But, Mark . . ." That's all she managed to get out. In the next moment, he was gone.

THIRTY-FOUR

In all the time she'd been there no one had bothered to bring her either food or drink. Nor had anyone demonstrated even enough compassion to release her long enough for her to relieve herself. Fortunately, she'd eaten so little in the last few days that she was scarcely bothered by such matters.

The dead mouse still lay on her chest like some mark of shame, and not all of her twisting and squirming seemed able to dislodge it. It was only a matter of time, she knew, before the boy would be back. Having had a taste of tormenting her, there was no doubt he would soon be craving more. She was certain that the next visit would be more of a trial than the first.

Overhead, the footsteps persisted, restless, unceasing, tracking back and forth. By then, she'd almost gotten used to the burning of her eyes and throat, and the cruel itch of the burlap next to her bare skin. She wondered about Borghini. Where was he? Why hadn't he come down to taunt her, too?

She guessed it was going on toward dusk, or roughly 7:00 P.M. The stream of air whistling through the pinhole behind her had grown cooler—hot days, cool nights, all typical of a Roman autumn. She wondered where the cat was. She longed to see it in much the same way someone in troubled times longs for the comforting presence of an old friend.

Behind the wall, beyond that fading pinprick of light, she could hear traffic noises—the wheeze of diesel trucks and buses, the vital buzz of the marketplace, where people came and went freely. She tried to imagine Fiesole and the Villa Tranquillo, all of its cozy dilapidation, and Erminia, frightened and wondering where she was.

Throughout that afternoon while her mind had wandered, full of regrets and unspoken fears, she had been working at her bonds, trying to loosen them by the simple act of stretching, then relaxing her muscles beneath them. It came down to mere mechanical repetition of identical movements. After a while, she did them automatically, not even aware of her actions as she turned, twisted, swiveled her wrists about until the edges of the belt had burned a raw red line into the back of her hand.

The noises from above appeared to increase, suggesting heightened activity. She was certain that activity had something to do with her, and knowledge of that served as a goad to her flagging strength and spirits.

When the cat finally did reappear, it was a blessing. Slinking its lank way up to her, it spied the mouse on her chest and stopped dead in its tracks. Eyes riveted to the maggoty little heap of fur, it crouched, tensing its powerful rear haunches, then sprang.

It seemed surprised, perhaps even disappointed, when the mouse neither ran nor attempted to resist. Mesmerized, Isobel watched the cat's jaw open, then clamp down hard, taking the animal headfirst into its mouth, leaving only the limp, stringy tail still dangling from its lips, switching right and left across the floor as the creature scurried off with its prize.

Isobel took that as a good omen and resumed with feverish zeal the business of attempting to work herself free. The incessant stretching of her muscles, constant expansion and then contraction, was exhausting. If only she could use her mouth, she thought, she might gnaw through her restraints with her teeth the way animals caught in the vise of hunters' traps have been known to gnaw off a limb in order to get free. She understood why animals would do that now. She would do that, she told herself, if only she could.

Her ordeal continued. Oddly enough, it was the bottom strap, the one wound round her ankles, that gave first. Odd, in that it was the strap upon which she'd been able to exert least pressure; throughout her ordeal, she'd been concentrating her efforts on those encircling her middle and upper body.

Now, in some surprising, totally unexpected way, the lower strap suddenly sagged and, like a fist loosening its grip, gave way. She wasn't sure how much until she started to stretch and wiggle her feet, and with that the belt yielded as if the buckle had failed. Almost at once, she found that she could raise her legs off the cot, raising them straight up from the waist like someone doing stomach exercises.

For all of her efforts, the remaining two straps were as begrudging as ever. They pinned her tightly to the cot, while her wrists, badly skinned, may as well have been cemented together. Having freed her legs, she wasn't sure what advantage, if any, she'd gained. But with time running out, she intended to test the question to its limit.

Trying several maneuvers, she concluded she'd not gained much. However, at the completion of a few more frantically acrobatic moves, she discovered that her now-freed legs enabled her to slowly arch her back, raising it slightly from the cot while at the same time applying somewhat greater pressure to the upper restraints.

In the next quarter hour, she waged a sweaty, harrowing battle between herself and the middle restraint, alternately arching her back, then throwing her legs up and back as far as they would go. She was like someone working out on a mat in a gymnasium. She had by then achieved a certain momentum, and with each thrust she went faster and faster, until finally hitting a near-frenzied pace.

The act of throwing her legs up and back over and over again failed to loosen the midstrap noticeably. However, the same action was not without a plus side; all of that frenzy had, with each thrust, the net effect of inching her body lower toward the bottom of the cot. Simultaneously, the top strap had begun to creep its way upward from breast level toward her shoulders. If she could get it to reach that point, she reasoned, she might conceivably manage to work that strap up over the top of her shoulders and thus into the shallow well between shoulder and throat. That might possibly give her upper body more purchase to push and heave against the midstrap. But even if that gave, she still had to contend with the upper strap, which was hanging somewhat more loosely around her neck, pinning her to the cot. Above all, there was still the rope around her wrists. To all intents and purposes, she was still very much a prisoner.

All the while she'd been flailing against the cords and leather, the cot had responded with much groaning and creaking. Several times, the legs actually moved, scraping against the bare concrete floor. In the past several minutes it had grown silent upstairs, and now she feared that to continue meant she risked being overheard.

She wondered if the sudden silence above indicated that whoever was there had begun to think about dinner, or if they'd actually gone out in search of some, or, more ominously, if they were now huddled together somewhere, preparing to do whatever it was they were planning to do with her.

The latter possibility brought her back to the struggle with renewed drive. Opting to run the risk of being heard (she had no other choice), she resumed arching her back and kicking her legs. Ten hard minutes of that left her winded, cold pockets of sweat chilling her armpits. She paused momentarily to rest. When she resumed the kicking, it seemed to her—or was it merely her imagination?—that each time she did so she was able to kick her legs back farther. With her last thrust, she'd been able to bring the tips of her toes back almost to ear level.

Maintaining that position for any length of time was almost impossible, since it so greatly increased the crushing pressure of belts against her chest and shoulder. A minute of it left her breathless.

But with each kick, she continued her agonizing inch-by-inch descent toward the bottom of the cot. After several additional thrusts, just as she'd calculated, the uppermost strap slipped over the tips of her shoulders and dropped into the hollow between scapula and throat. At the same time, the lower half of the strap sagged loose beneath the cot.

She had no way of knowing where all of this was leading. She was still securely lashed to the cot. All she knew was that she now had far more mobility within her restraints than she'd had a half hour ago.

The kicking and flailing went on for another ten minutes. She labored bravely. Her greatest deficit was the absence of any assistance from her hands. The cords that bound them were as tight as ever and the effect of all the kicking had badly abraded the skin on her wrists. They'd started to bleed; at first, it was only a trickle she could feel in the dark. Then it came somewhat more freely. With each kick and thrust of her legs, her wrists felt as though the hot blade of a knife had been drawn across them.

Yet that, too, had a plus side. During the same time she'd kept kicking and inching farther down the cot, the lower half of her face—namely, the chin and mouth—had slipped beneath the loose strap dangling from her neck. She reasoned that if she could continue that same frantic motion, her head would eventually slide beneath the strap, thereby freeing the upper part of her body. The question utmost in her mind was whether she had the time.

In the next several minutes, by alternately kicking and heaving, then twisting her head at a cruelly unnatural angle, she managed not only to continue her inch-by-inch descent down the length of the cot but, at the same time, to slip her head beneath the topmost belt. The upper half of her body was suddenly free.

She was pinned to the cot now by just one remaining lashing—the one bound around her middle, which she judged to be the tightest and most unrelenting. The frustration of having bound hands seemed suddenly harsher and far more perverse than ever.

For the next several minutes, she struggled valiantly against the middle strap, arching and stretching and thrusting against it. She hoped that, like the bottom strap, persistent, sheer brute force applied to it might undermine the buckle, finally causing it to give.

After five minutes more of desperate thrashing, she lay panting and exhausted on the cot. The silk gag round her mouth cutting off half of her air did little to help. But in the course of these exertions, her legs from roughly midcalf to toe hung out in midair over the bottom edge of the cot. Lying there in that clumsy, immobilized position, it occurred to her that she might possibly be able to stand.

It meant, of course, that the cot would still be lashed to her by means of the middle strap. But it was a light, flimsy thing, just sticks and some cheap white duck cloth stapled together. In all, it couldn't weigh more than three or four pounds. Assuming she'd be able to get to her feet, walking in the cluttered confines of the cellar would be extremely awkward. She wasn't sure what advantage it would gain her, but she was determined to find out.

The first few times she attempted to stand, she couldn't get her feet down to the floor. She stretched and writhed, trying to slide lower on the cot. But the lashing around her middle was far too tight. She tried to stand and fell backward, the rear legs of the cot clattering so noisily that she thought for sure someone above would have heard and be down at once to check.

She lay there panting in the half dark, waiting for the stairway door to fly open and footsteps to come clumping down. But when nothing happened, she whispered three Hail Marys (something she hadn't done since childhood).

The fact that there appeared to be no one upstairs for the moment made her more keenly aware than ever of time running out. If she was going to get out of this situation, it had to be within the next few minutes. She was certain her captors wouldn't run the risk of leaving her unguarded much longer.

She renewed her struggle. Heaving, thrashing, writhing on the flimsy cot, she resembled someone striding on air, her legs free and pumping powerful strokes. The burlap sacking she wore felt like the tips of a million needles piercing her bare skin. The cot clattered and shook while she spat and drooled into the silk gag. Her sides and ribs heaved like those of a winded hound having run too hard.

For all that exertion, it seemed to her she'd gotten precious little in return. The final lashing was no looser than when she'd first started. However, this time when she tried to stand, she felt, to her amazement, her bare feet graze the chill, damp floor of the cellar. In that same instant, the cot rose, wobbling through an upward rotation of ninety degrees.

She was standing.

She stood for some moments, slightly dizzy, unsteady, puzzled to find herself upright, her mind already leaping forward to anticipate the next move. When at last that came, it was a bumpy, lurching thing, with the bottom edge of the cot alternately banging her ankles and the floor.

Fortunately, the ceilings were high. She passed beneath them easily, only once or twice smashing the top of the cot into one of the overhead joists. The illumination was poor, only just enough so that she could make out the clutter of bizarre bric-a-brac scattered around the cellar.

She negotiated a treacherous path of sinks, tables, workbenches, shelves all chockablock with bottles and jars, many containing a murky broth she was loath to inspect.

Passing the area she first thought to be a large black floor stain, she discovered it to be a kind of subterranean pool, but not of water. It contained something else, a dark, still fluid, somewhat heavier than water. She had no idea what it was. All she knew was that as she passed in its vicinity, her eyes teared more and the burning sensation in her nostrils increased.

Turning to flee the spot, the tip of the cot on her back banged into a flensing table. On that, she saw what gradually took the form of a human shape. It lay spread-eagled on the table. Fully half the skin had been peeled like a fruit from the bony frame beneath and lay draped over the edges of the table like a discarded garment.

A wad of something undigested rose in her throat, and she turned to run. She had no idea where she was running or what she was looking for until she actually saw it. It lay on a table amid a lot of other debris she couldn't immediately identify. But once she saw it, nothing could deflect her eye. It glittered like a jewel in the gloomy light—a fine, light coping saw, its blade slim and graceful as a steel thread. It sat amid a chaos of other tools. She thought they were carpenter's tools, but some had a more clinical look, like surgical instruments.

Moving about now, the cot still lashed to her back, she found the going easier, the way she imagined one grows accustomed to crutches or an artificial limb. The sight of the coping saw lying there, so near, so accessible, sharpened her determination. Forgetting that her hands were bound, she lunged for it. As she did so, the top of the cot clipped a naked lightbulb dangling from a bare wire in the ceiling.

A dull, rushing pop followed and she was standing in a shower of glass. More startled than injured, she barged forward and nearly shrieked as the scattered shards of glass bit into the bare soles of her feet.

Reaching the saw was more difficult than she'd imagined. While her fingers were free, the cords round her wrists were so tight that her fingers had stiffened and grown numb. Moreover, the saw lay at a far corner of the worktable. With a low joist overhanging the table and the cot lashed to her back, it couldn't be reached by merely walking around to it. The only way to reach it was by stretching herself directly across the table from where she stood. That involved folding herself nearly in half over the table's edge and inching her way to it with the cot bouncing and bumping about on top of her.

Stretching and twisting until her limbs ached, when she actually touched the saw, numbed fingers grazing the cold, ridged metal of the blade, all she could manage was to slap and flail at it helplessly. Several times, she succeeded in pincering it between two fingers, but each time she dropped it and had to start in anew. That went on for a time, until she devised a method of using the cord that linked both wrists as a means of dragging the saw across the table toward her.

In the triumphant moment that she held the saw dangling between thumb and forefinger, she heard the outside door upstairs slam and the anxious, hurried tread of someone entering.

Panting heavily, still bent over the worktable, she peered up at the creaking ceiling above her, her eyes tracking the footsteps as they crossed overhead. She followed their sound as they moved off to another room to her left. Moments later, she heard something like a chair being pulled out from beneath a desk, followed by the rattle of a phone being dialed. Then someone was talking. The sound of it drifted to her in a rapid, breathy murmur. No one had to tell her who it was.

The thing she imagined would be the most difficult turned out to be the most simple. Perhaps it was the return of the boy, the prospect of awful things to come, and the terrible certainty that time was running out that focused the last of her dwindling energy.

Under no circumstances did she wish to encounter Beppe again, particularly not while strapped down to a cot in a filthy cellar. The numbness in her fingers still prevented her from holding the saw in her hands. Instead, she pinned it blade upward between her knees and proceeded to push down hard on the cord between her bound wrists, rubbing it back and forth over the blade. It was a matter of two or three strokes, no more. So sharp was the blade, the cords were no match for it. They yielded quickly.

With her hands suddenly free, numbness and prolonged lack of circulation made them feel distant and ungainly, as though they were no longer a part of her body. But clenching and unclenching them, a rush of warmth entered her hands. Circulation returned, and in the next moment she tore off her gag and was tearing at the last belt—the one around her middle. The buckle had been lashed so tightly she could scarcely budge it.

Overhead, the conversation had ended. She heard the phone bang back into the cradle and the chair scrape over the floor. The footsteps started back out from the other room. They crossed directly overhead, moving toward the cellar door at the top of the stair, roughly thirty feet away.

The door swung open with a hard, angry yank, sending a shaft of mote-filled light streaming down the stair. Inhaling deeply, she sucked her stomach inward as far as it could possibly go. All the while, her free right hand tugged hard at the belt. Still the prong would not disengage the buckle.

The first footstep hit with a thud at the top of the stair. She felt a rush of adrenaline surge through her. It moved like a current of electricity down the muscles in her arms and shoulders. She felt her hands and wrists tauten and, with a final desperate suck inward, she pulled, and the prong slid loose.

Through the slats of an upright ladder, she could see cut off at the waist the trousered legs of someone up ahead. They appeared and disappeared, then reappeared with each shift of position their owner made. The figure, halfway down the stairs, drove her backward into the dank gloom at the rear of the cellar.

THIRTY-FIVE

"I'm sorry I couldn't get to you sooner. I wish I had something to report, but I don't. Nothing tangible at least."

Manship listened to the clipped, syntactically perfect English of Ettore Foa.

"If it is of any comfort, Dr. Gigli, the Italian ambassador, is on the case himself."

"Did the Lloyd's people reach the British ambassador in Rome?"

"That's what I'm getting to. They have."

"And?"

"The news is not good."

It was shortly after midnight. Manship was already in bed, the earliest he'd gotten to bed in nine months. Maeve was asleep across the hall, she and Osgood and himself having had a quiet dinner at a restaurant over near Second Avenue.

"I tried to reach you at five o'clock at your office," Foa went on hastily, as though he, too, felt pressed. "Your assistant, Miss—"

"Taverner."

"*Giusto*. Taverner. She told me you were gone for the day."

"I was tied up with the conservator. We've been trying to get the last few pieces ready for the show. We're supposed to open in forty-eight hours. Listen—for God sake, tell me. What's this now with the British ambassador?"

"It's not the ambassador. He's a very good friend of Dr. Gigli. Eager and more than willing to help."

"Then, damn it, what's the problem?" Manship tried to subdue the edge in his voice. "Is there something I can do at this end?"

"No, no, dear fellow." Foa made a sympathetic clucking sound.

"At this point, I'm ready to fly over myself."

"I quite understand your anxiety. But your barging off

to Italy now would be rash, and, if you don't mind my saying so, counterproductive. Besides, you have your show.''

"Right. Of course. The show." Manship repeated the words without much enthusiasm.

"I didn't mean to weigh the girl's well-being against the show," Foa hastened to explain.

"But you agree there's reason for concern?"

"No doubt. The police have been in touch with Miss Cattaneo's housekeeper. The lady's missing all right. Fallen into the wrong hands."

"Wrong hands?"

"Wrong people, I should say. This Borghini—"

"Who?"

"Borghini—Ludovico Borghini. You know, the chap we spoke of, the one I told you I knew as a boy."

"Yes. Of course. Is it him?"

"It looks more and more that way. An unsavory character. Up to his ears in all sorts of mischief."

"Mischief?"

"Fascist mischief. Throughout Italy, with global connections to like organizations around the world. Everything from bombings and assassinations to simple kidnappings. The targets are mostly centrist and left-leaning political figures." Foa laughed bitterly. "They're also not above the desecration of priceless works of art—statuary, paintings of great masters—when it suits their purpose—their purpose in all of this being to intimidate the nation by discrediting the ability of the government to protect its national treasures. If you can walk into a museum and destroy a da Vinci or take a hammer to a Michelangelo, what, then, can't you do? I can assure you, it makes the government sit up and take notice. No government wants to look that weak and feckless."

Manship thought about the attacks on the Botticellis in Turkey and Italy. They'd start once it was publicly announced that he intended to bring the paintings home for exhibition in the United States. "These people must be insane."

"Many of them are. Certifiable lunatics with no place else to go. No one else would have them. A few years ago, we asked the federal police to investigate this organization. They actually infiltrated it. An unpleasant group of people made up largely of xenophobic rabble-rousers. They loathe foreigners. They suspect all non-Italians. They long to see the good old days of Il Duce and the blackshirts return. Mostly old men, along with a smattering of bored juveniles who know zero about fascism and shave their heads and affect bizarre dress. You have those quasi-militia groups in America, too. Mostly misfits. They crave excitement—violent excitement. But also among them are a few aspirants of genuine political genius."

"Such as Signor Borghini?"

"Precisely. People with carefully worked out ideological agendas. The police today don't find these people quite so laughable as they used to. For one thing, their numbers seem to be growing."

"Yes, yes. But what does all this have to do with Isobel Cattaneo?"

"I'm coming to that." Foa's slightly raspy voice betrayed signs of fatigue.

"Was Isobel one of these people?"

"At one time. In her student days. As you well know, when one is young, there's no limit to the seductiveness of stupid things. She had a slight brush with them. It was brief, and with her, it never had a strong political appeal. The appeal was more romantic, I'd say."

"Romantic? You mean with Borghini?"

Foa laughed a tired, world-weary laugh. "No, no. You misunderstand. If you saw Borghini, you'd know what I mean. By romantic, I mean the situation itself, the very clandestine nature of it. A small upstart group of outsiders full of grievances, banished to the periphery of respectable society, defiant of all authority, scornful of the daily circus of corruption and scandal that is Italian political life today. These people dream of returning to the discipline and grandeur of old Europe. Well, you can see for yourself, that sort of thing could well hold a certain allure to an idealistic young mind.''

Manship's mouth was dry. Sprawled in bed, propped against a stack of pillows, his hand reached for the glass of ice water on his night table. ''You mentioned something about the British ambassador.'' He gulped deeply. ''In Rome. Something about bad news.''

There was a pause at the other end of the line, as if the deputy ambassador had been anticipating yet dreading this part of the call. When he resumed talking, it was with a sigh of resignation. ''We've been watching Signor Borghini's movements with extreme interest. His palazzo on the Quirinal has been under surveillance since early today. The Lloyd's people, who have a particular interest in wanting your show to come off without further incident, have been watching the little framing establishment in Parioli.''

''The Quattrocento.''

''The very same. At this hour, the palazzo on the Quirinal appears to be dark. No one has gone in or out of there for the past sixteen hours. As for the framing shop—''

''Yes?''

''As I told you, this Fèrro Pugno bunch has a seventy-five-year lease on the place. It's set up to give the appearance of a business, but it isn't. It's what I believe you people call a 'front.' No business is conducted there. It's a meeting place for Borghini and his various business cronies from Italy and abroad. According to my contacts, there are people there during the day—aliens, foreigners. The carabinieri at this moment are trying to identify them. At night, there's a caretaker on the premises—a young boy, apparently, who goes in and out at odd hours. But for the most part, the place is in darkness. If Signorina Cattaneo is being held anywhere, it's there.''

''Then, by God, let's go in and find out.''

"That's the bad news I must tell you."

Manship's heart sank. Propped on an elbow, phone cradled between cheek and shoulder, scribbling notes on a pad, he listened, slightly out of breath.

"As I told you," Foa rushed on, "the name Borghini is an influential name in Italy. Perhaps not as influential as it once was, but in certain quarters, it still exerts a force. Apparently, the British ambassador, upon being informed of the situation today, immediately called the Italian foreign secretary, who at once notified the magistracy in Rome, directing them to issue warrants for the police to search not only the palazzo in Rome but the little gallery in Parioli as well."

"And?"

"I'm coming to that. Apparently, Borghini also has a friend or two in the magistracy, if not the chief magistrate himself." The deputy ambassador's voice dropped to a near whisper. "You didn't hear that from me. And if you say I told you so, I shall deny it. In any event, the moment the order to issue warrants was given, someone in the magistracy, someone obviously quite high up, immediately warned Borghini. He's now disappeared. Gone completely off the map."

"But what about the warrants? Can we get into the gallery?"

There was another lengthy pause, followed by the thick growl of Foa clearing his throat.

"The chief magistrate has ordered the warrants to be issued, but as of this moment, to the best of my knowledge, the police have received no warrants. They cannot move until the warrants are in hand."

"The magistrate is stalling," Manship reflected aloud.

"Obviously," Foa quickly agreed. "Someone there is clearly dragging his feet."

"But why? Unless there's something to hide."

"Precisely." Foa gave an angry burst of laughter. "And also to give Colonel Borghini enough time to make himself scarce—or, more probably, to get out of the country.''

"Leaving Miss Cattaneo to the tender mercies of the present occupants.''

"I'm afraid so.''

Manship struggled to absorb all that was coming at him so quickly. "Where do you suppose he is?''

"Borghini? With his resources and large circle of sympathetic friends, he could show up in any one of a half dozen places and find sanctuary.''

"New York?''

"Given his special antipathy to your exhibition, that would not surprise me.''

The decidedly pointed manner in which that had been revealed did not escape Manship. "And what about Isobel?''

"About her,'' Foa said guardedly, "we can do nothing for the moment but wait for the warrants and see.''

THIRTY-SIX

By the time the boy was halfway down the stairs, Isobel was crouched behind a huge armoire at the far end of the cellar.

Starting down, he'd punched the light switch at the head of the stair, flooding the place with blinding illumination. That was to Isobel's disadvantage. The place that she'd instinctively dived for was the darkest part of the cellar. Now it was no longer dark there.

To her advantage, however, was the fact that the cellar floor had been partitioned into at least a half dozen distinct areas, all set off by a maze of boundaries fashioned out of shelves, packing cases, and hulking pieces of discarded furniture. The arrangement offered opportunities to stay out of sight so long as one was quick on one's feet and stayed close to the ground.

She was certainly not quick. Several slivers of glass, no more than a millimeter or so long, stuck in her bare feet and pricked cruelly whenever she put pressure on them. In addition, she was in a state of near panic.

From behind the armoire, she watched the boy bound off the bottom stair and plunge into the cellar, heading toward the place where he'd left her hours before. He no longer wore his harlequin costume. He was now just another young street tough, full of swagger and pose. She watched him weave in and out of the clutter, alternately losing, then regaining sight of him as his figure emerged from behind some bulky obstacle.

As he moved back into the cellar, she continued to creep forward in the opposite direction, toward the foot of the stairs. She had no more fixed plan in mind than to keep the farthest possible distance between the two of them.

She could tell the instant he'd discovered she was gone. Unable to see him, she heard his scraping footsteps come to an abrupt halt, followed by a cry, almost feral, like an animal suddenly wounded. After that came a stream of obscenities, then the resumption of footsteps, only this time the tread heavier and far more hurried.

His search started at the rear of the cellar, not far from where she crouched. She could hear him muttering—a soft, angry chant that grew angrier as he went.

He had little doubt she was still down there. The door at the head of the stair had been locked when he came back and there was no other exit from the cellar to the street. It was only a matter of time until he found her. Swiftly, methodically, he worked his way from the rear to the forward part of the room.

All the while he pressed forward, she did, too, moving, stooped over, from one large encumbrance to the next, putting her foot down as lightly as possible to avoid the cruel bite of glass jabbing upward into her flesh.

The principal problem that lay before her now was how to cover the broad swath of open space running for approximately twenty feet from the head of the cellar to the bottom step of the stairway.

It meant coming out into the open. Reason dictated that if it was her intention to bolt for the stair, she'd best do it sooner than later, while he was still back some distance in the cellar.

"Bitch," he called softly after her, his voice a caress. "Bitch." He moved along like a terrier tracking a rat, running it to ground. She could hear the smothered rage in his voice, but also, oddly enough, the fear—not of her, but of Borghini, if by chance he'd have to explain her having slipped away.

Kneeling, she'd been dragging her right hand across the floor for balance when it inadvertently bumped into something cold and hard. Groping for it, she reached down and picked it up. It was one of those cheap ceramic dolls—a lurid cartoonlike figure with the face of a ventriloquist's dummy, the sort of thing you win at carnivals for knocking over ninepins with a rubber ball. A child's toy. She couldn't imagine a more improbable place to stumble on such a thing.

He came faster now, arms swinging wildly, a small cyclone, leaving in its wake a trail of wreckage. Certain that she was hidden in one of the big storage cupboards, he flung open their doors, then slammed them shut, taking out his wrath on them as if they'd personally insulted him. It was a fearful racket. She flinched with each sharp crack. Half-paralyzed with fear, she inched forward, trying to keep him in view.

"Bitch. Bitch." The half caress, half howl roiled the stale air. A cat, unlucky enough to get in his way, shrieked when he kicked it aside. By that time, he'd worked himself into a state of unreasoning rage.

Up until then, she'd been lucky. But now, he'd covered a great deal of territory in short order and was closing in on her fast. Her task was clear—keep the greatest distance between herself and the boy. The job was made more difficult by the fact that she had to move crablike, crouched over on all fours so he couldn't see her. Moreover, putting pressure on her foot, no matter how slight, was sheer agony, like walking on needles. Whenever she stepped down, she wanted to shriek. Wherever she moved, she left a spoor of bloody footprints behind her on the floor.

If she was fading, not so the boy. The zest for the hunt seemed to have quickened his adrenaline flow. He sought her now with a demented glee, whistling slightly as he swung in and out of those cluttered aisles.

He was no more than some fifteen or twenty feet from her when he must have spotted one of those blurred red outlines of her bleeding feet. From where she crouched, she heard him come to a shuddering halt, panting rapidly as he stooped to examine the print. Sensing the closeness of his prey, he yipped with excitement. It was at that moment she hefted the ceramic doll in her hand and, without a second thought, hurled it. It was as though someone else were guiding her hand. She hadn't tossed it at him, but, rather, lofted it over his head into a shadowy corner behind him. What followed was a dull, percussive thud. The boy wheeled instantly and plunged back in the direction of the sound. The moment he'd reached the place where the doll had landed, she rose and bolted for the stairs.

He saw the movement out of the corner of his eye and grasped at once that he'd been duped. Like an enraged panther, he came tearing out of the shadows, bellowing at the top of his lungs. It was a deep, hoarse, terrifying sound she could feel in the pit of her stomach—a sound full of rage combined with a strange, joyous excitement.

The distance between her and the stair was no more than twenty feet. He was nearly twice that distance back from where she stood, but the sound of him bounding after her was paralyzing. Moreover, each step she took on her bleeding feet was unbearable.

The open doorway at the top of the stair seemed light-years away, and she didn't know what she would find once she got beyond that door. No doubt more Beppes, and worse even than what she might have expected had she been content to lie below there in the dark, strapped to the cot, submissively accepting her fate.

He was halfway up the stair when she crossed the threshold, flung the door shut behind her, and threw the bolt. The full weight of him going flat out hit the opposite side of the door. With a terrible fascination, she watched the wood buckle down the midline, then bulge outward.

A succession of deafening cracks followed, like rifle shots, both fists impacting so rapidly on the door that the sound of each separate blow merged into one prolonged, unbroken hail. With each crack of his fist, she could see the door hinges straining from their anchors in the wall.

PART THREE

They finally found the hotel after circling the waterfront in the Battery Park area for well over an hour. The cabdriver, whose name on his livery license appeared to consist of nothing but consonants, spoke only marginal English. The colonel's English was accomplished, but he couldn't make head or tail of the driver's contrapuntal Arabic-English, thus turning their search into something of a shouting match.

The place they were looking for wasn't a hotel in the strict sense of the word. It was actually a home for retired seamen that happened to also let rooms out to merchant sailors in port for a night or two and in need of lodgings while their vessels took on or discharged cargos. Borghini had learned of it from a distant cousin whose political activities made it imperative that he remain in no locale for more than two days at a time. The same person had helped him acquire the forged passport and seaman's papers he'd used to enter the country on a Pakistani airliner late that afternoon.

The ride in from Kennedy had been uncharacteristically trouble-free—little traffic and no half-mile backups at the toll plazas. Once down in lower Manhattan, however, where the simple, logical grid system of midtown streets and avenues gives way to a labyrinth of demented traffic patterns, communication between passenger and driver broke down entirely.

Shortly, they were barking at each other, but in different tongues. In the end, of course, they found the place, called, somewhat unimaginatively, Harbor Rest. They didn't actually find it; they stumbled on it by accident when they asked directions of a homeless man who insisted on wiping their windshield with a soiled Kleenex. For the modest fee of a dollar, he literally walked them the distance of twenty paces to the front door.

The Harbor Rest sat square in the middle of a winding

little ribbon of cobblestone called End Street, which served as a transverse between Holme Street and Battery Park. The structure itself was an anachronism—an 1840s farmhouse with a wraparound porch, upon which sat huge cast-iron urns overflowing with blood-red geraniums. The place, wedged in between a sooty row of warehouses and derelict tenement buildings, was easy to miss. The twentieth century itself appeared to have bypassed it entirely.

One end of the street sat in the perpetual twilight cast by the World Trade Center several blocks east; the other end trickled down to its terminus at the Battery promenade. The only association the old sailors' Harbor Rest had with the sea was the thin patch of river barely visible between a pair of spavined Civil War brick structures listing dangerously toward each other from opposite corners of the street. The occasional moan of foghorns booming at night during the inclement fall and winter months was the extent of nautical atmosphere at the Harbor Rest.

The old Harbor Rest was like walking into something fixed in a distant time warp. Despite the rough surroundings of the neighborhood, the interior had a cozy farmhouse charm: rough pine furniture, overstuffed wing chairs, settees encased in badly frayed embroidered slipcovers, nests of tables upon which sat neat stacks of well-thumbed vintage *Life* and *National Geographic* magazines awaiting the unhurried browser. Converted hurricane lights hung as sconces on the mottled plaster walls.

From a chair behind the desk, a solitary clerk with muttonchop whiskers and sporting sleeve garters, snored lightly, threatening to topple from his high stool at any moment.

Still ruffled from his encounter with the cabdriver, Borghini entered and set his bag down on the freshly polished wood floors. Noting the drowsy, unattended look of the place, the colonel was not greatly encouraged. He was pleasantly surprised, however, to find that the dozing clerk, once roused, not only had a record of his reservation in the name of one Gaudio Favese but had already taken the liberty of opening and airing the room to make it ready for his visit.

Ushered upstairs (there was no elevator) by a squat, burly figure whose bowed legs suggested that he'd spent more than his share of years negotiating slippery decks in storm-tossed seas, Borghini found the lodging as well as its out-of-the-way location increasingly to his taste.

On first arriving, he had the impression from the virtually empty lobby that the place was vacant. But by 6:00 P.M. the same lobby overflowed with lodgers and permanent residents come down to chat, smoke, quaff a mug of ale before the little combination breakfast–dining room in the rear opened at 7:00 P.M. for dinner.

Amid this odd assembly, the colonel felt slightly out of place. He began to feel more comfortable, however, when he saw that no one bothered to approach him with an eye toward companionship or small talk.

It could have been a page out of Conrad—a public room in Limehouse at the turn of the century; the noisy, boisterous fellowship of merchant seamen out for a few hours of relaxation. Swedes, Kanaks, Filipinos, dour Finns, and burly lascars, all of them carousing at the long plank tables, pewter mugs of ale and steamy plates of stew heaped up before them. Afterward, following the coffee and cobblers, pipes and cigarillos were lit. Shortly, smoke coiled upward like serpents intertwining in the chain-hung pewter candelabras overhead.

With a bit of supper and a cognac under his belt, Borghini began to let himself relax. He even struck up a conversation with a paunchy Dutchman who spoke a guttural but passable Italian. He was at the Harbor Rest, he said, while his ship, a freighter of Panamanian registry, took on cargo. In the morning, they were bound for Lagos and the west coast of Africa.

Later, upstairs in his room, in pajamas and seated on his bed, Borghini removed from his bag a set of sharp krislike

knives of the type used at the Quattrocento galleries for
cutting canvas and mat. A wig of sandy-colored hair hung
on the bedpost. A short time after, windows open, foghorns
booming far out across the Verazzano Straits, he fell asleep
while reading a fairly long article in *The New York Times*.
It was a preview of the glittery opening to take place the
following night at the Metropolitan.

It was a rare day that found Manship home by 6:00 P.M.
Passing through the front door of number 5 East Eighty-
fifth, he stepped into the narrow hallway. A single lamp
glowed faintly on the telephone table and several messages
were propped up against the rotary dial. The first was from
Mrs. McCooch, who'd already left for the weekend, in-
forming him that he'd had a long distance call from Italy—
a Mr. Foa. (She apologized for the spelling of the name,
despite the fact she'd had it perfectly correct.) She went on
to explain that Mr. Foa and she had had a cordial conversation in which no information of any special note was
passed.

Manship muttered a few unrepeatables. It was just midnight in Rome. He had not the slightest idea where to begin
to look for the deputy ambassador in Italy at that hour.

Another message in Mrs. McCooch's spidery hand informed him that Emily Taverner had called, frantic to reach
him—something about the florist and floral arrangements
for the following morning. Would he please be sure to call
her?

There was a third message, from Osgood, asking him to
call first thing in the morning. He would be out for the
evening.

A final message, this one scratched out in Maeve's fierce,
elegant cursive. Her letters, like her painting, full of mys-
tical little glyphlike characters, informed him that she
would be spending the night with an old friend in Scarsdale.

The message, by chance juxtaposed with that of Osgood's announcing that he, too, would be unavailable till

the next day, made Manship smile. He felt no bitterness, but, rather, an odd sense of relief. He wished them well. Nothing was worth getting too sad over. Life was short, everything impermanent, no loss so awful that it couldn't be endured. All comes to nought. Everyone ends up essentially the same way. What's to fret? What's to grieve?

With still no word from Foa, he grew increasingly anxious over the fate of Isobel Cattaneo—to his surprise, far more anxious than over the fate of his show. Imagining several possible scenarios, none provided him much solace.

Later that night, too agitated to sleep, he tossed and turned for several hours, his mind churning with nagging suspicions regarding Van Nuys, as well as the myriad small details still waiting to be resolved at the museum.

Slightly past midnight, Manship threw in the towel. Too keyed up to sleep, he rose and dressed, intending to steal across to his office and have a last look at the show before zero hour tomorrow. At the back of his mind was a fast-fading hope that he would find a message waiting there from Foa, reporting that he'd located Isobel and that everything was all right.

Fifth Avenue was remarkably busy for that hour. For late September, the night air had a silkiness that was almost voluptuous—more like May. A fragrance of twice-bloomed honeysuckle wafted about from across the way in the park. It was as though New York, unwilling to accept approaching winter, was reinventing spring. People in shirtsleeves were out strolling the avenue—out for a breath of air, giving the dog a final sprinkle for the night. Cabs and buses lurched along, brakes shrieking as they shuddered at stops to pick up or discharge passengers. Hordes of people milled about, looking intent, purposeful. Where were they going at that hour? Manship wondered. Did no one in the city go to bed anymore?

But it was the museum that truly surprised him. Fully expecting to find that long expanse of masonry plunged in darkness, with perhaps a sporadic light twinkling here and there along the great facade, he found instead the building emblazoned in lights all along the upper stories.

Mounted above the columned entrance, pennants and banners in cerulean blue, swelling outward like great spinnakers, rode the gentle midnight breeze. In yard-high letters, they proclaimed for all the world to see: BOTTICELLI. 550. It sounded like an Italian bicycle race.

His immediate reaction was embarrassment. It was too big, too showy. It bordered on the cheaply theatrical. But then again, much to his dismay, there was something in it to which he responded. He couldn't bring himself to call it pride, but after all, wasn't it the culmination of a dream? Hadn't it cost the better part of five years of his life to put it together; to assemble in some coherent order all of its multiple and diverse parts; to bring it to the point where banners could fly? Come December, early January, he knew all too well the show would close, the paintings would come down, all packed away, crated in excelsior and wood to be shipped back to their respective owners. Then it would all be history. Quickly forgotten.

Out front, up and down the length of the great stone stairway, people, mostly the young, squatting on knapsacks and book bags, sprawled about in untidy little clusters.

He threaded his way through recumbent forms, assorted soda cans, and candy wrappers, up to the entrance and let himself in with a passkey. Save for two or three security lights providing minimal illumination, the Great Hall, divested of its daily horde of tramping visitors, appeared to slumber in the partial dark. A pair of security guards immediately converged on him as he entered, then, recognizing him, murmured respectful good evenings and moved off in the direction of the Sackler Wing on their nightly patrol.

Opposite him, in that cavernous gloom, the central stairway appeared to float downward through the airy silences of the main floor. At the very top of the stair, lights blazed and a low hum of activity filtered downward.

He'd intended to go first to his office, but the steady din drifting down from above roused his curiosity. With a sense of mounting excitement, Manship made his way into the first of the twelve central galleries that now housed the Botticelli exhibition.

He was startled by what he saw. For one thing, there was far more activity than anything he was prepared for at that hour. Lighting technicians moved about everywhere, coiled in great loops of wire; picture hangers poised on ladders rushed to make last-minute adjustments; photographers, camera technicians, and personnel from the department of conservators all went about applying final touches to their work.

Manship threaded his way among the ladders. He watched security experts mount plates of see-through bulletproof glass before world-class paintings. Up ahead, a pale blur of motion swam before his dazed eyes. At the center of it stood Taverner in the midst of the fray, issuing orders to a crew of exhausted assistants. She, too, looked pretty much at the end of her rope. At that moment, she happened to turn and see him.

"Mark. Thank heavens! . . ."

"What's going on here, anyway?"

"There's still so much to do." She came toward him, wailing a litany of complaint. "And then there's the florist."

"I know. I got your message."

"They want to do the table arrangements first thing in the morning."

"Impossible. Everything will be drooping by dinner."

"Don't even ask about Frettobaldi."

"What about him?"

"He insists that the lighting over the Predella panels is all wrong. And the lighting over the *Primavera*, he says, turns the blue to purple. He's had his people rip it out and do it over and over again. He stormed out of here an hour ago, and most of them are ready to snap.'' Her chin sagged to her chest. ''I can't tell you how relieved I am you're here.''

He thought she was about to cry, and he pushed a straying forelock from her brow.

''All these last details,'' she went on, close to tears. ''There was no one to turn to. You'd left for the day. Mr. Osgood had gone, too. Van Nuys is out of town till tomorrow evening. . . .''

''I had some things to work out,'' he offered by way of explanation. ''Come, show me the problem with the Predella panels.''

They set off at once for one of the galleries farther back on the floor. She walked slightly ahead of him, still reciting woes while leading him. When they reached the wall where the panels hung, they found three of Frettobaldi's assistants lounging on the floor, drinking coffee from a thermos.

''What are you gentlemen doing?'' Manship inquired.

''We're waiting for Mr. Frettobaldi.''

''You may have to wait a long time. I gather he's having one of his creative blocks.'' Manship gazed up at the panels. ''What seems to be the problem?''

Sensing authority, one of them scrambled to his feet. ''It's the glare we're getting when we reach the required brightness.''

''Show me.'' Manship planted himself squarely before the panels, folded his arms, and waited.

The fellow proceeded to run his dimmers through several degrees of brightness. The other two, judging it politic, had shambled to their feet, as well. Taverner hovered in the background.

''You see the glare,'' the first fellow explained, ''the way it comes off the glass?''

''I do, but it's not all that bad,'' Manship replied. ''Bring the floods up to maximum and then lower them slowly.'' Manship's voice was remarkably calm, considering the depth of his irritation. ''Down a bit more,'' he called over his shoulder to the assistant operating the dimmer. ''That's it. Fine.''

The assistant came up from behind him. Along with the two others, they stood studying the effect of the lights and shaking their heads.

''There's still glare there,'' one of them said.

''Maybe,'' Manship replied. ''But we can live with it. Look okay to you, Taverner?''

''Looks fine to me.'' She nodded.

''Mr. Frettobaldi will never approve—''

''He doesn't have to.'' Manship smiled frostily. ''You can tell him Mr. Manship has approved it for him. You gentlemen are free to go now.''

One of them, the largest of the three, shuffled forward. ''Beg pardon, sir, but we have our instructions. Mr. Frettobaldi told us to wait right here till he gets back.''

Manship shrugged. ''Suit yourself. But as of this moment''—he glanced at his watch—''one-fourteen A.M., you gentlemen are off the museum payroll. The meter has stopped running. Taverner, will you please note that in your log.''

Manship nodded cordially to the workmen, then turned on his heel. Taverner scurried along behind while Frettobaldi's three assistants, somewhat stunned, watched the two figures recede slowly down the aisle, then disappear.

The next gallery was devoid of workmen. A quiet, almost serene hush hovered over the space. Here resided the *Adoration of the Magi* from the Uffizi, the dazzling *Saint Sebastian* from the Staatliche Museum in Berlin, *The Virgin Teaching the Child to Read* from the Poldi-Pezzoli in Milan, *The Story of Nastagio degli Onesti,* only just arrived the day before from the Prado in Madrid. That was followed by the superstar, the *Birth of Venus,* carried across the Atlantic from the Uffizi in Florence by courier, then uncrated at the museum from specially constructed cartons with built-in humidity- and climate-control devices.

The Venus was bewitching. Any viewer, even a particularly acute one, could forgive the unnatural elongation of her neck, the impossibly steep fall of her shoulder, the queer manner in which her left arm is hinged to her body. Manship would have argued that all of those anatomical aberrations were intentional, that it was Botticelli's way of heightening the beauty and harmony of the design, and that, in the end, all one saw were the eyes—sad, tender, infinitely wise.

Taverner behind him, he moved farther along, past *St. Augustine in His Cell, Christ on the Mount of Olives,* a *Portrait of Lorenzo,* and then an empty space.

It lay between the *Portrait of Lorenzo* and the *Annunciation* from the Met's own permanent collection. More a gap than a space, it looked like a mismeasurement or an oversight on the part of the hangers. It called attention to itself like a missing tooth in an otherwise-lovely face.

He stood staring at it, a look of puzzlement on his lowering brow; then his expression darkened.

"What is this?"

"Mark—"

"What's going on here?"

"Mark, please. I don't want to get into the middle of anything."

"Don't worry. You won't." A line in his jaw began to throb. "Just tell me who's responsible."

"I had nothing to do with it. If you'd been here—"

"Was it Van Nuys? René? Where's my *Centurion*?"

She stared down at the floor miserably, wringing her hands.

"Who took it? Tell me." His voice was ominously soft. "You'd better tell me, Emily."

She stood there, kneading her hands, as close to tears as she'd come that night. At last, she nodded. "Both of them—Van Nuys and René."

Swallowing several times, she struggled for air. "They came around to your office late in the afternoon, looking for you. I told them you'd left for the day. I thought they'd be angry, but they seemed almost relieved. Then they left."

"They left?"

"Not the museum. Just your office."

"Where'd they go?"

Her tear-rimmed eyes opened wide, brimming with anger. "Where do you think?" She pointed to the gaping void near the center of the wall.

"Who took it down?" Manship demanded. "Which one? Was it René?"

"One of the hangers. René directed him."

"And Van Nuys?"

"Just stood there and watched. If you'd just been here."

"I wasn't. But I'm here now. Where did they take it?"

Taverner had been working fourteen-hour days throughout that whole week. She looked wobbly on her feet. She kept wringing her hands and shaking her head slowly back and forth. She was like a stutterer desperate to speak but unable to get words out.

"I don't know," she confessed at last.

"What do you mean, you don't know? You followed them down from my office. You followed them here to this gallery. Why didn't you follow them wherever they were taking the *Centurion*?"

She had the look of a child about to be punished, her head still shaking right to left. "Mark, I can't . . . I don't . . ."

"I know. You don't want to get into the middle of anything. You've already said that."

"I know I did. I just . . ."

She'd wadded a Kleenex in her fist, then crushed it to her mouth, stifling her sobs behind it. Tired tears slid downward from her eyes.

"Just one thing." He appeared to soften. "Just tell me one thing."

Her eyes watched him warily over the Kleenex.

"Do you know anyone here, other than Van Nuys or

René Klass, who might have some idea where they stashed my *Centurion*?''

In the moments just passed, the *Centurion* and its unusual cause had become exclusively *his*.

It was common knowledge at the museum that Manship's present status, for a variety of reasons, was shaky. It was the daily chatter of middle management, in cafeterias, rest rooms, wherever people who were apt to hear things gathered. Taverner, ambitious, and closely identified with Manship, had been forced to decide in a matter of seconds where to cast her lot.

''I can tell you this,'' she whispered, her eyes scanning the gallery, ''the *Centurion* is locked up in one of the storerooms.'' She'd made her choice, settling on a wise but craven middle course. ''That's all I know.'' She turned to go, but his hand encircled her upper arm.

''Just one more thing. How do you know it's in one of the storerooms?''

''Helen Mirkin told me,'' she said in a near whisper, then turned and fled the place.

Helen Mirkin was Walter Van Nuys's administrative assistant.

THIRTY-EIGHT

The task before him was daunting. Search each storeroom, each containing upward of a hundred paintings, all part of the Met's permanent collection. The reasons for mothballing a painting were manifold, but chiefly it came down to two things: either the canvas was awaiting restoration or no appropriate setting, historic or thematic, could be found in which to display it.

As a senior curator, with special administrative privileges, Manship held a master key to all the twenty-seven storerooms scattered in various locations throughout the museum. In the few hours remaining until dawn, he would have to tear around to each, fly through the hundred or so paintings stacked in deep wooden racks, then, assuming he found nothing, tear around to the next.

It seemed futile. He'd been up since three the previous morning and he was bone-weary from the relentless stress of last-minute activity surrounding the show.

There was no thought of going home now. Rest was out of the question. The injustice of the thing, as well as the petty, narrow-minded motivation behind it, made him seethe. He felt betrayed, not merely by Van Nuys and Klass but by everyone around him.

Before he did anything, he decided to check his office to see if Foa had tried again to reach him with news of Isobel. He hadn't. He noted with a sinking heart that his desk was entirely clear of messages. What does it matter? he asked himself. Why should I care? Surely his feelings—whatever they were—were far out of proportion to anything he'd actually shared with her. The urgency, the irrationality of them seemed adolescent. On the other hand, he was grateful for the feeling. It was like sensation returning to a numbed limb. He'd felt nothing like that since the early days with Maeve years before.

Then he was out of his office, slamming the door behind him. Determined to put everything out of his mind for the next few hours, he would now concentrate his last bit of energy on recovering the *Centurion*.

There was little chance Van Nuys would have been foolish enough to remove the painting from the museum. In the first place, the museum didn't own it. St. Stephen's in Istanbul did. Even mutilated beyond repair, it was nonetheless a Botticelli, granted a virtually unknown one. The mindless destruction it had sustained at the hands of a madman had greatly depreciated its monetary worth, but it still had enormous historic value, if only as a link in the artistic progression of a great genius.

Secondly, in removing the ruined canvas from the premises, Van Nuys would surely forfeit whatever potential liability for theft or additional damage the insurance people still had. In matters of money, Van Nuys, headstrong as he was, would never be so rash as that.

Manship felt reasonably certain the painting was still somewhere on the premises. But where? The Met was enormous. Some two hundred thousand square feet. Taverner had said it was in one of the storerooms. She'd had that from Helen Mirkin, and in matters regarding Van Nuys's day-to-day movements, no one knew better than she.

Forthwith, his ordeal began.

Since Van Nuys was the architect of this treachery, reason suggested that the search begin with the two storerooms closest to his office on the second floor. Manship was not greatly surprised, however, a short time later, to discover that what Van Nuys had done with the *Centurion* had little to do with reason. It was far more concerned with self-esteem and other factors born in the darker regions of the soul.

It had taken him the better part of an hour to cover three storerooms. Of necessity, his examination of the canvases contained in those three could be no more than cursory. A sloppy fly-by was the best he could manage under the circumstances.

He reasoned that if all he could cover were three storerooms per hour, he would need close to eight hours to complete the remaining twenty-four. It was now slightly past 3:00 A.M. Under the most ideal conditions, he could not hope to finish before 11:00 A.M. By then, the full daytime staff would be in. There would be those who would set off alarm bells immediately. Van Nuys would be informed and an awful row would follow. The police would be called in and Manship, no doubt, would be put off the premises. Whatever hope he still had of recovering the *Centurion* would be lost forever.

If he hoped to do what he'd planned, the deed would have to be accomplished between 3:00 A.M. and 6:00 A.M., roughly three hours away.

He resumed the search, ratcheting up anger along with speed. Each department had a storage area; some, depending on their size and importance, had several. In rapidly fleeting minutes, he tore through department after department: Greek and Roman Art, Musical Instruments, Twentieth Century Art, the American Wing. By 4:00 A.M. he was in Medieval Art, then Renaissance Arms and Armor, in a lather, his flying footsteps clacking through the large galleries where figures in chain mail, mounted on noble steeds, paraded beneath walls covered with heraldic banners and brightly painted shields.

By 4:30 A.M., he was in a fever of sweat. He'd been to no less than sixteen locked storage areas, flying through each like someone with his clothing on fire. But at the storage room for Arms and Armor, he confronted a different situation. When he put his master key in the lock of the storage room there, he discovered to his surprise that the lock rejected it entirely.

He pushed the key in several times. Each time, the lock balked. On at least one occasion, twisting the key harder, he nearly snapped it in half.

The clock ticked remorselessly onward. It was going on 4:45 A.M. The first gray streaks of dawn raked the sullen

skies above the terraced rooftop gardens stretching north
and southward along upper Fifth Avenue.

All the while he jiggled keys, he fumed, a stream of foul
words sputtering from his lips. Then, by chance, he happened to look down at the lock he'd been contending with
over the past quarter hour. Instead of the tarnished purplish
patina of decades-old dirt characteristic of each of the other
locks he'd tried, the face of this one was the fresh shiny
brass of one newly installed.

Not only was he certain that the lock had been changed
within the last several days, or possibly even the last several
hours (the face was that shiny and new), he was even more
certain his search was over and that his missing *Centurion*
lay just behind that door. But *that* door was a thick two
inches of sturdy oak, not easily forced. Several times, he
tried, jamming his full weight against it, succeeding only
in wrenching his shoulder.

He was at an impasse. In another two or two and a half
hours, the daytime staff would start straggling in. They
would be mostly kitchen, cafeteria, and janitorial personnel.
That would also be the time when the night security force
would shift to the day force—a fact, most definitely, to be
factored into the problem.

He was completely stymied. He had no idea what he was
going to do until he was actually doing it, walking, not
only quickly but with the sort of brisk, lunging gait that
prompts people to step quickly out of one's path. His tread
ricocheted off the cold travertine and boomed up into the
high-groined arches above him.

At the elevator, he made a sharp left, rejecting it in favor
of the stairs, ascending the half flight two steps at a time,
then glided through the swinging glass doors and on into
the museum's executive suites.

Passing his own office, he moved straight ahead to a
second half flight of stairs at the far end of the corridor. He
bounded up it without so much as a break in stride. At the
top of that flight, behind a tasteful but imposing set of glass

doors, lay the four-room suite of offices occupied by Walter Van Nuys, chairman of the board of directors of the Metropolitan Museum.

The outer office, a kind of antechamber-cum-reception area was the domain of Helen Mirkin, Van Nuys's personal assistant. Restrained in both layout and design, Helen Mirkin's office had no door, opening instead directly off the corridor through glass dividers. Opposite her desk, Van Nuys's office, with its authentic Corbusier furniture, rare Aubusson rugs, and priceless paintings, lay impregnable behind massive oak doors locked tighter than a bank vault.

Manship knew precisely what he was looking for but had no idea where to begin the search. Logic dictated that if the key to the storeroom was anywhere, it would be locked in a drawer or, possibly, a wall safe behind the stout oaken doors to Van Nuys's office. He didn't even wish to consider the possibility that Van Nuys might be carrying the key on his person, having taken it home for safekeeping.

His internal gyroscope took him on a beeline to Helen Mirkin's desk, where his feverish, bleary eyes swarmed across the desktop in search of the key. He found nothing unexpected there, Helen Mirkin being a compulsively fastidious type. Nothing was out of place—desk blotter, desk calendar, Rolodex, appointment book, a toby jug jammed tightly with freshly sharpened pencils. For the touch of importance, there was a pen and inkwell set of fake chalcedony, only slightly better than the sort of things banks give away with great fanfare whenever someone opens a new account. The closest thing to hint at some sort of personal life was a framed desk photograph of a nondescript middle-aged gentleman in a formal blue suit. This, one presumed, was Mr. Mirkin.

The top desk drawer, left unlocked, presented nothing more exotic than had the desktop—compulsively neat little trays of rubber bands, paper clips, a stapler, a pronged device for removing staples, a handheld, battery-powered plastic computer. Finally, there was a key. It hung on a

beaded brass chain, along with a small rectangular wood
plaque on which was written: "Women's Washroom. Staff
Only. MMA."

He muttered an obscenity, replaced everything in the
drawer precisely as he'd found it, then rolled the drawer
shut without making a sound. Above all, he had no wish
to alert the security people, who patrolled the area on a
strict regular basis.

Several drawers later, with hope fading fast, he found
what he was looking for. It sat in the lower right-hand
drawer in a little tin soapdish. His eye caught it at once,
even though a somewhat halfhearted attempt had been
made to cover it over with a small vest-pocket map of lower
Manhattan.

His heart actually leapt as he plucked it out and held it
up to the light. In the next moment, he was tracking at a
near trot across the floor to the big oak doors leading to
the chairman's office.

He wasn't prepared for what happened next. In his overwrought, overtired state of mind, it never occurred to him
that the key he held might quite possibly *not* be the key to
Walter Van Nuys's office. Just as before with the lock
downstairs, he stood there before Van Nuys's doors, jamming this key into the lock, and just as before, he felt its
immediate rejection, its clear lack of fit. He kept at it a
while, a look of disbelief on his face, twisting hard, willing
the tumblers to turn by means of oaths and a series of
complicated body gyrations.

It was then that something shamefully obvious occurred
to him. This key he was jamming and twisting, then fuming
and cursing at was a brass key. It had the same bright,
glittery, unmistakably new sheen to it as its counterpart, the
lock face on the storeroom door.

He had no recollection of departing Mirkin's office, storm-
ing back through the Greek and Roman galleries, past the
Great Hall and the galleries of Egyptian art, finding himself

at last standing before the storeroom door that scarcely less than an hour ago had denied him entry.

He laughed aloud at the ease with which the bright little brass key slipped into the shiny new face of the lock. A slight flick of the fingers and at once he felt the well-oiled tumblers mesh beneath his eager hand. He pushed, not with his hand but with the tip of a finger. The latch bolt clicked, slid backward into the frame plate, and the short, heavy door drifted open with a soft sigh.

A musty breath of airlessness and the odor of machine oil wafted outward from the darkened interior. His groping fingers reached inward and to the right. He found first the switch plate, then the switch itself. Flicking it up, his eyes, accustomed to darkness and shadow, were momentarily blinded. Seconds later, he stood there stunned.

It was like entering the arsenals of Charlemagne or Frederick the Great. A treasure-house of armor and weaponry glistened from within. The original owners of all that fearful panoply had been emperors and nomads, pirates and knights. Some had been famous, like Richard I and Bobadilla. Most had been anonymous warriors or jousting knights who'd tilted with Vikings and Saracenes.

Like a man hip-high in heavy brush, Manship waded in, starting his search. He pored through helmets of burnished gold, inlaid with cloisonné; blades of steel from the fifteenth century, with grips of jade and jewels; from eighteenth-century Mughal, diamond-and-emerald-studded scabbards; and fierce weaponry of every imaginable kind, crafted by the finest gunsmiths in the Islamic world; firearms from Morocco and the Balkans, all part of the once-sprawling Ottoman empire. But of the *Centurion,* there was no sign.

With the coming of dawn, he'd begun to doubt his initial instinct. Panicked, he toyed with the idea of moving on to other storerooms. But still, he couldn't overlook the bright little brass key and the freshly changed lock in the door. That had to mean something.

It was not until well past 5:00 A.M. that he found what he'd been seeking. It sat behind a stack of sixteenth-century German flintlocks; it was wrapped in chamois, like a piece of cast-off rubbish destined for burial in some landfill in New Jersey. When he lifted the chamois, the ruined canvas flowed outward in long, drooping strips. It had never been one of Botticelli's great paintings. But when Manship first saw it in Istanbul, recognizing at once all of its flaws, along with its quiet grandeur, he'd fallen for it without qualification or regret.

Coming across reproductions of it in dusty old portfolios while still a student at the Institute, Manship had felt an instant affinity with it, this painting of the good Centurion of Capernaum, whom both Matthew and Luke had gone out of their way to honor in the Gospels. He'd sensed the dignity, the strength, the inherent decency of the nobleman who'd sought out Christ to cure his ailing slave.

There it hung now in shreds and tatters, narrow strips that could never be sewn in such a way as to restore it to even a semblance of its former glory, having suffered the mindless destruction at the hands of a madman seething with a sense of personal grievance or, perhaps, thinking himself the instrument of some divine retribution.

Now that its function as exhibition art had been all but ended, Manship was determined to give the work another life. If it could no longer be a painting, it would become an educational tool, a public warning to the world, putting it on notice of the perishability of its most precious possessions.

Before leaving that morning, he dictated a message to Taverner over his phone mail. In it, he gave some last-minute instructions for the opening night and thanked her for the heroic efforts she'd made on behalf of the show, then authorized a salary increase for her on the occasion of her first anniversary at the museum.

He concluded with a simple sentence, as if it were an

afterthought: He was flying to Rome that evening on the 6:00 P.M. Alitalia flight from Kennedy. He offered no explanation for the trip or why he chose not to be in attendance at the opening of an exhibition that would no doubt stand as the pinnacle of his professional life. The message gave no address where he could be reached in Rome. Even he didn't know where he would be in the next twenty-four hours.

THIRTY-NINE

There was more traffic on the street at that hour, 6:00 A.M., than anyone might have reasonably expected. Fleets of taxis prowled Fifth Avenue for early fares. Lines of buses lumbered up to stops, brakes gasping, hydraulic doors flapping open where early risers waited to board.

It was no typical day for Manship. Far from it. The day of his show's opening—it should have been a joyous occasion. For Manship, it was quite the opposite, but he was determined not to brood too much about it.

About one thing, however, he had no doubts. He would tender his resignation to Van Nuys sometime within the next four weeks. For now, first in his mind was to get to Rome and see how he might help in the search for Isobel Cattaneo, his unreasoning need to do that still a mystery to him, but becoming less so with each passing day and hour.

The blare of a horn roused him from his musings to suddenly find himself in the middle of Eighty-fifth Street just as the lights were changing from yellow to red. He bounded the rest of the way across the street, landing safely on the other side, and brushed past a figure standing at the curb's edge. There was nothing particularly remarkable about the figure except for the space it occupied, so sharply defined that it created an island of distinct isolation in a sea of swarming humanity.

Manship hadn't actually seen the figure. It was a man glimpsed out of the corner of an eye. Still, there was something about him that had caught his attention. Nothing tangible—perhaps only the attitude conveyed in the posture—aloof and unapproachable, something off-putting enough to make one instinctively shy away.

It struck a cord in Manship, then was gone in an instant, disappearing like a puff of bad air. In the next moment, he was bounding up the stoop at 5 East Eighty-fifth, turning his key in the lock.

Mrs. McCooch was there at the door, startled as well as

relieved to see him, silently disapproving his unshaven face and rumpled suit. Where had he spent the night? she seemed to ask. Years in the service of various employers, she'd long ago learned to ask no questions. Instead, she urged him into the kitchen with the lure of fresh coffee, bacon, and eggs.

Manship had no further occasion to think of that phantom figure until some fifteen hours later, but by then it was too late.

The day of the exhibition passed like a dream. Manship had moved through it like a sleepwalker, legs a bit leaden, mind strangely disengaged.

After breakfast, a shave, and a shower, by 9:00 A.M. that morning he had nothing to do but wait until 4:00 P.M., when he would call for a taxi to take him out to the airport for his flight at six. Time crept and the hours wore on slowly.

He'd resolved that under no circumstances would he set foot back in the museum that day. Leave it to René and Van Nuys, Osgood and Taverner. Let them clash with the Leonardo of lighting and contend with Mr. Tsacrios over his phyllo dough. Let them squabble over who was to get the lion's share of accolades for mounting the show. Let them devour one another. Walk away, Manship. Walk away. Wash your hands of them.

Before leaving the museum that morning, he'd concealed his *Centurion*, but he had definite plans on that score. He owed it to Maestro Botticelli. Paying off his debt to the artist would require some inside cooperation, and he was by no means yet certain where he would find it.

Until the right moment, no one must learn that he'd penetrated Van Nuys's hiding place and walked off with the painting. After the show, it would no longer matter if his actions in the predawn hours of that morning were to become general knowledge. But for the moment, the element of surprise was paramount.

Throughout the rest of the day, he'd kept trying to contact Ettore Foa's office at the Italian embassy in Washington. He was repeatedly rebuffed each time by the same stubbornly uninformative assistant and told only that Mr. Foa was out of town and couldn't be reached.

Though Manship had never met Foa personally, his impression of the man from speaking with him several times on the phone was that he was dealing with an intelligent, worldly individual. More importantly, he also came across as someone entirely sympathetic to Isobel's predicament.

The total absence of any communication now from the deputy ambassador seemed uncharacteristic of the man and a bit ominous, as well.

Maeve breezed in somewhere near 10:00 A.M., still attired in the dressy outfit she'd obviously gone out in the day before. Seeing him there flustered her. It was embarrassing, yet she couldn't say exactly why. After all, weren't they free agents? Grown, consenting adults? Still, she could read his thoughts as his eyes perused all of the telltale signs of her evening with Osgood. Mrs. McCooch's silent judgment didn't help much, either.

Maeve excused herself and whisked upstairs to her room. Minutes later, winding up a few minor last-minute details in his own room, he heard her through the plaster walls talking on the phone to Tom Costain in La Jolla. Several times, her voice rose angrily; at other times, it sounded guarded, alternately tense and soothing. He imagined they were having some sort of spat, that Costain was shouting and that she was giving back as good as she was getting.

From what he could gather through snatches of conversation, it seemed that Costain felt she had stayed on far longer than was seemly. The funeral was over; the legal arrangements made. He was now insisting she return. It didn't sound as though she was quite ready to do that. In addition to which, Costain was unaware of the recent Osgood factor.

When she came downstairs again, she looked rattled and

white. She was in the process of exorcising all past fear of her second husband. Speaking to Manship, she was unaware that she spoke too fast and that her laughter was too frequent and seemed forced.

She wanted to show Manship the dress she'd bought at Bergdorf's for the opening that night. "Wait right there," she said, darting back upstairs to her room. She emerged moments later, descending the stairway. The stair was far too modest for the grandness of her descent.

The dress was a skintight black silk sheath that showed off her slim hips, small breasts, and thin, fine legs to great advantage. At age thirty-four, she still had the figure of a high school girl. How she'd maintained it locked up in a studio in Southern California, painting sixteen hours a day, was a mystery to him.

"Well?" She was a bit breathless standing there, hands on hips, feet pointed outward like a dancer in first position. There was a defiance in her carriage, as if she dared him not to like it. In spite of all her jauntiness, she seemed to hunger for his approbation, and he gave it.

"Beautiful, Maeve. Really."

"You mean it?"

"I wouldn't say it if I didn't."

"Sexy?"

"Very," he said, surprised at the pang of envy he felt for Osgood and the night he'd just spent with her.

Her laugh was a girlish giggle. She was clearly delighted. He'd not seen her quite so up in years. He knew she was going to the opening with Osgood. He didn't have to ask, although he knew that she wanted him to.

"I can't believe you're skipping out on your own show," she said moments later, following him into the library. "McCooch just told me," she fretted. "Probably the highlight of your career, and you're chucking it. Well, I guess that's what they call style, Marky." She shook her head at him in wonderment. "You always had it. Lots of style but little sense. Can't you say what this is all about?"

"It's too complicated to go into now."

"It has something to do with this Italian woman, doesn't it? This Isobel?"

"Yes," he conceded wearily. "But don't ask me any more. Not now at least. How's Tom?"

"Don't ask," she shot back, and they both laughed, genuinely fond of each other.

A short time later, Osgood arrived. He hadn't expected to find Manship there. He glanced at Maeve, his eyes seeking some hint of what Manship might know. The two of them were as nervous as two adolescents caught bundling in the attic.

Manship took all of that in with a glance.

Maeve went upstairs to change, leaving him and Osgood alone together in the library. When Manship said nothing, Osgood felt obliged to. Clearing his throat, he started awkwardly. "I s'pose you know."

"Look, don't feel you have to explain."

"I don't."

"Good."

"But I want to."

"If it makes you feel better," Manship offered expansively. "Whatever happens, I want you to know I'm pleased for both of you."

Osgood's taut, anxious look relaxed. He shrugged in that wry Texas way and laughed.

"But I should warn you," Manship quickly added, "you're not out of the woods yet. You're going to have to deal with Tom Costain. He'll teach you things about the art of litigation you scarcely dreamed possible."

Osgood was about to reply, but instead, Manship hurriedly informed him of his plans to go to Rome that evening, and why he felt he had to.

"Now listen, Bill. I need a favor, and you're the only one I can trust to do it without making a balls-up of everything."

Hastily and in half whispers, he explained the situation

with the *Centurion* and told Osgood what had to be done with it.

Osgood sat stonily, not speaking for several moments afterward. Manship sensed he was looking desperately for a graceful way to decline. After all, he had far more to lose than Manship.

At last, he unwound his loose, gangly legs and spoke. "You realize this will be the end of your career at the Met?"

"I certainly hope so. It will spare me the trouble of having to draft my own resignation."

"You'll never work in a museum again, Mark—at least, not in any responsible position."

"Sounds fine to me."

Osgood gazed at him skeptically. "His heart's not good, you realize. He could expire in an apoplectic seizure."

Manship pondered the possibility, then replied solemnly, "In which case, I'd be shortlisted for the Nobel Peace Prize."

Osgood reared back as if ducking a blow. Then, both of them were doubled over, howling.

FORTY

Long before sunrise, Borghini had set out from Battery Park, leaving the Harbor Rest shrouded in mist behind him. Armed with a small map he'd purchased at a cigar store, he'd made his way through the empty predawn streets of lower Broadway, Chinatown, through SoHo, narrow, silent lanes of warehouses and loading docks, and on to the Village. By the crack of dawn he'd crossed Washington Square Park and was starting up Fifth Avenue.

An hour later, he stood out front, across the street from the museum and watched the enormous pennant above the pillared entryway drift lazily up and down in the soft morning breeze. Imprinted on its silken folds was a huge blowup of the worldly, slightly jaded smile of the Primavera, along with the words BOTTICELLI. 550 emblazoned in large bold letters across the banner's full length.

Later, he walked into the park. He urinated behind a bush, then strolled the wooded, leaf-strewn paths. He sat idly on a bench and watched the joggers and children being walked to school, and young business types cutting briskly across the Sheep Meadow on their way to work.

There were hours to wait before he must swing into action. He would have to find ways to kill time. He didn't mind. Strangely, he felt a certain peace, a sense of divine approval in the benevolence of that bright autumn morning. The day, fully dawned, promised to be brilliant.

By 9:00 A.M., he was at the zoo, the first person there when the gate opened. A short time later, a busload of school children arrived for a day's outing in the park. Borghini stood there a while, full of a sense of secret pleasure, watching the elephants. Outside in their concrete patios, floors splattered with heaps of steaming dung, the elephants dozed on their feet. Tails switching, they dreamed of open skies and dimly-remembered broad savannahs a half-world away.

Going wherever his footsteps led him, he circled the seal

pool, watching the sleek, bullet-shaped silhouettes glide effortlessly over and under the oily surface of the water, their hoarse cries ringing on the silky air. Laughing to himself, he watched the polar bear with his dirty coat having an icy morning bath in his pool. Behind him, park attendants, slight-framed Ecuadorians and Peruvians in brown uniforms, made scratching music as they pushed rubbish along ahead of their massive straw brooms.

Later, he sat at a table beneath an umbrella outside the cafeteria. He had coffee and a roll and watched the mechanical bronze animals of the zoo clock promenade in circles to proclaim the passing of the hour.

He hadn't bathed for several days and took the opportunity to wash up in the men's room of the cafeteria. He removed his shirt and rinsed his face and under his arms. People coming in to use the facilities avoided his eyes and gave him a wide berth.

Later, outside on the footpaths, in his nearly full-length raincoat, a crumpled slouch hat pulled down low over his brow, he mingled with parents and strollers. The impression he conveyed was vaguely dissolute. He walked stiffly on his elevated shoes, one hand plunged deep in his pocket, that hand wrapped around the hilt of a razor-sharp kris.

Along about noon, he bought a frankfurter and an orange soda from a park vendor. Standing under the fellow's brightly striped umbrella, he chewed, scarcely tasting any of his food, and watched waves of ecstatic children scurrying up and down the paths.

It was past five when Borghini got back to the Met. A normal workday, the museum was scheduled to close at six and the reception for the show would start promptly at eight. All of that, he had carefully written down in a small black pad he carried in an inside jacket pocket.

The police were already there out front, setting up barricades, cordoning off the main entrance, where opening-night guests would start to arrive in less than ninety

minutes. An NBC mobile camera unit had parked its van
outside the entrance on Fifth Avenue. Its team of technicians ran spools of cable up the stone stairway, setting up
lights, drinking coffee from paper cups.

Small clots of curious onlookers had begun to form behind the barricades. They jockeyed up and down the line,
seeking out the best up-front positions.

Borghini joined the excited group of spectators. "What's
happening?" he asked a woman who'd obviously been
there some time.

She was eating an egg-salad sandwich out of a paper bag.
"They're having some kind of show."

"A show? What kind of show?"

"Some kind of big art show. Gonna be lots of celebrities.
Big names."

"Oh?" Borghini beamed happily.

"Some excitement, huh?" A daub of egg salad clung to
her lip.

"Yes, a lot of excitement." Borghini nodded, looking
around at the police patrol cars and the TV crews.

At promptly 6:00 P.M., those visitors who'd been touring
the museum that day began to stream out of the main entrance. Dozens of uniformed security guards took up their
positions at the ground-floor exits.

Borghini continued to watch the prereception activity. A
buzz of excitement had begun to radiate through the milling
crowd. Its numbers had grown noticeably over the past
quarter hour and continued to do so.

At several minutes past six, two paneled trucks pulled
up to the curb. Borghini watched seven or eight men spill
from the trucks, file around to the rear of the lead truck,
and proceed to unload enormous trays of food and chafing
dishes. The trucks were a bright, fresh garden green and
the lettering on their side panels identified them as the property of Tsacrios Bros. Purveyors of Fine Food and
Drink.

Borghini watched the men unload the trucks, each of

them marching trays and platters up the stairs and in through the heavily guarded entryway.

At a certain opportune moment, just as all of the Tsacrios personnel were preoccupied with the long trek up to the entrance, the two panel trucks were left unguarded.

It was then that Borghini had started to thread his way through the throng. He marched up to the lead truck and, with all of the assurance of the proprietor himself, removed from it a huge platter of smoked salmon and caviar. In the next moment, he was marching his platter up the stairs, trailing not too far behind the first phalanx of food and cup bearers.

When he reached the door, one of the three or four guards stationed there, noting that he wasn't dressed in the black-and-white houndstooth trousers and white monkey jackets of the other waiters, gave him a puzzled look. The man gazed at Borghini's raincoat and muddy shoes and frowned. He was about to ask questions but the colonel, anticipating that, headed him off.

"Which way?" he inquired brusquely.

The guard's gaze continued to assess the slightly disheveled man in the plastic raincoat, but the tray of canapés he carried finally conquered the fellow's doubt.

"Round the corner to your right. Palace of Dendur," the guard yielded and waved him on.

The colonel hoisted his tray onto his shoulder and swept into the museum.

FORTY-ONE

They were having cocktails in the first-class cabin and preparing to serve dinner when the Alitalia 747 New York-London-Rome flight began to descend. That was a bit off-putting, in that they hadn't been airborne more than an hour and a half since their liftoff from Kennedy.

No one paid much attention. Most people, like Manship, merely assumed that the pilots were making an altitude correction. Others thought they were simply imagining it, sinking deeper into their second martini or Bloody Mary.

Then the seat-belt signs came on, advising passengers to buckle up, as the rate of descent became faster and decidedly more purposeful. At that point, people began to glance questioningly at one another. Still no announcement came from the flight cabin.

The plane was clearly not out of control. The descent was orderly. The flight attendants, unfazed, made no dire announcements regarding life preservers or emergency exit doors. It looked like business as usual.

Manship, curiously uneasy, glanced out the window. Puffs of vapory clouds scudded past, leaving little droplets of condensation streaking down the glass. In the occasional breaks, he caught glimpses of tiny lights from what appeared to be widely scattered dwellings, suggesting a sparsely inhabited area.

Only when they landed and were taxiing up to an administration building did the captain come on over the PA system and, with that carefully studied nonchalance of airline captains, announce that they'd made an unscheduled landing in St. John's, Newfoundland. It was purely procedural, nothing mechanical. They would be there no more than a few minutes at most and would then be departing directly for London, then on to Rome.

The plane never reached the administration building, but, instead, taxied to a bumpy stop out on the runway. A good deal of murmuring and edgy laughter filled the cabin, but still no explanation seemed forthcoming.

If Manship was apprehensive, he couldn't say precisely why. A short time later, a pale, blond Milanese stewardess, more uneasy than he, moved nervously to his seat, knelt over, and whispered in his ear, "Please remove your belongings from the overhead compartment and follow me."

All conversation in the cabin ceased as people watched them move forward up the aisle in the direction of the flight cabin. Mystified, Manship followed the young woman, feeling like a recaptured escaped felon. When they entered the flight deck and closed the door, he was suddenly aware of a number of faces all directed at him.

The captain was a swarthy Calabrian with wavy dark hair and a handlebar mustache. Gazing up at Manship from the pilot's seat, he addressed him. "You are Mr. Manship?"

"I am."

The captain squinted down at a passenger manifest. "Mr. Mark Manship?"

"That's right."

For such a close area, the space was crowded. Most of the flight crew had jammed in, as well as two gentlemen in civilian dress.

"I am Captain Pratesi. I am sorry to have to inconvenience you, but these gentlemen"—he gestured with what Manship thought a look of disdain in the direction of two men in civilian dress—"have several questions to ask you."

"May I ask these gentlemen to identify themselves?" Manship addressed his question to the captain.

One of the men opened a large vest-pocket wallet and flashed what was unmistakably a federal seal of some sort. By then, Manship knew very well why the plane had been ordered down in Newfoundland.

"All right." Manship nodded, determined to remain calm. "Fire away."

"Not here, sir. Outside, if you please."

They filed out through the flight crew's cabin door and down a disembarkation ladder that had been rolled up to the plane moments before. A car waited at the bottom of the ladder, its motor idling, the driver at the wheel smoking and listening to country-western music sung in a highly nasal Quebecois.

As they sped off in the direction of the administration building, Manship glanced back in time to see the disembarkation ladder being wheeled off by a Jeep. From inside the plane, a flight attendant had begun to seal the cabin door in preparation for departure.

"May I ask what all this is about?" Manship inquired, certain now that Van Nuys had discovered the *Centurion* was missing and had extracted from a terrified Taverner Manship's flight plans for that evening. With the possible theft of a Botticelli involved, it would not have been difficult for a man of Van Nuys's connections to prevail on the federal authorities to have the plane forced down and Manship brought back to face charges of grand larceny before he could vanish somewhere into thin air on the Continent.

"We're instructed to say nothing, Mr. Manship."

"In that case, where are you taking me?"

"To the other side of the terminal," the other agent replied. "There's a private plane waiting there to fly you back to New York."

The customs officials at Kennedy must have been radioed from St. John's. They didn't bother with passports, but whisked him through a side door and out into a kind of alleyway where a private government car awaited him, its motor running. A pair of burly motorcycle police in white helmets stood by to escort them back into the city.

For Manship, the episode was more embarrassing than frightening.

*   *   *

He was certain their destination was Rikers Island or the Tombs. Instead, somewhere close on to 10:00 P.M. they rolled up to the museum. Avoiding the main entrance, they chose instead to slip unobtrusively down the ramp leading to the underground garage, where an elevator waited to take them up to the reception. By then, Manship's embarrassment had changed to a slow, simmering anger.

By the time he stepped from the elevator into the gaudy dazzle of a New York gala, he was in no mood for conciliation.

As such things go, it was a star-studded evening. The event had brought out politicians and pundits as well as celebrities and "Kultur vultures" in full cry. Luminaries from the theater and corporate worlds drank Pol Roger side by side and pretended they cared about one another's ideas as they mingled and elbowed their way throughout the galleries of dazzling Botticelli paintings.

At a glance, one could see the Honorable Mayor of New York City, Rudolph Giuliani, then Senator Patrick Moynihan framed against one of the gorgeous Lemmi frescoes, glad-handing potential backers. Ex-Governor Mario Cuomo, on his way to a roasting at the Friars, paused to chat with Mrs. Pamela Harriman. Waves of courtiers and sycophants encircled the frail, tiny, jewel-bedizened frame of Mrs. Brooke Astor—among them ex-Mayor John Lindsay, William Buckley, and Norman Mailer. A rumor had swept the galleries that Katharine Hepburn was there, but no one actually claimed to have seen her.

Manship turned, to find himself peering into the grinning countenance of Bill Osgood.

"Aren't you in Rome?" he asked, then glanced inquisitively at the two federal agents on either side of Manship and divined the situation at once. "Well, I guess you're not."

Manship ignored the attempt at humor. "I'd like a few words with Van Nuys," he murmured grimly.

"Come along. I know exactly where you'll find the great

man." Osgood glanced at the two federal agents. "I suppose you chaps will want to tag along, too."

All four of them set out, Osgood leading them through the milling throng. The Texan, at least a full head taller than anyone else in the room, served as a kind of beacon they could easily follow through the shifting human maze.

Friends and colleagues, oblivious to Manship's situation at the moment, rushed up to congratulate him.

"Dazzling, Mark."

"Well done, old man."

"Just like old times, Mark. Sumptuous. Give us one a year."

A tall, heavily scented woman kissed his cheek. "Mark dear. Ted and I are thrilled. Call us next week for dinner. There's someone dying to meet you."

It was in gallery thirteen, more crowded than any of the others, that Osgood suddenly began to wave them eagerly forward. Several television crews were up ahead filming something.

The two federal agents were now running a small phalanx of interference before Manship, anxious to carry out the final phase of the night's operation. Less genteel than others there, they became a flying wedge, before which waves of people fell away like the Red Sea parting.

Manship had a glimpse of cameras. A sizable group of people had all clustered together around a relatively small area. Osgood had already reached there, his tall, whip-thin figure having knifed a path through the crowd. Down that path, Manship and the two agents streamed, moving directly up to the focus of activity, which turned out to be a pack of reporters all barking questions at once. The target of their attention was Walter Van Nuys. There he stood, a small fireplug of a man in a tuxedo.

As they heaved into sight, Van Nuys had his back to them, declaiming to the assembled press. René Klass and Pat Colbert hovered officiously nearby. Emily Taverner hung somewhat farther back. The subject of the talk was a painting on the wall, at which Van Nuys kept gesturing. The painting was Botticelli's *Centurion*—the good soldier, eyeless and in tatters. Seeing it there, horribly ravaged but somehow ennobled by all of the frightful wounds it had sustained, took Manship's breath away. The impact of it amidst that setting of glitter and inviolable privilege was overwhelming.

At that moment, Manship's gaze met Osgood's and the one sent the other a silent message of gratitude across the mobbed and overheated space.

Beside the *Centurion,* and blown up into a six-foot-two glass-framed panel was Manship's essay on society's role as protector and preserver of great art.

"We here at the Museum feel strongly that we must put ourselves on the line," Van Nuys proclaimed to a rapt audience. "As a foremost repository of much of the world's great art, we must be leaders. We must join with other institutions . . ."

Sensing a public-relations triumph, Van Nuys grew rhapsodic over the spectacle of the ruined painting. The reporters encircling him dutifully scribbled his every word into their tiny pads.

"There were some of us here, well-meaning to be sure," he went on, "who were dead set against a display such as this. In a setting ostensibly a celebration of the works of a great Renaissance master, they claimed such wanton destruction would be deeply disturbing, strike a note of discord. Possibly even encourage copycat behavior in unbalanced individuals. I confess I, too, felt reservations. But I also felt that we in the art world—directors, curators, conservators, and, especially, artists—we above all had a special responsibility to speak out. This morning, I personally made a plea to the Secretary General for the establishment of an international commission to enact a study into the subject of theft and the desecration of great art. The need to enact international policy, global laws . . ."

In that moment, Van Nuys's gaze happened to fall on

Manship standing there, along with Osgood and the two federal agents. His voice trailed off; his mind appeared to go blank. Most of the newsmen standing there were not immediately aware of it, but Manship was. He could see the flush rise in the old man's jowls and hear the quaver in his voice as it struggled to regain its note of pious authority.

By then, both René Klass and Taverner had spotted Manship in the crowd and guessed the problem. In the next instant, Van Nuys flashed a queasy grin at Manship. His eyes made a silent plea, as if to say, Not here, not now. Please.

The fact that he'd reversed his position on displaying the *Centurion* and now appeared to be taking full credit for what had become hands down one of the dark-horse highlights of the exhibit hadn't fazed Van Nuys in the least.

"He's undergone a remarkable conversion in a short period of time," Manship muttered.

"Hasn't he, though," Osgood replied, and shot him a knowing wink. "If I know him, he probably doesn't even know he has."

"What's going on here?" One of the agents tilted his head at Van Nuys. "This isn't Mr. Foa."

"Foa?" Manship wheeled at the mention of the name. "What was that about Foa?"

"Our orders are to turn you over to a Mr. Ettore Foa from the Italian embassy. Not this guy here." He shot a disparaging look at Van Nuys, who by then had recovered sufficiently to resume the press conference.

"Mr. Foa's in one of the other rooms," Osgood explained in a whisper.

Manship's feet nearly left the ground. "You mean Foa's here right now? In the museum?"

"Isn't that what I just said?"

"Where? Where is he?"

"That's our guy, too," the agent added. "Can you take us to him?"

"He was over in gallery nine the last time I looked."
Osgood's face wore a sly grin.

The galleries had meanwhile filled to near capacity. The
throng of guests in evening dress, along with squadrons of
waiters plying salvers of champagne gridlocked the aisles
and made the going slow.

Manship chafed at Osgood. "Why didn't you say anything?"

"About what?"

"About Foa."

"I knew nothing about him. You said nothing about him.
I only met the man a half hour ago."

"A half hour?"

"That's when he showed up. Apparently, you sent him
an invitation. Nice chap," Osgood remarked offhandedly.

It was perfectly true, Manship had to concede. He'd told
him nothing about Foa, or why he'd gone barging off like
a loose cannon to Rome on his opening night. He'd never
mentioned a word of it to anyone, except to Taverner, and
possibly Maeve.

Gallery nine, by contrast with the others, seemed relatively
empty. Many of Botticelli's sketches and drawings hung
there along with some larger works. Rather than being filled
by large, surging waves of people on a celebrity safari, this
gallery appeared to be occupied by cozy little clusters of
individuals, some actually more interested in the drawings
and paintings than the power games and fashion shows under way in many of the adjoining galleries.

"This way," Osgood cried out. "Over here," he called
over his shoulder, and plunged ahead.

Manship and the two agents staggered after him.

Osgood had stopped and was now chatting with a tall,
thinly elegant man with wavy gray hair. He was pointing
back to where Manship and the two agents were weaving
their way toward them. The tall gentleman turned and

peered directly at them. In the next moment, he disengaged himself from several other people with whom he'd been chatting and strode briskly toward Manship. He came on fast, hand outstretched long before they'd actually come anywhere close enough to shake.

Ettore Foa had the sort of eye-riveted-to-eye smile typical of people in the diplomatic corps. He looked older, too, Manship noted, than he'd sounded on the phone.

"Don't tell me. I know. You're Mark Manship."

Foa's hand was bony and dry, a thin patrician hand, smooth but at the same time strong. "You look just like you sound on the phone. I'd have known you anywhere," he rattled on in his crisp, slightly accented English.

Just behind him and to his left stood two women. Both were approximately the same height, remarkably similar in build, but from that point on the resemblance ended. One was Maeve, looking breathtaking in emerald green. The other, he didn't recognize at once, or rather, some part of him did, but his mind could not accept what his eyes told him; the sudden rush of blood to his head did.

"Ah, forgive me," Foa said. Noting where Manship's gaze had fixed, he steered him in the direction of the two women. "Mrs. Costain, of course, you know." He made one of those ineffably Italian flourishes toward the other waiting quietly there. "And may I present Signorina Cattaneo. . . ."

When at last he spoke, his voice made a hoarse, croaking sound. "We've already met."

"Twice," Isobel said.

Foa bowed his head deeply. For any other mortal, the gesture would have bordered on the ridiculous. But as executed by the Italian deputy ambassador, it was poetry.

"I hope you don't mind that I came," Isobel said.

"Mind? God no," Manship blurted out. "A short while ago I was on a plane to Rome to . . ."

His voice trailed off, conscious of Maeve observing them, the trace of a smile playing wickedly at her lips.

"I decided to take you up on your invitation." She looked pale and depleted. It seemed an effort for her to speak. "Your wife—"

"My wife?"

"Mrs. Costain."

"Former wife." Maeve smiled archly.

"Yes, of course." The correction appeared to have flustered her. "Mrs. Costain . . . was kind enough to lend me something to wear."

She laughed nervously and looked down at the dress as though seeing it for the first time. "I had to leave Italy rather quickly. I was unprepared for anything as grand as this." She looked uneasily around the room.

The dress she wore was the plain black sheath Maeve had bought to wear to the opening. On Isobel, it gave the appearance of a light drape laminated to the hard angularity of her body.

"It took a bit of diplomatic doing to get her here." Foa expanded on the adventure he'd been having. "Your FAA was not all that eager to order an Italian airliner down in Newfoundland. It nearly required an act of Congress, plus a very stern phone call from your Justice Department to send the FBI up there to fetch you. You're still a free citizen, you know."

"You can't know how relieved I am to hear that," Manship replied, his eyes fixed Isobel.

Foa breezed on. "I hope you'll forgive me. The inconvenience I put you to. I didn't care to have you go by yourself to Italy. Not at this time. For one thing, Borghini is still at large. For another, Rome is crawling with his people, who, as you know, are mostly demented. I wouldn't depend much on their sympathy, if for some reason your paths happened to cross."

Like most of his countrymen, Foa had that seemingly effortless flow of talk that everyone is grateful for at tense moments. "The signorina has had a bit of an adventure herself. But I'm sure she'll tell you all about it, in her own good time.''

Manship's gaze came back to the woman under discussion. She had worn her hair down, Simonetta-style, for the occasion, and he wondered if that in any way had been an olive branch to him. She was standing directly beneath the *Chigi Madonna,* which had been loaned by Boston's Gardner Museum. Seeing her in juxtaposition to the full painting in all of its grandeur, his eye happened to stray along the wall to the series of Chigi sketches.

They hung there in such a pleasing arrangement that Manship failed to note that the deliberate gap he'd planned to leave open to indicate the three missing sketches was no longer there. For a fraction of a second, he sensed something askew, but he couldn't say what. Then he understood. Instead of the ten sketches intended to hang there, the full thirteen now occupied the space.

His first impulse was to get up close to them, to feel— or even to smell—them in order to make certain his eyes didn't deceive him. He moved from one to the other, his cheek at one point nearly brushing with his own flesh the pale gray tracery of the master's line. It was as though he were trying to breathe in the essence of paper and lead, until at last he felt a shock of connection with old Alessandro himself. He felt his eyes moisten, and he turned away.

When he turned back, he was aware of all of them watching him. But he was watching Isobel.

Foa glowed. ''That is Signorina Cattaneo's little surprise for you. She told us where we could find them.''

A small crowd had gathered behind them, studying the preliminary sketches as they worked their way along the wall to the full glory of the finished work. In their perfectly fluid order and balance, they looked as though they'd always occupied that space. They gave no hint of the five years of anger, frustration, and occasional despair involved in bringing all thirteen sketches together in culmination of this moment.

It would be hard to imagine a jaded old city like New York stirred up over the presence of a direct descendant of Alessandro Botticelli's favorite model. Nonetheless, the city roused itself to the occasion. In the mysterious way of such things, a combination of shrewd press agentry and word of mouth had suddenly put the name Simonetta on everyone's lips.

In no time, photographers and reporters were nosing about, sensing a new angle. They found it in Isobel. Most of them hadn't the faintest idea who the striking young lady was until her connection with the unforgettable countenance in such works as the *Primavera* and the *Chigi Madonna* was pointed out to them. From then on, the cameras clicked madly. Lights flashed. Questions were barked at her from every direction, and someone asked her to stand before the *Chigi Madonna* to have her picture taken. In that moment, the uncanny, eerily perfect resemblance to the famous face came home to Manship as never before.

Shortly, strolling musicians dressed in harlequin tunics and Tuscan pantaloons, strumming lutes and banging tambourines, came around, announcing that dinner was about to be served upstairs on the roof garden.

As they started up, Van Nuys and a stout woman Manship presumed to be Mrs. Van Nuys hustled up breathlessly. Van Nuys had heard that Signorina Cattaneo was there. He seemed miffed that he'd heard it by chance from an acquaintance and had not been officially notified.

Barely acknowledging the presence of anyone else, Van Nuys swept down on Isobel and proceeded to engulf her with unwanted attention. For some reason, he'd started to speak with a vaguely British accent as his conversation with her grew increasingly uplifted.

Isobel appeared to be embarrassed. Van Nuys took that to be a sign that she was flattered by the attentions of such a lofty personage as he. As for Manship and Osgood, the chief executive officer of the Metropolitan had completely forgotten the fact that the *Centurion* was at that moment, against his expressed wishes, on exhibition in gallery thirteen. In light of all the acrimony he'd whipped up over the painting, his attitude toward both men was remarkably benign. That may have had something to do with the fact that, having taken the unusual step of exhibiting a great painting irreparably vandalized, the museum had scored a sizable public-relations victory. Van Nuys had already accepted an invitation to appear on the *Today Show* to speak specifically about the painting's recent destruction in Istanbul and the museum's courage and determination to bring it to the United States in order to tell its story.

Van Nuys had by then appropriated Isobel for himself, leaving Manship to escort Mrs. Van Nuys up to dinner. Maeve and Osgood fell in behind the little procession.

The elevator doors slid noiselessly open at the roof garden level and they walked out into the soft glare of flickering lights. Before them, candlelit tables set with silver and crystal and rich napery shimmered in a perfect grid of rows and aisles. Fresh flowers adorned each table, while all about the roof stood huge stone urns and terracotta pots full of flowers and trees brought in especially for the occasion. Mr. Tsacrios, resplendent in tails, stood beaming at the entrance, brandishing a large scroll listing table assignments.

The evening, for late September, was mild, even springlike. Heavy rains from the night before had swept the clouds out to sea, leaving in their wake an air quality of such clarity that the legendary skyline from river to river produced the optical effect of being far closer than it actually was. Looking south, the sky above the Theater District glowed a brick red. A delicate calligraphy of lights etched a spidery pattern of intersecting footpaths meandering their way west across the darkened park. Where they ended, the West Side began, all ablaze in the raucous nocturnal life of the great city. Lights glittered everywhere. A billion megawatts radiated power and indestructability. So gay and welcoming it was, like some huge amusement park, one would never suspect the human dislocation and social breakdown roiling on the darkened streets below.

FORTY-TWO

Since shortly after 6:00 P.M., Borghini had been moving about the museum with complete freedom, observing much, staying out of sight. Having assumed the identity of one of the catering staff, he'd proceeded to play the part perfectly.

The staff was by no means permanent. Consisting mostly of private contractors hiring out for the night, the presence of a new face among them caused no stir.

Having carried his tray of canapés to the Temple of Dendur, where a bar had been set up for guests more eager for refreshment than for viewing art, Borghini then followed several of the waiters to the kitchen of the museum restaurant on the ground floor.

Most of the group had already assembled in the locker room, changing from street clothes into professional attire provided by the caterers for their personnel that evening. There had been a great deal of playful banter and horsing about as people donned smocks, toques, and the classic houndstooth trousers of the kitchen staff. Those at the more lofty levels of the hierarchy donned tails for the occasion.

Borghini slipped easily into the routine, even joshing with some of the more friendly types as he pulled off his street wear to slip into one of the waiters' costumes piled in a stack nearby. But when the others had reported directly back to the bar to pick up trays holding flutes of chilled champagne, Borghini instead had peeled off from the group and ducked down a stairway into the basement of the building.

The colonel's plan was to lose himself inside the vast sprawl of galleries and hallways until such time, he reasoned, he could blend in more easily with the gathering throng.

He idled for a while in the basement. Moving briskly through snaking corridors where generators, turbines, and transformers hummed with quiet authority, he looked like a senior member of the catering staff dispatched to the bowels of the building to carry out some highly critical function.

His eyes followed the unending lengths of wide-gauge pipe as they wound their way along the ceiling. At one point, he came to a wall of fuse boxes, literally hundreds of them, fastened by means of brackets into the concrete. A tangled maze of multicolored electrical wire sprouted from the tops of each box, shooting off in every conceivable direction. Each marked with a small white square of adhesive designated the specific area of the museum that particular box serviced. Borghini duly noted the place and location of the boxes that serviced the roof garden and second-floor galleries.

The sound of approaching voices and footsteps brought him around sharply. He had barely enough time to step into a nearby broom closet before a pair of security guards passed within two or three feet of him. He watched them through a crack in the door. They scarcely gave the closet a glance, then moved on, their lively talk fading into the distance.

Borghini groped for a light switch, quickly finding it on a wall to his right. Flicking it on, he found himself in one of those deep closets equipped with a sink used by porters. The floor was cluttered with pails and mops. The narrow space reeked of disinfectants. Flicking the light back off, he spent the next hour standing upright in darkness while soap fumes and detergents wafted upward all about him, causing his eyes to tear.

"What's wrong, Mark?"

"Wrong?"

"You're scowling. You ought to be delirious. I don't think the Met has ever produced a show more spectacular or intelligent."

"That's very kind of you, Maeve."

"I'm not saying it to be kind, you idiot. It happens to be true. Old Botticelli ought to be very pleased."

They'd gone through the first two courses of Mr. Tsacrios's projected six-course banquet. Across from them sat
Osgood, Foa, Isobel, and Van Nuys who, uninvited, had
appropriated a place for himself at their table. Short one
setting, Mrs. Van Nuys had been fobbed off to some other
table and apparently abandoned there.

Since the start of dinner, an endless procession of people
kept filing up to the table, greeting Osgood, paying court
to Van Nuys, but lavishing praise on Manship. The more
praises lavished, the more he seemed to shrink.

"Really, Mark," Maeve fretted as a couple departed
their table. "You're behaving strangely. What's wrong with
you?"

"Nothing's wrong. I keep telling you. It's just that—"

"It's just what?"

"It's all wrong. It's not what I wanted. I had something
else in mind," he said gloomily.

"What's wrong? You mean this?" Her hand swept
around the glittering room with its dazzling array of the
rich and powerful. A fanfare sounded and the sextet of
strolling players entered in procession, playing Renaissance
canzones on authentic period instruments.

Manship cringed. "All of this." He nodded his head ve-
hemently. "All this cheap theater. What the hell does it
have to do with anything?"

Overhearing his plaint, Osgood glanced up sharply. Manship attempted a smile, then lowered his voice.

Puzzled and annoyed, Maeve shook her head. "Okay, I
grant you, it is a bit glitzy. But part of your job is glitz.
That's how you hawk art nowadays. When will you learn
that? Show business goes with the territory, or haven't you
heard? You don't get to spend your life sequestered all day
with great painting and get off scot-free from all the grubby
striving of the commercial world. You pay a toll for that.
The toll happens to be marketing. It's the thing that makes
your gorgeous show possible. How many people do you
think will show up here tomorrow, line up to pay their

seven or eight dollars to see your Botticellis? You think they're coming to see Botticelli? They're coming because the show's been hyped to the sky—written about, spoken about. Those silly pipers in pantaloons will be all over the newspapers and television tomorrow. That's what keeps museums open and crowds lining up outside. That's what keeps people like you and me working. I love it. I love meeting my public at each opening. If that makes me superficial, so be it. Lighten up, Mark. Without them, we're nothing—zero. So don't sit there and whine to me about how your show turned out. It turned out precisely the way you wanted it to: a huge success. Just the way you planned it from the very start. Think how you'd have felt if no one had bothered to come."

Crestfallen, he gazed around at the shimmering crystal and candlelight, taking her criticism with uncharacteristic docility.

A waiter had begun to serve portions of lamb mignonette; another removed goblets of white wine and replaced them with red. Off to the side, another waiter had appeared. Drifting beneath the archway of a shadowy alcove, he paused, as though counting dinner guests, then stooped over beside a nearby cupboard, sorting out additional silverware. The cupboard stood nearly twenty yards away from where the Manship party sat. From time to time, the waiter glanced around that table, studying faces, but by far, the major share of his attention was fixed on the striking young woman seated next to Walter Van Nuys. The waiter's face was mostly in shadow, his features barely discernible.

His task of counting silver completed, he rose and moved off quickly. A short time later, Mr. Tsacrios himself appeared at the Manship table, his guest list unscrolled.

"Excuse me, is there a Miss Cattaneo at this table?"

"Yes," Isobel's voice fluttered. "I'm Miss Cattaneo."

"There's a phone call for you. It's just outside here. Come, I'll show you."

Looking somewhat rattled, Isobel rose. "Excuse me, please," she murmured, and followed Mr. Tsacrios's trim, brisk, figure down the aisle.

Mellowed by wine and lamb, Maeve watched Manship's gaze follow her receding figure. "I see now what sent you dashing back to Rome on the opening night of your show," she remarked, more amused than disturbed. "If I didn't have consolations of my own just now, I'd be a bit put out."

"Oh, cut it out, Maeve."

"I'm serious. I don't think you ever looked at me that way." Then, as if she didn't think the subject worth pursuing, she changed it. "I spoke to Tom tonight. I told him I was delaying my return."

"For how long?"

"Indefinitely." Her fork speared a chunk of lamb and guided it to her lips.

"How did he take that?"

"Can't you guess?" She moved the lamb around in her mouth. "Anyway, I'll be here at least until Christmas. I've decided that the Cosmos gallery is either incompetent or completely crooked. I lean more to the less charitable explanation."

"And you now conclude that your presence here at this time is indispensable?"

"Well, I certainly can't trust them to mount my show by themselves. And you needn't worry that I'm moving in on you for the next three months."

"You'd be more than welcome if you did."

"That's sweet of you, Mark, even if you don't mean it." Her eyes drifted across the table to where Osgood sat deep in conversation with Ettore Foa. "And besides, his place is bigger and more comfortable than yours."

"And the poor fellow has no one with whom to share it."

"He does now." She winked at him and speared another chunk of lamb.

It was at that moment the lights went out on the roof garden. It didn't happen all at once, but in a slow, orderly succession, from one row to the next, leaving only the pale orange glow of guttering candles looking like fiery wraiths dancing across the sudden darkness. A collective gasp went up, followed by laughter and some scattered applause.

Captain MacWirter, chief of security, and his deputy assistant, Roberto Santos, were just leaving the American Wing, making their rounds and heading toward the Lehman Collection, when Santos's beeper sounded at his hip.

"Lights seem to have blown on the roof, sir," the young man reported.

"Probably a fuse. Notify the electrician's office," MacWirter snapped, then tugged Santos back by the elbow. "What am I saying? The chief won't be here at this hour. I'll go down, have a look myself. You go on up to the roof. Make sure everything's okay up there."

Santos moved smartly out toward a nearby staircase.

"Take a few of the others with you," MacWirter called out after him. "It's probably nothing. But just to be on the safe side."

He turned and started down the stairs into the basement. "Damn. Wouldn't you know it? Right in the middle of Mr Manship's wingding."

Passing through the galleries of medieval art, Santos's footsteps echoed like rifle shots across the cold tile. Paintings of icons and triptychs of angels and saints with their sad eyes stared down at him. They caused in him a sense of growing unease.

Santos saw no sign of the sixty or seventy security guards on special duty that night. Most, he knew, were stationed at the main entryways and exits, or upstairs, on the roof garden, monitoring the movements of several hundred guests. For all of the human presence in the museum that night, the young man may as well have been on Mars, such was his sense of isolation.

Coming into the Great Hall, he turned and started up the Grand stairway. At the top of the stairs, he found himself at the entrance to the galleries of European painting, where an immense blowup of the *Primavera* marked the entrance to the exhibition.

Intending to continue on up to the roof, something stayed him. It was nothing he saw, but, rather, something he heard—nothing emphatic, but subtle and suggestive, a muffled sound like the movement of a curtain or a heavy fabric falling.

Fully expecting to see a guard, Santos ducked his head into the entryway of the first gallery. There was none. He thought that strange until he recalled that whatever security had been posted there had no doubt left in response to reports of the power failure.

At a quick glance, he could see nothing out of the ordinary. His inclination was to turn and get up to the banquet, where he felt he might be needed.

Then he heard the sound again. This time, it came from someplace farther back in one of the more distant galleries. As with the first sound, he couldn't quite put his finger on it, uncertain whether or not its source was even human. This time, it had about it a padded, muffled quality, quick, like a cat scurrying over the floor. His curiosity piqued, he moved slowly in the direction of the sound.

Roberto Sàntos was Catholic, not especially devout. But at the sight of scenes portraying Mary and the infant Jesus, the Magi, Peter denying Christ, Carafas and Herod, Christ, wreathed in thorns, stooped beneath the crushing weight of wood, walking the Stations of the Cross, a quiet awe descended upon him.

It was precisely that slowing of the senses that caused his usually keen eye to pass over the improbable image of a figure standing motionless beneath a painting some forty or fifty feet dead ahead of him. The figure was cloaked in a full-length garment open down the front. Possibly a rain-coat, it was made of a shiny fabric that reflected light. It was the light flashing off of that fabric that first caught Santos's eye. The second thing that caught his eye was that the figure was not alone. Another figure stood—or rather, crouched—beside the first, hands outstretched as though tethered to him.

What he saw made scarcely any sense, at least not in the context within which he viewed it. The figures were stand-ing behind a large, protective Lucite screen, which had the effect of magnifying them, distorting their shapes gro-tesquely. One figure, Santos now saw, was a man, the other a woman. The man stood with one hand upraised toward the painting, while with the other he appeared to hold the woman by her hair, all the while looking over his shoulder at the guard. In the next moment, the man's right arm moved. Santos watched it climb upward, something shiny glinting in its fist.

One part of Santos told him that whatever he was seeing wasn't real; another part said that it was. All too real. What would a man and a woman be doing behind the Lucite screen? The man was neither a guard nor a workman. And why was he holding the woman by the hair?

Suddenly, the man turned and faced him. That movement had the effect of turning the woman as well, so that she saw Santos for the first time, then screamed. It was then that Santos had a glimpse of the painting just behind them. It was the *Chigi Madonna*.

The next thing Santos heard was a hoarse growl. It took a moment before he realized that the sound had come from somewhere deep within himself and that he was charging toward the painting with the gathering momentum of a run-away locomotive.

FORTY-THREE

Mr. Tsacrios was supervising the candlelight presentation of small, individual-sized peach souffleés when the lights came back on. There was a burst of cheers and polite clapping, followed by gasps of delight on seeing the souffleés. Swirled across the face of each in a raspberry ganache were the words "Happy 550th, Sandro." Squadrons of waiters filed down the aisles with steamy pots of espresso and dark Darjeeling.

Sensing that he had obligations elsewhere, Van Nuys rose and excused himself. He was well aware he'd neglected many of the museum's leading benefactors, and he now set out to redress those wrongs.

Watching him go with a sense of relief, it occurred to Manship that Isobel Cattaneo's chair was still empty, and had been since even before the lights went out.

At the time she'd gone off with Mr. Tsacrios to take her phone call, Manship had thought nothing of it. Now, troubled by what seemed an overlong absence, a score of questions came to mind. Who, for instance, could be calling her here? Who even knew she was here? As far as he knew, she had no friends or family in the States. The only person in Italy who might know where she was that night was Erminia. But why would the housekeeper be calling her now? Was there some new trouble there? Or was it simply that Isobel was exhausted from the ordeal of the past several days and had gone back to the hotel to bed?

Then he recalled that Ludovico Borghini was still at large.

Looking up, Manship found Ettore Foa's gaze fixed intently on him. From the way the deputy ambassador looked at him, he guessed that he was thinking the same thing.

They both rose at the same time, but Manship was faster. Going around the table, he pressed Foa back into his chair, bowing slightly and whispering into the Italian's ear: "Where is she?"

"I don't know. It's a long time for just a phone call."

Manship's eyes scanned the roof. "I'm going to have a look around. Most likely, it's nothing at all. Probably just powdering her nose."

"I'll join you," Foa said, starting up.

"No. You stay. Don't let on to the others. Just keep everything calm here."

Sensing trouble, Maeve glanced up. "Problems?"

"Not really," Manship said, affecting a breezy manner. "I have to go downstairs for a minute."

She wasn't buying his breeziness. Her eyes ransacked his for information. All he could manage was a shrug and then hurried off.

On his way out, he stopped at the front desk, where Mr. Tsacrios was issuing orders like a field commander to a battery of assistants.

"Miss Cattaneo . . ." Manship began a bit breathlessly.

Mr. Tsacrios beamed one of those professional head-waiter smiles. "Yes, sir. What about her?"

"She was here a few minutes ago at the phone?"

"Yes, sir. Just over there." Mr. Tsacrios pointed to a phone a few feet away.

Manship looked across at it. There was no one there.

"You didn't happen to see where she went?" he asked.

"No, sir. I didn't. Hasn't she returned?" The smile never left his face. He said something else, but Manship never heard it. He'd already started out, certain, even as he went, that something was wrong. Isobel was gone, under questionable circumstances. Her absence, he felt sure, indicated that something was amiss. It had something to do with Borghini and the Chigi sketches, he reasoned, and with no other plausible explanations at hand, it was with the sketches he intended to start.

For the duration of an elevator ride between the rooftop and the second floor, Manship's head spun with half a dozen terrifying scenarios. When the doors of the elevator parted, he flinched from the glare of sudden light. Before him, and seemingly in every corner of the gallery, there was a great blur of motion.

Primed by his own overwrought imagination, Manship had fully expected to see something frightening—things overturned, paintings slashed, horrifying destruction.

To some extent, that's what he did see. But within the space of seconds, his eye filled with far more specific detail. The first item was Roberto Santos. He lay prone on the floor, struggling to rise with the aid of one hand while the other flapped about trying to stanch the flow of blood that fountained from between his fingers.

The next thing he saw was Isobel Cattaneo. She was standing to the left of the *Chigi Madonna,* trying to squirm free of the person who held her, his fist coiled in her hair. Even from where he stood, Manship could see she was white as parchment, watching the knife blade scything above her head.

"Let her go," Manship shouted across to him, trying to conceal the tremor in his voice. Instinct urging him forward to help her, he was keenly aware that to do so would endanger her even more.

"Not on your life, Mr. Manship."

The man's use of his name came as a shock to Manship. "You can go at any time. I promise no one will stop you. Just leave Miss Cattaneo and go."

The man he now knew to be Borghini laughed. "Only to have your police thugs leap on me the moment I step out the front door."

"I promise. No one—"

"Damn your promises. Why would I believe the promises of someone who goes about looting the national treasures of other countries? Besides, Miss Cattaneo and I are old friends. We have some unfinished business to complete."

"If you're talking about those three Chigi sketches, Miss Cattaneo had nothing to do with their being here."

"You're a liar, Mr. Manship. I know very well the part

Miss Cattaneo played in the removal of those drawings from my home. She and I will work that matter out together.''

They'd reached an impasse. Manship didn't mind that. He was content just to keep the man talking. Talk was certainly preferable to something more destructive.

Borghini's talk had gradually blossomed into a tirade. It was almost impossible to make any sense of what he was saying. Manship watched the count's fist coil more tightly in Isobel's hair. Each twist of his wrist had the effect of dragging her closer to him and bending her over, her head pointed at her assailant's midsection. All the while, the long, curved blade of the knife kept scything ever closer to her, making a soft wooshing sound with each sweep.

Several times, Borghini feinted at her with the blade, stopping each time just short of her eyes, which seemed to be his principal target. He appeared to enjoy tormenting her, as well as taunting his attackers, daring them to make some foolish move.

Yanking cruelly at Isobel's hair, he'd started to rant about racial mongrels, the desecration of civilization by "subspecies" befouling the world everyplace they went.

All the while he ranted on, he gave sharp twists to the knot of hair coiled in his fist. The tirade grew more irrational, disconnected, until suddenly he was talking about his mother, his voice grown strangely tender and caressing.

It seemed to go on and on—the tirade, the sweeping blade, Isobel bent over in a cruelly painful position. Manship kept looking round for MacWirter's people, hoping they would soon show. Then it occurred to him with a sinking sensation that no one upstairs had the remotest idea where they were. At the moment, from where things stood, Borghini, holding both the woman and the painting, held all of the winning cards.

"Won't you at least let me help this poor man?" Manship pointed to Santos, who was fading rapidly in a pool of his own blood. "If he doesn't have medical help soon . . ."

Borghini, behind the Lucite screen, seemed puzzled. He kept looking around, expecting to find someone behind him. The knife with which he'd been menacing Isobel appeared to halt in midair, as though some invisible hand had momentarily stayed it. The effect of that action had freed Isobel. She stood there now, wild-eyed, hair streaming down her face, transfixed on the scene before her.

Never much for physical activity, and not fast on his feet, something amounting to overdrive kicked in, and Manship started to move. Borghini stepped out in front of the screen to await him.

They met in midair, both of them actually off the ground—Manship in a flying tackle, not quite horizontal to the floor, Borghini, stepping off the shallow platform on which he'd stood, appearing to drop through space. The sound they made on impact was a soft thud, followed by a gentle sigh of air, like a balloon emptying.

Manship had expected Isobel to flee, to seek help. Amazingly, she didn't. Instead, she stood there, baffled, a deer frozen in the path of onrushing headlights.

"Isobel." Manship's half-smothered words rose from somewhere beneath Borghini. "Help. Get help. Quick."

She started to go, saw the knife levering back and forth between the two, then waded directly into the fray instead. She kicked Borghini, aiming her foot for the hand holding the knife. But the lurchings of the two men had grown so frantic that her kick missed entirely.

"Isobel," Manship gasped. "For Chrissake. Go."

This time, the message got through. Making a soft half-moaning, half-apologetic sound, she wheeled around and fled.

Amid writhings and grunts, the two figures scuffled. Light on his feet, Borghini bounded up, turning his back on Manship, still scrambling on the floor. The tails of his raincoat flared outward like a cape, revealing beneath it the uniform of one of the Tsacrios waiters. Manship rose, wobbling to his knees. At that moment, a booted foot shot straight out, the heel of it catching him in the side of the head. Stars exploded before his eyes as he went sprawling.

Renewing the attack, Borghini whirled, his outstretched arm inscribing a wide, clumsy arc. The bright point at the end of that arc glinted in and out of the beam of an overhead spotlight, then plunged swiftly.

Manship watched, transfixed, the bright point swoop through the air, soaring toward him. The point disappeared from his line of vision, then reappeared. In the next instant, he felt a faint nick above the cheek.

The colonel was moving toward him again. The full-length raincoat made a rattling sound, giving off a faint odor of rubber. Manship watched, mesmerized, as the blade of a knife, nearly six inches long, the last two inches of it angled at the tip, flailed in Borghini's hand.

Manship's immediate need was for something with which to protect himself. His eyes swept around the room. It was in that first desperate sweep of the eyes, and with that gray blocklike shape hurtling toward him, that he felt something warm slowly descending the side of his face. His hand jerked up automatically, as if he were about to swat a fly. He felt his finger glide over something wet and slippery.

He glanced at his hand and for an instant thought it was someone else's. It was smeared with blood. Next, he saw blood on his shirtfront and lapels, and then he realized the blood was his own.

The blur of the onrushing figure swarmed toward him again, gathering momentum as it came. The object nearest at hand was a vase of fresh-cut mums, hardly ideal as an instrument of self-defense, but by then there were no alternative choices. With one hand splayed across the side of his face to staunch the flow of blood, he hefted the vase with the other and flung it at the gray blur hurtling toward him.

The vase grazed Borghini's head at the temple, barely fazing him. It didn't stop him so much as slow him long enough for Manship to regain his footing and retreat, drawing the man away from the painting, Borghini's blade switching in the air as he followed him.

By then, Manship was simply playing for time. Behind him, Santos lay on the floor, all color drained from his face, panting heavily from blood loss, going into shock.

Manship's chief hope was that Isobel had found help and would return with it shortly. The person bearing down hard on him appeared to have divined that thought and was just as determined that this man whose recent activities had obsessed him would never live to savor the triumph of his dream.

In a half crouch, Borghini stalked Manship, slashing his blade through the air, trying to drive him into a corner from which there'd be no escape.

Bleeding freely, using himself as a lure, Manship attempted to draw the man out of the gallery, away from the paintings. But when he reached the gallery entrance and dashed from it, Borghini failed to take the bait. Instead of following him, the colonel dashed back into the gallery, in the direction from which he'd just come. Manship had little doubt where he was headed—back to the *Chigi Madonna* to finish the job he'd come for. With the whole right side of his face drenched in blood, Manship lunged back into the gallery after him.

By then, characteristic caution and practical good sense had been replaced by a sense of outrage and plain injustice. Manship no longer thought of his own safety, nor of the safety of the painting that had been one of his principal preoccupations for the past five years. If he thought of anyone's safety, it was that of the young security guard, possibly fatally disabled on the floor, with a demented madman careening through the galleries, waving a knife, slashing the air before him.

It was that madman Manship wanted. With every fiber

of his being, he wanted to get his hands on that person. Looking for whatever was in reach, he grabbed a light-weight bridge chair that had been used by one of the ticket collectors at the door, then barged ahead.

The man was precisely where he'd found him the first time, standing on the shallow platform before the *Chigi Madonna*. His back was to the entrance, that curved, lethal blade of his again upraised. Flashing before Manship's eyes at that instant was the *Centurion* hanging in limp, unres-torable strips, and the Pallavicini painting, the eyes gouged, horribly mutilated. "Sick. Sick. Sick," he heard himself say; then something in him snapped.

Borghini must have sensed it, too. Momentarily dis-tracted, he whirled around, a look of sharp annoyance on his face, to see the person he'd just driven from the gallery back again and rushing him.

Brandishing the bridge chair, its four legs thrust out be-fore him, Manship roared at the top of his lungs and charged.

FORTY-FOUR

In the brief time it took for the EMS technicians to fetch Borghini and whisk him, as well as Manship and Santos, off to the hospital, a squad of porters armed with pails and mops had swarmed into the gallery and restored the place to pristine condition.

Several banquet guests, oblivious to the turmoil that had transpired there not more than a quarter hour before, had strayed back down into the gallery for a last look before calling it a night.

Rushing into the gallery and sweeping past several important patrons, Osgood barely acknowledged their greetings. He never paused or slowed once, coming finally to rest before the *Chigi Madonna* and the thirteen sketches. He stood rooted to the spot, scarcely breathing; all the while, his keen, well-practiced eye scoured the canvas for any signs of damage. Satisfied there were none, he moved next to the *Centurion,* several galleries away.

It hung there, roped off, in splendid isolation, in all of its tatters and ruins, unbowed. No one had tried to remove it; nor was there any sign of additional damage. A few more guests had gathered there behind him, awed, not speaking, the way one views the devastation of a car crash and finally grasps the meaning of loss.

When he turned, he found MacWirter's anxious gaze on him.

"Is it all right, sir?"

"Looks okay to me," Osgood murmured grimly.

They walked back together through the galleries gradually filling with returning guests. "What about this lunatic? This slasher?"

"EMS and the police took him off to hospital. Took four of our people to hold him down till they got here. Hauled him off, knife still sticking in his eye."

"Any idea who he is?"

"Foreign national, sir. Italian passport. Name of—"

"Don't tell me," Osgood interrupted. "I'll tell you. The name was Borghini." That was the name Foa had given him upstairs.

"No, sir. Something else. Gaudio something. From Messina, he claims. Had seaman's papers on him. Police can't hold him indefinitely, being a foreign national and all. We'll have to notify the Italian consulate, I think, sir."

"It just so happens, Captain, the deputy Italian ambassador is our guest here tonight."

MacWirter appeared to inflate. A delighted smile crimsoned his jowly features. "Pleasant coincidence, wouldn't you say, sir?"

"I'd say so," Osgood nodded.

"And the young lady, sir, Miss Cattaneo," MacWirter went on, "what about her?"

"Mrs. Costain took her back to her hotel. Aside from being a bit shaken, she seems okay. Would you be good enough to send one of your people up to fetch Mr. Foa and appraise him of the situation here. If anyone wants me, I'm on my way up to Mount Sinai to look in on both Santos and Mr. Manship."

From that point on, the night became a kind of phantasmagoria. A police officer took Osgood on a near-reckless ride in a patrol car, sirens screaming, tearing up to Mount Sinai, where he was taken directly to the Emergency Ward, there to find Manship, his face bandaged and twirling his thumbs impatiently.

"How bad is it?" Osgood asked.

"Nothing. Lost some blood is about all." Manship's thumbs spun faster. "I'm waiting for the chief resident to come up and discharge me. What about her?"

"You mean Cattaneo? Other than a few bruises, she's fine. Maeve took her back to the hotel."

"And Borghini?"

"He's here, too. Surgeons are trying to save his eye. Foa's on his way over to make a positive identification.

According to his passport and seaman's papers, his name is Gaudio something—''

"Favese." At that moment, Foa strode in, all breezy efficiency. "Gaudio Favese," he said. "The Faveses are closely related to the Borghinis. Our question is to determine whether we have here a Favese or a Borghini."

"Ask Isobel," Manship replied grimly. "She'll tell you."

"She doesn't have to," Foa said. "All I need is a quick peek at the fellow and I'll know for myself."

Shortly after, the chief resident bustled in, asked Manship several questions, studied the nurse's chart, then signed him out.

The consulate must have called ahead to Mount Sinai. No sooner had Manship been released than a pallid young man hurried nervously forward, identified himself as an assistant administrator, then led them directly up to a small private waiting area outside the operating room.

"How long should this take?" Manship asked.

The young administrator seemed overwhelmed by what he took to be three important visitors. "I don't know exactly what's ailing this fellow, but I gather from the resident, it's something pretty serious. He's been in there an hour and a half already. I'd count on three, four additional hours at least."

The waiting room had a couch, several plastic chairs, a large wall TV, and a table stacked with outdated magazines. The three of them took up their positions there.

Near dawn, a harried-looking young man, gowned and capped in hospital green, stuck his head in the door. Osgood had dozed off but woke the instant the fellow appeared.

"Which one of you gentlemen is Mr. Foa?" the young man asked.

"I am." Foa rose and stepped forward.

"I'm Dr. Kramer, the resident surgeon. Are you related

to this man?'' He glanced down at the hospital admittance card. ''Mr. Favese?''

''No, I'm not,'' Foa explained. ''This man's an Italian national. I represent the Italian consulate here. What's the fellow's present status?''

''Guarded. But he'll live.'' The surgeon studied them warily, as if he resented having to say anything.

''How badly was he injured?'' Manship asked.

''He enucleated himself.''

''He what?''

''He plunged a knife into his eye. Severed the optic nerve. Yanked the pupil out. He'll be all right, but we couldn't save the eye.''

The young man looked at them again, this time as if they were all not only suspicious but possibly felons. ''You know the guy at all?''

None of them replied, thereby raising the young resident's suspicions even more.

''What did he do?'' the surgeon asked. ''The place is crawling with cops.''

''He tried to destroy a very valuable painting,'' Manship replied.

''Where?''

''At the Metropolitan Museum,'' Manship said. ''When can we see him?''

The surgeon shook his head wearily. ''You can see him now. They have him down in the recovery room. But he won't be out of the anesthesia for at least another hour.''

''That's all right.'' Foa swept past him. ''We don't have to talk. We just need to look.''

It was nearly 6:00 A.M. when they left the hospital. Already the big sanitation trucks were creeping down Fifth Avenue like prehistoric insects, spouting jets of water on the curbs and sidewalks, their huge, twirling brushes pushing mounds of trash before them.

Manship hailed a cab and invited Osgood and the deputy

ambassador back to 5 East Eighty-fifth Street for a spot of breakfast.

"How did your reunion with Miss Cattaneo go last evening?" Foa made pleasant talk as they glided south along Fifth Avenue in the first pale pink streaks of morning.

"Reasonably well, under the circumstances."

"You can't really know the circumstances, my friend. Horrific. Truly horrific. Has she told you anything?"

"Not yet. I had the distinct impression she'd prefer to leave that to you."

Foa gazed out the cab window, staring ruefully at the long column of plane trees whirring past, their branches still swathed in rags of morning mist.

"I suggest you fortify yourself with two very strong martinis before you face that," he said. "The name Borghini in Italy would be like the name Rockefeller or Kennedy here. The name was exalted during the Renaissance, identified with wealth and privilege. However, since World War Two, it's been somewhat sullied by the colonel's activities."

Manship sat grimly, staring straight ahead as they rumbled southward.

"It's common knowledge to Romans of a certain class that Borghini is a bit unbalanced," Foa went on. "What he put Isobel through, you could not begin to imagine. She told me everything on the plane coming over. When the carabinieri searched Borghini's residence, they found hundreds of photos of her. Candid shots—all taken without her knowledge. Something of a voyeur, he'd been following her about everywhere, taking these pictures. Had his eye on her for years. There were newspaper photos of you, as well—and clippings from the Italian press, describing your show, your activities in Europe, what paintings you were seeking to take home with you, where you were going next, a complete itinerary of your trip. You can't imagine the detail."

Manship gave a weary wave of the hand. "I'm afraid

much of what happened to that poor woman is my fault."

Foa appeared puzzled by his remarks. "Ah, you mean your pursuit of those three little sketches?"

"Yes. She more or less told me where to find them, or at least she sent me to the man who knew where they were to be found. Her friend, Pettigrilli—it was he who sent me to the Quattrocento, which, I'm certain, set the whole awful thing in motion."

Osgood pondered that a while. "I wouldn't be too hard on myself for what happened to Isobel, old buddy. Sounds to me as if this Borghini was only looking for an excuse. If it hadn't been you, it would have been someone else."

They rumbled past the massive gray facade of the Metropolitan, where a crew of sanitation workers was already sweeping up the mounds of litter left behind by the crowds from the night before.

"Tell me one thing." Manship turned to the deputy ambassador. "How the hell did you get her to consent to come over here?"

Foa laughed. "Well, for one thing, it wasn't the power of my considerable charms, if that's what you're thinking. And for another, Borghini was still on the loose when we reached her, and the thought of going back to Fiesole by herself could not have been all that appealing."

FORTY-FIVE

Mrs. McCooch was just turning the key in the lock of 5 East Eighty-fifth when the cab drew up outside the front door. Foa exited first. Not recognizing the tall, imposing figure, she reared back, until she saw Manship stepping out behind him. Osgood followed.

At first, she frowned, wondering what on earth her employer was doing bringing home guests at this hour of the morning. Then she noticed the bandage on his face and nearly wept. She could barely get her key in the lock to get him indoors.

Twenty minutes later, they were sitting around the table in the cozy ground-floor kitchen while she and Mrs. McCooch fried bacon and eggs and served copious cups of steaming coffee.

Hearing noise below in the kitchen, Maeve came down in a robe, rubbing sleep-filled eyes. Then seeing Foa and Osgood, she fled back upstairs to put a comb through her hair and just enough makeup to appear presentable.

Shortly after breakfast, Foa was in the library, on the phone to Washington, speaking with his boss, the ambassador, at his residence. Foa advised the ambassador that Ludovico Borghini, of the illustrious Borghini family, had been apprehended in New York by federal authorities while attempting to destroy a priceless Botticelli at the Metropolitan Museum of Art. He was also wanted by the carabinieri in Rome. After linking him to a long series of unsolved murders and disappearances of itinerants, they'd finally been able to secure warrants to search the Quattrocento galleries in Parioli and the Palazzo Borghini on the Quirinal, where they had uncovered the existence of a "house of horrors."

Arrangements were set in motion then and there to extradite Borghini back to Italy.

While in Italy, Foa had learned that the carabinieri had picked up a young man by the name of Beppe Falco at the

Quattrocento galleries. In an effort to reduce the charges against himself, the young man had led them on a tour of the cellar area beneath the galleries and then again of the upper floor of the Palazzo Borghini.

As things stood now, the story that would most certainly be breaking in the newspapers that day would involve an extreme right-wing Italian nobleman, a known neofascist from a splinter group of the National Alliance party, who'd been apprehended in New York just as he was about to mutilate one of the priceless Botticellis currently on exhibition at the Metropolitan. A major embarrassment for the Italian government, the most pressing task for Foa and the ambassador now came down to a matter of damage control. They would have to move quickly, since both the Italian and Turkish governments had already moved to extradite the colonel for similar crimes committed within their sovereign boundaries.

That morning, all of the major newspapers were full of accounts of the Botticelli exhibition. The TV showed extensive clips of seemingly endless lines of long black and gray limousines arriving and departing the museum.

The New York Times gave the show full coverage on their art page, comparing the scale and importance of the show to the Met's big Degas exhibition some years before. Repeatedly cited as the coup of the evening were the thirteen preliminary sketches for the *Chigi Madonna,* never all seen together before.

The review ended with an anguished paean to the desecrated *Centurion:* "displayed in all of the savage, mindless rage wreaked upon it." The shock of actually seeing the consequences of "such wanton idiocy" on display made a shambles of what most people had always assumed was a rational universe. Virtually all of the credit for making this point so tellingly was given to Walter Van Nuys, president and chief executive officer of the Metropolitan Museum.

No mention appeared anywhere of the attempted attack on the *Chigi Madonna* the night before, since all of the

morning papers had already gone to press before the incident had actually occurred.

That night, however, the story exploded everywhere. The
evening news and all the dailies featured the story of the
"mad Italian Count" who'd not only attempted to mutilate
the *Chigi Madonna* the night before but was now definitely
identifed as the destroyer of the *Centurion* at St. Stephen's
in Istanbul and the *Transfiguration* in the Pallavicini.

Roberto Santos, the plucky little security guard who'd
had an ear severed holding off the crazed colonel until help
arrived, found himself an overnight hero. Microsurgeons,
working through the night, were able to reattach the ear,
and Santos was expected to make a complete recovery.

Ettore Foa, back in Washington, was quoted at length.
Van Nuys gave interviews and press conferences at the
drop of a hat. Only Manship declined all invitations to appear on news shows and kept his silence.

In the days that followed, a flood of details emerged,
revealing the character and past of the shadowy neofascist
Ludovico Borghini. The reporters had by then dubbed him
"the master slasher."

The week following the opening, Isobel stayed on as guest
of the Metropolitan, with Manship as an unofficial personal
tour guide. Manship had naïvely assumed that, on her first
visit to New York, she would want to see the sights, all the
typical things and places first-time visitors gravitated to—
the World Trade Center, the Empire State Building, the
Statue of Liberty, Chinatown, Little Italy. In addition, he
had planned a number of small dinner parties in her honor,
inviting lively, amiable people, many from the theater,
thinking she would enjoy that most.

He was relieved when she asked, almost apologetically,
if they could "skip all that." The itinerary he'd worked on
so diligently had struck him as a bit trite, anyway. The
World Trade Center and the Statue of Liberty, after the

horrific ordeal she'd just been through, also seemed hope-
lessly inappropriate.

Though Foa had gone to some pains to apprise him in
advance of the Roman horrors, Manship could only guess
at the true depths of the ordeal. The young woman he saw
before him now—subdued, withdrawn, just barely socia-
ble—struck him as very sad. Hardly the feisty, self-assured
young woman he'd met in Fiesole, she was in a state of
shock and in the process of trying to heal.

She seemed most at peace when they walked out in the
park together, or prowled the museum during off-hours,
losing themselves in its endless wings and sparsely popu-
lated galleries.

She found it particularly pleasing to sit in the little garden
out back of 5 East Eighty-fifth Street. She would perch on
the tiny white marble bench beneath the pergola where
Manship grew grapes, from which he occasionally made
bad wine. It reminded her of Italy.

Sometimes she would go off with Maeve for an afternoon of shopping, or go with her to her small rented studio
on Greene Street and marvel at her energy as she scrambled
up and down ladders, dressed in paint-spattered jeans and
sneakers, putting the final touches on paintings scheduled
to be shown at her upcoming exhibition.

Isobel had been taking most of her meals at the hotel.
Finally, Manship asked one night if she would consent to
have dinner at number 5, where Mrs. McCooch would be
happy to prepare a bird, or perhaps one of her savory Irish
stews that they might eat before the fire in the library.

That was the first time he'd seen her light up since her
coming to New York, and he felt encouraged. It was then
he understood that it wasn't *he* who was being rejected,
but, more likely, noise, excitement, glitter. What she
wanted now, needed more than ever, was calm.

One night toward the end of the week, Manship kissed
her. Like a man long out of touch with romance, he had
planned it. It was a clumsy kiss, occurring in the dark en-

tryway of a dental office on the corner of Eighty-third and
Fifth. A chaste, fumbling thing, it had taken her by surprise,
and he regretted it the instant it was under way. When he
attempted something more ambitious, she turned her head
away and gently drew him out of the shadows of the doorway. She seemed miserable, utterly crestfallen.

He had the sense of a humiliating defeat. They were
standing now on Fifth Avenue, just at the entrance to the
Stanhope. Light from the lobby streamed across his anguished features.

"Tomorrow?" he asked hopefully.

"Do you really want to? Or are you just being kind?
You don't have to, you know. There's no need—"

He watched her with a sense of infuriating helplessness.
She was shaking her head back and forth as if she'd lost
for the moment the power of speech. But it was her eyes
that nailed him—the Chigi eyes, full of mystery and sorrow. They'd finally overtaken him, so slowly, so gently, he
could scarcely recall the moment when he'd first suc-
cumbed to their lovely sadness.

"I *do* want to," he said. "And kindness has never been
one of my strong points."

He kissed her again. This time, it went better. Deeper,
harder, more satisfying. They'd both fallen into it, occasionally jarred and bumped by the crowds streaming in and
out the revolving front doors as they spun past them into
waiting taxis and the night.

FORTY-SIX

The end of her visit loomed, as he knew it must. It was Thursday. She'd booked a seat on the Alitalia flight from New York to Rome for Saturday evening.

It was Mrs. McCooch's night off. That last night, Isobel wanted to "do dinner," as she said. She longed to putter at a stove. She missed her kitchen back in Fiesole.

She cooked him a risotto with fresh porcini mushrooms imported from Tuscany that she'd found at a little Italian greengrocer around the corner on Madison Avenue. She simmered these in a pale sauce of *pomadora* sprinkled with a dash of freshly ground Parmesan.

Afterward, she tossed a salad of endive and radicchio in olive oil and balsamic vinegar. She'd roasted a chicken and the odor of thyme and fresh garlic drifted on the warm currents of air suffusing the kitchen.

Manship brought up a fine old barolo from his tiny cellar, and they finished off with a dark, bitter espresso, fresh raspberries, and hard almond biscotti, dipped Tuscan-style in a saucer of golden amber Vin Santos.

"I don't suppose," he said, shifting uneasily in his chair, "I could prevail on you to stay a bit longer?"

They hadn't talked much during dinner. The absence of talk never seemed to bother her. Now, its sudden intrusion into the meal made her visibly uncomfortable. She peered into the bottom of her espresso cup as though she were reading some melancholy tidings in the calligraphy of dregs spattered there.

"Do you recall that night in Florence? You took me to dinner and I made a great pig of myself."

He smiled in spite of his sense of gathering gloom.

"You asked me to go to New York with you," she went on.

"And you politely declined my offer just as you're about to do now."

Despite the painted smile on his face, she was determined

to finish. "I had the feeling then that you were reaching out to me, that there was something more on your mind than just having me in New York as some kind of center-piece for your show." She looked down again into her cup. "I confess I thought the worst."

He was about to protest, then conceded in his mind that much of what she said may have been true.

"I liked you," she went on. "That's why I sent that note to you about Pettigrilli. As it turned out, I nearly got myself killed in the bargain."

He smiled sadly. "I'm sure I offended you with all of my grand talk of theater connections. I was certain you wanted to get rid of me as quickly as possible. Besides, there was that young man."

"Young man?"

"The fellow I saw at your place that afternoon. . . ."

"Tino?" She laughed. "One of my bigger mistakes. He had some very bad habits. I sent him off."

Manship pondered that a while. "Is there someone else?"

She shook her head, sending a shower of ash-blond hair sliding across her cheek. "No, there's no one else."

"Then why not stay with me a bit longer? Much longer. As long as you want." He was surprised at the sudden ardor and at how quickly he'd upped the ante.

"I must get home," she said with her typical quiet firm-ness. "I must get about my work, make something of my life."

"I have to make something of mine, too. Why can't we do it together?" It sounded to him like a proposal of sorts.

She leaned slightly backward, fixing him shrewdly with her gaze. "What's kept you alone so long?"

"You mean since Maeve?"

"Yes. That would be how long?"

"Over ten years." He divided the last of the espresso between their two cups, then raised his eyes toward the ceiling as though reading his thoughts from there. "When

you're a bachelor about town"—he groped for words—
"and have a certain kind of high-profile job . . ."

"High-profile?"

"Visible—talked about. Occasionally written about.
That sort of thing."

"Ah, yes. I see."

"Everyone you meet then has a woman they're certain
is perfect for you."

"Yes." She nodded. "I see."

"You do?"

"Yes, of course. That's the way in Italy, too."

"So," he went on, "what inevitably happens is that you
find yourself in lots of places you don't care to be, and
often among people you don't particularly care to be with.
It's a distraction and usually a waste of time. Then, when
you finally realize what you've been doing, it's too late.
You can't have that time back."

Listening, she gnawed her lower lip.

Manship dropped a lump of sugar into his cup and began
to slowly stir it. "For the last year or so, it's occurred to
me I don't have much more time to squander. And so, when
I had dinner with you that night in Florence, I confess that
what started out with entirely commercial motives, getting
you over here as a centerpiece for the show, as you say,
became something else. Don't ask me to explain. It's completely irrational."

"What did it become exactly?"

"I don't know. At least I didn't know then. I'm not sure
I know now. All I know is that something in me has
changed. Call it a shift of priorities. My feeling about
things—my work, my life. Everything."

She looked at him sympathetically, he thought, for the
first time. "How so? Tell me."

"If I could put it into words, it would sound ridiculous."
He laughed, more at himself than anything else. Then, el-
bows on the table, he leaned forward. "It feels very natural
sitting here in this kitchen with you, having dinner together

like this. It's as if we've been sitting here this way for years, and that we'll still be sitting here together like this for years to come."

She looked at the table with its uncleared dishes and cozy disorder.

"At this same table," he went on, "with the same chipped china, the same tarnished flatware, the same old cut-glass cruet of oil and vinegar, full of thumbprints that Mrs. McCooch refuses to clean, and that same bowl of lump sugar she refuses to fill more than halfway."

She looked up, about to say something, then changed her mind. "I really should be going."

"It's early." Manship glanced at his watch. "Not quite eleven."

"I still have some packing. Letters to write . . ."

Her eagerness to be off saddened him. It was, he thought, as if in her mind she'd finally settled some long-standing and deeply unpleasant problem.

"Tomorrow's your last day," he said. "How would you like to spend it? I thought we might—"

She lay a light tremulous hand on his sleeve. "If it's all the same to you, I must attend to some matters by myself."

It was as though the legs had been cut out from beneath him. Never before had he known such thorough rejection. Its terrible gentleness was especially hurtful. As if she pitied him.

He shrugged it off with seeming ease. "If that's what you want. But I insist on taking you out to the airport tomorrow evening."

She looked at him doubtfully, a hint of reproach in her eyes, then shook her head. "I do think it's better I go myself."

"But why?" The question tore from him, full of exasperation and regret. "Is it me? Is it something I've done? Am I so awful?"

She put a finger to his lips in order to calm him.

"It is," she said in a tone of quiet authority, "to prevent me from once more making one of my big mistakes."

Two days after Isobel's departure, Manship was summoned upstairs to the boardroom, then ushered into the sanctum sanctorum by Helen Mirkin, who was uncharacteristically flustered by events that morning.

He entered a large, airy room, encircled by windows giving onto panoramic views of the city sweeping east and west.

Though it was a cool October day, bright and crisp, there was a sense of heat in the room, and the vaguely unpleasant odor of nervous sweat hovered all about. Upon entering, Manship could feel the tension rise at once.

Thirteen people sat around a long mahogany Duncan Phyfe table. It was one of those typical boardroom tables that took itself very seriously; it exuded self-importance. The thirteen who sat there were silent, glaring into papers, shuffling reports, fiddling with eyeglass frames as they worked hard at the job of being unperturbed.

At one end of the table sat Van Nuys in his shirtsleeves, somewhat redder in the face than usual. At the other end was Osgood, smiling and looking very much in command of himself.

Manship had the impression he'd come in on the tail end of a fight. He had no doubt that he had been the subject of it.

Osgood finally broke the awkward silence when it appeared no one else would. "Walter, perhaps you'd be good enough to tell Mark why he was called here this morning."

Scarcely able to contain his pique, Van Nuys shuffled papers a while longer, the red of his face deepening to an apoplectic purple.

"Before we go any further, Mark," Van Nuys began (the use of his Christian name when usually Van Nuys addressed him only by his surname was in itself portentous). "You're aware, I'm sure, that Bill Osgood has elected to resign the directorship of the museum on the first of the year in order to pursue personal interests.''

"I am," Manship replied without much enthusiasm.

"I should then inform you that the board this morning, by a tally of seven to six, has voted to appoint you to the position of director. A vote," he added, "that I strongly oppose. May we have at this time your reaction to the proposal?"

Manship had known for the past eighteen months that he'd been shortlisted for one of the most coveted positions in the elite, highly rarefied world of museum administration. He also knew that ever since Bill Osgood had made known his intention to take early retirement, the board had initiated a search for a suitable replacement. Thousands of dollars had been spent employing the services of top headhunters in the field to locate precisely the right man. A combination of credentials, meaning a graduate degree—that is, a full doctorate from a top school—and a minimum of ten years of practical administrative experience at a leading institution, was taken for granted. Lastly, and perhaps most importantly, a distinguished and luminous old family name instantly recognizable to people of wealth and social standing was deemed to be indispensable. As of yet, no suitable candidate had emerged at the conclusion of the search.

At the first two levels, Manship more than qualified for the job. It was at the third, however, where he knew he fell down. Consequently, he never took the rumor of his candidacy too seriously.

Sitting there at a corner of the table, where an extra chair had been quickly moved in for him, he felt the suffocating weight of all eyes turned upon him. It occurred to him that what was happening was unreal—much like a dream in which the mind tells you that what you're seeing is all just imagined. Now that at last the moment had come (and he had thought about it for years), he felt a curious absence of any feeling at all.

After some seconds, Manship pushed his chair back and rose to his feet. Resting the tips of his fingers lightly on the table's edge, he directed his response to the question eye-to-eye at Walter Van Nuys.

"I am pleased that the board has chosen to award me this position. You honor me greatly. Of all comparable positions in this highly special, unrealistically privileged world we're lucky enough to inhabit, directorship of this institution is the single position I've coveted most."

The words flowed from him with surprising ease, his gaze never once leaving the engorged red face of his employer. "But were I to accept this position," he went on, "it would mean that Walter Van Nuys would have to leave his. Since he is the antithesis of everything I think a museum should be, we could never function together in the same professional climate. And so, knowing that Mr. Van Nuys is not about to leave the Metropolitan, I must respectfully decline. . . ."

A short time later, Manship walked out through the pillared main entrance, down the long stone stairway, a jaunty bounce to his step, and out into the bright crisp morning. Having tendered his resignation, leaving behind him a dozen mouths agape, he was then, for all intents and purposes, unemployed, a little nervous about the future perhaps, but marvelously free.

EPILOGUE

The following spring, Manship found himself in Lugano, the recipient of a quickie consultancy job for Thyssen-Bornemisza. He'd come to authenticate a Giotto, finished earlier than had been anticipated, and, finding himself with nearly five days to kill before he was due back in New York, he decided to drive down through the lakes, where he hadn't been since the early days with Maeve.

He rented a small car and struck south for Maggiore. The plan was to spend several days on the shore of the lake, prowl forest paths and possibly, do some boating. Then he would strike south again for Milan, from where he would fly home.

But his plan was not to be. An old friend, chief curator at the Poldi-Pezzoli, tracked him down at his hotel and invited him to Milan. It appeared that the Poldi had been offered a highly prized Pontormo at a very attractive price. The offer had been tendered by a Florentine aristocrat with cash-flow problems and a reputation for shifty trading. Eager for the painting, the Poldi man was reluctant to move without someone of Manship's stature to certify it.

With certain misgivings, Manship agreed to have a look at the painting. It happened to be in Florence, and possibly that had something to do with his accepting the job.

Driving in his rented Audi, Manship and his friend set out on the autostrada for Florence the following morning. As it turned out, the Pontormo was a copy, and not a very good one at that. Manship advised his friend against it. Effusively grateful for helping him to avoid a catastrophic gaffe, Manship's colleague placed an overly generous check in his hand and boarded the next train back to Milan.

Manship had no reason to go to Fiesole—certainly not Isobel Cattaneo. On a conscious level, he'd written that off months ago and scarcely thought of her anymore. To all intents and purposes, it was now a dead issue. Still, he had a whole afternoon to kill (he was flying back to New York the next day), and he thought he might like to go up to the Bandini and look once more at the Fra Angelico and Filippo Lippi, both long favorites of his. The fact that the Bandini happened to be in Fiesole did not strike him as particularly significant.

Driving up from the Piazza San Marco, he found to his disappointment that the Bandini was closed. A cardboard placard nailed to the front door explained that the museum was undergoing refurbishment and would reopen in the fall.

Somewhat at a loss, he sat at an outdoor café in the central square, sipping a Campari beneath a large striped umbrella, his eyes scanning the blue haze of Tuscan mountains in the distance.

Having exhausted that activity, and with an impatient waiter hovering nearby, silently demanding he either order another Campari or have the decency to pay his bill and clear out to make room for the next party, Manship decided to leave.

From that point on, his recollection of events was sketchy. He liked to think that the direction he'd taken from the town square was entirely random. But it was no more random than the daily rise and fall of tides. Starting out with nothing special in mind, he found his pace gradually quickening and his breath coming more rapidly. Approaching his destination, it was as though he were tethered to an invisible leash tugging him inexorably forward.

It was no more than five or six minutes by foot from the town square. When he looked up, he wasn't in the least surprised to see there before him the Villa Tranquillo, just as shabby and down-at-the-heels as it had been that first time. Peeling paint slowly drifted downward into the orange-globed trumpet vines that crept along its water-stained outer walls.

Despite all that, the place still had a kind of easy, slap-dash charm. Come in, if you care to, it seemed to say. It didn't particularly care what you thought of it.

He lingered there, wavering between two choices. It was

so close. What could be the harm? She'd be annoyed, of course. It might be embarrassing. He'd feel like a fool. And what if she had someone with her, someone new?

He rang the bell, at first tentatively, then three or four times somewhat more insistently. The sound of it rattling through the upper halls echoed with a gloomy vacancy. To his relief, no one answered.

He walked around the side and through a rusty wrought-iron gate. A tiny cowbell tinkled as he entered. He saw her instantly. She was there in the garden, stooped over, elbow-deep in a stand of poppies. The cracked cupid trickled a stream of water through its tiny genitals, making a pleasant plashing sound into the stone basin just beneath it.

He stood there for a while, having no wish to disturb her. Instead, he sat down on one of the half-sprung chaises on the flagged patio, where they'd sipped tea together that first time.

She worked on for several minutes, not noticing him, the click of her pruning shears wafting up to him. When at last she looked up, an expression of mild surprise crossed her features. Nothing more demonstrative than that. Moments later, to his surprise, she smiled and waved. It was one of those ineffably Italian gestures that manage to say everything without the need for words. This one said, Wait there. I'll be right with you. It was that easy, as though they'd seen each other the day before, as if she'd been expecting him.

Kneeling, she clamped the stem of one vibrantly pink poppy between her teeth as she pruned and snipped at others. At last, she gathered the bunches of them, along with cosmos and ranunculus and blue cornflowers she'd cut to bring into the house.

As she came toward him beneath a battered old straw hat, he saw that she was nodding. She'd taken the poppy from her mouth and held it out to him, while with the other arm she bundled the big bouquet to her breast. It was the Simonetta look to be sure, but centuries removed from that mythological orange grove where the Primavera had stood while the spring months, bearing flowers, all came swarming around her.

Once again, he had the strange sensation of having lived it before—just as in those final days of September as they sat together in the ground-floor kitchen on Eighty-fifth Street, the crumbs and scraps of unfinished dinner on the china plates between them. Like then, this moment had that same air of well-worn familiarity, that sense of drowsy timelessness, as though sitting there with her in that garden had always been, would always be.

When she came up on the patio, she laid her flowers on the nearby table and flopped down into the chaise beside him. The light at that moment had the soft, perfect clarity of Tuscan spring afternoons, when the days have grown longer and the darkness holds off for a time.

She didn't speak, nor had he felt any particular need to. But just when he thought he could feel the quiet perfection of the moment slipping away and the old stiffness and distrust returning between them, she stirred. "You're really serious about this?"

"I've had enough time to think about it."

"And?"

"I'd like to give it a try."

"It won't be easy. I'm not easy."

"Neither am I, God knows."

"Well, so at least we start even."

"Even." He nodded while she rolled the stem of the poppy dreamily between her fingers.

After a while, she rose and placed her bouquet in his arms. "Will you carry those in for me? I'll get a vase."

Manship rose and followed her.

POSTSCRIPT

An Italian circus owner and entrepreneur acquired today the entire collection of stuffed human figures discovered in the attic rooms of the Palazzo Borghini in Rome, or, as it came to be known during the recent trial of Count Ludovico Borghini, the notorious "house of horrors."

The Italian government has decided to grant a license to Signor Attilo Zampano to purchase for the sum of 230 million lire the entire collection of *tableaux vivants*, which had been impounded in warehouses for eight months throughout the course of the trial. According to Culture Minister Ronchey, the money derived from the sale is to be used to restore and maintain what he described as "museum-class" works of art.

Signor Zampano has acquired permission to take the collection on tour with his Circo Magico throughout Europe and North America. He reports that as early as last week he'd already arranged for as many as sixty bookings in cities throughout the world, including in the United States.

Characterized as Grand Guignol, the Borghini studies, fashioned from the skins of once-living individuals and posed to replicate famous works of art, have already become the source for a certain kind of black humor that has become all the rage throughout Italy. Also, a dance called the *tableau vivant,* in which the participants assume for long periods of time the poses of famous subjects in master paintings, is currently sweeping the discotheques of Rome, Paris, London, and New York. As recently as two days ago, the Vatican released a statement expressing its horror at the commercialization of such material.

When questioned regarding the propriety of publicly displaying such ghastly subjects for profit and gain, Signor Zampano disputed the notion that his motives were in any way venal. "These are great works of art," he insisted. "And as such, they have great educational value. In a free society," he went on, "the public has a right to view what they choose without government or church interference. Like it or not, that is the essence of a free society."

—*Il Messagero*, Rome
9 July 1995